HARL VINCENT RESURRECTED

The Astounding Stories of Harl Vincent

By Harl Vincent
Edited by Greg Fowlkes

HARL VINCENT RESURRECTED

The Astounding Stories of Harl Vincent

Published by Resurrected Press

This classic book was handcrafted by Resurrected Press. Resurrected Press is dedicated to bringing high quality classic books back to the readers who enjoy them. These are not scanned versions of the originals, but, rather, quality checked and edited books meant to be enjoyed!

Please visit ResurrectedPress.com to view our entire catalogue!

ISBN 13: 978-1-937022-15-0

Printed in the United States of America

FOREWORD

Though he was one of the more prolific science fiction writers during the 30's, Harl Vincent is not as well known today as some of his contemporaries such as Edmond Hamilton, Jack Williamson, and Murray Leinster. Perhaps this is because he stopped writing in the early 40's and thus did not have a presence during the "Golden Age" of science fiction that occurred after World War II.

In many ways, Vincent was a typical writer of the era. His stories are full of monsters from outer space, mad scientists, evil from other dimensions, and his heroes must confront space pirates, death rays, and mad monarchs intent on ruling the earth, the solar system, or the universe. It's also fair to say that his stories were longer on the descriptions of the incredible inventions and futuristic devices than on character development. As a working engineer, this is not surprising, and with some seventy stories published this was obviously what his readers (and his editors) wanted.

But there was also some depth to his stories that was missing from much of the fiction of the period. In a number of the works in this volume, his scientists meddle in forces that would be better left untouched, only to lead to disastrous consequences. He viewed technology and science as a two edged sword with both benefits and dangers. Particularly poignant is the "Wanderer of Infinity," who like a "Flying Dutchman" from another dimension is doomed to wander forever trying to prevent cross dimensional disasters after his experiments cause the destruction of his own world and his family.

In his stories the Ramapo Mountains in up-state New York are filled with the secret lairs of mad scientists, who in their hubris, carry out dangerous experiments resulting in invasions from other dimensions, the importation of deadly lunar flora that nearly destroy the Earth, and other disasters. In others, the moons of Jupiter are the home to space pirates or worse and Mars maintains a hell-hole of a prison on the planet Vulcan within the orbit of Mercury.

Given the time that these stories were written, this is not surprising. Knowledge of the other bodies in our solar system was sketchy at best and many writers of the time pictured the various planets and satellites as being much more Earth like than we know them to be today. With technology, Vincent was a bit more realistic, if not accurate. He was a working engineer with Westinghouse and therefore familiar with the technology of the day. He describes various electrical and electronic devices drawing on his professional knowledge. Though he mentions Einstein's theories in several of his stories, his physics is perhaps on shakier ground than his engineering. Still, he does no worse, and often much better than the writers of other stories that appeared in the same magazines.

Whatever his flaws and virtues, Harl Vincent was an important part of a period that saw the birth of modern science fiction. For this reason, Resurrected Press is pleased to offer this collection of some of Vincent's best stories for the enjoyment of its readers.

About the Author

Harl Vincent was the pen name of Harold Vincent Schoepflin, an early American science fiction author. Born in Buffalo, New York on October 19, 1893, he worked as an mechanical engineer for Westinghouse specializing in large electrical apparatus before turning to writing in the late 1920's. His first story was published in *Amazing Stories* in 1928, and during the next fourteen years more than seventy of his stories were published before he stopped writing in the early 1940's. He resumed writing shortly before his death in the mid 1960's. He died in Los Angeles on May 5, 1968.

Greg Fowlkes
Editor-In-Chief
Resurrected Press
www.ResurrectedPress.com

TABLE OF CONTENTS

Old Crompton's Secret

**Originally Published in *Astounding Stories*
February 1930**

Old Crompton's Secret

Two miles west of the village of Laketon there lived an aged recluse who was known only as Old Crompton. As far back as the villagers could remember he had visited the town regularly twice a month, each time tottering his lonely way homeward with a load of provisions. He appeared to be well supplied with funds, but purchased sparingly as became a miserly hermit. And so vicious was his tongue that few cared to converse with him, even the young hoodlums of the town hesitating to harass him with the banter usually accorded the other bizarre characters of the streets.

The oldest inhabitants knew nothing of his past history, and they had long since lost their curiosity in the matter. He was a fixture, as was the old town hall with its surrounding park. His lonely cabin was shunned by all who chanced to pass along the old dirt road that led through the woods to nowhere and was rarely used.

His only extravagance was in the matter of books, and the village book store profited considerably by his purchases. But, at the instigation of Cass Harmon, the bookseller, it was whispered about that Old Crompton was a believer in the black art—that he had made a pact with the devil himself and was leagued with him and his imps. For the books he bought were strange ones; ancient volumes that Cass must needs order from New York or Chicago and that cost as much as ten and even fifteen dollars a copy; translations of the writings of the alchemists and astrologers and philosophers of the dark ages.

It was no wonder Old Crompton was looked at askance by the simple-living and deeply religious natives of the small Pennsylvania town.

But there came a day when the hermit was to have a neighbor, and the town buzzed with excited speculation as to what would happen.

*   *   *   *   *

The property across the road from Old Crompton's hut belonged to Alton Forsythe, Laketon's wealthiest resident—hundreds of acres of scrubby woodland that he considered well nigh worthless. But Tom Forsythe, the only son, had returned from college and his ambitions were of a nature strange to his townspeople and utterly incomprehensible to his father. Something vague about biology and chemical experiments and the like is what he spoke of, and, when his parents objected on the grounds of possible explosions and other weird accidents, he prevailed upon his father to have a secluded laboratory built for him in the woods.

When the workmen started the small frame structure not a quarter of a mile from his own hut, Old Crompton was furious. He raged and stormed, but to no avail. Tom Forsythe had his heart set on the project and he was somewhat of a successful debater himself. The fire that flashed from his cold gray eyes matched that from the pale blue ones of the elderly anchorite. And the law was on his side.

So the building was completed and Tom Forsythe moved in, bag and baggage.

For more than a year the hermit studiously avoided his neighbor, though, truth to tell, this required very little effort. For Tom Forsythe became almost as much of a recluse as his predecessor, remaining indoors for days at a time and visiting the home of his people scarcely oftener than Old Crompton visited the village. He too became the target of village gossip and his name was ere long linked with that of the old man in similar animadversion. But he cared naught for the opinions of his townspeople nor for the dark looks of suspicion that greeted him on his rare appearances in the public places. His chosen work engrossed him so deeply that all else counted for nothing. His parents remonstrated with him in vain. Tom laughed away their recriminations and fears, continuing with his labors more strenuously than ever. He never troubled his mind over the nearness of Old Crompton's hut, the existence of which he hardly noticed or considered.

*   *   *   *   *

It so happened one day that the old man's curiosity got the better of him and Tom caught him prowling about on his property, peering wonderingly at the many rabbit hutches, chicken coops, dove cotes and the like which cluttered the space to the rear of the laboratory.

Seeing that he was discovered, the old man wrinkled his face into a toothless grin of conciliation.

"Just looking over your place, Forsythe," he said. "Sorry about the fuss I made when you built the house. But I'm an old man, you know, and changes are unwelcome. Now I have forgotten my objections and would like to be friends. Can we?"

Tom peered searchingly into the flinty eyes that were set so deeply in the wrinkled, leathery countenance. He suspected an ulterior motive, but could not find it within him to turn the old fellow down.

"Why—I guess so, Crompton," he hesitated: "I have nothing against you, but I came here for seclusion and I'll not have anyone bothering me in my work."

"I'll not bother you, young man. But I'm fond of pets and I see you have many of them here; guinea pigs, chickens, pigeons, and rabbits. Would you mind if I make friends with some of them?"

"They're not pets," answered Tom dryly, "they are material for use in my experiments. But you may amuse yourself with them if you wish."

"You mean that you cut them up—kill them, perhaps?"

"Not that. But I sometimes change them in physical form, sometimes cause them to become of huge size, sometimes produce pigmy offspring of normal animals."

"Don't they suffer?"

"Very seldom, though occasionally a subject dies. But the benefit that will accrue to mankind is well worth the slight inconvenience to the dumb creatures and the infrequent loss of their lives."

*   *   *   *   *

Old Crompton regarded him dubiously. "You are trying to find?" he interrogated.

"The secret of life!" Tom Forsythe's eyes took on the stare of fanaticism. "Before I have finished I shall know the nature of the vital force—how to produce it. I shall prolong human life indefinitely; create artificial life. And the solution is more closely approached with each passing day."

The hermit blinked in pretended mystification. But he understood perfectly, and he bitterly envied the younger man's knowledge and ability that enabled him to delve into the mysteries of nature which had always been so attractive to his own mind. And somehow, he acquired a sudden deep hatred of the coolly confident young man who spoke so positively of accomplishing the impossible.

During the winter months that followed, the strange acquaintance progressed but little. Tom did not invite his neighbor to visit him, nor did Old Crompton go out of his way to impose his presence on the younger man, though each spoke pleasantly enough to the other on the few occasions when they happened to meet.

With the coming of spring they encountered one another more frequently, and Tom found considerable of interest in the quaint, borrowed philosophy of the gloomy old man. Old Crompton, of course, was desperately interested in the things that were hidden in Tom's laboratory, but he never requested permission to see them. He hid his real feelings extremely well and was apparently content to spend as much time as possible with the feathered and furred subjects for experiment, being very careful not to incur Tom's displeasure by displaying too great interest in the laboratory itself.

*   *   *   *   *

Then there came a day in early summer when an accident served to draw the two men closer together, and Old Crompton's long-sought opportunity followed.

He was starting for the village when, from down the road, there came a series of tremendous squawkings, then a bellow of dismay in the voice of his young neighbor. He turned quickly and was astonished at the sight of a monstrous rooster which had escaped and was headed straight for him with head down and wings fluttering wildly. Tom followed close behind, but was unable to catch the darting monster. And monster it was, for this rooster stood no less than three feet in height and appeared more ferocious than a large turkey. Old Crompton had his shopping bag, a large one of burlap which he always carried to town, and he summoned enough courage to throw it over the head of the screeching, over-sized fowl. So tangled did the panic-stricken bird become that it was a comparatively simple matter to effect his capture, and the old man rose to his feet triumphant with the bag securely closed over the struggling captive.

"Thanks," panted Tom, when he drew alongside. "I should never have caught him, and his appearance at large might have caused me a great deal of trouble—now of all times."

"It's all right, Forsythe," smirked the old man. "Glad I was able to do it."

Secretly he gloated, for he knew this occurrence would be an open sesame to that laboratory of Tom's. And it proved to be just that.

*   *   *   *   *

A few nights later he was awakened by a vigorous thumping at his door, something that had never before occurred during his nearly sixty years occupancy of the tumbledown hut. The moon was high and he cautiously peeped from the window and saw that his late visitor was none other than young Forsythe.

"With you in a minute!" he shouted, hastily thrusting his rheumatic old limbs into his shabby trousers. "Now to see the inside of that laboratory," he chuckled to himself.

It required but a moment to attire himself in the scanty raiment he wore during the warm months, but he could hear Tom muttering and impatiently pacing the flagstones before his door.

"What is it?" he asked, as he drew the bolt and emerged into the brilliant light of the moon.

"Success!" breathed Tom excitedly. "I have produced growing, living matter synthetically. More than this, I have learned the secret of the vital force—the spark of life. Immortality is within easy reach. Come and see for yourself."

They quickly traversed the short distance to the two-story building which comprised Tom's workshop and living quarters. The entire ground floor was taken up by the laboratory, and Old Crompton stared aghast at the wealth of equipment it contained. Furnaces there were, and retorts that reminded him of those pictured in the wood cuts in some of his musty books. Then there were complicated machines with many levers and dials mounted on their faces, and with huge glass bulbs of peculiar shape with coils of wire connecting to knoblike protuberances of their transparent walls. In the exact center of the great single room there was what appeared to be a dissecting table, with a brilliant light overhead and with two of the odd glass bulbs at either end. It was to this table that Tom led the excited old man.

"This is my perfected apparatus," said Tom proudly, "and by its use I intend to create a new race of supermen, men and women who will always retain the vigor and strength of their youth and who can not die excepting by actual destruction of their bodies. Under the influence of the rays all bodily ailments vanish as if by magic, and organic defects are quickly corrected. Watch this now."

*   *   *   *   *

He stepped to one of the many cages at the side of the room and returned with a wriggling cottontail in his hands. Old Compton watched anxiously as he picked a nickeled instrument from a tray of surgical appliances and requested his visitor to hold the protesting animal while he covered its head with a handkerchief.

"Ethyl chloride," explained Tom, noting with amusement the look of distaste on the old man's face. "We'll just put him to sleep for a minute while I amputate a leg."

The struggles of the rabbit quickly ceased when the spray soaked the handkerchief and the anaesthetic took effect. With a shining scalpel and a surgical saw, Tom speedily removed one of the forelegs of the animal and then he placed the limp body in the center of the table, removing the handkerchief from its head as he did so. At the end of the table there was a panel with its glittering array of switches and electrical instruments, and Old Crompton observed very closely the manipulations of the controls as Tom started the mechanism. With the ensuing hum of a motor-generator from a corner of the room, the four bulbs adjacent to the table sprang into life, each glowing with a different color and each emitting a different vibratory note as it responded to the energy within.

"Keep an eye on Mr. Rabbit now," admonished Tom.

From the body of the small animal there emanated an intangible though hazily visible aura as the combined effects of the rays grew in intensity. Old Crompton bent over the table and peered amazedly at the stump of the foreleg, from which blood no longer dripped. The stump was healing over! Yes—it seemed to elongate as one watched. A new limb was growing on to replace the old! Then the animal struggled once more, this time to regain consciousness. In a moment it was fully awake and, with a frightened hop, was off the table and hobbling about in search of a hiding place.

*   *   *   *   *

Tom Forsythe laughed. "Never knew what happened," he exulted, "and excepting for the temporary limp is not inconvenienced at all. Even that will be gone in a couple of hours, for the new limb will be completely grown by that time."

"But—but, Tom," stammered the old man, "this is wonderful. How do you accomplish it?"

"Ha! Don't think I'll reveal my secret. But this much I will tell you: the life force generated by my apparatus stimulates a certain gland that's normally inactive in warm blooded animals. This gland, when active, possesses the function of growing new members to the body to replace lost ones in much the same manner as this is done in case of the lobster and certain other crustaceans. Of course, the process is extremely rapid when the gland is stimulated by the vital rays from my tubes. But this is only one of the many wonders of the process. Here is something far more remarkable."

He took from a large glass jar the body of a guinea pig, a body that was rigid in death.

"This guinea pig," he explained, "was suffocated twenty-four hours ago and is stone dead."

"Suffocated?"

"Yes. But quite painlessly, I assure you. I merely removed the air from the jar with a vacuum pump and the little creature passed out of the picture very quickly. Now we'll revive it."

Old Crompton stretched forth a skinny hand to touch the dead animal, but withdrew it hastily when he felt the clammy rigidity of the body. There was no doubt as to the lifelessness of this specimen.

*   *   *   *   *

Tom placed the dead guinea pig on the spot where the rabbit had been subjected to the action of the rays. Again his visitor watched carefully as he manipulated the controls of the apparatus.

With the glow of the tubes and the ensuing haze of eery light that surrounded the little body, a marked change was apparent. The inanimate form relaxed suddenly and it seemed that the muscles pulsated with an accession of energy. Then one leg was stretched forth spasmodically. There was a convulsive heave as the lungs drew in a first long breath, and, with that, an astonished and very much alive rodent scrambled to its feet, blinking wondering eyes in the dazzling light.

"See? See?" shouted Tom, grasping Old Crompton by the arm in a viselike grip. "It is the secret of life and death! Aristocrats, plutocrats and beggars will beat a path to my door. But, never fear, I shall choose my subjects well. The name of Thomas Forsythe will yet be emblazoned in the Hall of Fame. I shall be master of the world!"

Old Crompton began to fear the glitter in the eyes of the gaunt young man who seemed suddenly to have become demented. And his envy and hatred of his talented host blazed anew as Forsythe gloried in the success of his efforts. Then he was struck with an idea and he affected his most ingratiating manner.

"It is a marvelous thing, Tom," he said, "and is entirely beyond my poor comprehension. But I can see that it is all you say and more. Tell me—can you restore the youth of an aged person by these means?"

"Positively!" Tom did not catch the eager note in the old man's voice. Rather he took the question as an inquiry into the further marvels of his process. "Here," he continued, enthusiastically, "I'll prove that to you also. My dog Spot is around the place somewhere. And he is a decrepit old hound, blind, lame and toothless. You've probably seen him with me."

* * * * *

He rushed to the stairs and whistled. There was an answering yelp from above and the pad of uncertain paws on the bare wooden steps. A dejected old beagle blundered into the room, dragging a crippled hind leg as he fawned upon his master, who stretched forth a hand to pat the unsteady head.

"Guess Spot is old enough for the test," laughed Tom, "and I have been meaning to restore him to his youthful vigor, anyway. No time like the present."

He led his trembling pet to the table of the remarkable tubes and lifted him to its surface. The poor old beast lay trustingly where he was placed, quiet, save for his husky asthmatic breathing.

"Hold him, Crompton," directed Tom as he pulled the starting lever of his apparatus.

And Old Crompton watched in fascinated anticipation as the ethereal luminosity bathed the dog's body in response to the action of the four rays. Somewhat vaguely it came to him that the baggy flesh of his own wrinkled hands took on a new firmness and color where they reposed on the animal's back. Young Forsythe grinned triumphantly as Spot's breathing became more regular and the rasp gradually left it. Then the dog whined in pleasure and wagged his tail with increasing vigor. Suddenly he raised his head, perked his ears in astonishment and looked his master straight in the face with eyes that saw once more. The low throat cry rose to a full and joyous bark. He sprang to his feet from under the restraining hands and jumped to the floor in a lithe-muscled leap that carried him half way across the room. He capered about with the abandon of a puppy, making extremely active use of four sound limbs.

"Why—why, Forsythe," stammered the hermit, "it's absolutely incredible. Tell me—tell me—what is this remarkable force?"

*   *   *   *   *

His host laughed gleefully. "You probably wouldn't understand it anyway, but I'll tell you. It is as simple as the nose on your face. The spark of life, the vital force, is merely an extremely complicated electrical manifestation which I have been able to duplicate artificially. This spark or force is all that distinguishes living from inanimate matter, and in living beings the force gradually decreases in power as the years pass, causing loss of health and strength. The chemical composition of bones and tissue alters, joints become stiff, muscles atrophied, and bones brittle. By recharging, as it were, with the vital force, the gland action is intensified, youth and strength is renewed. By repeating the process every ten or fifteen years the same degree of vigor can be maintained indefinitely. Mankind will become immortal. That is why I say I am to be master of the world."

For the moment Old Crompton forgot his jealous hatred in the enthusiasm with which he was imbued. "Tom—Tom," he pleaded in his excitement, "use me as a subject. Renew my youth. My life has been a sad one and a lonely one, but I would that I might live it over. I should make of it a far different one— something worth while. See, I am ready."

He sat on the edge of the gleaming table and made as if to lie down on its gleaming surface. But his young host only stared at him in open amusement.

"What? You?" he sneered, unfeelingly. "Why, you old fossil! I told you I would choose my subjects carefully. They are to be people of standing and wealth, who can contribute to the fame and fortune of one Thomas Forsythe."

"But Tom, I have money," Old Crompton begged. But when he saw the hard mirth in the younger man's eyes, his old animosity flamed anew and he sprang from his position and shook a skinny forefinger in Tom's face.

"Don't do that to me, you old fool!" shouted Tom, "and get out of here. Think I'd waste current on an old cadger like you? I guess not! Now get out. Get out, I say!"

Then the old anchorite saw red. Something seemed to snap in his soured old brain. He found himself kicking and biting and punching at his host, who backed away from the furious onslaught in surprise. Then Tom tripped over a wire and fell to the floor with a force that rattled the windows, his ferocious little adversary on top. The younger man lay still where he had fallen, a trickle of blood showing at his temple.

"My God! I've killed him!" gasped the old man.

With trembling fingers he opened Tom's shirt and listened for his heartbeats. Panic-stricken, he rubbed the young man's wrists, slapped his cheeks, and ran for water to dash in his face. But all efforts to revive him proved futile, and then, in awful fear, Old Crompton dashed into the night, the dog Spot snapping at his heels as he ran.

*　　*　　*　　*　　*

Hours later the stooped figure of a shabby old man might have been seen stealthily re-entering the lonely workshop where the lights still burned brightly. Tom Forsythe lay rigid in the position in which Old Crompton had left him, and the dog growled menacingly.

Averting his gaze and circling wide of the body, Old Crompton made for the table of the marvelous rays. In minute detail he recalled every move made by Tom in starting and adjusting the apparatus to produce the incredible results he had witnessed. Not a moment was to be wasted now. Already he had hesitated too long, for soon would come the dawn and possible discovery of his crime. But the invention of his victim would save him from the long arm of the law, for, with youth restored, Old Crompton would cease to exist and a new life would open its doors to the starved soul of the hermit. Hermit, indeed! He would begin life anew, an active man with youthful vigor and ambition. Under an assumed name he would travel abroad, would enjoy life, and would later become a successful man of affairs. He had enough money, he told himself. And the police would never find Old Crompton, the murderer of Tom Forsythe!

He deposited his small traveling bag on the floor and fingered the controls of Tom's apparatus.

He threw the starting switch confidently and grinned in satisfaction as the answering whine of the motor-generator came to his ears. One by one he carefully made the adjustments in exactly the manner followed by the now silenced discoverer of the process. Everything operated precisely as it had during the preceding experiments. Odd that he should have anticipated some such necessity! But something had told him to observe Tom's movements carefully, and now he rejoiced in the fact that his intuition had led him aright. Painfully he climbed to the table top and stretched his aching body in the warm light of the four huge tubes. His exertions during the struggle with Tom were beginning to tell on him. But the soreness and stiffness of feeble muscles and stubborn joints would soon be but a memory. His pulses quickened at the thought and he breathed deep in a sudden feeling of unaccustomed well-being.

*   *   *   *   *

The dog growled continuously from his position at the head of his master, but did not move to interfere with the intruder. And Old Crompton, in the excitement of the momentous experience, paid him not the slightest attention.

His body tingled from head to foot with a not unpleasant sensation that conveyed the assurance of radical changes taking place under the influence of the vital rays. The tingling sensation increased in intensity until it seemed that every corpuscle in his veins danced to the tune of the vibration from those glowing tubes that bathed him in an ever-spreading radiance. Aches and pains vanished from his body, but he soon experienced a sharp stab of new pain in his lower jaw. With an experimental forefinger he rubbed the gum. He laughed aloud as the realization came to him that in those gums where there had been no teeth for more than twenty years there was now growing a complete new set. And the rapidity of the process amazed him beyond measure. The aching area spread quickly and was becoming really uncomfortable. But then—and he consoled himself with the thought—nothing is brought into being without a certain amount of pain. Besides, he was confident that his discomfort would soon be over.

He examined his hand, and found that the joints of two fingers long crippled with rheumatism now moved freely and painlessly. The misty brilliance surrounding his body was paling and he saw that the flesh was taking on a faint green fluorescence instead. The rays had completed their work and soon the transformation would be fully effected. He turned on his side and slipped to the floor with the agility of a youngster. The dog snarled anew, but kept steadfastly to his position.

*   *   *   *   *

There was a small mirror over the wash stand at the far end of the room and Old Crompton made haste to obtain the first view of his reflected image. His step was firm and springy, his bearing confident, and he found that his long-stooped shoulders straightened naturally and easily. He felt that he had taken on at least two inches in stature, which was indeed the case. When he reached the mirror he peered anxiously into its dingy surface and what he saw there so startled him that he stepped backward in amazement. This was not Larry Crompton, but an entirely new man. The straggly white hair had given way to soft, healthy waves of chestnut hue. Gone were the seams from the leathery countenance and the eyes looked out clearly and steadily from under brows as thick and dark as they had been in his youth. The reflected features were those of an entire stranger. They were not even reminiscent of the Larry Crompton of fifty years ago, but were the features of a far more vigorous and prepossessing individual than he had ever seemed, even in the best years of his life. The jaw was firm, the once sunken cheeks so well filled out that his high cheek bones were no longer in evidence. It was the face of a man of not more than thirty-eight years of age, reflecting exceptional intelligence and strength of character.

"What a disguise!" he exclaimed in delight. And his voice, echoing in the stillness that followed the switching off of the apparatus, was deep-throated and mellow—the voice of a new man.

Now, serenely confident that discovery was impossible, he picked up his small but heavy bag and started for the door. Dawn was breaking and he wished to put as many miles between himself and Tom's laboratory as could be covered in the next few hours. But at the door he hesitated. Then, despite the furious yapping of Spot, he returned to the table of the rays and, with deliberate thoroughness smashed the costly tubes which had brought about his rehabilitation. With a pinch bar from a nearby tool rack, he wrecked the controls and generating mechanisms beyond recognition. Now he was absolutely secure! No meddling experts could possibly discover the secret of Tom's invention. All evidence would show that the young experimenter had met his death at the hands of Old Crompton, the despised hermit of West Laketon. But none would dream that the handsome man of means who was henceforth to be known as George Voight was that same despised hermit.

He recovered his satchel and left the scene. With long, rapid strides he proceeded down the old dirt road toward the main highway where, instead of turning east into the village, he would turn west and walk to Kernsburg, the neighboring town. There, in not more than two hours time, his new life would really begin!

*   *   *   *   *

Had you, a visitor, departed from Laketon when Old Crompton did and returned twelve years later, you would have noticed very little difference in the appearance of the village. The old town hall and the little park were the same, the dingy brick building among the trees being just a little dingier and its wooden steps more worn and sagged. The main street showed evidence of recent repaving, and, in consequence of the resulting increase in through automobile traffic; there were two new gasoline filling stations in the heart of the town. Down the road about a half mile there was a new building, which, upon inquiring from one of the natives, would be proudly designated as the new high school building. Otherwise there were no changes to be observed.

In his dilapidated chair in the untidy office he had occupied for nearly thirty years, sat Asa Culkin, popularly known as "Judge" Culkin. Justice of the peace, sheriff, attorney-at-law, and three times Mayor of Laketon, he was still a controlling factor in local politics and government. And many a knotty legal problem was settled in that gloomy little office. Many a dispute in the town council was dependent for arbitration upon the keen mind and understanding wit of the old judge.

The four o'clock train had just puffed its labored way from the station when a stranger entered his office, a stranger of uncommonly prosperous air. The keen blue eyes of the old attorney appraised him instantly and classified him as a successful man of business, not yet forty years of age, and with a weighty problem on his mind.

"What can I do for you, sir?" he asked, removing his feet from the battered desk top.

"You may be able to help me a great deal, Judge," was the unexpected reply. "I came to Laketon to give myself up."

"Give yourself up?" Culkin rose to his feet in surprise and unconsciously straightened his shoulders in the effort to seem less dwarfed before the tall stranger. "Why, what do you mean?" he inquired.

*　　*　　*　　*　　*

"I wish to give myself up for murder," answered the amazing visitor, slowly and with decision, "for a murder committed twelve years ago. I should like you to listen to my story first, though. It has been kept too long."

"But I still do not understand." There was puzzlement in the honest old face of the attorney. He shook his gray locks in uncertainty. "Why should you come here? Why come to me? What possible interest can I have in the matter?"

"Just this, Judge. You do not recognize me now, and you will probably consider my story incredible when you hear it. But, when I have given you all the evidence, you will know who I am and will be compelled to believe. The murder was committed in Laketon. That is why I came to you."

"A murder in Laketon? Twelve years ago?" Again the aged attorney shook his head. "But—proceed."

"Yes. I killed Thomas Forsythe."

The stranger looked for an expression of horror in the features of his listener, but there was none. Instead the benign countenance took on a look of deepening amazement, but the smile wrinkles had somehow vanished and the old face was grave in its surprised interest.

"You seem astonished," continued the stranger. "Undoubtedly you were convinced that the murderer was Larry Crompton—Old Crompton, the hermit. He disappeared the night of the crime and has never been heard from since. Am I correct?"

"Yes. He disappeared all right. But continue."

Not by a lift of his eyebrow did Culkin betray his disbelief, but the stranger sensed that his story was somehow not as startling as it should have been.

"You will think me crazy, I presume. But I am Old Crompton. It was my hand that felled the unfortunate young man in his laboratory out there in West Laketon twelve years ago to-night. It was his marvelous invention that transformed the old hermit into the apparently young man you see before you. But I swear that I am none other than Larry Crompton and that I killed young Forsythe. I am ready to pay the penalty. I can bear the flagellation of my own conscience no longer."

*   *   *   *   *

The visitor's voice had risen to the point of hysteria. But his listener remained calm and unmoved.

"Now just let me get this straight," he said quietly. "Do I understand that you claim to be Old Crompton, rejuvenated in some mysterious manner, and that you killed Tom Forsythe on that night twelve years ago? Do I understand that you wish now to go to trial for that crime and to pay the penalty?"

"Yes! Yes! And the sooner the better. I can stand it no longer. I am the most miserable man in the world!"

"Hm-m—hm-m," muttered the judge, "this is strange." He spoke soothingly to his visitor. "Do not upset yourself, I beg of you. I will take care of this thing for you, never fear. Just take a seat, Mister—er—"

"You may call me Voight for the present," said the stranger, in a more composed tone of voice, "George Voight. That is the name I have been using since the mur—since that fatal night."

"Very well, Mr. Voight," replied the counsellor with an air of the greatest solicitude, "please have a seat now, while I make a telephone call."

And George Voight slipped into a stiff-backed chair with a sigh of relief. For he knew the judge from the old days and he was now certain that his case would be disposed of very quickly.

With the telephone receiver pressed to his ear, Culkin repeated a number. The stranger listened intently during the ensuing silence. Then there came a muffled "hello" sounding in impatient response to the call.

"Hello, Alton," spoke the attorney, "this is Asa speaking. A stranger has just stepped into my office and he claims to be Old Crompton. Remember the hermit across the road from your son's old laboratory? Well, this man, who bears no resemblance whatever to the old man he claims to be and who seems to be less than half the age of Tom's old neighbor, says that he killed Tom on that night we remember so well."

*   *   *   *   *

There were some surprised remarks from the other end of the wire, but Voight was unable to catch them. He was in a cold perspiration at the thought of meeting his victim's father.

"Why, yes, Alton," continued Culkin, "I think there is something in this story, although I cannot believe it all. But I wish you would accompany us and visit the laboratory. Will you?"

"Lord, man, not that!" interrupted the judge's visitor. "I can hardly bear to visit the scene of my crime—and in the company of Alton Forsythe. Please, not that!"

"Now you just let me take care of this, young man," replied the judge, testily. Then, once more speaking into the mouthpiece of the telephone, "All right, Alton. We'll pick you up at your office in five minutes."

He replaced the receiver on its hook and turned again to his visitor. "Please be so kind as to do exactly as I request," he said. "I want to help you, but there is more to this thing than you know and I want you to follow unquestioningly where I lead and ask no questions at all for the present. Things may turn out differently than you expect."

"All right, Judge." The visitor resigned himself to whatever might transpire under the guidance of the man he had called upon to turn him over to the officers of the law.

*   *   *   *   *

Seated in the judge's ancient motor car, they stopped at the office of Alton Forsythe a few minutes later and were joined by that red-faced and pompous old man. Few words were spoken during the short run to the well-remembered location of Tom's laboratory, and the man who was known as George Voight caught at his own throat with nervous fingers when they passed the tumbledown remains of the hut in which Old Crompton had spent so many years. With a screeching of well-worn brakes the car stopped before the laboratory, which was now almost hidden behind a mass of shrubs and flowers.

"Easy now, young man," cautioned the judge, noting the look of fear which had clouded his new client's features. The three men advanced to the door through which Old Crompton had fled on that night of horror, twelve years before. The elder Forsythe spoke not a word as he turned the knob and stepped within. Voight shrank from entering, but soon mastered his feelings and followed the other two. The sight that met his eyes caused him to cry aloud in awe.

At the dissecting table, which seemed to be exactly as he had seen it last but with replicas of the tubes he had destroyed once more in place, stood Tom Forsythe! Considerably older and with hair prematurely gray, he was still the young man Old Crompton thought he had killed. Tom Forsythe was not dead after all! And all of his years of misery had gone for nothing. He advanced slowly to the side of the wondering young man, Alton Forsythe and Asa Culkin watching silently from just inside the door.

"Tom—Tom," spoke the stranger, "you are alive? You were not dead when I left you on that terrible night when I smashed your precious tubes? Oh—it is too good to be true! I can scarcely believe my eyes!"

*   *   *   *   *

He stretched forth trembling fingers to touch the body of the young man to assure himself that it was not all a dream.

"Why," said Tom Forsythe, in astonishment. "I do not know you, sir. Never saw you in my life. What do you mean by your talk of smashing my tubes, of leaving me for dead?"

"Mean?" The stranger's voice rose now; he was growing excited. "Why, Tom, I am Old Crompton. Remember the struggle, here in this very room? You refused to rejuvenate an unhappy old man with your marvelous apparatus, a temporarily insane old man—Crompton. I was that old man and I fought with you. You fell, striking your head. There was blood. You were unconscious. Yes, for many hours I was sure you were dead and that I had murdered you. But I had watched your manipulations of the apparatus and I subjected myself to the action of the rays. My youth was miraculously restored. I became as you see me now. Detection was impossible, for I looked no more like Old Crompton than you do. I smashed your machinery to avoid suspicion. Then I escaped. And, for twelve years, I have thought myself a murderer. I have suffered the tortures of the damned!"

Tom Forsythe advanced on this remarkable visitor with clenched fists. Staring him in the eyes with cold appraisal, his wrath was all too apparent. The dog Spot, young as ever, entered the room and, upon observing the stranger, set up an ominous growling and snarling. At least the dog recognized him!

"What are you trying to do, catechise me? Are you another of these alienists my father has been bringing around?" The young inventor was furious. "If you are," he continued, "you can get out of here—now! I'll have no more of this meddling with my affairs. I'm as sane as any of you and I refuse to submit to this continual persecution."

The elder Forsythe grunted, and Culkin laid a restraining hand on his arm. "Just a minute now, Tom," he said soothingly. "This stranger is no alienist. He has a story to tell. Please permit him to finish."

*   *   *   *   *

Somewhat mollified, Tom Forsythe shrugged his assent.

"Tom," continued the stranger, more calmly now, "what I have said is the truth. I shall prove it to you. I'll tell you things no mortals on earth could know but we two. Remember the day I captured the big rooster for you—the monster you had created? Remember the night you awakened me and brought me here in the moonlight? Remember the rabbit whose leg you amputated and re-grew? The poor guinea pig you had suffocated and whose life you restored? Spot here? Don't you remember rejuvenating him? I was here. And you refused to use your process on me, old man that I was. Then is when I went mad and attacked you. Do you believe me, Tom?"

Then a strange thing happened. While Tom Forsythe gazed in growing belief, the stranger's shoulders sagged and he trembled as with the ague. The two older men who had kept in the background gasped their astonishment as his hair faded to a sickly gray, then became as white as the driven snow. Old Crompton was reverting to his previous state! Within five minutes, instead of the handsome young stranger, there stood before them a bent, withered old man—Old Crompton beyond a doubt. The effects of Tom's process were spent.

"Well I'm damned!" ejaculated Alton Forsythe. "You have been right all along, Asa. And I am mighty glad I did not commit Tom as I intended. He has told us the truth all these years and we were not wise enough to see it."

"We!" exclaimed the judge. "You, Alton Forsythe! I have always upheld him. You have done your son a grave injustice and you owe him your apologies if ever a father owed his son anything."

"You are right, Asa." And, his aristocratic pride forgotten, Alton Forsythe rushed to the side of his son and embraced him.

The judge turned to Old Crompton pityingly. "Rather a bad ending for you, Crompton," he said. "Still, it is better by far than being branded as a murderer."

"Better? Better?" croaked Old Crompton. "It is wonderful, Judge. I have never been so happy in my life!"

*　　*　　*　　*　　*

The face of the old man beamed, though scalding tears coursed down the withered and seamed cheeks. The two

Forsythes looked up from their demonstrations of peacemaking to listen to the amazing words of the old hermit.

"Yes, happy for the first time in my life," he continued. "I am one hundred years of age, gentlemen, and I now look it and feel it. That is as it should be. And my experience has taught me a final lasting lesson. None of you know it, but, when I was but a very young man I was bitterly disappointed in love. Ha! ha! Never think it to look at me now, would you? But I was, and it ruined my entire life. I had a little money—inherited—and I traveled about in the world for a few years, then settled in that old hut across the road where I buried myself for sixty years, becoming crabbed and sour and despicable. Young Tom here was the first bright spot and, though I admired him, I hated him for his opportunities, hated him for that which he had that I had not. With the promise of his invention I thought I saw happiness, a new life for myself. I got what I wanted, though not in the way I had expected. And I want to tell you gentlemen that there is nothing in it. With developments of modern science you may be able to restore a man's youthful vigor of body, but you can't cure his mind with electricity. Though I had a youthful body, my brain was the brain of an old man—memories were there which could not be suppressed. Even had I not had the fancied death of young Tom on my conscience I should still have been miserable. I worked. God, how I worked—to forget! But I could not forget. I was successful in business and made a lot of money. I am more independent—probably wealthier than you, Alton Forsythe, but that did not bring happiness. I longed to be myself once more, to have the aches and pains which had been taken from me. It is natural to age and to die. Immortality would make of us a people of restless misery. We would quarrel and bicker and long for death, which would not come to relieve us. Now it is over for me and I am glad—glad—glad!"

*   *   *   *   *

He paused for breath, looking beseechingly at Tom Forsythe. "Tom," he said, "I suppose you have nothing for me in your heart but hatred. And I don't blame you. But I wish—I wish you would try and forgive me. Can you?"

The years had brought increased understanding and tolerance to young Tom. He stared at Old Crompton and the long-nursed anger over the destruction of his equipment melted into a strange mixture of pity and admiration for the courageous old fellow.

"Why, I guess I can, Crompton," he replied. "There was many a day when I struggled hopelessly to reconstruct my apparatus, cursing you with every bit of energy in my make-up. I could cheerfully have throttled you, had you been within reach. For twelve years I have labored incessantly to reproduce the results we obtained on the night of which you speak. People called me insane—even my father wished to have me committed to an asylum. And, until now, I have been unsuccessful. Only to-day has it seemed for the first time that the experiments will again succeed. But my ideas have changed with regard to the uses of the process. I was a cocksure young pup in the old days, with foolish dreams of fame and influence. But I have seen the error of my ways. Your experience, too, convinces me that immortality may not be as desirable as I thought. But there are great possibilities in the way of relieving the sufferings of mankind and in making this a better world in which to live. With your advice and help I believe I can do great things. I now forgive you freely and I ask you to remain here with me to assist in the work that is to come. What do you say to the idea?"

At the reverent thankfulness in the pale eyes of the broken old man who had so recently been a perfect specimen of vigorous youth, Alton Forsythe blew his nose noisily. The little judge smiled benevolently and shook his head as if to say, "I told you so." Tom and Old Crompton gripped hands—mightily.

The Terror of Air-Level Six

Originally Published in *Astounding Stories*,
July 1930

The Terror of Air-Level Six

It was a sweltering evening in mid-August, during that unprecedented heat wave which broke Weather Bureau records in 2011. New York City had simmered under a blazing sun for more than three weeks, and all who were able had deserted the city for spots of lesser torridity. But I was one of those unfortunates who could not leave on account of the pressing urgency of business matters and, there being nothing else to do, kept doggedly at my work until it seemed that nerves and body must soon give way under the strain. To-night, as I boarded the pneumatic tube, I dropped into the nearest seat and could not even summon the energy to open my newspaper.

For some minutes I sat as in a daze, wishing merely that the journey was over, and that I was on my own front porch out in Rutherford. After awhile I stirred and looked around. Seeing none of my acquaintances in the car, I finally opened the newspaper and was considerably startled by the screaming headlines that confronted me from its usually conservative first page:

SECOND COAST TRANSPORT PLANE LOST!
Disaster Like First in Air-Level Six!

No wonder the newsboys had been crying an extra on Broadway! I had given no heed to the import of their shoutings, but this was real news and well worthy of an extra edition. Since the mysterious loss of the SP-61, only four days previously, the facilities of the several air transportation systems were seriously handicapped on account of the shaken confidence of the general public. It was not surprising that there was widespread reluctance at trusting human lives and valuable merchandise to the mercies of the inexplicable power which had apparently wiped out of existence the SF-61, together with its twenty-eight passengers and the consignment of one-half million dollars in gold. And now the NY-18 had gone the way of the other!

Details were meager. Both ships had failed to reply to the regular ten-minute radio calls from headquarters and had not since been seen or heard from. In both cases the last call had been answered when the ship was proceeding at full speed on its regular course in air-level six. The SF-61 last reported from a position over Mora in New Mexico, and four days of intensive search by thousands of planes had failed to locate ship or passengers. To-day, in the early hours of the morning, the NY-18 reported over Colorado Springs, on the northern route, and then, like the SF-61, dropped out of existence insofar as any attempts at communicating with or locating her were concerned. She, too, carried a heavy consignment of specie, though only eleven passengers had risked the westward journey.

*   *   *   *   *

Someone had dropped into a seat at my side, and I looked up from my reading to meet the solemn eyes of Hartley Jones, a young friend whom I had not seen for several months.

"Why, hello, Hart," I greeted him. "Glad to see you, old man. Where in Sam Hill have you been keeping yourself?"

"Glad to see you, too, Jack," he returned warmly. "Been spending most of my time out at the hangar."

"Oh, that's right. You fellows built a new one at Newark Airport, didn't you?"

"Yeah. Got a great outfit there now, too. Why don't you drop around and see us one of these days?"

"I will, Hart, and I want you to take me up some time. You know I have never been in one of these new ships of yours. But what do you think of this mess?" I pointed to the black headlines.

He grinned joyously and flipped back the lapel of his coat, displaying a nickeled badge. "George and I are starting out to-night to look around a little," he gloated. "Just been appointed deputy air commissioners; and we got a couple of guns on our newest plane. Air Traffic Bureau thinks there's dirty work afoot. Twelve-motored planes don't disappear without leaving a trace. Anyhow, we've got a job, and we're going to try and find out what's wrong. How'd you like to come along?"

"What?" I replied. "You know darn well I'm too busy. Besides, I'd be no good to you. Just extra load, and not pay load at that. And then, I'm broke—as usual."

* * * * *

Hartley Jones grinned in his engaging way. "You'd be good company," he parried; "and, what's more, I think the trip would do you a lot of good. You look all shot to pieces."

"Forget it," I laughed. "It's just the heat. And I'll have to leave you here, Hart. Drop in and see us, will you? The wife was asking for you only yesterday."

"Jack, dear," my wife greeted me at the door of my modest suburban home, "Mr. Preston just called, and he wants you to call him right back."

"Oh, Lord," I groaned, "can't I forget the office for one evening?" Preston was manager of the concern for which I worked.

Nevertheless, though our two fine youngsters were clamoring for their dinner, I made the telephone call at once.

"Makely," came the voice of the boss, when the connection was completed, "I want you to take the night plane for Frisco. Hate to ask you, but it must be done. Townley is sick and someone has to take those Canadian Ex. bonds out to Farnsworth. You're the only one to do it, and after you get there, you can start on that vacation you need. Take a month if you wish."

The thought of Hartley Jones' offer flashed through my mind. "But have you read of the loss of the NY-18?" I asked Preston.

"I have, Makely. There'll be another hundred a month in your check, too, to make up for the worry of your family. But the government is sending thirty Secret Service men along on the SF-22, which leaves to-night. In addition, there will be a convoy of seven fighting planes, so there is not likely to be a repetition of the previous disasters."

That hundred a month sounded mighty good, for expenses had been mounting rapidly of late. "All right, Mr. Preston," I agreed. "I will be at the airport before midnight. But how about the bonds?"

"I'll drive around after dinner and deliver them to you. And thanks for your willingness, Makely. You'll not be sorry."

*   *   *   *   *

My wife had listened intently and, from my words, she knew what to expect. Her face was a tragic mask when I replaced the receiver on its hook, and my heart sank at her expression.

Then there came the ring of the telephone and, for some reason, my pulse raced as I went to the hall to answer it. Hartley Jones' cheerful voice greeted me and he was positively gleeful when I told him of my projected trip.

"Hooray!" he shouted. "But you'll not take the SF-22. You'll take the trip with me as I wanted. I tell you what: You be out at Newark Airport at eleven-thirty, but come to my hangar instead of to that of the transportation company. We'll leave at the same time as the regular liner, and we'll get your old bonds to Frisco, regardless of what might happen to the big ship. Also we might learn something mighty interesting."

I argued with him, but to no avail. And the more I argued, the greater appeal was presented by his proposition. Finally there was nothing to do but agree.

*   *   *   *   *

Preston arrived with the bonds shortly after the children were tucked in their beds. I did not tell him of my change in plans. He did not stay long, and I could see that he was uncomfortable under the accusing eyes of Marie, for all his own confidence in the safety of the trip in the closely-guarded SF-22.

At precisely eleven-thirty I reached the great steel and glass hangar where Hart Jones and George Boehm carried on their experiments with super-modern types of aircraft. Hart Jones had inherited more than two million dollars, and was in a fair way to spend it all on his favorite hobby, though those who knew him best vowed that he would make many times that amount through royalties on his ever-growing number of valuable inventions.

The immense doors were open, and I gazed for the first time into the hangar whose spacious interior provided storage and manufacturing facilities for a dozen or more planes of Hart Jones' design. A curiously constructed example of his handiwork stood directly before me, and several mechanics were engaged in making it ready for flight. My friend advanced from their midst to meet me, a broad smile on his grease smeared countenance.

"Greetings, Jack," he said, taking my small bag from my hands. "Right on time, I see. And I can't tell you how glad I am that you are coming with us. So is George."

"Well, I didn't expect to," I admitted; "but there is no need of telling you that I had far rather be in your ship than in the big one."

*   *   *   *   *

George Boehm, the same jolly chap I had several times met in Hart's company, but fatter than ever, crawled from beneath the shiny metal body of the plane and scrambled to his feet at my side.

"Going in for a bit of adventuring, Mr. Makely?" he asked, wiping his hand with a piece of cotton waste before extending it.

"Yes," I replied, as I squeezed his chubby fingers. "Can't stick in the mud all my life, George. And I wouldn't want to be in better company for my first attempt either."

"Nor we," he returned, a mischievous twinkle in his eyes. "Rather have a greenhorn on the Pioneer than some government agent, who'd be butting in and trying to run everything. Think you'll be scared?"

"Probably," I admitted; "but I guess I can stand it."

"Hear the latest news broadcast?" interrupted Hart Jones.

"No. What was it?" I asked.

"There has been a report from out near Cripple Creek," said Hart solemnly, "that a pillar of fire was observed in the mountains shortly after the time the NY-18 last reported. The time and the location coincide with her probable position and the report was confirmed by no less than three of the natives of that locality. Of course the statements are probably extravagant, but they claim this pillar of fire extended for miles into the heavens and was accompanied by a tremendous roaring sound that ceased abruptly as the light of the flame disappeared, leaving nothing but blackness and awe-inspiring silence behind."

*   *   *   *   *

"Lot of bunk!" grunted George, who was vigorously scrubbing the back of his neck.

"Sounds like a fairy tale," I commented.

"Nevertheless, there may be something in it. In fact, there must be. Three of these mountaineers observed practically the same phenomenon from quite widely separated points, though one of them said there were three pillars of fire and that these looked more like the beams of powerful search-lights. All agreed on the terrific roar. And, after all, these two liners did disappear. There must be something quite out of the ordinary about the way in which they were captured or destroyed, and this occurrence may well be supposed to have a bearing on the matter."

"Possibly they were destroyed by some freak electrical storm," I suggested.

"Where then are the wrecked vessels?" asked Hart. "No, Jack, electrical storms do not destroy huge air liners and then suck them out into space beyond our vision. These two ships are no longer on the surface of the earth, else they would have been long since located. The magnetic direction finders of the transportation people have covered every inch of the United States, as well as Mexico and Canada."

"Of course they might have been carried halfway around the world by a wind of unprecedented velocity." I commenced a silly argument in favor of the theory that the elements had accounted for the two vessels, but was interrupted by the mounting roar of great engines throbbing overhead.

"Hurry up there, George!" shouted Hart. "It's the SF-22 coming in. We have to be ready for the take-off in five minutes!"

*   *   *   *   *

He hastened to take George's place at the washbowl and all was activity within the confines of our hangar. George and I left the office and went out to the landing field, which was now brilliant with the glare of floodlights. The *Pioneer* had been trundled into the open and stood ready for the flight. Not a hundred feet above the field, the huge silver moth that was the SF-22 swept by in a wide circle that would bring her into the wind. The roar of her engines died as she swung out of the circle of light into the surrounding darkness.

The crowds which had gathered to witness her landing buzzed with excited comment and speculation. Her nose brought slightly up, she dropped to a perfect three-point landing, the brakes screeching as she was brought to a standstill at the hangar of the transportation company.

"Come on now, you fellows," came the voice of Hart Jones from the hangar entrance, "there's no time to lose. The *Pioneer* takes off immediately after the big fellow."

We hurried to the waiting ship, which seemed like a tiny toy when compared with the giant SF-22. I had observed very little of the construction of the *Pioneer*, but I could now see that she was quite different in design from the ordinary plane. A monoplane she was, but the wing structure was abnormally short and of great thickness, and there were a number of tubes projecting from the leading edge that gave the appearance of a battery of small cannon. The body, like all planes designed for travel in air-level six, was cigar-shaped, and had hermetically sealed ports and entrance manholes. A cluster of the cannon-shaped tubes enclosed the tail just back of the fins and rudder and, behind the wing structure atop the curved upper surface of the body, there was a sphere of gleaming metal that was probably three feet in diameter.

*   *   *   *   *

Before I could formulate questions regarding the unusual features of the design, we were within the *Pioneer's* cabin and Hart Jones was engaged in clamping the entrance manhole cover to its rubber seat. A throbbing roar that penetrated our double hull attracted my attention and, looking through a nearby porthole, I saw that the convoy of army planes had taken off and was circling over the SF-22 in anticipation of her start. Trim, speedy fighting ships these were, with heavy caliber machine-guns in turrets fore and aft and normally manned by crews of twelve each. The under surfaces of their bodies glistened smooth and sleek in the light from the field, for the landing gears had been drawn within and the openings sealed by the close-fitted armor plate that protected these ordinarily vulnerable portions when in flight.

The SF-22 was ready to take off and the crowds were drawing back into the obscurity beyond the huge circle of blinding light. One after another her twelve engines sputtered into life, and ponderously she moved over the field, gathering speed as the staccato barking of the exhausts gradually blended into a smooth though deafening purr. The tail of the great vessel came up, then the wheels, and she was off into the night.

*   *   *   *   *

Hart Jones sat at a bewildering array of instruments that covered almost the entire forward partition of the cabin. He pressed a button and the starting motor whined for a moment. Then the single engine of the *Pioneer* coughed and roared. Slowly we taxied in the direction taken by the SF-22, whose lights were now vanishing in the darkness. I saw George open a valve on the wall and Hart stretched the fingers of his left hand to what appeared to be the keyboard of a typewriter set into the instrument board. He pressed several of the keys and pulled back his stick. There was a whistling scream from astern and I was thrown back in my seat with painful force. With that, the motor roared into full speed and we had left the airport far behind.

"What on earth?" I gasped.

"Rocket propulsion," laughed Hart. "I should have warned you. Those tubes you saw outside at the tail and along the leading edge of the wings. Only used three of them, but that was sufficient for the take-off."

"But I thought this rocket business was not feasible on account of the wastage of fuel due to its low efficiency," I objected.

"We should worry about fuel," said Hart.

I looked about me and saw that there was very little space for the storage of this essential commodity. "Why?" I inquired. "What fuel do you use?"

"Make our own," he replied shortly. He was busy at the moment, maneuvering the *Pioneer* into a position above and behind the SF-22 and her convoy.

"You make your own fuel enroute?" I asked in astonishment.

"Yes. That sphere you saw on top. It is the collecting end of an electrical system for extracting nitrogen and other elements, from the air. This extraction goes on constantly while we are in the atmosphere and my fuel is an extremely powerful explosive of which nitrates are the base. The supply is replenished continuously, so we have no fear of running short even in the upper levels."

*   *   *   *   *

George had crawled through a small opening into some inaccessible region in the stern of the vessel. I pondered over what Hart had just told me, still keeping my eyes glued to the port, through which could be seen the fleet we were following. The altimeter registered thirty-five thousand feet. We were entering air-level six—the stratosphere! Below us the troposphere, divided into five levels, each of seven thousand feet, teemed with the life of the air. The regular lanes were filled with traffic, the lights of the speeding thousands of freight and pleasure craft moving in orderly procession along their prescribed routes.

Up here in the sixth level, which was entirely for high-speed traffic of commercial and government vessels making transcontinental or transoceanic voyages, we were the only adventurers in sight—we and the convoyed liner we were following. The speed indicator showed six hundred miles an hour, and the tiny spot of light that traveled over the chart to indicate our position showed that we were nearing Buffalo.

Glancing through one of the lower ports, I saw the lights of the city shining dimly through a light mist that fringed the shore of Lake Erie and extended northward along the Niagara. Then we were out over the lake, and the luminous hue was slipping rapidly behind. I looked ahead and saw that the distance to the SF-22 and her convoy had somewhat increased. We were a mile behind and some two thousand feet above them. Evidently Hart was figuring on keeping at a safe distance for observation of anything that might happen.

*   *   *   *   *

Our motor was running smoothly and the angle of the propeller blades had been altered to take care of the change in air density from the lower altitudes. It flashed across my mind that this was an ideal location for an attack, if such was to be made on the SF-22.

Then, far ahead, I saw a beam of light stab through the darkness and strike the tossing surface of the lake. Another and another followed, and I could see that the SF-22 and her convoy were surrounded by these unearthly rays. They converged from high above to outline a brilliant circle where they met on the surface of the waters, and in the midst of the cone formed by the beams, the liner and its seven tiny followers could be seen to falter, and huddle more closely together.

It all happened in the twinkling of an eye—so quickly, in fact, that Hart and I had not the time to exchange remarks over the strange occurrence. For a moment the eight vessels hovered, halted suddenly by this inexplicable force from out the heavens. Then there rose from the apex of the inverted cone of light a blinding column of blue-white radiance that poured skyward an instant and was gone. To our ears came a terrific roaring that could be likened to nothing we had heard on earth. The *Pioneer* was tossed and buffeted as by a cyclone, and George came tumbling from the opening he had entered, his round face grown solemn. Then came eery silence, for the *Pioneer's* motor had gone dead. Ahead there was utter darkness. The liner and her convoy had completely vanished and the *Pioneer* was slipping into a spin!

*   *   *   *   *

"What's up?" asked George of Hart, who was tugging frantically at the controls.

"The liner has gone the way of the first two," he replied: "and the yarn about the pillar of fire was not so far wrong after all."

"You saw the same thing?" asked George incredulously.

"Yes, and so did Jack. There came some beams of light from the sky; then the pillar of fire and the roaring you heard, after which the vessels were gone and our electrical system paralyzed."

"Holy smoke!" ejaculated George. "What to do now?"

As he spoke, the *Pioneer* came out of the spin, and we were able to resume our positions in the seats. None of us was strapped in, and we had been clinging to whatever was handiest to keep from being tossed about in the cabin. Hart wiped his forehead and growled out an oath. The instrument board was still illuminated, for its tiny lamps were supplied with current from the storage battery. But the main lights of the cabin and the ignition system refused to function. We were gliding now, but losing altitude rapidly, having already dropped to the lower limits of level five.

"Can't you use the rocket tubes?" I inquired hesitatingly.

"They are fired in the same manner as the motor," replied Hart; "but we might try an emergency connection from the storage battery, which is ordinarily used only in starting and for the panel lights."

*   *   *   *   *

George was already fussing with the connections in a small junction box from which he had removed the cover. Meanwhile, the black waters of Lake Erie were rushing upward to meet us, and the needle of the altimeter registered twelve thousand feet.

"Here's the trouble!" shouted George, triumphantly holding up a small object he had removed from the junction box. "Ignition fuse is blown."

"Probably by some radiations from the cone of light and the column that destroyed the liner. Lucky we were no closer," were Hart's muttered comments.

George produced a spare fuse and inserted it in its proper place. The cabin lights glowed instantly and the motor started at once.

"Well, I'm going up after the generators of this mysterious force that is destroying our cross-country ships and killing our people," asserted Hart. "The rays came from high above, but the *Pioneer* can go as high as anything that ever flew—*higher*."

He snapped a switch and a beam of light that rivalled the so-called pillar of fire bored far into the night, dimming the stars by its brilliance. Again his fingers strayed to the rows of white keys and the rocket tubes shrieked in response to his pressure. This time I was prepared for the shock of acceleration, but the action was maintained for several seconds and I found the pressure against my back growing painful. Then it was relieved, and I glanced at the altimeter. Its needle had reached the end of the scale, which was graduated to eighty thousand feet!

"Good Lord!" I exclaimed. "Do you mean to tell me that we are more than sixteen miles in the air?"

"Nearly thirty," replied Hart, pointing to another dial which I had not seen. This one was graduated in miles above sea-level, and its needle wavered between the twenty-nine and thirty mark!

*   *   *   *   *

Again Hart pressed the rocket buttons, and we shot still higher into the heavens. Thirty, forty, fifty miles registered the meter, and still we climbed.

"Great Scott!" blurted a voice I knew was my own, though I had no consciousness of willing the speech. "At this rate we'll reach the moon!"

"We could, if we wished," was Hart's astounding reply; "I wish you wouldn't say too much about it when we return. We have oxygen to breathe and an air-tight vessel to retain it. With the fuel we are using, we could easily do it, provided a sufficient supply were available. However, the *Pioneer* does not have large enough storage tanks as yet, and, of course, we cannot now replenish our supply with sufficient rapidity, for the atmosphere has become very rare indeed—where we are. My ultimate object, though, in building the *Pioneer*, was to construct a vessel that is capable of a trip to the moon."

"You think you could reach a great enough velocity to escape the gravitational pull of the earth?" I asked, marveling more and more at the temerity and resourcefulness of my science-minded friend.

"Absolutely," he replied. "The speed required is less than seven miles a second, and I have calculated that the *Pioneer* can do no less than twenty."

Mentally I multiplied by sixty. I could hardly credit the result. Twelve hundred miles a minute!

"But, how about the acceleration?" I ventured. "Could the human body stand up under the strain?"

"That is the one problem remaining," he replied; "and I am now working on a method of neutralizing it. From the latest results of our experiments, George and I are certain of its feasibility."

*   *   *   *   *

The *Pioneer* was now losing altitude once more, and Hart played the beam of the searchlight in all directions as we descended. He and George watched through one of the floor ports and I followed suit. We were falling, unhampered by air resistance, and our bodies were practically weightless with reference to the *Pioneer*. It was a strange sensation: there was the feeling of exhilaration one experiences when inhaling the first whiff of nitrous oxide in the dentist's chair—a feeling of absolute detachment and care-free confidence in the ultimate result of our precipitous descent.

I found considerable amusement in pushing myself from side to side of the cabin with a mere touch of a finger. There was no up nor down, and sometimes it seemed to me that we were drifting sideways, sometimes that we fell upward rather than downward. Hart and George were unconcerned. Evidently they were quite accustomed to the sensations. They bent their every energy toward discovering what had caused the disaster to the SF-22 and its convoy.

For several hours we cruised about on the strangest search ever made in the air. Alternately shooting skyward to unconscionable altitudes and dropping to levels five and six to replenish our fuel supply, we covered the greater portion of the United States before the night was over. But the powerful searchlight of the *Pioneer* failed to disclose anything that might be remotely connected with the disappearance of the SF-22.

For me it was a never-to-be-forgotten experience. Lightning dashes from coast to coast which required but a few minutes of time—circling many miles above New York or Washington or Savannah in broad daylight with the sun low on the up-curved horizon; then shooting westward into the darkness and skirting the Pacific coast less than fifteen minutes later, but with four hours' actual time difference. Space and time were almost one.

*   *   *   *   *

Hart had not provided the *Pioneer* with a radio or television transmitter, but there was an excellent receiver, and, through its agency we learned that the world was in a veritable uproar over the latest visitation of the mysterious terror of the sixth air level. All commercial traffic in levels four, five and six was ordered discontinued, and the government air control stations were flashing long messages in code, the import of which could but be guessed. Vision flashes showed immense gatherings at the large airports and in the public squares of the great cities, where the general populace become more and more excited and terrified by the awful possibilities pictured by various prominent speakers.

The governments of all foreign powers made haste to disclaim responsibility for the air attacks or for any attempt at making war on the United States. News broadcasts failed to mention Hart Jones or the *Pioneer*, since the mission had been kept secret. The phenomenon of the rays and the roaring column of light had been observed from many points on this occasion and there was no longer any doubt as to the nature of the terror as visible to the eye, though theories as to the action and source of the rays conflicted greatly and formed the basis of much heated discussion.

Eventually the advancing dawn reached San Francisco, and with its advent Hart decided to make a landing in that city so that my bonds could be delivered.

*   *   *   *   *

Jones was apparently a very much mystified and discouraged man. "Jack," he said, "it seems to me that this thing is but the beginning of some tremendous campaign that is being waged against our country by a clever and powerful enemy. And I feel that our work in connection with the unraveling of the mystery and overcoming the enemy or enemies is but begun. It's a cinch that the thing is organized by human minds and is not any sort of a freak of the elements. Our work is cut out for us, all right, and I wish you would stick to George and me through the mess. Will you?"

"Sure," I agreed, readily enough. "After these bonds are delivered I am free for a month."

"Ha! Ha!" cackled George, without mirth. "A month! We're doggoned lucky if we get to the bottom of this in a year."

"Nonsense!" snapped Hart, who was considerably upset by the failure to locate the source of the disastrous rays. "There is nothing supernatural about this, and anything that can be explained on a scientific basis can be run to earth in short order. These rays are man-made and, as such, can be accounted for by man. Our greatest scientists must be put to work on the problem at once—in fact, they have quite probably been called in by the government already."

*　　*　　*　　*　　*

He was maneuvering the *Pioneer* to a landing on the broad field of the San Francisco airport. Hundreds of idle planes of all sizes lined the field, and, unmindful of the earliness the hour, a great crowd was collected in expectation of sensational reports from the occupants of arriving ships. The unusual construction of the *Pioneer* attracted considerable attention and it was with difficulty that the police kept back the crowd when she rolled to a stop near the office of the local government supervisor. We hustled inside and were greeted by that official with open arms.

"Glory be!" he exclaimed. "Hart Jones and the *Pioneer*. Every airport in the land has been on the lookout for you all night. It was feared you had been lost with the SF-22 and the others. Code messages to the supervisors of all districts advised of your mission, though it has been kept out of the general news, as has the message from the enemy."

"Message from the enemy!" gasped Hart, George and I, echoing the words like parrots.

"Yes. A demand that the United States surrender, and a threat to descend into the lower levels if the demand is not complied with in twenty-four hours!"

"Who is this enemy?" asked Hart, "and where?"

"Who they are is not known," replied the official gravely; "and as to the location, the War Department is puzzled. Direction finders throughout the country took readings on the position of their radio transmitter and these readings differed widely in result. But the consensus of opinion is that the messages originate somewhere out in space, probably between fifty and one hundred thousand miles from our earth."

"Great guns!" Hart glanced at George and me, where we stood with stupidly hanging jaws. "And what does the government want of me now?"

"You are considered to be the one man who might be able to cope with the problem, and are ordered to report to the Secretary of War, in person, immediately."

*   *   *   *   *

Hart was electrified into instant activity. "Here," he said in a voice of authority that commanded the official's attention and respect, "see that this package of bonds is delivered at once to the addressee and that the addressor is advised of its safe arrival. We're off at once."

Suiting action to the words, he thrust my packet into the hands of the astonished supervisor. Then, turning sharply on his heel, he flung back, "Advise the Secretary of War that I shall report to him in person in less than one hour."

As we stepped through the entrance of the *Pioneer*, he shot a final look at the official and laughed heartily at his sudden accession of energy. We had not the slightest doubt that Hart's orders would be immediately and efficiently carried out.

*   *   *   *   *

In precisely forty-five minutes, we stood before the desk of Lawrence Simler, then Secretary of War, in Washington.

"You are Mr. Hartley Jones?" inquired the stern-visaged little man.

"I am, Mr. Secretary, and these are my friends and co-workers, George Boehm and John Makely."

The Secretary acknowledged the introduction gravely, then plunged into the heart of the matter at hand with the quick energy for which he was famed.

"It may or may not be a serious situation," he said, "but certainly it has thus far been quite alarming. In any event, we have taken the matter out of the hands of the Air Traffic Bureau. We are prepared to defy the ultimatum of the enemy, whoever he may be. But we want your help, Mr. Jones. Every ship of the Air Navy will be in the upper levels within the prescribed twenty-four hours, and we will endeavor to stave off their attacks until such time as you can fit the *Pioneer* for a journey to their headquarters."

"How can your antiquated war vessels, capable of hurling a high explosive shell no more than fifty miles, fight off an enemy that is thousands of miles distant?" asked Hart.

"It is believed by the research engineers of the government that, though their headquarters may be located at a great distance, the raiders drop to a comparatively low altitude at the time of one of their attacks, returning immediately thereafter to their base."

Hart Jones shook his head. "The engineers may be correct," he stated; "but how on earth can you expect a little vessel like the *Pioneer* to battle an enemy who is possessed of these terribly destructive weapons and who has sufficient confidence in his own invulnerability to declare war on the greatest country on earth?"

*　　*　　*　　*　　*

Secretary Simler dropped his voice to a confidential tone, and his keen gray eyes flashed excitement as he unfolded the details of the discoveries and plans of the War Department. We three listened in undisguised amazement to a tale of the unceasing labors of our Secret Service agents in foreign countries, of elaborate experiments with deadly weapons and the chemicals of warfare.

We heard of marvelous new rays that could be projected for many miles and destroy whole armies at a single blast; rays that would, in less time than that required to tell of the feat, reduce to a mass of fused metal the greatest firstline battleships of the old days of ocean warfare. We heard of preparations for defensive warfare throughout the civilized world, preparedness that insured so terrible and final a war that it was literally impossible for a great world conflagration to again break out. We learned that the present mysterious signs of a coming war could not possibly have originated in any country on earth, else they would have been known of long in advance, due to the network of the Secret Service system. This war, so unexpectedly thrust upon us, was undoubtedly a war of planets!

"But," objected Hart, "the messages were in English, were they not?"

"They were," continued Secretary Simler, "and that puzzled our experts in the beginning. But, it may well be that our enemy from out the skies has had spies among us for many years and could thus have learned our languages and radio codes. In any event, we are to meet destructive rays with others equally destructive, and you, Hartley Jones, are the man who can make our effectiveness certain."

"I?"

"Yes. How long a time will be required in fitting out the *Pioneer* for reliable space flying?"

*   *   *   *   *

Hart Jones pondered the matter and I could see that he was overjoyed at the prospect of getting into the thing in earnest. "About one week," he replied, "providing you can send a force of fifty expert mechanics to my hangar at once and supply all material as fast as I shall require it."

"Excellent," said the Secretary. "We'll have the men there in a few hours and will obtain whatever you need, regardless of cost, for immediate delivery. Incidentally, there will be several scientists as well, who will supervise the installation of two types of ray generators and their projecting mechanisms on the *Pioneer*. You will need them later."

"I don't doubt we shall," said Hart. "And now, with your permission, we shall leave for the hangar. I'm ready to start work."

"Capital!" Secretary Simler pressed every one of a row of buttons set in his desk top. We were dismissed.

"Well," said I, when we reached the outside, "he has given you quite a job, Hart!"

"You said something," he replied. "But, if this threat from the skies proves as real and as calamitous as I think it will, we all have our work cut out for us."

"Do you really believe this enemy comes from another planet?" asked George as we entered the *Pioneer* for the trip home.

"Where else can they be from?" countered Hart. "But, really it makes no difference to us now. We have to go after them in earnest. Don't want to quit, do you, George?"

"Wha-a-at?" shouted George, as he jerked savagely at the main switch of the *Pioneer*. "You know me better than that, Hart. Did I ever let you down in anything?"

"No," admitted the smiling Hart, "you never did, bless your heart. But Jack here is another matter. He has a wife and two kids to look after. That lets him out automatically."

* * * * *

My heart sank at the words, for I knew that he meant what he said. And, truth to tell, I saw the justice in his remarks.

"But, Hart," I faltered, "I'd like to be in on this thing."

"I know you would, old man. But I think it's out of the question, for the present at least. You can help with the reconstruction of the *Pioneer*, however."

And meekly I accepted his dictum, though with secretly conflicting emotions. Little did I realize at the time that Hart knew far more than he pretended and that he had merely attempted to salve his own conscience in this manner.

I was very anxious to return to my family, and, as I sped homeward in a taxicab after the *Pioneer* landed at her own hangar, my mind was filled with doubts and fears. Secretary Simler had been very brief in his talk, but his every word carried home the gravity of the situation. What if these invaders carried the war to the surface? Suppose they seared the countryside and the cities and suburbs with rays of horrible nature that would shrivel and blast all that lay in their path? My heart chilled at the thought and it was a distinct relief when I gazed on my little home and saw that it was safe—so far. I paid the driver with a much too large bank note and dashed up my own front steps two at a time.

A few hours later I tore myself away and returned to the hangar, where the *Pioneer* now reposed in a scaffolded cradle. The sight which met my eyes was astonishing in the extreme, for the hangar had been transformed into a huge workshop with seemingly hundreds of men already at work. It was a scene of furious activity, and, to my utter amazement, I observed that the *Pioneer* was already in an advanced stage of disassembly.

*   *   *   *   *

I had no difficulty in locating Hart Jones, for he was striding from lathe to workbench to boring mill, issuing his orders with the sureness and decision of a born leader of men. He welcomed me in his most brisk manner and immediately assigned me to a portion of the work in the chemical laboratory—something I was at least partly fitted for.

We labored far into the night, when a siren called us to rest and food. This was to be a night and day job, and not a man of those on duty gave thought to the intense nervous and physical strain. Sixty-five of us I learned there were, though it had seemed there were several times that number.

During the rest period, Hart switched on the large television and sound mechanism of the public news broadcasts. Great excitement prevailed throughout the United States, for there had been a leak and the news had gone abroad regarding the message from the enemy. There was widespread panic and disorder and the government was besieged with demands for authentic news. The twenty-four hours of grace had nearly expired.

Finally the public was told of what actually was happening. Our entire fleet of one thousand air cruisers was in air-level six, waiting for the enemy. America was going to fight in earnest!

*   *   *   *   *

Flashes of our air cruisers in construction and in action came over the screen; voice-vision records of the popular officers of the fleet followed in quick succession. Then came the blow—the first of the strange war.

Two vessels of the air fleet had been destroyed by the triple rays and pillar of fire! Fifty cruisers rushing to the scene had been unable to find any traces of the source of the deadly rays. And, this time, there was an alarming added element. The pillar of fire had risen from a point near Gadsden in Alabama and, in its wake, there spread a sulphurous, smoldering fire that crept along the ground and destroyed all in its path. Farms, factories, and even the steel rails of the railroads were consumed and burned into the ground as if by the breath of some tremendous blast furnace. Hundreds of inhabitants of the section perished, and it was reported that the fumes from the strange fires were drifting in the direction of Birmingham, terrifyingly visible in blue-green clouds of searing vapor.

With the first news of the disaster came a wave of fear that spread over the country with the rapidity of the ether waves that carried the news. Then came stern determination. This enemy must be swept from the skies! Gatherings in public places volunteered en masse for whatever service the government might ask of them. The entire world was in an uproar, and from Great Britain, France, Germany and Russia, came immediate offers of their air fleets to assist in fighting off the Terror.

*   *   *   *   *

In less than an hour there were nearly five thousand cruisers in air-level six, patroling its entire depth from thirty-five thousand to one hundred thousand feet altitude.

We resumed work in the hangar, but the news service was kept in operation as far as the amplifiers were concerned, though the television screen was switched off on account of the likelihood of its distracting the workers.

Again came the report of a major disaster, this time over Butte in Montana. Four American vessels and one British were the victims in level six. And the city of Butte was in flames; blue, horrible flames that literally melted the city into the ground. Again there was no trace of the invaders.

How puny were the efforts of the five thousand air cruisers! Marvels of engineering and mechanical skill, these vessels were. Deadly as were the weapons they carried—weapons so terrible that war on earth was considered impossible since their development—they were helpless against an enemy who could not be located. Though our vessels were capable of boring high into the stratosphere, the enemy worked from still higher.

"Holy smoke!" gasped Hart Jones, who had stopped at my side. "What a contract I have on my hands!"

*   *   *   *   *

He looked in the direction of the partly dismantled *Pioneer*, and I could see by the fixedness of his stare that he was thinking of her insignificant size in comparison with the job she was to undertake.

Above the din of the machines in the hangar rang the startled voice of a news announcer. Panic-stricken he seemed, and we stopped to listen. Another blow of the terror of the skies—and now close by! Over Westchester County in New York State there was a repetition of the previous attacks. Only two of the cruisers had vanished this time; but several towns, including Larchmont and Scarsdale, were pools of molten fire!

Sick at heart, I thought of my little home in Rutherford and of the dear ones it contained. I thought of telephoning, but, what was the use? There was no warding off of this terrible thing that had so suddenly come to our portion of the world. It was the blowing of the last trumpet, the way things looked.

The announcer had calmed himself. His voice droned tonelessly now, as was the custom. Another raid, on the Mexican Border now. We were stupefied by the rapidity of the enemy's attacks; then electrified once more by the most astounding news of all. Alexandria, in Egypt, was the base of a pillar of fire! Fully half of the city was wiped out, and the remainder in a mortal funk, terrorized and riotous. The United States was not alone in the war!

The foreign fleets which reinforced our own were ordered home immediately. But to what avail? The world was doomed!

*   *   *   *   *

In the morning, after nine fearful attacks during the night, there came another message from the enemy and this was repeated in five languages and addressed to the entire world:

"People of Earth," it read, "this is our final warning. One chance has been given and you have proved stubborn. Consider well that your civilization be not entirely destroyed, and answer as the expiration of forty-eight hours, using our transmitting frequency. Our hand is to be withheld for that period only, when, unless our demands are met, all of your large cities and towns will be destroyed. Our terms for peace are that we be permitted to land without resistance on your part; that you surrender farm and forest lands, cities and towns, able-bodied men of twenty to forty, selected women of seventeen to thirty, and tribute in the form of such supplies and precious metals as we may specify, all to the extent of forty per cent of your resources. No compromise will be accepted."

That was all. It was during a rest period at the Jones hangar and I had brought Hart and George to my home for breakfast. We sat at the table when the news instrument brought the message. Marie was pouring the coffee, and my two small boys, Jim and Jack, had gone to the playroom, from whence their joyous voices could be heard. We four were struck dumb at the announcement, and Marie looked at me with so awful an expression of dread that my coffee turned bitter in my mouth. Marie was just twenty-eight!

"What beasts!" cried Hart. "Allow them to land without resistance? I should say not! Rather we should fight them off until all of us perish."

*   *   *   *   *

He had risen from his chair in his anger. Now he sat down suddenly and shook a forefinger in my face.

"Say!" he exploded. "You can't tell me that some master mind of our own world is not back of this!"

"I'm not telling you," I replied, startled at the fierce fire that flashed from his eyes.

"I know. I'm just trying to think aloud and I'm liable to say anything. But this sort of business is the work of humans as sure as you're born. Still I believe that what Simler says is true. I can't believe that any country on earth is back of the thing. It must be an attack from beings of another planet, but I think they have as a leader a man who is of our own earth."

Marie's eyes opened wide at this. "But how could that be?" she asked. "Surely no one from our earth has made the trip to one of the other planets?"

"It may be that someone has," replied Hart. "Do you remember Professor Oradel? Remember, about ten years ago, I think it was, when he and a half dozen or more of extremely radical scientists built a rocket they claimed would reach the moon? They were ridiculed and hissed and relegated to the position of half-baked, crazy inventors. But Oradel had a large private fortune, and he and his crowd built themselves a workshop and laboratory in a secluded region in the Ozarks. Here they labored and experimented and eventually the rocket ship was constructed. No person was in their confidence, but when the machine was completed they issued a statement to the press to the effect that they were ready for the voyage to the moon, and that, when they returned, a reckoning with the world was to be made for its disbelief and total lack of sympathy. Again the press subjected Oradel to a series of scathing denunciations, and the scientific publications refused to take cognizance of his claims in any way, shape or form."

*   *   *   *   *

"Then, one night, a great rocket roared into the heavens, leaving a terror-stricken countryside in the wake of its brilliantly visible tail. Several observatories whose telescopes picked up and followed the trail of the contraption reported that it described a huge parabola, mounting high into the stratosphere and falling back to earth, where it was lost in the depths of the Pacific Ocean. There the thing ended and it was soon forgotten. But I believe that this rocket ship of Oradel's reached Mars or Venus and that the peoples of whichever planet they reached have been prevailed upon and prepared to war upon the world."

"That would explain their knowledge of our languages and codes." I ventured, "and would likewise account for the fact that the first of our ships to be attacked were those carrying large shipments of currency. Though if these were destroyed by the fire columns, I can not see what good the money would do them."

"Don't believe the first three were destroyed," grunted Hart. "You'll remember that in these cases the pillars of fire, or whatever you want to call them, were of a cold light, whereas now they are viciously hot and leave behind them the terrible destructive fires that spread and spread and seemingly never are extinguished. No, I think that the force used is something of the nature of an atom-disrupting triad of beams and that these set up the column as a veritable tornado, a whirling column of roaring wind rushing skyward with tremendous velocity. The first ships, I believe, were carried into the stratosphere and captured intact by the enemy.

"Since the declaration of war the nature of the column has altered. The three beams, instead of meeting at or near the surface of the earth, now join high in the heavens and the column strikes downward instead of expending its force upward. An added energy is used which produces the terribly destructive force below. And now we are able to locate fragments of the ships destroyed above, whereas previously there were no traces."

*   *   *   *   *

"Sounds reasonable," commented George. "But why have they not landed and waged their war right here without warning, if that is what they now intend to do?"

"A natural question, George. But I have a hunch that the space flier or fliers of the enemy are conserving fuel by remaining beyond gravity. You know, in space flying, the greatest expenditures of energy are in leaving or landing on a body and, once landed, they might not have sufficient fuel for a getaway. They know we are not exactly helpless, once they are in our midst, and are taking this means of reducing us to the point of complete subjection before risking their precious selves among us."

The telephone startled us by its insistent ring. It was a call from the hangar for Hart. The news broadcast announcer was in the midst of a long dissertation regarding the discovery only this morning that there were certain apparent discrepancies in the movements of the tides and unwonted perturbations of the moon's orbit. There flashed on the screen a view of the great observatory at Mount Wilson, and Professor Laughlin of that institution stepped into the foreground of the scene to take up the discussion so mechanically repeated by the announcer.

"Must leave for the hangar at once," declared Hart, returning from the telephone. "Simler and his staff are there and we are wanted immediately."

"Oh, Jack!" Marie begged with her eyes.

"Got to be done, Honey," I responded, "and, believe me, I am going to do what little I can to help. Suppose we surrendered!"

*   *   *   *   *

I shuddered anew at the very thought and took hurried leave of my family, Hart and George awaiting me in the hall. Had I known what was to transpire before the end of the war, I am certain I would have been in much less of a hurry.

We rushed to the hangar, where Secretary Simler and his party awaited us in the office. Rather, I should say, they waited for Hart Jones.

"Mr. Jones," said the Secretary of War, when the introductions were over, "it is up to you to get the *Pioneer* in shape to go out after these terrible creatures before the forty-eight hours have expired. We have replied to their ultimatum and have told them we will have our answer ready within the appointed time, but it is already agreed between the nations of the World Alliance that our reply is to be negative. Better far that we submit to the utter destruction of our civilization than agree to their terms."

"I believe I can do it, Mr. Secretary," was Hart Jones' simple comment. "At least I will try. But you must let me have an experienced astronomer at once with whom to consult."

"Astronomer?"

"Yes—immediately. I have a theory, but am not enough of a student of astronomy myself to work it out."

"You shall have the best man in the Air Naval Observatory at once." Secretary Simler chewed his cigar savagely. "And anything else you might need," he concluded.

"There is nothing else, sir." Hart turned from the great men who regarded him solemnly, some with expressions of hope, others with plain distrust written large on their countenances.

* * * * *

They left in silence and we returned to our work with renewed vigor. Within an hour there arrived by fast plane an undersized, thick-spectacled man can who presented himself as Professor Linquist from the government observatory. He was immediately taken into the office by Hart and the two remained behind closed doors for the best part of four hours.

Meanwhile the hangar hummed with activity as usual. We in the chemical laboratory were engaged in compounding the high explosive used as fuel in the *Pioneer*. This was being compressed to its absolute limit and was stored in long steel cylinders in the form of a liquid of extremely low temperature. These cylinders were at once transferred to a special steel vault where the temperature was kept at a low enough point to prevent expansion and consequent loss of the explosive, not to speak of the danger of destroying the entire lot of us in its escape.

The generating apparatus of the *Pioneer* was to be dispensed with for this trip, since it was of no value outside the atmosphere where there was no air from which to extract the elements necessary for the production of the explosive. Instead, the entire supply of fuel for the trip was to be carried aboard the vessel in the cylinders we were engaged in filling. Hart had calculated that there was just sufficient room to store fuel for a trip of about two hundred thousand miles from the earth and a safe return. We hoped this would be enough.

* * * * *

On the scaffolding around the *Pioneer* there were now so many workers that it seemed they must forever be in one another's way. But the work was progressing with extreme rapidity. Already there projected from her blunt nose a slender rod of shining metal which was the projector of one of the destructive rays whose generator and auxiliaries were being installed under the supervision of the government experts. The force had been trebled and was now working in shifts of two hours each, the pace being so exhausting that highest efficiency was obtained by using these short periods.

Additional rocket tubes were being installed, and the steel framework of a bulge now showed on the hull, this bulge being an additional fuel storage compartment that would provide a slight additional resistance and consequently lower speed in the lower levels, but would prove little hindrance in level six and none at all in outer space.

When Hart emerged from his office he appeared to be very tired, indeed, but his face bore an expression of triumph that could not be mistaken. He and this little scientist from Washington had evidently arrived at some momentous conclusion regarding the enemy.

"Jack," he said, when he reached my bench during his first round of the hanger, "celestial mechanics is a wonderful thing. I had a hunch, and this astronomer chap has proved it correct with his mathematics. Our friend the enemy is out there in space at a point where his own mass and velocity are exactly counteracted by those of the earth and its satellite, the moon. He is just floating around in space, doing no work whatsoever to maintain his own position. He has temporarily assumed the rôle of a second satellite to us and is revolving around us at a definite period that was calculated by Lindquist. The gravitational pull of the moon keeps him from falling to the earth and that of the earth keeps him from approaching the moon. The resultant of the set of forces is what determines his orbit and the disturbance in the normal balance is what has been observed by the astronomers who reported changes in the tides and in the moon's orbit."

*   *   *   *   *

"But Lindquist's figures prove that the vessel or fleet of the enemy must be of tremendous size to produce such discrepancies, infinitesimally small though they might seem. We have a big fellow with whom to deal, but we know where to find him now."

"How can he work from a fixed position to make his attacks on the earth at such widely separated points?" I asked.

"It isn't a fixed position in the first place, and besides the earth rotates once in twenty-four hours, while the moon travels around the earth once in about twenty-eight days. But, even so, the widespread destruction could not be accounted for. He must send out scouting parties or something of that sort. That is one of the things we are to learn when we get out there. We'll have some fun, Jack."

"Will the *Pioneer* be ready?" I asked. Evidently I was to go.

"She will, with the exception of the acceleration neutralizers. But I'm having some heavily-cushioned and elastic supports made that will, I believe, save us from injury. And I guess we can stand the discomfort for once."

"Yes," I agreed, "in such a cause, I, for one, am willing to go through anything to help keep this overwhelming disaster from our good old world."

"Jack," he whispered, "we must prevent it. We've got to!"

Then he was gone, and I watched him for a moment as he dashed headlong from one task to another. He was a whirlwind of energy once more.

*　　*　　*　　*　　*

Forty-three hours and twenty minutes had passed since the receipt of the enemy's ultimatum. The last bolt was being tightened in the remodeled *Pioneer*, and Secretary Simler and his staff were on hand to witness the take-off of the vessel on which the hopes of the world were pinned. The news of our attempt had been spread by cable and printed news only, for there was fear that the enemy might be able to pick up the broadcasts of the news service and thus be able to anticipate us. As usual, there were many scoffers, but the consensus of opinion was in favor of the project. At any rate, what better expedient was there to offer?

The huge airport, now unused on account of the complete cessation of air traffic, was closed to the public. But there was quite a crowd to witness the take-off, the visitors from Washington, the officials of the field, and the two hundred workers who had enabled us to make ready for the adventure in time. There were four to enter the *Pioneer*: Hart, George, Professor Lindquist, and myself. And when the entrance manhole was bolted home behind us, the watchers stood in silence, waiting for the roar of the *Pioneer's* motor. As the starter took hold, Hart waved his hand at one of the ports and every man of those two hundred and some watchers stood at attention and saluted is if he were a born soldier and Hart a born commander-in-chief.

*　　*　　*　　*　　*

We taxied heavily across the field, for the *Pioneer* was much overloaded for a quick take-off. She bumped and bounced for a quarter-mile before taking to the air and then climbed very slowly indeed, for several minutes. Our speed was a scant two hundred miles an hour when we swung out over New York and headed for the Atlantic. And then Hart made first use of the rocket tubes, not daring to discharge the hot gases below while over populated land at so low an altitude. He touched one button, maintaining the pressure for but a fraction of a second. The ocean slipped more rapidly away from beneath our feet and he touched the button once more. Our speed was now nearly seven hundred miles an hour and we made haste to buckle ourselves into the padded, hammocklike contrivances which had been substituted for the former seats. In a very few minutes we entered level six and the motor was cut off entirely.

A blast from a number of the tail rockets drove me into my supporting hammock so heavily that I found difficulty in breathing, and could scarcely move a muscle to change position. The rate of acceleration was terrific, and I am still unable to understand how Hart was able to manipulate the controls. For myself, I could not even turn my head from its position in the padding and I felt as if I were being crushed by thousands of tons of pressure. Then, the pressure was somewhat relieved and I glanced to the instruments. We were more than a thousand miles from our starting point and the speed indicator read seven thousand miles an hour. We were traveling at the rate of nearly two miles a second!

*　　*　　*　　*　　*

Another blast from the rockets, this one of interminable length, and I must have lost consciousness. For when I next took note of things I found that we had been out for nearly two hours and that the tremendous pressure of acceleration was relieved. I moved my head, experimentally and found that my senses were normal, though there was a strange and alarming sensation of being wrong side up. Then I remembered that I had experienced the same thing when we first searched the upper levels of the atmosphere for the origin of the destructive rays of the enemy.

But this was different! I gazed through a nearby port and saw that the sky was entirely black, the stars shining magnificently brilliant against their velvet background. Streamers of brilliant sunlight from the floor ports struck across the cabin and patterned the ceiling. Looking between my feet I saw the sun as a flaming orb with streamers of incandescence that spread in every direction with such blinding luminosity that I could not bear the sight for more than a few seconds. Off to what I was pleased to think of as our left side, there was a huge globe that I quickly made out as our own earth. Eerily green it shone, and, though a considerable portion of the surface was obscured by patches of white that I recognized as clouds, I could clearly make out the continents of the eastern hemisphere. It was a marvelous sight and I lost several minutes in awed contemplation of the wonder. Then I heard Hart laugh.

"Just coming out of it, Jack?" he asked.

*   *   *   *   *

I stared at him foolishly. It had seemed to me that I was alone in this vast universe, and the sound of his voice startled me. "Guess I'm not fully out of it yet," I said. "Where are we?"

"Oh, about sixty thousand miles out," he replied carelessly; "and we are traveling at our maximum speed—that is, the maximum we need for this little voyage."

"Little voyage!" I gasped. And then I looked at George and the professor and saw that they, too, were grinning at my discomfiture. I laughed crazily, I suppose, for they all sobered at once.

Traveling through space at more than forty thousand miles an hour, it seemed that we were stationary. Movement was now easy—too easy, in fact, for we were practically weightless. The professor was having a time of it manipulating a pencil and a pad of paper on which he had a mass of small figures that were absolutely meaningless to me. He was calculating and plotting our course and, without him, we should never have reached the object we sought.

Time passed rapidly, for the wonders of the naked universe were a never-ending source of fascination. Occasionally a series of rocket charges was fired to keep our direction and velocity, but these were light, and the acceleration so insignificant that we were put to no discomfort whatever. But it was necessary that we keep our straps buckled, for, in the weightless condition, even the slightest increase or decrease in speed or change in direction was sufficient to throw us the length of the cabin, from which painful bruises might be received.

*   *   *   *   *

The supports to which we were strapped and which saved us from being crushed by the acceleration and deceleration, were similar to hammocks, being hooked to the floor and ceiling of the cabin rather than suspended horizontally in the conventional manner. This was for the reason that the energy of the rockets was expended fore and aft, except for steering, and the forces were therefore along the horizontal axis of the vessel. The supports were elastic and the padding deep and soft. Being swiveled at top and bottom, they could swing around so that deceleration as well as acceleration was relieved. For this reason the controls had been altered so that the flexible support in which Hart was suspended could rotate about their pedestal, thus allowing for their operation by the pilot either when accelerating or decelerating. How he could control the muscles of his arms and hands under the extreme conditions is still a mystery to me, however, and George agrees with me in this. We found ourselves to be utterly helpless.

My next impression of the trip is that of swinging rapidly around and finding myself facing the rear wall of the cabin. Then the tremendous pressure once more at a burst from the forward tubes. We had commenced deceleration. For me there were alternate periods of full and semi-consciousness and, to this

day, I can remember no more than the high spots of that
historical expedition.

*   *   *   *   *

Then we were free to move once more, and I turned to face
the instrument board. Our relative velocity had become
practically zero; that is, we were traveling through space at
about the same speed and in the same direction as the earth.
The professor and Hart were consulting a pencil chart and
excitedly looking first through the forward ports and then into
the screen of the periscope.

"This is the approximate location," averred the professor.

"But they are not here," replied Hart.

George and I peered in all directions and could see nothing
excepting the marvels of the universe we had been viewing. The
moon now seemed very close and its craters and so-called seas
were as plainly visible as in a four-inch telescope on earth. But
we saw nothing of the enemy.

The earth was a huge ball still, but much smaller than when
I had first observed it from the heavens. The sun's corona—the
flaming streamers which the professor declared extended as
much as five million miles into space—was partly hidden behind
the rim of the earth and the effect was blinding. A thin crescent
of brilliant light marked the rim of our planet and the rest was
in shadow, but a shadow that was lighted awesomely in cold
green by reflected light from her satellite.

"I have it!" suddenly shouted the professor. "We are all in
very nearly the same line with reference to the sun, and the
enemy is between the blazing body and ourselves. We must shift
our position, move into the shadow of the earth. We have missed
our calculation by a few hundred miles, that is all."

All! I thought. These astronomers, so accustomed to dealing
in tremendous distances that must be measured in light-years,
thought nothing of an error of several hundred miles. But I
suppose it was really an inconsiderable amount, at that.

At any rate, we shifted position and looked around a bit
more. We saw nothing at first. Then Hart consulted the
chronometer.

"Time is up!" he shouted.

*   *   *   *   *

On the instant there was a flash of dazzling green light from a point not a hundred miles from our position, a flash that was followed by a streaking pencil of the same light shooting earthward with terrific velocity. Breathlessly we followed its length, saw it burst like a bomb and hurl three green balls from itself which sped at equally spaced angles to form a perfect triangle. They hovered a moment at about two thousand miles above the surface of the earth, according to the professor, who was using the telescope at the time, and shot their deadly rays toward our world. We were too late to prevent the renewal of hostilities!

Another and another streak of green light followed and we knew that great havoc was being wrought back home. But these served to locate the enemy's position definitely and we immediately set about to draw nearer. We were still somewhat on the dark side of the object, which had prevented our seeing it. Now we swung about so that it was plainly visible. And, what a strange appearance it presented, out here in space!

Fully fifteen miles in diameter, it was a huge doughnut, a great ring of tubing with a center-opening that was at least eighty per cent of its maximum diameter. There it hovered, sending out those deadly missiles in a continuous stream toward our poor world. As we approached the weird space flier, we saw that a number of objects floated about within the great circle of its inner circumference. The NY-18, the SF-61 and the SF-22, without doubt! The theory of Hart's was correct in every detail.

*   *   *   *   *

We were still at about ten miles distance from the great ring and the streaking light pencils were speeding earthward at the rate of one a minute now. There was no time to lose. Already there was more destruction on its way than had been previously wrought—several times over.

Hart was sighting along a tiny tube that projected into the forward partition and he maneuvered the *Pioneer* until she was nose on to the great ring. He pulled a switch and there came a purring that was entirely new. A row of huge vacuum tubes along the wall lighted to vivid brilliancy and a throbbing vibration filled the artificial air of the cabin.

He pulled a small lever at the side of the tube and the vessel rocked to the energy that was released from those vacuum tubes. The thin rod which had been installed at the *Pioneer's* nose burst into brilliant flame—orange tinted luminescence that grew to a sphere of probably ten feet in diameter. Then there was a heavy shock and the ball of fire left its position and, with inconceivable velocity, sprang straight for the side of the great ring. It was a fair hit and, when the weird missile found its mark, it simply vanished—swallowed up in the metal walls of the monster vessel. For a moment we thought nothing was to result. Then we burst into shouts of joy, for a great section of the ring fused into nothingness and was gone! Fully a quarter of the circumference of the ring had disappeared into the vacuum of space. Truly, the governments of Earth had developed some terrible weapons of their own!

We watched, breathless.

*   *   *   *   *

The green light pencils no longer streaked their paths of death in the direction of our world, which now seemed so remote. The great ring with the vacant space in its rim wabbled uncertainly for a moment as though some terrific upheaval from within was tearing it asunder. Then it lurched directly for the *Pioneer*. We had been observed!

But Hart was equal to the occasion and he shot the *Pioneer* in the direction of the earth with such acceleration that we all were flattened into our supports with the same old violence. Then, with equal violence, we decelerated. The ring was following so closely that it actually rushed many hundreds of miles past us before it was brought to rest. From it there sprang one of the light pencils, and the *Pioneer* was rocked as by a heavy gale when it rushed past on its harmless way into infinity. The enemy had missed.

Meanwhile, Hart was operating another mechanism that was new to the *Pioneer* and again he sighted along the tiny tube. This time there was no sound within, no ball of fire without, no visible ray. But, when he had pressed the release of this second energy, the ring seemed to shrivel and twist as if gripped by a giant's hand. It reeled and spun. Then, no longer in a balance of forces, it commenced its long drop earthward.

His job finished and finished well, Hart Jones collapsed.

*   *   *   *   *

Following his more than three days and four nights of superhuman endeavor, it seemed strange to see Hart slumped white and still over the control pedestal. He who had energy far in excess of that of any of the rest of us had worn himself out. Having had no rest or sleep in nearly a hundred hours, the body that housed so wonderful a spirit simply refused to carry on. Tenderly we stretched him on the cabin floor, the *Pioneer* drifting in space the while. The professor, who was likewise something of a physician, listened to his heart, drew back his eyelids, and pronounced him in no danger whatever.

We slapped his wrists, sprinkled his face and neck with cold water from the drinking supply, and were soon rewarded by his return to consciousness. He smiled weakly and fell sound asleep. No war in the universe could have wakened him then, so we lifted him to his feet—rather I should say, we guided his practically floating body—and strapped him in George's hammock, preparing for the homeward journey. Though dangling from the straps in a position that would be vertical were we on earth, he slept like a baby. George took the controls in Hart's place and the professor and I returned to our accustomed supports.

The return trip was considerably slower, as George did not wish to push the *Pioneer* to its limit as had been necessary when coming out to meet the enemy, nor was he able to keep control of the ship against a too-rapid acceleration. Consequently, the rate of acceleration was much lower and we were not nearly as uncomfortable as on the outgoing trip. Thus, nearly ten hours were required for the return. And Hart slept through it all.

*   *   *   *   *

In order to make best use of the small amount of fuel still in the cylinders, George circled the earth five times before we entered the upper limits of the atmosphere, the circles becoming of smaller diameter at each revolution and the speed of the ship proportionately reduced. An occasional discharge from one of the forward rocket tubes assisted materially in the deceleration, yet, when we slipped into level five, our speed was so great that the temperature of the cabin rose alarmingly, due to the friction of the air against the hull of the vessel. It was necessary to use the last remaining ounce of fuel to reduce the velocity to a safe value. A long glide to earth was then our only means of landing and, since we were over the Gulf of Mexico at the time, we had no recourse other than landing in the State of Texas.

Passing over Galveston in level three, we found that the Humble oil fields and a great section of the surrounding country had been the center of one of the enemy bombardments. All was blackness and ruin for many miles between this point and Houston. At Houston Airport we landed, unheralded but welcome.

The lower levels were once more filled with traffic, and one of the southern route transcontinental liners had just made its stop at this point. The arrival of the *Pioneer* was thus witnessed by an unusually large crowd, and, when the news was spread to the city, their numbers increased with all the rapidity made possible by the various means of transportation from the city.

So it was that Hart Jones, after we finally succeeded in awakening him and getting him to his feet, was hailed by a veritable multitude as the greatest hero of all time. The demonstrations become so enthusiastic that police reserves, hastily summoned from the city, were helpless in their attempts to keep the crowd in order.

*   *   *   *   *

It was with greatest difficulty that Hart was finally extricated from the clutches of the mob and conveyed to the new Rice Hotel in Houston, where it was necessary to obtain medical attention for him immediately. He was in no condition at the time to receive the richly deserved plaudits of the multitude, and, truth to tell, we others from the *Pioneer* were in much the same shape.

To me that night will always be the most terrible of nightmares. My first thought was of my family and, when I had been assigned to a room, I immediately asked the switchboard operator for a long-distance connection to my home in Rutherford. There was complete silence for a minute and I jangled the hook impatiently, my head throbbing with a thousand aches and pains. Then, to my surprise, the voice of the hotel manager greeted me.

"Mr. Makely," he said softly, and I thought there was a peculiar ring in his voice, "I think you had better not try to get Rutherford this evening. We are sending the house physician to your room at once and—there are orders from Washington, you know—you are to think of nothing at the present but sleep and a long rest."

"Why—why—" I stammered, "can't you see? I must communicate with my family. They must know of my return. I must know if they're safe and well."

"I'm sorry, sir," apologized the manager, "Government orders, you know." And he hung up.

Something in that soft voice brought to me an inkling of the truth. An icy hand gripped my heart as I heard a knock at the door. With palsied fingers I turned the key and admitted the professor and a kindly-faced elderly gentleman with a small black bag. One look at the professor told me the truth. I seized his two arms in a grip that made him wince.

"Tell me! Tell me!" I demanded, "Has anything happened to my family?"

"Jack," said the professor slowly, "while we were out there watching Hart destroy the enemy vessel, Rutherford was destroyed!"

*   *   *   *   *

It must be that I frightened him by my answering stare, for he backed away from me in apparent fear. I noticed that the doctor was rummaging in his bag. I know I did not speak, did not cry out, for my tongue clove to the roof of my mouth. It seemed I must go mad. The professor still backed away from me; then, wiry little athlete that he was, he sprang directly for my knees in a beautiful football tackle. I remember that point clearly and how I admired his agility at the time. I remember the glint of a small instrument in the doctor's hand. Then all was blackness.

Eight days later, they tell me it was, I returned to painful consciousness in a hospital bed. But let me skip the agony of mind I experienced then. Suffice it to say that, when I was able, I set forth for Washington. Hart Jones was there and he had sent for me. But I took little interest in the going; did not even bother to speculate as to the reason for his summons. I had devoured the news during my convalescence and now, more than two weeks after the destruction of the Terror, I knew the extent of the damage wrought upon our earth by those deadly green light pencils we had seen issuing from the huge ring up there in the skies. The horror of it all was fresh in my mind, but my own private horror overshadowed all.

*   *   *   *   *

I was glad that Hart had been so signally honored by the World Peace Board, that he was now the most famous and popular man in the entire world. He deserved it all and more. But what cared I—I who had done least of all to help in his great work—that the Terror had been found where it buried itself in the sand of the Sahara when falling to earth? What cared I that the discoveries made in the excavating of the huge metal ring were of inestimable value to science?

It gave me passing satisfaction to note that all of Hart Jones' theories were borne out by the discoveries; that Oradel and his minions were responsible for this terrible war; that the planet they aligned against us was Venus and that more than a hundred thousand of the Venerians had been carried in that weird engine of destruction which had been brought down by Hart.

It was interesting to read of the fall of that huge ring; how it was heated to incandescence when it entered our atmosphere at such tremendous velocity; of the tidal waves of concentric billows in the sand that led to its discovery by Egyptian Government planes. The broadcast descriptions and the television views of the stunted and twisted Venerians whose bodies were recovered from the partly consumed wreckage were interesting. But it all left me cold. I had no further interest in life. That the world had escaped an overwhelming disaster was clear, and it gave me a certain pleasure. But for me it might as well have been completely destroyed.

Nevertheless, I went to Washington. I felt somehow that I owed it to Hart Jones, the greatest world hero since Lindbergh. I would at least listen to what he had to say.

*   *   *   *   *

A fast plane carried me, a plane chartered by the government. To me it seemed that it crawled, though it was a sixth-level ship, and made the trip in record time. Why I was impatient to reach Washington I do not know, for I was absolutely disinterested in anything that might occur there. It was merely that my nerves were on edge, I suppose, and everything annoyed me.

Hart met me at the airport and greeted me like a long-lost brother. He talked incessantly and jumped from one subject to the other with the obvious intention of trying to get my mind off my troubles until we reached his office in the Air Traffic building.

On his door there was the legend, "Director of Research," and, when we had entered, I observed that the office was furnished with all the luxury that suited his new position. I dropped into a deeply upholstered chair at the side of his mahogany desk, and, for the space of several minutes, Hart regarded me with concern, speaking not a word.

"Jack, old man," he finally ventured. "I can't talk to you of this thing. But it makes me feel very badly to see you take it so hard. There are many things you have to live for, old top, and it is to talk about these that I sent for you."

"You mean work?" I asked.

"Yes. That is the best thing for us all, in any emergency or under any circumstances whatever. Preston wants you back for one thing, and he authorized me to tell you that the job of office manager is waiting for you at double your former salary."

*　　*　　*　　*　　*

My eyes misted at this. Preston was a good old scout! But I could never bear it to return to the old surroundings, even in the city. "No, Hart," I said, "I'd rather be away from New York and from that part of the country. Associations, you know."

"I understand," he replied, "and that is just what I had hoped you would decide. Because I have a job for you in the Air Service. A good one, too.

"You know there is much reconstruction work to be done on earth. More than forty cities and towns have been wiped out of existence and these must be rebuilt. That will occupy the minds and energies of thousands who have been bereaved as you have. But, in the Air Service, we have a program that I believe will be more to your liking. The log of the *Terror*, in Oradel's handwriting, was found intact, as were a number of manuscripts pertaining to plans of the Venerians.

"These misshapen creatures were quite evidently educated by Oradel to a hatred of our world. We have reason to believe that other attacks may follow, for they were obviously intending to migrate here in millions. And, according to records found aboard the *Terror*, they are of advanced scientific accomplishment. We may expect them to construct other vessels similar to the *Terror* and to come here again. We must be prepared to fight them off, to carry the war to their own planet if necessary. My work is to organize a world fleet of space ships for this purpose, and I'd like you to help me in this. The work will take you all over the world and will keep you too busy to think about—things."

It was just like Hart, and I thanked him wordlessly, but from the bottom of my heart. Yes, I would accept his generous offer. Though I was no engineer, I had a knowledge of scientific subjects a little above the average, and I could follow instructions. By George, it was the very thing! Suddenly I grew enthusiastic.

*　　*　　*　　*　　*

There was the sound of voices in the outer office, and Hart's secretary entered to announce the arrival of George Boehm and Professor Lindquist. This was great!

Chubby George, red-faced and smiling as ever, embraced me with one short arm and pounded me on the back with his other fist in his jovial, joking manner. It was good to have friends like these! The professor held forth his hand timidly. He was thinking of that tackle and the half-Nelson he had used on me while the doctor slipped that needle into my arm back there in Houston.

"Don't remove your glasses, Professor," I laughed; "I'm not going to hit you. That was a swell tackle of yours, and you did me a big service down there in the Rice Hotel."

He beamed with pleasure and gripped my hand—mightily, for such a little fellow. George was whispering to Hart, and I could see that they were greatly excited over something.

"Jack," said Hart, when the professor and I finished talking things over, "George here wants you to take a little trip over to Philly with him. He has something there he wants to show you."

I looked from one to the other for signs of a hoax. These two, under normal circumstances, were always up to something. But what I saw in their expressions convinced me that I had better go, and somehow, there rose in my breast a forlorn hope.

"All right," I agreed. "Let's go!"

*   *   *   *   *

Once more we four took off together, this time in a speedy little first-level cabin plane of Hart's design, piloted by the irrepressible George. I was brimming with questions, but George kept up such a running fire of small talk that I was unable to get in a single word throughout the short trip to the Quaker City. It was quite evident that something was in the wind.

Instead of landing at the airport, George swung across the city and dropped to the roof landing space of a large building which I recognized as the Germantown Hospital. We had no sooner landed when I was rushed from the plane to the penthouse over the elevator shafts. We were soon on the main floor and George went immediately to the desk at the receiving office, where he engaged in earnest conversation with the nurse in charge.

"What are you doing—committing me?" I asked, half joking only. For, from the mysterious expression of my friends' faces, I was not sure what to expect.

"No," laughed Hart. "George learned of the existence of a patient here who may turn out to be a very good friend of yours."

I turned this over in my mind, which did not yet function quite normally. A friend? Why, I had very few that could really be termed good friends outside of those that accompanied me. It could mean but one thing. Possibly one of my children—or even my dear wife—might have escaped somehow. I followed in a daze as a white-capped and gowned nurse led us along the corridor and into a ward where there were dozens of high, white beds.

* * * * *

Some of the patients were swathed in bandages; some sat up in their beds, reading or just staring; others lay inert and pale. The reek of iodoform pervaded the large room.

We stopped at the bedside of one of the staring patients, a young woman who looked unseeingly at our party. Great heavens, it was Marie!

A physician stood at the other side of her bed, finger on her pulse. The others drew back as I approached her side, raised her free hand to my lips and spoke to her.

"Marie, dear," I asked gently, forcing the lump from my throat as best I could, "don't you know me? It's Jack, Honey."

The fixed stare of the great blue eyes shifted in my direction. It seemed that they looked through and past me into some terrible realm where only horror held sway. She drew her hand from my grasp and passed it before those staring, unnatural eyes. There was an audible gulp from George. But the doctor smiled encouragement to me. I tried once more.

"Marie," I said, "where are Jim and Jackie?"

* * * * *

The hand fluttered to her lap, where it lay, blue-veined and pitifully thin. The stare focussed on me, seemed to concentrate.

Then the film was gone from the eyes and she saw—she knew me!

"Oh, Jack!" she wailed, "I have been away. Don't you know where they are?"

My heart nearly stopped at this, but I sat on the edge of the bed and took her in my arms, looking at the doctor for approval. He nodded his head brightly and beckoned to the nurse.

"Bring the children," I heard him whisper.

My cup was full. But I must be calm for Marie's sake. She had closed her eyes now and great tears coursed down her waxen cheeks. Her body shook with sobs.

"She'll recover?" I asked the doctor.

"You bet. Just an aggravated case of amnesia. Hasn't eaten. Didn't even know her children. Cured now, but she'll need a few weeks to build up." He snapped shut the lid of his watch.

Those succinct sentences were the finest I had ever heard.

Marie clung to me like an infant to its mother. Her sobs gradually ceased and she looked into my eyes. Little Jim and Jack had come in and were clamoring for recognition.

"Oh, Jack," Marie whispered, "I'm so happy."

She relinquished me and turned her attention to the children. I saw that my friends had left and that an orderly was placing screens about us. So I'll close the screen on the remainder of this most happy reunion.

*   *   *   *   *

It was several days before I had the complete story. Being lonesome during my absence when we were preparing for the voyage into space, and not knowing just when I would return, Marie had packed a grip and taken the train for Philadelphia, deciding to spend a few days with her Aunt Margaret, or at least to remain there with the children until I returned.

She had boarded the train at Manhattan Transfer at about the time we reached the location of the *Terror* and the train was just pulling out of the station when there came the first of the new attacks of the enemy. She thought that the pillar of fire rose from the approximate location of Rutherford, but was not sure until they reached Newark, when the news was spread throughout the train by passengers who boarded it there. She worried and cried over the loss of our little home and had worked herself into a state of extreme nervousness and near-hysteria by the time they reached New Brunswick.

Then, as the long train left New Brunswick, there was another attack, this one on the town they had just left. The last two cars of the train were blown from the track by the initial concussion, and the remainder of the train brought to a grinding, jerking stop that threw the passengers into a panic.

Already hysterical, Marie was in no condition to bear up under the shock, and the loss of memory followed. Jack and Jim clung to her, of course, and were taken to the Germantown Hospital with her when the wreck victims were transferred to that point. She had no identification on her person, and it was by sheerest luck that George, who was visiting a friend in the same hospital, chanced to see her and thought he recognized her.

That was all of it, but to me it was more than enough. From the depths of despondency, I rose to the peaks of elation. It was true that we would have to establish a new home, but this would be a joy as never before. Those I had given up as lost were restored to me and I was content. Hart would have to make some changes in the duties of that new job—the world travel was out of the picture. I had had my fill of adventure.

Besides, the hot spell was over.

Silver Dome

Originally Published in *Astounding Stories*
Aughust 1930

Silver Dome

In a secluded spot among the hills of northern New Jersey stood the old DeBost mansion, a rambling frame structure of many wings and gables that was well-nigh hidden from the road by the half-mile or more of second-growth timber which intervened. High on the hill it stood, and it was only by virtue of its altitude that an occasional glimpse might be obtained of weatherbeaten gable or partly tumbled-down chimney. The place was reputed to be haunted since the death of old DeBost, some seven years previously, and the path which had once been a winding driveway was now seldom trod by human foot.

It was now two years since Edwin Leland bought the estate for a song and took up his residence in the gloomy old house. And it had then been vacant for five years since DeBost shot himself in the northeast bedroom. Leland's associates were sure he would repent of his bargain in a very short time, but he stayed on and on in the place, with no company save that of his man-servant, an aged hunch-back who was known to outsiders only as Thomas.

Leland was a scientist of note before he buried himself in the DeBost place, and had been employed in the New York research laboratory of one of the large electrical manufacturers, where he was much admired and not a little envied by his fellow workers. These knew almost nothing of his habits or of his personal affairs, and were much surprised when he announced one day that he had come into a sizable fortune and was leaving the organization to go in for private research and study. Attempts to dissuade him were of no avail, and the purchase of the DeBost property followed, after which Leland dropped from sight for nearly two years.

*   *   *   *   *

Then, on a blustery winter day, a strange telephone call was received at the laboratory where he had previously worked. It was from old Thomas, out there in the DeBost mansion, and his quavering voice asked for Frank Rowley, the genial young engineer whose work had been most closely associated with Leland's.

"Oh, Mr. Rowley," wailed the old man, when Frank responded to the call, "I wish you would come out here right away. The master has been acting very queerly of late, and to-day he has locked himself in his laboratory and will not answer my knocks."

"Why don't you break in the door?" asked Frank, looking through the window at the snow storm that still raged.

"I thought of that, Mr. Rowley, but it is of oak and very thick. Besides, it is bound with steel or iron straps and is beyond my powers."

"Why not call the police?" growled Frank. He did not relish the idea of a sixty or seventy mile drive in the blizzard.

"Oh—no—no—no!" Old Thomas was panicky at the suggestion. "The master told me he'd kill me if I ever did that."

Before Frank could formulate a reply, there came a sharp gasp from the other end of the line, a wailing cry and a thud as of a falling body; then silence. All efforts to raise Leland's number merely resulted in "busy" or "line out of order" reports.

Frank Rowley was genuinely concerned. Though he had never been a close friend of Leland's, the two had worked on many a knotty problem together and were in daily contact during the nearly ten years that the other man had worked in the same laboratory.

"Say, Tommy," said Frank, replacing the receiver and turning to his friend, Arnold Thompson, who sat at an adjoining desk, "something has happened out at Leland's place in Sussex County. Want to take a drive out there with me?"

"What? On a day like this? Why not take the train?"

"Don't be foolish, Tommy," said Frank. "The place is eight miles from the nearest station, which is a flag stop out in the wilds. And, even if you could find a cab there—which you couldn't—there isn't a taxi driver in Jersey who'd take you up into those mountains on a day like this. No, we'll have to drive.

It'll be okay. I've got chains on the rear and a heater in the old coupe, so it shouldn't be so bad. What do you say?"

So Tommy, who usually followed wherever Frank led, was prevailed upon to make the trip. He had no particular feeling for Leland, but he sensed an adventure, and, in Frank's company, he could ask for no more.

* * * * *

Frank was a careful driver, and three hours were required to make the sixty-mile journey. Consequently, it was late in the afternoon when they arrived at the old DeBost estate. It had stopped snowing, but the drifts were deep in spots, and Frank soon found that the car could not be driven through the winding path from the road to the house. So they left it half buried in a drift and proceeded on foot.

It was a laborious task they had undertaken, and, by the time they set foot on the dilapidated porch, even Frank, husky and athletic as was his build, was puffing and snorting from his exertions. Little Tommy, who tipped the scales at less than a hundred and twenty, could hardly speak. They both were wet to the waist and in none too good humor.

"Holy smoke!" gasped Tommy, stamping the clinging snow from his sodden trouser legs and shoes, "if it snows any more, how in Sam Hill are we going to get out of this place?"

"Rotten trip I let you in for Tommy," growled Frank, "and I hope Leland's worth it. But, darn it all, I just had to come."

"It's all right with me, Frank. And maybe it'll be worth it yet. Look—the front door's open."

* * * * *

He pointed to the huge oaken door and Frank saw that it was ajar. The snow on the porch was not deep and they saw that footprints led from the open door to a corner of the porch. At that point the snow on the railing was disturbed, as if a hurrying man had clung to it a moment before jumping over and into the drifts below. But the tracks led no further, for the drifting snow had covered all excepting a hollow where some body had landed.

"Thomas!" exclaimed Frank. "And he was in a hustle, by the looks of the tracks. Bet he was frightened while at the telephone and beat it."

They entered the house and closed the door behind them. It was growing quite dark and Frank searched for the light switch. This was near the door, and, at pressure on the upper button, the spacious old hall with its open staircase was revealed dimly by the single remaining bulb in a cluster set in the center of the high ceiling. The hall was unfurnished, excepting for a telephone table and chair, the chair having fallen to the floor and the receiver of the telephone dangling from the edge of the table by its cord.

"You must have heard the chair fall," commented Tommy, "and it sure does look as if Thomas left in a hurry. Wonder what it was that frightened him?"

The house was eerily silent and the words echoed awesomely through the adjoining rooms which connected with the hall through large open doorways.

"Spooky place, isn't it?" returned Frank.

*   *   *   *   *

And then they were both startled into immobility by a rumble that seemed to shake the foundations of the house. Heavier and heavier became this vibration, as if some large machine was coming up to speed. Louder and louder grew the rumble until it seemed that the rickety old house must be shaken down about their ears. Then there came a whistling scream from the depths of the earth—from far underground it seemed to be—and this mounted in pitch until their eardrums tingled. Then abruptly the sounds ceased, the vibration stopped, and once more there was the eery silence.

Rather white-faced, Tommy gazed at Frank.

"No wonder old Thomas beat it!" he said. "What on earth do you suppose that is?"

"Search me," replied Frank. "But whatever it is, I'll bet it has something to do with Leland's strange actions. And we're going to find out."

He had with him the large flashlamp from the car, and, by its light, the two made their way from room to room searching for the iron-bound door mentioned by Thomas.

They found all rooms on the first and second floors dusty and unused with the exception of two bedrooms, the kitchen and pantry, and the library. It was a gloomy and spooky old house. Floor boards creaked startlingly and unexpectedly and the sound of their footsteps echoed dismally.

"Where in time is that laboratory of Leland's?" exclaimed Frank, his ruddy features showing impatient annoyance, exaggerated to an appearance of ferocity by the light of the flashlamp.

"How about the cellar?" suggested Tommy.

"Probably where it is," agreed Frank, "but I don't relish this job so much. I'd hate to find Leland stiff down there, if that's where he is."

"Me, too," said Tommy. "But we're here now, so let's finish the job and get back home. It's cold here, too."

"You said it. No steam in the pipes at all. He must have let the fire go out in his furnace, and that's probably in the cellar too—usually is."

*   *   *   *   *

While talking, Frank had opened each of the four doors that opened from the kitchen, and the fourth revealed a stairway that led into the blackness beneath. With the beam of his torch directed at the steps, he proceeded to descend, and Tommy followed carefully. There was no light button at the head of the stairs, where it would have been placed in a more modern house, and it was not until they had reached the furnace room that they located a light fixture with a pull cord. An ordinary cellar, with furnace, coal bin, and a conglomeration of dust-covered trunks and discarded furniture, was revealed. And, at its far end, was the iron-bound door.

The door was locked and could not be shaken by the combined efforts of the two men.

"Have to have a battering ram," grunted Frank, casting about for a suitable implement.

"Here you are," called Tommy, after a moment's search. "Just the thing we are looking for."

*   *   *   *   *

He had come upon a pile of logs, and one of these, evidently a section of an old telephone pole, was of some ten or twelve inches diameter and about fifteen feet long. Frank pounced upon it eagerly, and, supporting most of the weight himself, led the attack on the heavy oak door with the iron bands.

No sound from within greeted the thunderous poundings. Clearly, if Leland was behind that door, he was either dead or unconscious.

Finally the double lock gave way and Tommy and Frank were precipitated headlong into the brightly lighted room beyond. Recovering their balance, they took stock of their surroundings and were amazed at what they saw—a huge laboratory, fitted out with every modern appliance that money could buy. A completely equipped machine shop there was; bench after bench covered with the familiar paraphernalia of the chemical and physical laboratory; huge retorts and stills; complicated electrical equipments; dozens of cabinets holding crucibles, flasks, bottles, glass tubing, and what not.

"Good Lord!" gasped Tommy. "Here's a laboratory to more than match our own. Why, Leland's got a fortune invested here!"

"I should say so. And a lot of stuff that our company does not even have. Some of it I don't know even the use of. But where is Leland?"

*   *   *   *   *

There was no sign of the man they had come to help. He was not in the laboratory, though the door had been locked from within and the lights left burning throughout.

With painstaking care they searched every nook and cranny of the large single room and were about to give up in despair when Tommy happened to observe an ivory button set into the wall at the only point in the room where there were no machines or benches at hand. Experimentally he pressed the button, and, at the answering rumble from under his feet, jumped back in alarm. Slowly there opened in the paneled oak wall a rectangular door, a door of large enough size to admit a man. From the recess beyond there came a breath of air, foul with the musty odor of decayed vegetation, dank as the air of a tomb.

"Ah-h-h!" breathed Frank. "So that is where Ed Leland is hiding! The secret retreat of the gloomy scientist!"

He spoke half jestingly, yet when he squeezed his stalwart bulk through the opening and flashed the beam of his light into the darkness of a narrow passage ahead he was assailed with vague forebodings. Tommy followed close behind and spoke not a word.

* * * * *

The passage floor was thick with dust, but the marks of many footsteps going and returning gave mute evidence of the frequency of Leland's visits. The air was heavy and oppressive and the temperature and humidity increased as they progressed along the winding length of the rock-walled passageway. The floor sloped, ever downward and, in spots, was slippery with slimy seepage. It seemed that they turned back on their course on several occasions but were descending deeper and deeper into the heart of the mountain. Then, abruptly, the passage ended at the mouth of a shaft, which dropped vertically from almost beneath their feet.

"Whew!" exclaimed Frank. "Another step and I'd have dropped into it. That's probably what happened to Leland."

He knelt at the rim of the circular opening and looked into the depths of the pit, Tommy following suit. The feeble ray of the flashlight was lost in the blackness below.

"Say, Frank," whispered Tommy, "turn off the flash. I think I saw a light down there."

And, with the snapping of the catch, there came darkness. But, miles below them, it seemed, there was a tiny pin-point of brilliance—an eery green light that was like a wavering phosphorescence of will-o'-the-wisp. For a moment it shone and was gone. Then came the dreadful vibration they had experienced in the hall of the house—the whistling scream that grew louder and louder until it seemed they must be deafened. The penetrating wail rose from the depths of the pit, and the vibration was all around them, in the damp rock floor on which they knelt, and in the very air of the cavern. Hastily Frank snapped on the light of his flash.

"Oh boy!" he whispered. "Leland is certainly up to something down there and no mistake! How're we going to get down?"

"Get down?" asked Tommy. "You don't want to go down there, do you?"

"Sure thing. We're this far now and, by George, we're going to find out all there is to learn."

"How deep do you suppose it is?"

"Pretty deep, Tommy. But we can get an idea by dropping a stone and counting the seconds until it strikes."

*   *   *   *   *

He played the light of the flash over the floor and soon located a smooth round stone of the size of a baseball. This he tossed over the rim of the pit and awaited results.

"Good grief!" exclaimed Tommy. "It's not falling!"

What he said was true, for the stone poised lightly over the opening and drifted like a feather. Then slowly it moved, settling gradually into oblivion. Frank turned the flash downward and they watched in astonishment as the two-pound pebble floated deliberately down the center of the shaft at the rate of not more than one foot in each second.

"Well, I'll be doggoned," breathed Frank admiringly. "Leland has done it. He has conquered gravity. For, in that pit at least, there is no gravity, or at any rate not enough to mention. It has been almost completely counteracted by some force he has discovered and now we know how to follow him down there. Come on Tommy, let's go!"

And, suiting action to his words, Frank jumped into the mouth of the pit where he bobbed about for a moment as if he had jumped into a pool of water. Then slowly he sank from view, and Tommy followed him.

*   *   *   *   *

It was a most unique experience, that drop into the heart of the mountain. Practically weightless, the two young men found it quite difficult to negotiate the passage. For the first hundred or more feet they continued to bump about in the narrow shaft and each sustained painful bruises before he learned that the best and simplest method of accommodating himself to the strange condition was to remain absolutely motionless and allow the greatly weakened gravity to take its course. Each movement of an arm or leg was accompanied by a change in direction of movement, and contact with the hard stone walls followed. If they endeavored to push themselves from the contact the result was likely to be an even more serious bump on the opposite side of the shaft. So they continued the leisurely drop into the unknown depth of the pit.

Frank had turned off the flashlamp, for its battery was giving out and he wished to conserve its remaining energy for eventualities. Thus they were in Stygian darkness for nearly a half-hour, though the green luminosity far beneath them grew stronger with each passing minute. It now revealed itself as a clearly defined disc of light that flickered and sputtered continually, frequently lighting the lower end of the shaft with an unusual burst of brilliance. Remotely distant it seemed though, and unconscionably slow in drawing nearer.

"How far do you think we must drop?" called Tommy to Frank, who was probably fifty feet below him in the shaft.

"Well, I figure we have fallen about a thousand feet so far," came the reply, "and my guess is that we are about one third of the way down."

"Then this shaft is over a half-mile deep, you think?"

"Yes, at least a thousand yards, I should say. And I hope his gravity neutralizing machinery doesn't quit all of a sudden and let us down."

"Me, too," called Tommy, who had not thought of that possibility.

* * * * *

This was no joke, this falling into an unknown region so far beneath the surface of good old mother earth, thought Tommy. And how they would ever return was another thing that was not so funny. Frank was always rushing into things like this without counting the possible cost and—well—this might be the last time.

Gradually the mysterious light became stronger and soon they could make out the conformation of the rock walls they were passing at such a snail's pace. Layers of vari-colored rock showed here and there, and, at one point there was a stratum of gold-bearing or mica-filled rock that glistened with a million reflections and re-reflections. The air grew warmer and more humid as they neared the mysterious light source. They moved steadily, without acceleration, and Frank estimated the rate at about forty feet a minute. Then, with blinding suddenness, the light was immediately below and they drifted into a tremendous cavern that was illuminated by its glow.

Directly beneath the lower end of the shaft through which they had passed, there was a glowing disc of metal about fifteen feet in diameter. They drifted to its surface and sprawled awkwardly where they fell. Scrambling to gain a footing, they bounced and floated about like toy balloons before realizing that it would be necessary to creep slowly from the influence of that repelling force which had made the long drop possible without injury. Gravity met them at the disc's edge with what seemed to be unusual violence.

*   *   *   *   *

At first it seemed that their bodies weighed twice the normal amount, but this feeling soon passed and they looked about them with incredulous amazement. The metal disc was quite evidently the medium through which the repelling force was set up in the shaft, and to this disc was connected a series of heavy cables that led to a pedestal nearby. On the pedestal was a controlling lever and this moved over a quadrant that was graduated in degrees, one end of the quadrant being labeled "Up" and the other "Down." The lever now stood at a point but a very few degrees from the center or "Zero" mark and on the down side. Frank pulled this lever over to the full "Down" position and they found that they could walk over the disc with normal gravity.

"I suppose," said Frank, "that if the lever is at the other end of the scale one would fall upward with full gravity acceleration—reversed. At zero, gravity is exactly neutralized, and the intermediate positions are useful in conveying materials or human beings up and down the shaft as desired. Very clever; but what is the reason for it all?"

In the precise center of the great cavern there was a dome or hemisphere of polished metal, and it was from this dome that the eery light emanated. At times, when the light died down, this dome gleamed with dull flickerings that threatened to vanish entirely. Then suddenly it would resume full brilliance, and the sight was marvelous beyond description. A slight hissing sound came from the direction of the dome, and this varied in intensity as did the light.

"Gosh!" said Tommy. "That looks like silver to me. And, if it is, what a wealthy man our friend Leland has become. He has spent his fortune well, even if he used it all to get to this."

"Yes, but where is he?" commented Frank. Then: "Leland! Leland!" he called.

*   *   *   *   *

His voice echoed through the huge vault and re-echoed hollowly. But there was no reply save renewed flickerings from the dome.

Leaving the vicinity of the gravity disc, the two men advanced in the direction of the shining dome, which was about a quarter-mile from where they stood. Both perspired freely, for the air was very close and the temperature high. But the light of the dome was as cold as the light of a firefly and they had no hesitancy in drawing near. It was a beautiful sight, this dome of silver with its flickering lights and perfect contour.

"By George, I believe it *is* silver," exclaimed Frank, when they were within a few feet of the dome. "No other metal has that precise color. And look! There is a wheelbarrow and some mining tools. Leland has been cutting away some of the material."

Sure enough, there was indisputable evidence of the truth of his statement. And the material was undoubtedly silver!

"Silver Dome," breathed Tommy, holding a lump of the metal in his hand. "A solid dome of pure silver—fifty feet high and a hundred in diameter. How much does that figure in dollars and cents, Frank?"

"Maybe it isn't solid," said Frank dryly, "though it's worth a sizeable fortune even if it is hollow. And we haven't found Leland."

*   *   *   *   *

They circled the dome twice and looked into every corner of the great cavern, but there was no sign of the man for whom they searched. The wheelbarrow was half filled with lumps of the heavy metal, and maul and drill lay where they had been dropped by the lone miner. A cavity three feet across, and as many deep, appeared in the side of the dome to show that considerably more than one wheelbarrow load had been removed.

"Funny," grunted Tommy. "Seems almost like the old dome had swallowed him up."

At his words there came the terrific vibration. The light of the dome died out, leaving them in utter darkness, and from its interior there rose the mounting scream that had frightened old Thomas away. From so close by it was hideous, devastating; and the two men clung to each other in fright, expecting momentarily that the earth would give way beneath their feet and precipitate them into some terrible depth from which there could be no return.

Then the sound abruptly ceased and a gleam of light came from under the dome of silver. A crack appeared between its lower edge and the rocky floor of the cavern, and through this crack there shone a light of dazzling brilliancy—a warm light of rosy hue. Wider grew the opening until there was a full three feet between the floor and the bottom of the dome. Impelled by some irresistible force from within, the two men stumbled blindly to the opening, fell to the floor and rolled inside.

There was a heavy thud and the dome had returned to its normal position, with Frank and Tommy prisoners within its spacious hollow. The warm light bathed them with fearful intensity for a moment, then faded to a rosy glow that dulled their senses and quieted their nerves. Morpheus claimed them.

*   *   *   *   *

When Frank awoke he found himself between silken covers, and for a moment he gazed thoughtfully at a high arched ceiling that was entirely unfamiliar. Then, remembering, he sprang from the downy bed to his feet. The room, the furnishings, his silken robe, everything was strange. His bed, he saw, was a high one, and the frame was of the same gleaming silver as the dome under which they had been trapped. The arched ceiling glowed softly with the same rosy hue as had the inner surface of the dome. A large pool of water invited him, the surface of the pool being no more than a foot below the point where it was built into the tile floor of the room. A large open doorway connected with a similar adjoining room, where he suspected Tommy had been taken. On his bare toes, he moved silently to the other room and saw that his guess had been correct. Tommy lay sleeping quietly beneath covers as soft as his own and amidst equal luxury of surroundings.

"Well," he whispered, "this doesn't look as though we would come to any harm. And I might as well take a dive in that pool."

Returning to his own room, he removed the silken garment with which he had been provided and was quietly immersed in the cool, invigorating water of the bath. His head cleared instantly.

"Hi there!" called Tommy from the doorway. "Why didn't you wake me up? Where are we, anyway?"

With dripping head and shoulders above the water, Frank was compelled to laugh at the sleepy-eyed, wondering expression on the blue-jowled face of his friend. "Thought you were dead to the world," he returned, "you old sleepy-head. And I don't know where we are, excepting that it is somewhere under the silver dome. What's more, I don't much care. You should get into this water. It's great!"

*   *   *   *   *

So saying, he dived to the bottom of the pool and stood on his hands, his feet waving ludicrously above the surface. Tommy sniffed once and then made a quick dash for the pool in his own room. He was not to be outdone by his more energetic partner.

A half-hour later, shaved and attired in their own garments, which had been cleaned and pressed and hung neatly in the closets, they settled themselves for a discussion of the situation. Having tried the doors of both rooms and found them locked from the outside, there was no other course open to them. They must await developments.

"Looks like Leland has quite an establishment down here inside the mountain," ventured Tommy.

"Hm!" snorted Frank, "this place it none of Leland's work. He is probably a prisoner here, as are we. He just stumbled on to the silver dome and was captured by whatever race is living down here beneath it, the same as we were. Who the real inhabitants are, and what the purpose of all this is, remains to be seen."

"You think we are in friendly hands?"

"These quarters do not look much like prison cells, Tommy, but I must admit that we are locked in. Anyhow, I'm not worrying, and we will soon learn our fate and have to be ready to meet it. The people who own this place must have everything they want, and they sure have some scientific knowledge that is not known to us on the surface."

"Wonder if they are humans?"

"Certainly they are. You never heard of wild beasts sleeping in beds like these, did you?"

*   *   *   *   *

Tommy laughed at he examined the exquisite hand-wrought figures on the silver bedstead. "No, I didn't," he admitted; "but where on earth did they come from, and what are they doing here?"

"You ask too many questions," replied Frank, shrugging his broad shoulders. "We must simply wait for the answers to reveal themselves."

There was a soft rap at the door of Frank's room, where the two men were talking.

"Come in," called Frank, chuckling at the idea of such consideration from their captors.

A key rattled in the lock and the door swung open to admit the handsomest man they had ever set eyes on. He was taller than Frank by several inches, standing no less than six feet five in his thin-soled sandals, and he carried himself with the air for an emperor. His marble-white body was uncovered with the exception of a loin cloth of silver hue, and lithe muscles rippled beneath his smooth skin as he advanced to meet the prisoners. His head, surmounted by curly hair of ebon darkness, was large, and his forehead high. The features were classic and perfectly regular. The corners of his mouth drew upward in a benign smile.

"Greetings," he said, in perfect English and in a soft voice, "to the domain of Theros. You need fear no harm from our people and will be returned to the upper world when the time comes. We hope to make your stay with us enjoyable and instructive, and that you will carry back kind memories of us. The morning meal awaits you now."

*   *   *   *   *

So taken aback were the two young Americans that they stared foolishly agape for a space. Then a tinkling laugh from the tall stranger set them once more at ease.

"You will pardon us, I hope," apologized Frank, "but this is all so unexpected and so unbelievable that your words struck me speechless. And I know that my friend was similarly affected—We place ourselves in your hands."

The handsome giant nodded understanding. "No offense was taken," he murmured, "since none was intended. And your feelings are not to be wondered at. You may call me Orrin."

He turned toward the open door and signified that they were to follow him. They fell in at his side with alacrity, both suddenly realizing that they were very hungry.

They followed in silent wonderment as Orrin led the way to a broad balcony that overlooked a great underground city—a city lighted by the soft glow from some vast lighting system incorporated in its vaulted ceiling high overhead. The balcony was many levels above the streets, which were alive with active beings of similar appearance to Orrin, these speeding hither and yon by means of the many lanes of traveling ways of which the streets were composed. The buildings—endless rows of them lining the orderly streets—were octagonal in shape and rose to the height of about twenty stories, as nearly as could be judged by earthly standards. There were no windows, but at about every fifth floor there was an outer silver-railed balcony similar to the one on which they walked. The air was filled with bowl-shaped flying ships that sped over the roof tops in endless procession and without visible means of support or propulsion. Yet the general effect of the busy scene was one of precise orderliness, unmarred by confusion or distracting noises.

*   *   *   *   *

Orrin vouchsafed no explanations and they soon reentered the large building of which the balcony was a part. Here they were conducted to a sumptuously furnished dining room where their breakfast awaited them.

During the meal, which consisted of several courses of fruits and cereals entirely strange to Frank and Tommy, they were tended by Orrin with the utmost deference and most painstaking attention. He anticipated their every want and their thoughts as well. For, when Frank endeavored to ask one of the many questions with which his mind was filled, he was interrupted by a wave of the hand and a smile from their placid host.

"It is quite clear to me that you have many questions to propound," said Orrin, "and this is not a matter of wonder. But it is not permitted that I enlighten you on the points you have in mind. You must first finish your meal. Then it is to be my privilege to conduct you to the presence of Phaestra, Empress of Theros, who will reveal all. May I ask that you be patient until then?"

So friendly was his smile and so polished his manner that they restrained their impatience and finished the excellent breakfast in polite silence.

And Orrin was as good as his word, for, no sooner had they finished when he led them from the room and showed the way to the elevator which conveyed them to the upper floor of the building.

From the silver-grilled cage of the lift they stepped into a room of such beauty and magnificence of decoration that they gazed about them in wondering admiration. The paneling and mouldings were of hammered silver that gleamed with polished splendor in the soft rose glow of the hidden lights. The hangings were of heavy plush of deep green hue and bore intricate designs of silver thread woven into the material. At the opposite side of the room there was a pair of huge double doors of chased silver and on either side of this pretentious portal there stood an attendant attired as was Orrin, but bearing a silver scepter to denote his official capacity.

"Phaestra awaits the visitors from above," intoned one of the attendants. Both bowed stiffly from the waist when Orrin led the two young scientists through the great doors which had opened silently and majestically at their approach.

*　　*　　*　　*　　*

If the outer room was astonishing in its sumptuousness of decoration and furnishing, the one they now entered was positively breath-taking. On every side there were the exquisite green and silver hangings. Tables, divans, and rugs of priceless design and workmanship. But the beauty of the surroundings faded into insignificance when they saw the empress.

A canopied dais in the center of the room drew their attention and they saw that Phaestra had risen from her seat in a deeply cushioned divan and now stood at its side in an attitude of welcome. Nearly as tall as Frank, she was a figure of commanding and imperious beauty. The whiteness of her body was accentuated by the silver embroidered and tightly fitted black vestments that covered yet did not conceal its charms. A halo of glorious golden hair surmounted a head that was poised expectantly alert above the perfectly rounded shoulders. The exquisite oval of her face was chiseled in features of transcendent loveliness. She spoke, and, at sound of her musical voice, Frank and Tommy were enslaved.

*　　*　　*　　*　　*

"Gentlemen of the upper world," she said gently, "you are welcome to Theros. Your innermost thoughts have been recorded by our scientists and found good. With a definite purpose in mind, you learned of the existence of the silver dome of Theros, yet you came without greed or malice and we have taken you in to enlighten you on the many questions that are in your minds and to return you to mankind with a knowledge of Theros—

which you must keep secret. You are about to delve into a mystery of the ages; to see and learn many things that are beyond the ken of your kind. It is a privilege never before accorded to beings from above."

"We thank you, oh, Queen," spoke Frank humbly, his eyes rivetted to the gaze of those violet orbs that seemed to see into his very soul. Tommy mumbled some commonplace.

"Orrin—the sphere!" Phaestra, slightly embarrassed by Frank's stare, clapped her hands.

At her command, Orrin, who had stood quietly by, stepped to the wall and manipulated some mechanism that was hidden by the hangings. There was a musical purr from beneath the floor, and, through a circular opening which appeared as if by magic, there rose a crystal sphere of some four feet in diameter. Slowly it rose until it reached the level of their eyes and there it came to rest. The empress raised her hands as if in invocation and the soft glow of the lights died down, leaving them in momentary darkness. There came a slight murmur from the sphere, and it lighted with the eery green flickerings they had observed in the dome of silver.

*   *   *   *   *

Fascinated by the weaving lights within, they gazed into the depths of the crystal with awed expectancy. Phaestra spoke.

"Men from the surface," she said, "you, Frank Rowley, and you, Arnold Thompson, are about to witness the powers of that hemisphere of metal you were pleased to term 'Silver Dome.' As you rightly surmised, the dome is of silver—mostly. There are small percentages of platinum, iridium, and other elements, but it is more than nine-tenths pure silver. To you of the surface the alloy is highly valuable for its intrinsic worth by your own standards, but to us the value of the dome lies in its function in revealing to us the past and present events of our universe. The dome is the 'eye' of a complicated apparatus which enables us to see and hear any desired happening on the surface of the earth, beneath its surface, or on the many inhabited planets of the heavens. This is accomplished by means of extremely complex vibrations radiated from the hemisphere, these vibrations penetrating earth, metals, buildings, space itself, and returning to our viewing and sound reproducing spheres to reveal the desired past or present occurrences at the point at which the rays of vibrations are directed.

*   *   *   *   *

"In order to view the past on our own planet, the rays, which travel at the speed of light, are sent out in a huge circle through space, returning to earth after having spent the requisite number of years in transit. Instantaneous effect is secured by a connecting beam that ties together the ends of the enormous arc. This, of course, is beyond your comprehension, since the Ninth Dimension is involved. When it is desired that events of the present be observed, the rays are projected direct. The future can not be viewed, since, in order to accomplish this, it would be necessary that the rays travel at a speed greater than that of light, which is manifestly impossible."

"Great guns!" gasped Frank. "This crystal sphere then, is capable of bringing to our eyes and ears the happenings of centuries past?"

"It is, my dear Frank," said Phaestra, "and I would that I were able to describe the process more clearly." She smiled, and in the unearthly light of the sphere she appeared more beautiful than before, if such a thing were possible.

On the pedestal which supported the sphere there was a glittering array of dials and levers. Several of these controls were now adjusted by Phaestra, the delicate motions of her tapered fingers being watched by the visitors with intense admiration. There came a change in the note of the sphere, a steadying of the flickerings within.

"Behold!" exclaimed Phaestra.

*   *   *   *   *

They gazed into the depths of the sphere and lost all sense of detachment from the scene depicted therein. It seemed they were at a point several thousand miles from the surface of a planet. A great continent spread beneath them, its irregular shore line being clearly outlined against a large body of water.

Here and there the surface was obscured by great white patches of clouds that cast their shadows below.

"Atlantis!" breathed Phaestra reverently.

The lost continent of mythology! The fabled body of land that was engulfed by the Atlantic thousands of years ago—a fact!

Tommy glanced at Frank, noting that he had withdrawn his gaze from the sphere and was devouring Phaestra with his eyes. As if drawn by the ardor of his observation, she raised her own eyes from the sphere to meet those of the handsome visitor. Obviously confused, she dropped her long lashes and turned nervously to the controls. Tommy experienced a sudden feeling of dread. Surely his pal was not falling in love with this Theronian empress!

Then there came another change in the note of the sphere and once more they lost themselves in contemplation of the scene within. The surface of the lost continent was rushing madly to meet them. With terrific velocity they seemed to be falling. An involuntary gasp was forced from Tommy's lips. Mountains, valleys, rivers could now be discerned.

*   *   *   *   *

Then the scene shifted slightly and they were stationary, directly above a large seacoast city. A city of great beauty it was, and its buildings were of the same octagonal shape as were those of Theros! There could be but one inference—the Theronians were direct descendants of those inhabitants of ancient Atlantis.

"Yes," sighed Phaestra, in answer to the thought she had read, "our ancestors were those you now see in the streets of this city of Atlantis. A marvelous race they were, too. When the rest of the world was still savage and unenlightened, they knew more of the arts and sciences than is known on the surface to-day. The mysteries of the Fourth Dimension they had already solved. Their telescopes were of such power that they knew of the existence of intelligent beings on Mars and Venus. They had conquered the air. They knew of the relation between gravity and magnetism but recently propounded by your Einstein. They were prosperous, happy. Then—but watch!"

Faint sounds of the life of the city came to their ears. A swarm of monoplanes roared past just beneath them. The streets were crowded with rapidly moving vehicles, the roof-tops with air-craft. Then suddenly the scene darkened; a deep rumbling came from the sea. As they watched in fascinated wonder, a great chasm opened up through the heart of the city. Tall buildings swayed and crumbled, falling into heaps of twisted metal and crushed masonry and burying hundreds of the populace in their fall. The confusion was indescribable, the uproar terrific, and within the space of a very few minutes the entire city was a mass of ruins, fully half of the wrecked area having been swallowed up by the heaving waters of the ocean.

*   *   *   *   *

Phaestra stifled a sob. "Thus it began," she stated. "Trovus was first—the city you just saw—then came three more of the cities of the western coast in rapid succession. Computations of the scientists showed that the upheaval was widespread and that the entire continent was to be engulfed in a very short time. The exodus began, but it was too late, and only a few hundred people were able to escape the continent before it was finally destroyed. The ocean became the tomb of two hundred millions. The handful of survivors reached the coast of what is now North America. But the rigors of the climate proved severe and more than three-quarters of them perished within a few days after their planes landed. Then the rest took to the caves along the shore, and for a while were safe."

She manipulated the controls once more and there was a quick shift to another coast, a rugged, wave-beaten shore. Closer they drew until they observed a lofty palisade that extended for miles along the barren waterfront. They saw a fire atop this elevation and active men and women at various tasks within the narrow circle of its warmth. A cave mouth opened at the brink of the precipice near the spot they occupied.

Then came a repetition of the upheaval at Trovus. The ocean rushed in and beat against the cliff with such ferocity that its spray was tossed hundreds of feet in the air. The earth shook and the group of people around the fire made a hasty retreat to the mouth of the cave. The sky darkened and the winds howled with demoniac fury. Quake after quake rent the rugged cliffs: huge sections toppled into the angry waters. Then a great tidal wave swept in and covered everything, cliffs, cave mouths and all. Nought remained where they had been but the seething waters.

*   *   *   *   *

"But some escaped!" exulted Phaestra, "and these discovered Theros. Though many miles of the eastern seaboard of your United States were submerged and the coastline entirely altered, these few were saved. Their cave connected with a long passage, a tunnel that led into the bowels of the earth. With the outer entrance blocked by the upheaval they had no alternative save to continue downward."

"They traveled for days and days. Some were overcome by hunger and fell by the wayside. The most hardy survived to reach Theros, a series of enormous caverns that extends for hundreds of miles under the surface of your country. Here they found subterranean lakes of pure water; forests, game. They had a few tools and weapons and they established themselves in this underground world. From that small beginning came this!"

Phaestra's slim fingers worked rapidly at the controls. The scenes shifted in quick succession. They were once more in the present, and seemed to be traveling speedily through the underground reaches of Theros. Now they were racing through a long lighted passage; now over a great city similar to the one in which they had arrived. Here they visited a huge workshop or laboratory; there a mine where radium or cobalt or platinum was being wrested from the vitals of the unwilling earth. Then they visited a typical Theronian household, saw the perfect peace and happiness in which the family lived. Again they were in a large power plant where direct application of the internal heat of the earth as obtained through deep shafts bored into the interior was utilized in generating electricity.

They saw vast quantities of supplies, fifty-ton masses of machinery, moved from place to place as lightly as feathers by use of the gravity discs, those heavily charged plates whose emanations counteracted the earth's attraction. In one busy laboratory they saw an immense television apparatus and heard scientists discussing moot questions with inhabitants of Venus, whose images were depicted on the screen. They witnessed a severe electrical storm in the huge cavern arch over one of the cities, a storm that condensed moisture from the artificially oxygenated and humidified atmosphere in such blinding sheets as to easily explain the necessity for well-roofed buildings in the underground realm. And, in all the speech and activities of the Theronians, there was evident that all-pervading feeling of absolute contentment and freedom from care.

"What I can not understand," said Frank, during a quiet interval, "is why the Theronians have never migrated to the surface. Surely, with all your command of science and mechanics, that would be easy."

"Why? Why?" Phaestra's voice spoke volumes. "Here—I'll show you the reason."

*   *   *   *   *

And again the scene in the sphere changed. They were on the surface and a few years in the past—at Chateau Thierry. They saw their fellow men mangled and broken; saw human beings shot down by hundreds in withering bursts of machine-gun fire; saw them in hand-to-hand bayonet fights; gassed and in delirium from the horror of it all.

They traveled over the ocean; saw a big passenger liner the victim of torpedo fire; saw babies tossed into the water by distracted mothers who jumped in after them to join them in death.

A few years were passed by and they saw gang wars in Chicago and New York; saw militia and picketing strikers in mortal combat; saw wealthy brokers and bank presidents turn pistols on themselves following a crash in the stock market; government officials serving penitentiary terms for betrayal of the people's trust; opium dens, speakeasies, sex crimes. It was a fearful indictment.

"Ah, no," said Phaestra kindly, "the surface world has not yet emerged from savagery. We should be unwelcome were we to venture outside. And now we come to the reason for your visit. You come in search of one Edwin Leland, a fellow worker at one time. Your motives are above reproach. But Leland came as a greedy searcher of riches. We brought him within to teach him the error of his ways and to beg him to desist from his efforts at destroying the dome of silver. He alone knew the secret."

"Then you followed him and we took you in for similar reasons, though our scientists found very quickly that your mental reactions were of entirely different type from Leland's and that the secret would be safe in your keeping. Leland remains obdurate. He threatens us with physical violence, and his reactions to the thought-reading machines are of the most treacherous sort. We must keep him with us. He shall remain unharmed, but he must not be allowed to return. That is the story. You two are free to leave when you choose. I ask not that you give your word to keep the secret of 'Silver Dome.' I know it is not necessary."

*   *   *   *   *

The lights had resumed their normal glow, and the marvelous sphere returned to its receptacle beneath the floor. Phaestra resumed her seat on the canopied divan. Frank dropped to a seat on the edge of the dais. Tommy and Orrin remained standing, Tommy lost in thought and Orrin stolidly mute. The empress avoided Frank's gaze studiously. Her cheeks were flushed; her eyes bright with emotion.

Frank was first to break the silence. "Leland is in solitary confinement?" he asked.

"For the present he is under guard," replied Phaestra. "He was quite violent and it was necessary to disarm him after he had killed one of my attendants with a shot from his automatic pistol. When he agrees to submit peacefully, he shall be given the freedom of Theros for the remainder of his life."

"Perhaps," suggested Frank, "if I spoke to him...."

"The very thing." Phaestra thanked him with her wondrous eyes.

A high pitched note rang out from behind the hangings, and, in rapid syllables of the language of Theros, a voice broke forth from the concealed amplifiers. Orrin, startled from his stoicism, sprang to the side of his empress. She rose from her seat as the voice completed its excited message.

"It is Leland," she said calmly. "He has escaped and recovered his pistol. I have been told that he is now at large in the palace, terrorizing the household. We have no weapons here, you see."

"Good God!" shouted Frank. "Suppose he should come here?"

* * * * *

He jumped to his feet just as a shot rang out in the antechamber. Orrin dashed to the portal when a second shot spat forth from the automatic which must certainly be in the hands of a madman. The doors swung wide and Leland, hair disarranged and bloodshot eyes staring, burst into the room. Orrin went down at the next shot and the hardly recognizable scientist advanced toward the dais.

When he saw Frank and Tommy he stopped in his tracks. "So you two have been following me!" he snarled. "Well, you won't keep me from my purpose. I'm here to kill this queen of hell!"

Once more he raised his automatic, but Frank had been watching closely and he literally dove from the steps of the dais to the knees of the deranged Leland. As beautiful a tackle as he had ever made in his college football days laid the maniac low with a crashing thud that told of a fractured skull. The bullet intended for Phaestra went wide, striking Tommy in the shoulder.

Spun half way around by the impact of the heavy bullet, Tommy fought to retain his balance. But his knees went suddenly awry and gave way beneath him. He crumpled helplessly to the floor, staring foolishly at the prostrate figure of Leland and at Frank, who had risen to his feet and now faced the beautiful empress of Theros. Strange lights danced before Tommy's eyes, and he found it difficult to keep the pair in focus. But he was sure of one thing—his pal was unharmed. Then the two figures seemed to merge into one and he blinked his eyes rapidly to clear his failing vision. By George, they were in each other's arms! Funny world—above or below—it didn't seem to make any difference. But it was a tough break for Frank—morganatic marriage and all that. No chance—well—

Tommy succumbed to his overpowering drowsiness.

* * * * *

The awakening was slow, but not painful. Rather there was a feeling of utter contentment, of joy at being alive. A delicious languor pervaded Tommy's being as he turned his head on a snow white silken pillow and stared at the figure of the white-capped nurse who was fussing with the bottles and instruments that lay on an enameled table beside the bed. Memory came to him immediately. He felt remarkably well and refreshed. Experimentally he moved his left shoulder. There was absolutely no pain and it felt perfectly normal. He sat erect in his surprise and felt the shoulder with his right hand. There was no bandage, no wound. Had he dreamed of the hammer blow of that forty-five caliber bullet?

His nurse, observing that her patient had recovered consciousness, broke forth in a torrent of unintelligible Theronian, then rushed from the room.

He was still examining his unscarred shoulder in wonder, when the nurse returned, with Frank Rowley at her heels. Frank laughed at the expression of his friend's face.

"What's wrong, old-timer?" he asked.

"Why—I—thought that fool of a Leland had shot me in the shoulder," stammered Tommy, "but I guess I dreamed it. Where are we? Still in Theros?"

"We are." Frank sobered instantly, and Tommy noted with alarm that his usually cheerful features were haggard and drawn and his eyes hollow from loss of sleep. "And you didn't dream that Leland shot you. That shoulder of yours was mangled and torn beyond belief. He was using soft nosed bullets, the hell-hound!"

"Then how—?"

*   *   *   *   *

"Tommy, these Theronians are marvelous. We rushed you to this hospital and a half-dozen doctors started working on you at once. They repaired the shattered bones by an instantaneous grafting process, tied the severed veins and arteries and closed the gaping wound by filling it with a plastic compound and drawing the edges together with clamps. You were anaesthetized and some ray machine was used to heal the shoulder. This required but ten hours and they now say that your arm is as good as ever. How does it feel?"

"Perfectly natural. In fact I feel better than I have in a month." Tommy observed that the nurse had left the room and he jumped from his bed and capered like a school boy.

This drew no sign of merriment from Frank, and Tommy scrutinized him once more in consternation. "And you," he said, "what is wrong with you?"

"Don't worry about me," replied Frank impatiently. Then, irrelevantly, he said "Leland's dead."

"Should be. I knew we shouldn't have started out to help him. But, Frank, I'm concerned about you. You look badly." Tommy was getting into his clothes as he spoke.

"Forget it, Tommy. You've been sleeping for two days, you know—part of the cure—and I haven't had much rest during that time. That is all."

"It's that Phaestra woman," Tommy accused him.

"Well, perhaps. But I'll get over it, I suppose. Tommy, I love her. But there's no chance for me. Haven't seen her since the row in the palace. Her council surrounds her continually and I have been advised to-day that we are to be returned as quickly as you are up and around. That means immediately now."

"Good. The sooner the better. And you just forget about this queen as soon as you are able. She's a peach, of course, but not for you. There's lots more back in little old New York." But Frank had no reply to this sally.

*　　*　　*　　*　　*

There came a knock at the door and Tommy called, "Come in."

"I see you have fully recovered," said the smiling Theronian who entered at the bidding, "and we are overjoyed to know this. You have the gratitude of the entire realm for your part in the saving of our empress from the bullets of the madman."

"I?"

"Yes. You and your friend. And now, may I ask, are you ready to return to your own land?"

Tommy stared. "Sure thing," he said, "or rather, I will be in a few minutes."

"Thank you. We shall await you in the transmitting room."
The Theronian bowed and was gone.

"Well, I like that," said Tommy. "He hands me an undeserved
compliment and then asks how soon we can beat it. A 'here's
your hat, what's your hurry' sort of thing."

"It's me they're anxious to be rid of," remarked Frank,
shrugging his broad shoulders, "and perhaps it is just as well."

"You bet it is!" agreed Tommy enthusiastically, "and I'm in
favor of making it good and snappy." He completed his toilet as
rapidly as possible and then turned to face the down-hearted
Frank.

"How do we go? The way we came?" he asked.

*   *   *   *   *

"No, Tommy. They have closed off the shaft that led from the
cavern of the silver dome. They are taking no more chances. It
seems that the shaft down which we floated was constructed by
the Theronians; not by Leland. They had used it and the gravity
disc to transport casual visitors to the surface, who occasionally
mixed with our people in order to learn the languages of the
upper world and to actually touch and handle the things they
were otherwise able to see only through the medium of Silver
Dome and the crystal spheres. Further visits to the surface are
now forbidden, and we are to be returned by a remarkable
process of beam transmission of our disintegrated bodies."

"Disintegrated?"

"Yes. It seems they have learned to dissociate the atoms of
which the human body is composed and to transmit them to any
desired point over a beam of etheric vibrations, then to
reassemble them in the original living condition."

"What? You mean to say we are to be shot to the surface
through the intervening rock and earth? Disintegrated and
reintegrated? And we'll not even be bent, let alone busted?"

*   *   *   *   *

This time he was rewarded by a laugh. "That's right. And I
have gone through the calculations with one of the Theronian

engineers and can find no flaw in the scheme. We're safe in their hands."

"If you say so, Frank, it's okay with me. Let's go!"

Reluctantly his friend lifted his athletic bulk from the chair. In silence he led the way to the transmitting room of the Theronian scientists.

Here they were greeted by two savants with whom Frank was already acquainted, Clarux and Rhonus by name. A bewildering array of complex mechanisms was crowded into the high-ceilinged chamber and, prominent among them, was one of the crystal spheres, this one of somewhat smaller size than the one in the palace of Phaestra.

"Where do you wish to arrive?" asked Clarux.

"As near to my automobile as possible," replied Frank, taking sudden interest in the proceedings. "It is parked in the lane between Leland's house and the road."

Tommy looked quickly in his direction, encouraged by the apparent change in his attitude. The scientists proceeded to energize the crystal sphere. They were bent upon speeding the parting guests. Their beloved empress was to be saved from her own emotions.

Quick adjustments of the controls resulted in the locating of Frank's car, which was still buried to its axles in snow. The scene included Leland's house, or rather its site, for it appeared to have been utterly demolished by some explosion within.

$$* \quad * \quad * \quad * \quad *$$

Tommy raised questioning eyebrows.

"It was necessary," explained Rhonus, "to destroy the house in obliterating all traces of our former means of egress. It has been commanded that you two be returned safely, and we are authorized to trust implicitly in your future silence regarding the existence of Theros. This is satisfactory, I presume?"

Both Tommy and Frank nodded agreement.

"Are you ready, gentlemen?" asked Clarux, who was adjusting a mechanism that resembled a huge radio transmitter. Its twelve giant vacuum tubes glowed into life as he spoke.

"We are," chimed the two visitors.

They were requested to step to a small circular platform that was raised about a foot from the floor by means of insulating legs. Above the table there was an inverted bowl of silver in the shape of a large parabolic reflector.

"There will be no alarming sensations," averred Clarux. "When I close the switch the disintegrating energy from the reflector above will bathe your bodies for a moment in visible rays of a deep purple hue. You may possibly experience a slight momentary feeling of nausea. Then—presto!—you have arrived."

"Shoot!" growled Frank from his position on the stand.

Clarux pulled the switch and there was a murmur as of distant thunder. Tommy blinked involuntarily in the brilliant purple glow that surrounded him. Then all was confusion in the transmitting room. Somebody had rushed through the open door shouting, "Frank! Frank!" It was the empress Phaestra.

*   *   *   *   *

In a growing daze Tommy saw her dash to the platform, seize Frank in a clutch of desperation. There was a violent wrench as if some monster were twisting at his vitals. He closed his eyes against the blinding light, then realized that utter silence had followed the erstwhile confusion. He sat in Frank's car—alone.

The journey was over, and Frank was left behind. With awful finality it came to him that there was nothing he could do. It was clear that Phaestra had wanted his pal, needed him—come for him. From the fact that Frank remained behind it was evident that she had succeeded in retaining him. A sickening fear came to Tommy that she had been too late; that Frank's body was already partly disintegrated and that he might have paid the price of her love with his life. But a little reflection convinced him that if this were the case a portion of his friend's body would have reached the intended destination. Then, unexplainably, he received a mental message that all was well.

*   *   *   *   *

Considerably heartened, he pressed the starter button and the cold motor of Frank's coupe turned over slowly, protestingly. Finally it coughed a few times, and, after considerable coaxing by use of the choke, ran smoothly. He proceeded to back carefully through the drifts toward the road, casting an occasional regretful glance in the direction of the demolished mansion.

He would have some explaining to do when he returned to New York. Perhaps—yes, almost certainly, he would be questioned by the police regarding Frank's disappearance. But he would never betray the trust of Phaestra. Who indeed would believe him if he told the story? Instead, he would concoct a weird fabrication regarding an explosion in Leland's laboratory, of his own miraculous escape. They could not hold him, could not accuse him of murder without producing a body—the *corpus delicti*, or whatever they called it.

Anyway, Frank was content. So was Phaestra.

Tommy swung the heavy car into the road and turned toward New York, alone and lonely—but somehow happy; happy for his friend.

Vagabonds of Space

Originally Published in *Astounding Stories*,
November 1930

Vagabonds of Space

CHAPTER I
The Nomad

Gathered around a long table in a luxuriously furnished director's room, a group of men listened in astonishment to the rapid and forceful speech of one of their number.

"I tell you I'm through, gentlemen," averred the speaker. "I'm fed up with the job, that's all. Since 2317 you've had me sitting at the helm of International Airways and I've worked my fool head off for you. Now—get someone else!"

"Made plenty of money yourself, didn't you, Carr?" asked one of the directors, a corpulent man with a self-satisfied countenance.

"Sure I did. That's not the point. I've done all the work. There's not another executive in the outfit whose job is more than a title, and you know it. I want a change and a rest. Going to take it, too. So, go ahead with your election of officers and leave me out."

"Your stock?" Courtney Davis, chairman of the board, sensed that Carr Parker meant what he said.

"I'll hold it. The rest of you can vote it as you choose: divide the proxies pro rata, based on your individual holdings. But I reserve the right to dump it all on the market at the first sign of shady dealings. That suit you?"

The recalcitrant young President of International Airways had risen from the table. The chairman attempted to restrain him.

"Come on now, Carr, let's reason this out. Perhaps if you just took a leave of absence—"

"Call it anything you want. I'm done right now."

Carr Parker stalked from the room, leaving eleven perspiring capitalists to argue over his action.

*   *   *   *   *

He rushed to the corridor and nervously pressed the call button of the elevators. A minute later he emerged upon the roof of the Airways building, one of the tallest of New York's mid-town sky-scrapers. The air here, fifteen hundred feet above the hot street, was cool and fresh. He walked across the great flat surface of the landing stage to inspect a tiny helicopter which had just settled to a landing. Angered as he was, he still could not resist the attraction these trim little craft had always held for him. The feeling was in his blood.

His interest, however, was short lived and he strolled to the observation aisle along the edge of the landing stage. He stared moodily into the heavens where thousands of aircraft of all descriptions sped hither and yon. A huge liner of the Martian route was dropping from the skies and drifting toward her cradle on Long Island. He looked out over the city to the north: fifty miles of it he knew stretched along the east shore of the Hudson. Greatest of the cities of the world, it housed a fifth of the population of the United States of North America; a third of the wealth.

Cities! The entire world lived in them! Civilization was too highly developed nowadays. Adventure was a thing of the past. Of course there were the other planets, Mars and Venus, but they were as bad. At least he had found them so on his every business trip. He wished he had lived a couple of centuries ago, when the first space-ships ventured forth from the earth. Those were days of excitement and daring enterprise. Then a man could find ways of getting away from things—next to nature— out into the forests; hunting; fishing. But the forests were gone, the streams enslaved by the power monopolies. There were only the cities—and barren plains. Everything in life was made by man, artificial.

*   *   *   *   *

Something drew his eyes upward and he spotted an unusual object in the heavens, a mere speck as yet but drawing swiftly in from the upper air lanes. But this ship, small though it appeared, stood out from amongst its fellows for some reason. Carr rubbed his eyes to clear his vision. Was it? Yes—it was—

surrounded by a luminous haze. Notwithstanding the brilliance of the afternoon sun, this haze was clearly visible. A silver shimmering that was not like anything he had seen on Earth. The ship swung in toward the city and was losing altitude rapidly. Its silvery aura deserted it and the vessel was revealed as a sleek, tapered cylinder with no wings, rudders or helicopter screws. Like the giant liners of the Interplanetary Service it displayed no visible means of support or propulsion. This was no ordinary vessel.

Carr watched in extreme interest as it circled the city in a huge spiral, settling lower at each turn. It seemed that the pilot was searching for a definite landing stage. Then suddenly it swooped with a rush. Straight for the stage of the Airways building! The strange aura reappeared and the little vessel halted in mid-air, poised a moment, then dropped gracefully and lightly as a feather to the level surface not a hundred feet from where he stood. He hurried to the spot to examine the strange craft.

"Mado!" he exclaimed in surprise as a husky, bronzed Martian squeezed through the quickly opened manhole and clambered heavily to the platform. Mado of Canax—an old friend!

"Devils of Terra!" gasped the Martian, his knees giving way, "—your murderous gravity! Here, help me. I've forgotten the energizing switch."

*   *   *   *   *

Carr laughed as he fumbled with a mechanism that was strapped to the Martian's back. Mado, who tipped the scales at over two hundred pounds on his own planet, weighed nearly six hundred here. His legs simply couldn't carry the load!

"There you are, old man." Parker had located the switch and a musical purr came from the black box between the Martian's broad shoulders. "Now stand up and tell me what you're doing here. And what's the idea of the private ship? Come all the way from home in it?"

His friend struggled to his feet with an effort, for the field emanating from the black box required a few seconds to reach the intensity necessary to counteract two-thirds of the earth's gravity.

"Thanks Carr," he grinned. "Yes, I came all the way in that bus. Alone, too—and she's mine! What do you think of her?"

"A peach, from what I can see. But how come? Not using a private space-flier on your business trips, are you?"

"Not on your life! I've retired. Going to play around for a few years. That's why I bought the Nomad."

"Retired! Why Mado, I just did the same thing."

"Great stuff! They've worked you to death. What are you figuring on doing with yourself?"

Carr shrugged his shoulders resignedly. "Usual thing, I suppose. Travel aimlessly, and bore myself into old age. Nothing else to do. No kick out of life these days at all, Mado, even in chasing around from planet to planet. They're all the same."

*   *   *   *   *

The Martian looked keenly at his friend. "Oh, is that so?" he said. "No kick, eh? Well, let me tell you, Carr Parker, you come with me and we'll find something you'll get a kick out of. Ever seen the Sargasso Sea of the solar system? Ever been on one of the asteroids? Ever seen the other side of the Moon—Uranus— Neptune—Planet 9, the farthest out from the sun?"

"No-o." Carr's eyes brightened somewhat.

"Then you haven't seen anything or been anywhere. Trouble with you is you've been in the rut too long. Thinking there's nothing left in the universe but the commonplace. Right, too, if you stick to the regular routes of travel. But the *Nomad's* different. I'm just a rover when I'm at her controls, a vagabond in space—free as the ether that surrounds her air-tight hull. And, take it from me, there's something to see and do out there in space. Off the usual lanes, perhaps, but it's there."

"You've been out—how long?" Carr hesitated.

"Eighty Martian days. Seen plenty too." He waved his arm in a gesture that seemed to take in the entire universe.

"Why come here, with so much to be seen out there?"

"Came to visit you, old stick-in-the-mud," grinned Mado, "and to try and persuade you to join me. I find you footloose already. You're itching for adventure; excitement. Will you come?"

Carr listened spellbound. "Right now?" he asked.

"This very minute. Come on."

"My bag," objected Carr, "it must be packed. I'll need funds too."

"Bag! What for? Plenty of duds on the *Nomad*—for any old climate. And money—don't make me laugh! Vagabonds need money?" He backed toward the open manhole of the *Nomad*, still grinning.

Carr hesitated, resisting the impulse to take Mado at his word. He looked around. The landing stage had been deserted, but people now were approaching. People not to be tolerated at the moment. He saw Courtney Davis, grim and determined. There'd be more arguments, useless but aggravating. Well, why not go? He'd decided to break away. What better chance? Suddenly he dived for the manhole of Mado's vessel; wriggled his way to the padded interior of the air-lock. He heard the clang of the circular cover. Mado was clamping it to its gasketed seat.

"Let's go!" he shouted.

CHAPTER II
Into the Heavens

The directors of International Airways stared foolishly when they saw Carr Parker and the giant Martian enter the mysterious ship which was a trespasser on their landing stage. They gazed incredulously as the gleaming torpedo-shaped vessel arose majestically from its position. There was no evidence of motive power other than a sudden radiation from its hull plates of faintly crackling streamers of silvery light. They fell back in alarm as it pointed its nose skyward and accelerated with incredible rapidity, the silver energy bathing them in its blinding luminescence. They burst forth in excited recrimination when it vanished into the blue. Courtney Davis shook his fist after the departing vessel and swore mightily.

Carr Parker forgot them entirely when he clambered into the bucket seat beside Mado, who sat at the Nomad's controls. He was free at last: free to probe the mysteries of outer space, to roam the skies with this Martian he had admired since boyhood.

"Glad you came?" Mado asked his Terrestrial friend.

"You bet. But tell me about yourself. How you've been and how come you've rebelled, too? I haven't seen you for a long time, you know. Why, it's been years!"

"Oh, I'm all right. Guess I got fed up with things about the same way you did. Knew last time I saw you that you were feeling as I did. That's why I came after you."

"But this vessel, the *Nomad*. I didn't know such a thing was in existence. How does it operate? It seems quite different from the usual ether-liners."

*   *   *   *   *

"It's a mystery ship. Invented and built by Thrygis, a discredited scientist of my country. Spent a fortune on it and then went broke and killed himself. I bought it from the executors for a song. They thought it was a pile of junk. But the plans and notes of the inventor were there and I studied 'em well. The ship is a marvel, Carr. Utilizes gravitational attraction and reversal as a propelling force and can go like the Old Boy himself. I've hit two thousand miles a second with her."

"A second! Why, that's ten times as fast as the regular liners! Must use a whale of a lot of fuel. And where do you keep it? The fuel, I mean."

"Make it right on board. I'm telling you Carr, the *Nomad* has no equal. She's a corker."

"I'll say she is. But what do you mean—make the fuel?"

"Cosmic rays. Everywhere in space you know. Seems they are the result of violent concentrations of energy that cause the birth of atoms. Thrygis doped out a collector of these rays that takes 'em from their paths and concentrates 'em in a retort where there's a spongy metal catalyst that never deteriorates. Here there is a reaction to the original action out in space and new atoms are born, simple ones of hydrogen. But what could be sweeter for use in one of our regular atomic motors? The energy of disintegration is used to drive the generators of the artificial gravity field, and there you are. Sounds complicated, but really isn't. And nothing to get out of whack either."

*   *   *   *   *

"Beats the rocket motors and bulky fuel of the regular liners a mile, doesn't it? But since when are you a navigator, Mado?"

"Don't need to be a navigator with the *Nomad*. She's automatic, once the controls are set. Say we wish to visit Venus. The telescope is sighted on that body and the gravity forces adjusted so we'll be attracted in that direction and repelled in the opposite direction. Then we can go to bed and forget it. The movement of the body in its orbit makes no difference because the force follows wherever it goes. See? The speed increases until the opposing forces are equal, when deceleration commences and we gradually slow down until within ten thousand miles of the body, when the *Nomad* automatically stops. Doesn't move either, until we awaken to take the controls. How's that for simple?"

"Good enough. But suppose a wandering meteor or a tiny asteroid gets in the way? At our speed it wouldn't have to be as big as your fist to go through us like a shot."

"All taken care of, my dear Carr. I told you Thrygis was a wiz. Such a happenstance would disturb the delicate balance of the energy compensators and the course of the *Nomad* would instantly alter to dodge the foreign object. Once passed by, the course would again be resumed."

"Some ship, the *Nomad*!" Carr was delighted with the explanations. "I'm sold on her and on the trip. Where are we now and where bound?"

*   *   *   *   *

Mado glanced at the instrument board. "Nearly a million miles out and headed for that Sargasso Sea I told you about," he said. "It isn't visible in the telescope, but I've got it marked by the stars. Out between the orbits of Mars and Jupiter, a quarter of a billion miles away. But we'll average better than a thousand miles a second. Be there in three days of your time."

"How can there be a sea out there in space?"

"Oh, that's just my name for it. Most peculiar thing, though. There's a vast, billowy sort of a cloud. Twists and weaves around as if alive. Looks like seaweed or something; and Carr, I swear there are things floating around in it. Wrecks. Something damn peculiar, anyway. I vow I saw a signal. People marooned there or something. Sorta scared me and I didn't stay around for long as there was an awful pull from the mass. Had to use full reversal of the gravity force to get away."

"Now why didn't you tell me that before? That's something to think about. Like the ancient days of ocean-going ships on Earth."

"Tell you? How could I tell you? You've been questioning me ever since I first saw you and I've been busy every minute answering you."

Carr laughed and slid from his seat to the floor. He felt curiously light and loose-jointed. A single step carried him to one of the stanchions of the control cabin and he clung to it for a moment to regain his equilibrium.

"What's wrong?" he demanded. "No internal gravity mechanism on the *Nomad*?"

"Sure is. But it's adjusted for Martian gravity. You'll get along, but it wouldn't be so easy for me with Earth gravity. I'd have to wear the portable G-ray all the time, and that's not so comfortable. All right with you?"

"Oh, certainly. I didn't understand."

*   *   *   *   *

Carr saw that his friend had unstrapped the black box from his shoulders. He didn't blame him. Glad he wasn't a Martian. It was mighty inconvenient for them on Venus or Terra. Their bodies, large and of double the specific gravity, were not easily handled where gravity was nearly three times their own. The Venusians and Terrestrials were more fortunate when on Mars, for they could become accustomed to the altered conditions. Only had to be careful they didn't overdo. He remembered vividly a quick move he had made on his first visit to Mars. Carried him twenty feet to slam against a granite pedestal. Bad cut that gave him, and the exertion in the rarefied atmosphere had him gasping painfully.

He walked to one of the ports and peered through its thick window. Mado was fussing with the controls. The velvety blackness of the heavens; the myriad diamond points of clear brilliance. Cold, too, it looked out there, and awesomely vast. The sun and Earth had been left behind and could not be seen. But Carr didn't care. The heavens were marvelous when viewed without the obstruction of an atmosphere. But he'd seen them often enough on his many business trips to Mars and Venus.

"Ready for bed?" Mado startled him with a tap on the shoulder.

"Why—if you say so. But you haven't shown me through the *Nomad* yet."

"All the time in the universe for that. Man, don't you realize you're free? Come, let's grab some sleep. Need it out here. The ship'll be here when we wake up. She's flying herself right now. Fast, too."

Carr looked at the velocity indicator. Seven hundred miles a second and still accelerating! He felt suddenly tired and when Mado opened the door of a sleeping cabin its spotless bunk looked very inviting. He turned in without protest.

CHAPTER III
A Message

The days passed quickly, whether measured by the Martian chronometer aboard the *Nomad* or by Carr's watch, which he was regulating to match the slightly longer day of the red planet. He was becoming proficient in the operation of all mechanisms of the ship and had developed a fondness for its every appointment.

Behind them the sun was losing much of its blinding magnificence as it receded into the ebon background of the firmament. The Earth was but one of the countless worlds visible through the stern ports, distinguishable by its slightly greenish tinge. They had reached the vicinity of the phenomenon of space Mado had previously discovered. Carr found himself seething with excitement as the *Nomad* was brought to a drifting speed.

Mado, who had disclaimed all knowledge of navigation, was busy in the turret with a sextant. He made rapid calculations based on its indications and hurried to the controls.

"Find it?" Carr asked.

"Yep. Be there in a half hour."

The nose of the vessel swung around and Mado adjusted the gravity energy carefully. Carr glued his eye to the telescope.

"See anything?" inquired Mado.

"About a million stars, that's all."

"Funny. Should be close by."

Then: "Yes! Yes! I see it!" Carr exulted. "A milky cloud. Transparent almost. To the right a little more!"

The mysterious cloud rushed to meet them and soon was visible to the naked eye through the forward port. Their speed increased alarmingly and Mado cut off the energy.

"What's that?" Mado stared white-faced at his friend.

"A voice! You hear it too?"

"Yes. Listen!"

Amazed, they gazed at each other. It was a voice; yet not a sound came to their ears. The voice was in their own consciousness. A mental message! Yet each heard and understood. There were no words, but clear mental images.

"Beware!" it seemed to warn. "Come not closer, travelers from afar. There is danger in the milky fleece before you!"

$$* \quad * \quad * \quad * \quad *$$

Mado pulled frantically at the energy reverse control. The force was now fully repelling. Still the billowing whiteness drew nearer. It boiled and bubbled with the ferocity of one of the hot lava cauldrons of Mercury. Changing shape rapidly, it threw out long streamers that writhed and twisted like the arms of an octopus. Reaching. Searching for victims!

"God!" whispered Carr. "What is it?"

"Take warning," continued the voice that was not a voice. "A great ship, a royal ship from a world unknown to you, now is caught in the grip of this mighty monster. We can not escape, and death draws quickly near. But we can warn others and ask that our fate be reported to our home body."

A sudden upheaval of the monstrous mass spewed forth an object that bounced a moment on the rippling surface and then was lost to view. A sphere, glinting golden against the white of its awful captor.

"The space-ship!" gasped Mado. "It's vanished again!"

They hurtled madly in the direction of this monster of the heavens, their reverse energy useless.

"We're lost, Mado." Carr was calm now. This was excitement with a vengeance. He'd wished for it and here it was. But he'd much rather have a chance to fight for his life. Fine ending to his dreams!

"Imps of the canals! The thing's alive!" Mado hurled himself at the controls as a huge blob of the horrible whiteness broke loose from the main body and wobbled uncertainly toward them. A long feeler reached forth and grasped the errant portion, returning it with a vicious jerk.

"Turn back! Turn back!" came the eery warning from the golden sphere. "All is over for us. Our hull is crushed. The air is pouring from our last compartment. Already we find breathing difficult. Turn back! The third satellite of the fifth planet is our home. Visit it, we beseech you, and report the manner of our going. This vile creature of space has power to draw you to its breast, to crush you as we are crushed."

*   *   *   *   *

The *Nomad* lurched and shuddered, drawn ever closer to the horrid mass of the thing. A gigantic jellyfish, that's what it was, a hundred miles across! Carr shivered in disgust as it throbbed anew, sending out those grasping streamers of its mysterious material. As the *Nomad* plunged to its doom with increasing speed, Mado tried to locate some spot in the universe where an extreme effect could be obtained from the full force of the attracting or repulsive energies. They darted this way and that but always found themselves closer to the milky billows that now were pulsating in seeming eagerness to engulf the new victim.

Once more came the telepathic warning, "Delay no longer. It is high time you turned back. You must escape to warn our people and yours. Even now the awful creature has us in its vitals, its tentacles reaching through our shattered walls, creeping and twining through the passages of our vessel. Crushing floors and walls, its demoniac energies heating our compartment beyond belief. We can hold out no longer. Go! Go quickly. Remember—the third satellite of the fifth planet—to the city of golden domes. Tell of our fate. Our people will understand. You—"

The voice was stilled. Mado groaned as if in pain and Carr saw in that instant that each knob and lever on the control panel glowed with an unearthly brush discharge. Not violet as of high frequency electricity, but red. Cherry red as of heated metal. The emanations of the cosmic monster were at work on the *Nomad*. A glance through the forward port showed they had but a few miles to go. They'd be in the clutches of the horror in minutes, seconds, at the rate they were traveling. Mado slumped in his seat, his proud head rolling grotesquely on his breast. He slid to the floor, helpless.

*   *   *   *   *

Carr went mad with fury. It couldn't be! This thing of doom was a creature of his imagination! But no—there it was, looming close in his vision. By God, he'd leave the mark of the *Nomad* on the vicious thing! He remembered the ray with which the vessel was armed. He was in the pilot's seat, fingering controls that blistered his hands and cramped his arms with an unnameable force. He'd fight the brute! Full energy—head on—that was the way to meet it. Why bother with the reversal? It was no use.

A blood-red veil obscured his vision. He felt for the release of the ray; pulled the gravity energy control to full power forward. In a daze, groping blindly for support, he waited for the shock of impact. The mass of that monstrosity must be terrific, else why had it such a power of attraction for other bodies? Or was it that the thing radiated energies unknown to science? Whatever it was, the thing would know the sting of the *Nomad's* ray. Whatever its nature, animate or inanimate, it was matter. The ray destroyed matter. Obliterated it utterly. Tore the atoms asunder, whirling their electrons from their orbits with terrific velocity. There'd be some effect, that was certain! No great use perhaps. But a crater would mark the last resting place of the *Nomad*; a huge crater. Perhaps the misty whiteness would close in over them later. But there'd be less of the creature's bulk to menace other travelers in space.

His head ached miserably; his body was shot through and through with cramping agonies. The very blood in his veins was liquid fire, searing his veins and arteries with pulsing awfulness. He staggered from the control cabin; threw himself on his bunk. The covers were electrified and clung to him like tissue to rubbed amber. The wall of the sleeping cabin vibrated with a screeching note. The floors trembled. Madness! That's all it was! He'd awaken in a moment. Find himself in his own bed at home. He'd dreamed of adventures before now. But never of such as this! It just couldn't happen! A nightmare—fantasy of an over-tired brain—it was.

There came a violent wrench that must have torn the hull plates from their bracings. The ship seemed to close in on him and crush him. A terrific concussion flattened him to the bunk. Then all was still. Carr Parker's thoughts broke short abruptly. He had slipped into unconsciousness.

CHAPTER IV
Europa

When Carr opened his eyes it was to the normal lighting of his own sleeping cabin. The *Nomad* was intact, though an odor of scorched varnish permeated the air. They were unharmed—as yet. He turned on his side and saw that Mado was moving about at the side of his couch. Good old Mado! With a basin of water in his hand and a cloth. He'd been bathing his face. Brought him to. He sat up just as Mado turned to apply the cloth anew.

"Good boy, Carr! All right?" smiled the Martian.

"Little dizzy. But I'm okay." Carr sprang to his feet where he wabbled uncertainly for a moment. "But the *Nomad?*" he asked. "Is she—are we safe?"

"Never safer. What in the name of Saturn did you do?"

Carr passed his hand across his eyes, trying to remember. "The D-ray," he said. "I turned it on and dived into the thing with full attraction. Then—I forget. Where is it—the thing, I mean?"

"Look!" Mado drew him to the stern compartment.

Far behind them there shone a misty wreath, a ring of drifting matter that writhed and twisted as if in mortal agony.

"Is that it?"

"What's left of it. You shot your way through it; through and out of its influence. D-ray must have devitalized the thing as it bored through. Killed its energies—for the time, at least."

Already, the thing was closing in. Soon there would be a solid mass as before. But the *Nomad* was saved.

"How about yourself?" asked Carr anxiously. "Last time I saw you you were flat on the floor."

"Nothing wrong with me now. A bit stiff and sore, that's all. When I came to I put all the controls in neutral and came looking for you. I was scared, but the thing's all over now, so let's go."

"Where?"

"Europa."

"Where's that?"

"Don't you remember? The third satellite of the fifth planet. That's Europa, third in distance from Jupiter, the fifth planet. It is about the size of Terra's satellite—your Moon. We'll find the city of the golden domes."

*   *   *   *   *

Carr's eyes renewed their sparkle. "Right!" he exclaimed. "I forgot the mental message. Poor devils! All over for them now. But we'll carry their message. How far is it?"

"Don't know yet till I determine our position and the position of Jupiter. But it's quite a way. Jupiter's 483 million miles from the Sun, you know."

"We're more than half way, then."

"Not necessarily. Perhaps we're on the opposite side of the sun from Jupiter's present position. Then we'd have a real trip."

"Let's figure it out." Carr was anxious to be off.

Luck was with them, as they found after some observations from the turret. Jupiter lay off their original course by not more than fifteen degrees. It was but four days' journey.

Again they were on their way and the two men, Martian and Terrestrial, made good use of the time in renewing their old friendship and in the study of astronomy as they had done during the first leg of their journey. Though of widely differing build and nature, the two found a close bond in their similar inclinations. The library of the Nomad was an excellent one. Thrygis had seen to that, all of the voice-vision reels being recorded in Cos, the interplanetary language, with its standardized units of weight and measurement.

*   *   *   *   *

The supplies on board the *Nomad* were ample. Synthetic foods there were for at least a hundred Martian days. The supply of oxygen and water was inexhaustible, these essential items being produced in automatic retorts where disassembled electrons from their cosmic-ray hydrogen were reassembled in the proper structure to produce atoms of any desired element. Their supply of synthetic food could be replenished in like manner when necessity arose. Thrygis had forgotten nothing.

"How do you suppose we'll make ourselves understood to the people of Europa?" asked Carr, when they had swung around the great orb of Jupiter and were headed toward the satellite.

"Shouldn't have any trouble, Carr. Believe me, to a people who have progressed to the point of sending mental messages over five hundred miles of space, it'll be a cinch, understanding our simple mental processes. Bet they'll read our every thought."

"That's right. But the language. Proper names and all that. Can't get those over with thought waves."

"No, but I'll bet they'll have some way of solving that too. You wait and see."

Carr lighted a cigar and inhaled deeply as he gazed from one of the ports. He'd never felt better in his life. Always had liked Martian tobacco, too. Wondered what they'd do when the supply ran out. One thing they couldn't produce synthetically. The disc of the satellite loomed near and it shone with a warmly inviting light. Almost red, like the color of Mars, it was. Sort of golden, rather. Anyway, he wondered what awaited them there. This was a great life, this roaming in space, unhampered by laws or conventions. The *Nomad* was well named.

"Wonder what they'll think of our yarn," he said.

"And me. I wonder, too, what that ungodly thing was back there. The thing that is now the grave of some of their people. And what the golden sphere was doing so far from home. It's a mystery."

*   *   *   *   *

They had gone over the same ground a hundred times and had not reached a satisfactory conclusion. But perhaps they'd learn more in the city of golden domes.

"Another thing," said Carr, "that's puzzled me. Why is it that Europa has not been discovered before this; that it's inhabited, I mean?"

"Rocket ships couldn't carry enough fuel. Besides, our astronomers've always told us that the outer planets were too cold; too far from the sun."

"That is something to think about. Maybe we'll not be able to stand the low temperature; thin atmosphere; low surface gravity."

"We've our insulated suits and the oxygen helmets for the first two objections. The G-rays'll hold us down in any gravity. But we'll see mighty soon. We're here."

They had entered the atmosphere as they talked and the *Nomad* was approaching the surface in a long glide with repulsion full on. It was daytime on the side they neared. Pale daylight, but revealing. The great ball that was Jupiter hung low on the horizon, its misty outline faintly visible against the deep green of the sky.

*   *   *   *   *

The surface over which they skimmed was patchworked with farm-lands and crisscrossed by gleaming ribbons. Roadways! It was like the voice-vision records of the ancient days on Mars and Terra before their peoples had taken to the air. Here was a body where a person could get out in the open; next to nature. They crossed a lake of calm green water fringed by golden sands. At its far side a village spread out beneath them and was gone; a village of broad pavements and circular dwellings with flat rooms, each with its square of ground. A golden, mountain range loomed in the background; vanished beneath them. More fields and roads. Everywhere there were yellows and reds and the silver sheen of the roads. No green save that of the darkening sky and the waters of the streams and ponds. It was a most inviting panorama.

Occasionally they passed a vessel of the air—strange flapping-winged craft that soared and darted like huge birds. Once one of them approached so closely they could see its occupants, seemingly a people similar to the Venusians, small of stature and slender.

"How in time are we to find this city of golden domes?" Carr ejaculated.

As if in answer to his question there came a startling command, another of the mental messages.

"Halt!" it conveyed to their mind. "Continue not into our country until we have communed with you."

Obediently Mado brought up the nose of the *Nomad* and slowed her down to a gradual stop. They hovered at an altitude of about four thousand feet, both straining their ears as if listening for actual speech.

"It is well," continued the message. "Your thoughts are good. You come from afar seeking the city of golden domes. Proceed now and a fleet of our vessels will meet you and guide you to our city."

"Now wouldn't that jar you?" whispered Carr. "Just try to get away with anything on this world."

Mado laughed as he started the generators of the propelling energy. "I'd hate to have a wife of Europa," he commented. "No sitting-up-with-sick-friend story could get by with her!"

CHAPTER V
The City of Golden Domes

With the *Nomad* cruising slowly over the surface of the peaceful satellite, Mado sampled the atmosphere through a tube which was provided for that purpose. The pressure was low, as they had expected; about twenty inches of mercury in the altitude at which they drifted. But the oxygen content was fairly high and the impurities negligible. A strange element was somewhat in evidence, though Mado's analysis showed this to be present in but minute quantity. They opened the ports and drew their first breath of the atmosphere of Europa.

"Good air, Carr." Mado was sniffing at one of the ports. "A bit rare for you, but I think you'll get along with it. Temperature of forty-five degrees. That's not so bad. The strangest thing is the gravity. This body isn't much more than two thousand miles in diameter, yet its gravity is about the same as on Venus—seven eighths of that of Terra. Must have a huge nickel-iron core."

"Yes. It'll be a cinch for me. But you, you big lummox—it's the G-ray for you as long as we're here."

"Uh-huh. You get all the breaks, don't you?"

Carr laughed. He was becoming anxious to land. "What sort of a reception do you suppose we'll get?" he said.

"Not bad, from the tone of that last message. And here they come, Carr. Look—a dozen of them. A royal reception, so far."

Suddenly they were in the midst of a flock of great birds; birds that flapped their golden wings to rise, then soared and circled like the gulls of the terrestrial oceans. And these mechanical birds were fast. Carr and Mado watched in fascination as they strung out in V formation and led the way in the direction of the setting sun. Six, seven hundred miles an hour the *Nomad's* indicator showed, as they swung in behind these ships of Europa.

*   *   *   *   *

They crossed a large body of water, a lake of fully five hundred miles in width. More country then, hardly populated now and with but few of the gleaming roadways. The sun had set, but there was scarcely any diminution of the light for the great ball that was Jupiter reflected a brilliance of far greater intensity than that of the full Moon on a clear Terrestrial night. A marvelous sight the gigantic body presented, with its alternate belts of gray-blue and red and dazzling white. And it hung so low and huge in the heavens that it seemed one had but to stretch forth a hand to touch its bright surface.

Another mountain range loomed close and was gone. On its far side there stretched the desolate wastes of a desert, a barren plain that extended in all directions to the horizon. Wind-swept, it was and menacing beneath them. Europa was not all as they had first seen it.

A glimmer of brightness appeared at the horizon. The fleet was reducing speed and soon they saw that their journey was nearly over. At the far edge of the desert the bright spot resolved itself into the outlines of a city, the city of golden domes. Cones they looked like, rather, with rounded tops and fluted walls. The mental message had conveyed the most fitting description possible without words or picture.

The landing was over so quickly that they had but confused impressions of their reception. A great square in the heart of the city, crowded with people. Swooping maneuvers of hundreds of the bird-like ships. An open space for their arrival. The platform where a committee awaited them. The king, or at least he seemed to be king. The sea of upturned faces, staring eyes.

*   *   *   *   *

Mado fidgeted and opened his mouth to voice a protest but Carr nudged him into silence. The king had risen from his seat in the circle on the platform and was about to address them. There was no repetition of the telepathic means of communication.

"Welcome, travelers from the inner planets," said the king. He spoke Cos perfectly! "Cardos, emperor of the body you call Europa, salutes you. Our scientists have recorded your thoughts with their psycho-ray apparatus and have learned that you have a message for us, a message we fear is not pleasant. Am I correct?"

Carr stared at the soft-voiced monarch of this remarkable land. It was incredible that he spoke in the universal language of the inner planets!

"Your Highness," he replied, "is correct. We have a message. But it amazes us that you are familiar with our language."

"That we shall explain later. Meanwhile—the message!"

"The message," Carr said, "is not pleasant. A golden sphere out in space. Helpless in the clutches of a nameless monster, a vast creature of jellylike substance but possessed of enormous destructive energy. A mental message to our vessel warning us away and bidding us to come here; to tell you of their fate. We escaped and here we are."

The face of Cardos paled. He reached for an egg-shaped crystal that reposed on the table; spoke rapidly into its shimmering depths. Hidden amplifiers carried his voice throughout the square in booming tones. It was a strange tongue he spoke, with many gutturals and sibilants. A groan came up from the assembled multitude.

Cardos tossed the crystal to the table with a resigned gesture, then tottered and swayed. Instant confusion reigned in the square and the emperor was assisted from the platform by two of his retainers. They never saw him again.

*   *   *   *   *

One of the counsellors, a middle-aged man with graying russet hair and large gray eyes set in a perfectly smooth countenance, stepped from the platform and grasped the two adventurers as the confusion in the square increased to an uproar.

"Come," he whispered, in excellent Cos; "I'll explain all to you in the quiet of my own apartments. I am Detis, a scientist, and my home is close by."

Gently he clung to them as the larger men forced their way between the milling groups of excited Europans. No one gave them much attention. All seemed to be overcome with grief. A terrible disaster, this loss of the golden sphere must be!

They were out of the square and in one of the broad streets. The fluted sides of the unpointed cones shone softly golden on all sides. Alike in every respect were these dwellings of the people of Europa, and strangely attractive in the light of the mother planet.

Not a word was spoken when they reached the abode of their guide. They entered an elaborate hall and were whisked upward in an automatic elevator. Detis ushered them into his apartment when they alighted. He smiled gravely at their looks of wonder as they cast eyes on the maze of apparatus before them. It was a laboratory rather than a living room in which they stood.

Detis led them to an adjoining room where he bid them be seated. They exchanged wondering glances as their host paced the floor vigorously before speaking further.

"Friends," he finally blurted, "I hope you'll excuse my emotion but the news you brought is a terrible blow to me as to all Europa. Carli, our prince, beloved son of Cardos, was commander of the ship you reported lost. We deeply mourn his loss."

*   *   *   *   *

Carr and Mado waited in respectful silence while their host made effort to control his feelings.

"Now," he said, after a moment, "I can talk. You have many questions to ask, I know. So have I. But first I must tell you that Carli's was an expedition to your own worlds. A grave danger hangs over them and he was sent to warn them. He has been lost. Our only space-ship capable of making the journey also is lost. Six Martian years were required to build it, so I fear the warning will never reach your people. Already the time draws near."

"A grave danger?" asked Mado. "What sort of a danger?"

"War! Utter destruction! Conquest by the most warlike and ambitious people in the solar system."

"Not the people of Europa?" asked Carr.

"Indeed not. There is another inhabited satellite of Jupiter, next farthest from the mother planet. Ganymede, you call it. It is from there that these conquerors are to set forth."

"Many of them?" inquired Mado.

"Two million or so. They're prepared to send an army of more than a tenth of that number on the first expedition."

"A mere handful!" Carr was contemptuous.

"True, but they are armed with the most terrible of weapons. Your people are utterly unprepared and, unless warned, will be driven from their cities and left in the deserts to perish of hunger and exposure. This is a real danger."

"Something in it, Carr, if what he says is true. We've no arms nor warriors. Haven't had for two centuries. You know it as well as I do."

"Bah! Overnight we could have a million armed and ready to fight them off."

*　　*　　*　　*　　*

Detis raised his hand. "You offend me," he said gravely. "I have told you this in good faith and you reward me with disbelief and boastful talk. Your enemies are more powerful than you think, and your own people utterly defenceless against them."

"I'm sorry," Carr apologized, "and I'll listen to all you have to say. Surely your prince has not given his life in vain." He was ashamed before this scientist of Europa.

A tinkling feminine voice from the next room called something in the Europan tongue.

Detis raised his head proudly and his frown softened at the sound of dainty footsteps. His voice was a caress as he replied.

A vision of feminine loveliness stood framed in the doorway and the visitors rose hastily from their seats. Carr gazed into eyes of the deepest blue he had ever seen. Small in stature though this girl of Europa was—not more than five feet tall—she had the form of a goddess and the face of an angel. He was flushing to the roots of his hair. Could feel it spread. What an ass he was anyway! Anyone'd think he'd never seen a woman in all his thirty-five years!

"My daughter, Ora, gentlemen," said Detis.

The girl's eyes had widened as she looked at the huge Martian with the funny black box on his back. They dropped demurely when turned to those of the handsome Terrestrial.

"Oh," she said, in Cos, "I didn't know you had callers."

CHAPTER VI
Vlor-urdin

The time passed quickly in Pala-dar, city of the golden domes. Detis spent many hours in the laboratory with his two visitors and the fair Ora was usually at his side. She was an efficient helper to her father and a gracious hostess to the guests.

The amazement of the visitors grew apace as the wonders of Europan science were revealed to them. They sat by the hour at the illuminated screen of the rulden, that remarkable astronomical instrument which brought the surfaces of distant celestial bodies within a few feet of their eyes, and the sounds of the streets and the jungles to their ears. It was no longer a mystery how the language of Cos had become so familiar to these people.

They learned of the origin of the races that inhabited Europa and Ganymede. Ages before, it was necessary for the peoples of the then thickly populated Jupiter to cast about for new homes due to the cooling of the surface of that planet. Life was becoming unbearable. In those days there were two dominant races on the mother body, a gentle and peaceful people of great scientific accomplishment and a race of savage brutes who, while very clever with their hands, were of lesser mental strength and of a quarrelsome and fighting disposition.

Toward the last the population of both main countries was reduced to but a few survivors, and the intelligent race had discovered a means of traversing space and was prepared to leave the planet for the more livable satellite—Europa. Learning of these plans, the others made a treaty of perpetual peace as a price for their passage to another satellite—Ganymede. The migration began and the two satellites were settled by the separate bands of pioneers and their new lives begun.

*   *   *   *   *

The perpetual treaty had not been broken since, but the energies of the warlike descendants of those first settlers of Ganymede were expended in casting about for new fields to conquer. Through the ages they cast increasingly covetous eyes on those inner planets, Mars, Terra and Venus. Not having the advantage of the Rulden, they knew of these bodies only what could be seen through their own crude optical instruments and what they had learned by word of mouth from certain renegade Europans they were able to bribe.

While their neighbors of the smaller satellite were engaged in peaceful pursuits, tilling the soil and making excellent homes for themselves, the dwellers on Ganymede were fashioning instruments of warfare and building a fleet of space-ships to carry them to their intended victims. It was a religion with them; they could think of nothing else. An unscrupulous scientist of Europa sold himself to them several generations previously and it was this scientist who had made the plans for their space-fliers and had contrived the deadly weapons with which they were armed. He likewise taught them the language of Cos and it now was spoken universally throughout Ganymede in anticipation of the glorious days of conquest.

"You honestly believe them able to do this?" asked Carr, still skeptical after two days of discussion.

"I know it as a certainty," Detis replied solemnly. "It is only during the past generation we have learned of the completeness and awfulness of their preparations. Your people can not combat their sound-ray. With it they can remain outside the vision of those on the surface and set the tall buildings of your cities in harmonic vibrations that will bring them down in ruins about the ears of the populace."

*   *   *   *   *

"There'll be nothing left for them to take if they destroy all our cities: nowhere for them to live. I don't get it."

"Only a few will be destroyed completely, to terrify the rest of the inhabitants of your worlds. Others will be depopulated by means of vibrations that will kill off the citizens without harming the cities themselves—vibrations which are capable of blanketing a large area and raising the body temperature of all living things therein to a point where death will ensue in a very few minutes. Other vibrations will paralyze all electrical equipment on the planet and make it impossible for your ships of the air to set out to give battle, even were they properly armed."

"Looks bad, Carr," said Mado glumly.

"It does that. We've got to go back and carry the warning."

"I fear it is too late," said Detis. "Much time will be needed in which to develop a defense and surely it can not be done within the three isini before they set forth—about four of your days."

"They leave that soon?" Carr was taken aback.

"Yes, with their one hundred and twenty vessels; forty to each of your three planets; seventeen hundred men to a vessel."

Carr jumped to his feet. "By the heat devils of Mercury!" he roared, "well go to their lousy little satellite and find a way to prevent it!"

*   *   *   *   *

Ora gazed at his flushed face with unconcealed admiration.

"You're crazy!" exploded Mado. "What can we do with the *Nomad*?"

"Her D-ray can do plenty of damage."

"Yes, but they'd have us down before we could account for five of their vessels. It's no use, I tell you."

But Carr was stubborn. "We'll pay them a call anyway. I'll bet we can dope out some way of putting it over on them. Are you game?"

"Of course I'm game. I'll go anywhere you will. But it's a fool idea just the same."

"Maybe so. Maybe not. Anyway—let's go."

"Just a moment, gentlemen," Detis interposed. "How about me?"

Carr stared at him and saw that his eyes shone with excitement. "Why, I believe you'd like to go with us!" he exclaimed admiringly.

"I would, indeed."

"Come on then. We're off." He was impatient to be gone.

Detis busied himself with a small apparatus that folded into a compact case, explaining that it was one that might prove useful. Ora left the room but quickly returned. She too carried a small case, and she had donned a snug fitting leather garment that covered her from neck to knees.

"What's this?" demanded Carr. "Surely Miss Ora does not intend to come with us?"

"She never leaves my side," said Detis proudly.

"Nothing doing!" Carr stated emphatically. "There'll be plenty of danger on this trip. We'll have no woman along—least of all your charming daughter."

*   *   *   *   *

Mado was leaving everything to his friend, but he grinned in anticipation when he saw the look of anger on the girl's face.

She stamped her little foot and faced Carr valiantly. "See here, Mr. Carr Parker!" she stormed. "I'm no weakling. I'm the daughter of my father and where he goes I go. You'll take me or I'll never speak to you again."

Carr flushed. He was accustomed to his own way in most things and entirely unused to the ways of the gentler sex. He could have shaken the little vixen! But now she was standing before him and there was something in those great blue eyes besides anger; something that set his heart pounding madly.

"All right!" he agreed desperately, "have your own way."

He turned on his heel and strode to the door. Giving in to this slip of a girl! What a fool he was! But it would be great at that to have her along in the *Nomad*.

They found the public square deserted, the gilded dwellings hung with somber colors in mourning for Carli. Ora and Detis were very quiet and preoccupied when they entered the *Nomad*. The five isini of lamentation for the young prince had not yet passed.

The two Europans were delighted with the appointments and mechanisms of the little vessel from Mars. They investigated every nook and cranny of its interior during the journey and were voluble in their praise of its inventor and builder. Neither had ever set foot in a space-flier and each was seized with a longing to explore space with these two strangers from the inner planets. They would make a couple of good vagabonds along with Mado and himself, Carr thought as they expressed their feelings. But there was more serious business at hand. They were nearing Ganymede.

"Where'll we land, Detis?" Mado called from the control cabin.

"Vlor-urdin. That is their chief city. I'll guide you to the location."

*   *   *   *   *

They took up their places at the ports and scanned the surface of the satellite as Mado dropped the ship into its atmosphere. A far different scene was presented than on Europa. The land was seamed and scarred, the colors of the foliage somber. Grays and browns predominated and the jungles seemed impenetrable. A river swung into view and its waters were black as the deepest night, its flow sluggish. A rank mist hung over the surface.

"The river of Charis!" exclaimed Detis. "Follow it, Mado. No, the other direction. There! It leads directly to Vlor-urdin."

By good chance they had entered the atmosphere at a point not far from their destination. In less than an hour by the *Nomad's* chronometer the towers of Vlor-urdin were sighted.

It was a larger city than Pala-dar and of vastly different appearance. A hollow square of squat buildings enclosed the vast workshops and storage space of the fleet of war vessels. Their huge spherical bulks rose from their cradles in tier after tier that stretched as far as the eye could reach when the *Nomad* had dropped to a level but slightly above the tips of the highest spires. The spires were everywhere, decorative towers at the corners of the squat buildings. Everything was black, the vessels of the fleet, the squat buildings and the spires of Vlor-urdin. Death was in the air. Rank vapor drifted in through the opened ports. There was silence in the city below them and silence in the *Nomad*.

Ora shuddered and drew closer to him. Carr was aware of her nearness and a lump rose in his throat. A horrible fear assailed him. Fear for the safety of the dainty Europan at his side. He found her hand; covered it protectingly with his own.

CHAPTER VII
Rapaju

Detis was setting up and adjusting the complicated mechanisms of his little black case. A dozen vacuum tubes lighted, and a murmur of throbbing energy came from a helix of shining metallic ribbon that topped the whole. Flexible cables led to a cap-like contrivance which Detis placed on his head. He frowned in concentration.

"The psycho-ray apparatus." Ora explained. "He's sending a message to the city."

Evidently the influence of the ray was directive. They had no inkling of the thoughts transmitted from the alert brain of the scientist but, from the look of satisfaction on his face, they could see that he was obtaining the desired contact.

"Rapaju," he exclaimed, switching off the power of his instrument, "commander of the fleet of the Llotta. I have advised him of our arrival. Told him that a Martian and a Terrestrial wish to treat with him concerning the proposed invasion of their planets. His answering thought first was of fiercest rage, then conciliatory in nature. He'll receive you and listen to your arguments, though he promises nothing. Is that satisfactory?"

"Yes." Carr and Mado were agreed. At least it would give them a chance to look over the ground and to make plans, should any occur to them.

The *Nomad* circled over the heart of the city and soon Mado saw a suitable landing space. They settled gracefully in an open area close by the building indicated by Detis as that of the administration officials of the city.

*   *   *   *   *

A group of squat, sullen Llotta awaited them and, without speaking a word either of hatred or welcome, led them into the forbidding entrance of the building. Close-set, beady eyes; unbelievably flat features of chalky whiteness; chunky bowed legs, bare and hairy; long arms with huge dangling paws—these were the outstanding characteristics of the Llotta. Mado stared straight before him, refusing to display any great interest in the loathsome creatures, but Carr was frankly curious and as frankly disapproving.

Rapaju leered maliciously when the four voyagers stood before him. He looked the incarnation of all that was evil and vile, a monster among monsters. Sensing him to be the more aggressive of the two visitors from doomed planets, he addressed his remarks to Carr.

"You come to plead with Rapaju," he sneered, his Cos tinged with an outlandish accent, "to beg for the worthless lives of your compatriots; for the wealth of your cities?"

"We come to reason with you," replied Carr haughtily, "if you are capable of reasoning. What is this incredible thing you are planning?"

Mado gasped at the effrontery of his friend. But Carr was oblivious of the warning looks cast in his direction.

"Enough of that!" snapped Rapaju. "I'll do the talking—you the reasoning. I've a proposition to make to you, and if you know what's best, you'll agree. Otherwise you'll be first of the Terrestrials to die. Is that clear?"

"Clear enough, all right," growled Carr. "What do you mean—a proposition?"

"Ha! I thought you'd listen. My offer is the lives of you and your companion in exchange for your assistance in guiding my fleet to the capital cities of your countries. Not that our plans will be changed if you refuse, but that much time will be saved in this manner and quick victory made certain without undue sacrifice of valuable property."

"You—you—!" Carr stammered in anger. But there was no use in raising a rumpus—now. They'd only kill him. Something might be accomplished if he pretended to accede. "Go on with your story," he finished lamely.

"In addition to sparing your lives I'll place you both in high position after we seize your respective planets. Make you chief officers in the prison lands we intend to establish for your countrymen. What do you say?"

"Will you give us time to talk it over and think about it?"

"Until the hour of departure, if you wish."

*   *   *   *   *

Carr bowed, avoiding Mado's questioning eyes. He looked at Ora where she stood at the side of Detis. She flashed him a guarded smile. He knew that she understood.

Rapaju relaxed. He was confident he could bribe these puerile foreigners to help him in the great venture. And sadly he needed such help. The Llotta were not navigators. Their knowledge of the heavens was sadly incomplete. They had no maps of the surfaces of the planets to be visited. Their simultaneous blows would be far more effective and the campaign much shorter if they could choose the most vital centers for the initial attacks.

"Now," he said, "that we understand one another, let us talk further of the plans. Then you will be able to consider carefully before making your decision."

Rapaju could be diplomatic when he wished. Carr longed to sink his fingers in the hairy throat. But he smiled hypocritically and found an opportunity to wink meaningly at Mado. This was going to be good! And who knew?—perhaps they might find some way to outwit these mad savages. To think of them in control of the inner planets was revolting.

They retired to a small room with Rapaju and four of his lieutenants, Detis and Ora accompanying them. Ora sat close to Carr at the circular table in Rapaju's council. Carr thought grimly of the board meetings in far away New York.

Rapaju talked. He told of the armament of his vessels, painting vivid pictures of the destruction to be wrought in the cities of Terra, of Mars and Venus. His great hairy paws clutched at imaginary riches when he spoke glowingly of the plundering to follow. He spoke of the women of the inner planets and Carr half rose from his seat when he observed the lecherous glitter in his beady eyes. Ora! Great God, was she safe here? He stole a glance at the girl and a recurrence of the awful fear surged through him. In her leather garment, close fitting and severe, she looked like a boy. Perhaps they would not know. Besides, there was the perpetual treaty with Europa. It always had been observed, Detis said.

*   *   *   *   *

As Rapaju expanded upon the glories to come he told perforce of many of the details of the plans. One thing stood out in Carr's mind: the vessels of the Llotta were not equal to the *Nomad* in many respects. They must carry their entire supply of fuel from the starting point and this was calculated as but a small percentage in excess of that required to carry them to their destinations. Their speed was not as great as the *Nomad's* by at least a third. If the *Nomad* led the fleet from Ganymede they might be able to get them off their course; cause them to get them off their course; cause them to run out of fuel out in the vacuum and absolute zero of space. He kicked Mado under the table and arose to ask a few leading questions.

Ora was whispering to her father and he nodded his head as if in complete agreement with what she was saying. These two were not deceived by his apparent traitorous talk, but Mado was aghast. Carr wondered if Rapaju believed him as did his friend.

"We'll do it, Rapaju," he stated finally. "In our ship, the *Nomad*, we'll guide you across the trackless wastes of the heavens. We'll take you to our capital cities; point out to you the richest of the industrial centers. We have no love for our own worlds. Mado and I deserted them for a life of vagabondage amongst the stars. We ask no reward other than that we be permitted to leave once more on our travels, to roam space as we choose."

Mado attempted to voice an objection but Carr's hand was heavy on his shoulder. "Shut up, you fool!" he hissed in his ear. "Can't you trust me?"

*   *   *   *   *

Rapaju's eyes seemed to draw closer together as he returned Carr's unflinching stare. He walked around the table and stood at the side of the tall Terrestrial. Suddenly he grasped Ora's jacket, tore it open at the throat. He ran his hairy fingers over the bare shoulder of the shrinking girl and gurgled his delight at the velvet smoothness of her skin.

With a roar like a wild animal Carr was upon him, bearing him to the floor. His fingers were in that hairy throat, where they had itched to twine.

"Dirty, filthy beast!" he was snarling. "Lay your foul hands on Ora, will you? Say your prayers, if you know any, you swine!"

Then his muscles went limp and he was jerked to his feet by a terrible force, a force that sent him reeling and gasping against the wall. One of Rapaju's lieutenants stood before him with a tiny weapon in his hand, the weapon which had released the paralyzing gas he breathed. He was choking; suffocating. A black mist rose before him. He felt his knees give way. Dimly, as in a dream, he saw that Ora was in Detis' arms. Rapaju was on his feet, fingering his neck and laughing horribly.

"The treaty, Rapaju!" Detis was shouting.

Ora was sobbing. Mado was in the hands of two of the vile Llotta, struggling wildly to free himself. The Martian's eyes accused him. He shut his own and groaned. Opened them again. But it was no use. Everything in the room was whirling now, crazily. He fought to regain his senses, crawled weakly toward the squat figure of Rapaju where it swayed and twisted and spun around. Then all was darkness. The gas had taken its toll.

CHAPTER VIII
The Expedition

Carr awakened to a sense of wordless disgust. Fool that he was to spill the beans as he had! All set to put one over on the leader of the Llotta, then to come a cropper like this! He knew he had been spared for a purpose. The gas was not intended to kill, only to render him helpless for a time. He opened his eyes to the light of a familiar room. He had awakened before in this bed. It was his own cabin on board the *Nomad*. What had happened?

Had he dreamed it all. Europa, Ora, Rapaju—all of it? He sat up and felt of his aching head.

"Oh, are you awake?" a soft voice greeted him.

"Ora!" he exclaimed. It was indeed she, beautiful as ever.

"Sh-h," she warned, placing the tip of a finger to his lips. "They'll hear us."

"Who?" he whispered.

"Rapaju—his two guards. They're in the control cabin with father and Mado."

"What? They've taken the *Nomad*?"

"Yes. We're under way. They've forced Mado to guide them but do not trust him. Rapaju spared you as he believes you more capable. He'll hold you to your word."

"Lord! But what are you doing here?"

Ora dropped her eyes. "He—Rapaju—" she said, "inferred from your action in assaulting him that you were very fond of me. He holds me as a hostage for your good behavior. Father volunteered to come along. He persuaded Rapaju to allow it. Swore allegiance to his cause. Of course he wouldn't leave me."

*   *   *   *   *

Carr gazed at her in admiration of her courage. She had been nursing him, too! What a girl she was!

"Ora," he said huskily, "Rapaju was right. I am fond of you. More than fond: I love you. I never knew I could feel this way."

"Oh Carr, you mustn't!" She drew back as he scrambled to his feet. "They'll find us. We must not show that we care. Rapaju is a beast. He wants me for himself and is delaying the time only until you have brought the fleet safely to the inner planets and to their great cities. He—"

"The skunk! Wants you himself, does he? Why, why didn't I kill him? But Ora, you said—you do care—"

"Ha! I thought so!" Rapaju stood in the doorway, grinning mockingly at the pair. "The impetuous Terrestrial is up and about. Back at his old game!"

"Please, please, for my sake, Carr!" Ora pressed him back as he tensed his muscles for a spring.

"Sorry I was so slow," Carr grated, over her shoulder. "Another five seconds, Rapaju, and I'd have had your windpipe out by the roots."

Rapaju scowled darkly and fingered his throat. "But, my dear Carr, you were too slow," he said, "and I live—and shall live— while you shall die. Meanwhile you'll carry out your agreement. Come, Ora."

The girl hesitated a moment, then with a pleading glance at Carr stepped from the room.

"All right now, Parker," snapped Rapaju. "Into your clothes and into the pilot's seat. You'll stay there, too, till the journey's over. Get busy!"

One of his guards had appeared in the doorway. Carr knew that resistance was useless. Besides, seated at those controls, he might think of something. Rapaju'd never get Ora if he could help it!

*   *   *   *   *

Mado's shoulders drooped and his face was haggard and drawn, but he summoned a smile when he saw Carr.

"Hello, Carr," he said. "You all right?"

"Sure. Rapaju says I've got to take the controls."

"Very well." Mado shrugged his broad shoulders and slipped from the pilot's seat. Two ugly Llotta guards were watching, ray-pistols in hand. "The chart is corrected, Carr, and—"

"Never mind the conversation!" Rapaju snarled. "There'll be no talk between you at all. Beat it to your cabin, Mado."

The Martian glowered and made as if to retort hotly.

"But Rapaju," Detis interposed, speaking from his position at one of the ports, "they'll have to consult regarding the course of the vessel. Mado is more familiar than Carr with the navigation of space."

"Shut up!" roared Rapaju. "I know what I am doing. And, what's more, you'll not converse with them, either! I'm running this expedition, and I'm not taking any chances."

Detis subsided and followed Mado through the passage to the sleeping cabins.

*   *   *   *   *

The ensuing silence was ominous. Carr could feel the eyes of the Llotta upon him as he examined the adjustments of the controls and peeped through the telescope. A glance at the velocity indicator showed him they were traveling at a rate of eight hundred miles a second. He studied the chart and soon made out their position. Jupiter was a hundred million miles behind them and they were heading almost due sunward. The automatic control mechanism was not functioning. Evidently Mado had kept this a secret—and for a purpose. He wished he could talk with his friend. They'd plan something.

"Like your job?" Rapaju was gloating over this Terrestrial who had dared to lay hands upon him.

"Yes, but not the company." Carr was disdainful.

"You'll like it less before I've finished with you. And get this straight. You think we're dependent on you to guide us to the inner planets, and that we'll not harm any of you until they are reached. Don't fool yourself! I've watched Mado and I've spent much time in the excellent library of the *Nomad*. I've learned plenty about the navigation of space and can reach those planets as quickly and directly as you. But it pleases me to see you work, so work you shall. I'll check you carefully, and don't think you can deceive me. Don't try to depart from the true course. The sun is my check as it is yours, and I'll keep constant tab on our position. Get it?"

"A rather long speech, Rapaju." Carr grinned into the evil face of the commander.

"Still defiant, eh? Suits me, Carr Parker. We'll have some nice talks here, and then—when it pleases me—you'll suffer. You shall live to see your home city crash in utter ruin; your people slain, starved, beaten. And, above all, there's Ora—"

"Don't defile her name in your ugly mouth, you—!"

*   *   *   *   *

Carr bit his tongue to keep back the torrent of invectives that sprang to his lips. This would never do! He'd get himself bumped off before they were well started. And while there was life there was hope. He'd stick to his guns and think; think and plan. If only he could have a few words with Mado. They must get out of this mess. There must be a way! There must!

Rapaju was laughing in triumph. Thought he had cowed him, did he? Boastful savage! If he could navigate the *Nomad* himself, why didn't he? Liar! He and Mado were godsends to him, and he knew it! His speech at the council table had been the real truth.

Foreign thoughts entered his mind. Detis, good old Detis, was using his thought apparatus in his own cabin! He paid no attention to the words of Rapaju when he left the control room. Detis was on the job! Between them they'd outwit this devil of Ganymede.

"Keep your courage," came the message. "I've read the thoughts of Mado and he bids you examine the chart carefully. He's made some notations in the ancient language of Mars. The automatic control of the *Nomad* can be used when necessary. He has not advised Rapaju of its existence."

Carr was encouraged and he concentrated on a suitable reply. But, though he did not consciously will it, his thoughts were of Ora.

Instantly there came the reassurance of her father. "Ora is not in immediate danger. Rapaju is saving her for his revenge on you. And I'm watching her constantly. A ray-pistol is concealed in my clothing, its charge ready for the foul creature in case he should lay hands on her. But you must plan an escape, and salvation for your worlds. Examine the chart at once."

*　　*　　*　　*　　*

He looked from the corner of his eye and saw that one of the Llotta guards was watching intently. He peered into the eye-piece of the telescope; made an inconsequential change in one of the adjustments. The guard stirred but did not arise. He looked at the chart with new interest, scanned its markings carefully. What had Mado marked for his attention? There were hundreds of notations, some in Cos and a few in the ancient Martian, all in Mado's painstaking chirography.

Ah, there it was! A tiny spot almost on their course, with Mado's minute notation. Sargasso Sea! What did it mean? Did Mado intend to lead the fleet into the embrace of that dreadful monster they had so fortunately escaped? An excellent idea to save the inner planets. But suicide for them! He'd do it though, if it weren't for Ora. She was so sweet and innocent. She must not die; must not suffer. Another way must be found. He groaned aloud as he realized that her predicament was the result of his own bullheadedness. If only he hadn't insisted on the trip to Ganymede. But then there was the problem of preserving the civilization of the inner planets. It had to be met.

There was a commotion behind him; a feminine shriek from the after cabins; loud shoutings from the beast called Rapaju. Carr's heart skipped a beat. He was paralyzed with fear. But only for an instant. With a bellow of rage he whirled around and started for the door, charging the two guards with head down and arms flailing.

CHAPTER IX
Nemesis

The Llotta did not use their ray-pistols. They were too busy attempting to elude the mad rushes of the powerful Terrestrial. Besides, there were good reasons they should not kill him—yet. Carr drove one of them halfway down the passageway with a well-planted punch. The other was on his back, hairy legs twined around his waist, an arm under his chin, drawing his head back with a steady and terrible pressure. He whirled around, trying to shake off his beastly antagonist.

But these powerful legs and arms held fast. He tore at the hairy ankles where they crossed in the pit of his stomach; wrenched them free. Still the creature clung to him, twisting his head until it seemed his neck must break. He found a waving foot with his right hand; wrenched it mightily. There was a sharp snap and the foot dangled limp in his fingers. He had broken the ankle. With a howl of pain his assailant let go and dropped to the floor to crawl away like a whipped cur.

In a flash Carr saw that the brute was reaching for his ray-pistol where it had dropped during the encounter. He kicked it from the reach of that hairy paw and sprang after it. With one of those little weapons in his hands the odds would change! His fingers closed on its grip just as Ora rushed into the room, closely followed by Rapaju, whose distorted features were terrible to behold. The cabin was full of them now; the guard he had first knocked down; the lust-crazed commander—the one with the broken ankle. All but Detis and Mado. Carr faced them alone.

So close was Rapaju to the girl that he dared not use the pistol, and now the uninjured guard was circling him, trying to get in a position where he could use his ray-pistol without endangering his commander. Carr fumbled for the release of the weapon he held in his hand; found it. The guard threw himself to the floor when he saw it raised; shouted a warning. But it was too late. The deadly ray had sped on its mission of death; struck him full in the middle. The twisted body lay still a moment and then collapsed like a punctured balloon, leaving his scant clothing in a limp heap—empty. A worthy miniature of the D-ray, this little weapon!

* * * * *

He turned to face Rapaju and saw that he was shielding himself with Ora's body. She had fainted and now hung drooping in the arms of the beast. Where was Mado? Detis? Good God—he'd killed them! Carr thought of that little spot on the chart. Must be very close now. They'd pass so near there'd be no escape. But he could not reach the controls without taking his eyes from Rapaju. That would have to wait.

Rapaju was backing toward the door, still holding the limp figure of the girl before him. The injured guard lay moaning on the floor.

"Drop her, you devil!" Carr shouted desperately as he saw that Rapaju soon would reach the passageway.

Then suddenly he reached for the controls and pushed the energy lever to full speed forward. He braced himself for the shock of acceleration and saw Rapaju and Ora thrown backward into the passageway, the girl's body cushioned by that of her captor as they were flung violently to the floor. Madly he rushed to the narrow entrance and tore at the hairy arms that encircled the slender waist of the girl. He jerked the snarling commander of the Llotta expedition to his feet and slammed him against the metal wall.

"Now, you damn pig," he grunted, "I'll finish the job. Dirty scum of a rotten world!"

He dragged his victim into the control cabin and threw him to the floor. But Rapaju was like an eel. He wriggled from under him and snatched from the heap of clothing the ray-pistol of the disintegrated guard. With a yelp of triumph he rose to his knees and leveled the weapon.

A well placed kick sent it spinning and Carr was upon him. He snapped back the head with a terrible punch; then lifted the dazed creature to his feet and stepped back.

"Stand up and take it like a man!" he roared.

*   *   *   *   *

Rapaju shook his head to clear it and rushed in with a bellow of rage. Just what Carr wanted! Starting almost from the floor, his right came up to meet the vicious jaw with a crack that told of the terrific power behind it. Lifted from his feet and hurled half way across the room by the impact, Rapaju lay motionless where he fell.

Carr was at the telescope. Their speed was close to fifteen hundred miles a second. The monstrous mass of Mado's Sargasso Sea loomed close in his vision. Off their course by a hundred miles or more. They'd miss it all right. He had the situation in hand now on board the *Nomad*. But how about the fleet behind them? He thought fast and furiously. Another two minutes and they'd pass the thing; the inexplicable horror which had accounted for the golden sphere of the Europans. Could he use it? Suppose the fleet of the enemy—

The idea was full of possibilities.

He rushed to the stern compartment, and scanned the heavens for the massed body of spheres he knew would be the fleet of the Llotta. At this speed they must have fallen far behind. Yes, there they were. Not so far behind at that. The battle in the control room must have been a shorter one than it had seemed. He returned quickly to the controls and reversed the energy, to give the fleet a chance to catch up to him.

Closer came that mass of whitish jelly. And now it was much larger than before. The terrible creature, for living matter it was, beyond doubt, was growing with the rapidity of a rising flood. Great tentacles of its horrid translucent substance reached in all directions for possible victims. He sickened at the sight. But what a fate for the fleet of the Llotta! If only he could maneuver them into its influence.

*   *   *   *   *

He changed his course slightly and headed directly for the monster, again increasing speed. Perhaps—if he calculated the forces correctly—he could dive through it again with the D-ray to clear a path. But no. It was a miracle they had escaped before, and now the vicious thing was more than double its previous size. Once more he altered his course. He'd cross in front of the thing; skim it as close as he dared and shoot from its influence on the far side. The greater mass of the enemy vessels and their lack of a quick-acting repulsive force would prove their undoing.

Full speed ahead. A rapid mental calculation—an educated guess, rather—and he set the automatic control. Turning around to start for the stern compartment, he saw that Ora had recovered from her swoon and now stood swaying weakly in the passageway.

"Ora!" he exclaimed delightedly. He rushed to her side and supported her in a tender embrace.

"Rapaju?" she questioned with horror in her eyes.

"Won't bother you for a while, dear. But your father—Mado?"

"He gassed them. They'll recover." The brave girl had regained her composure.

"Good! But, come! Time's short." He half carried her to the rear, berating himself the while for his inability to pay her closer attention. With arms still around her he placed her at one of the stern ports.

"What is it, Carr?" She sensed his excitement.

"The fleet—see! We'll destroy them."

The spherical vessels were close behind, huddled together in mass formation and following the *Nomad* blindly.

"How, Carr?"

"Lead them into it. Wait tall you see! There's a—"

*   *   *   *   *

The *Nomad* lurched, and changed direction. Cold fear clutched at his throat. That devil of a guard! Why hadn't he killed him? He dashed through the passage, Ora at his heels.

Sure enough, the crippled guard had dragged himself to the controls; was manipulating the energy director as he had seen Mado do. They were heading directly for the terrible monster of the heavens!

No need now to peer through the telescope. The thing was visible to the naked eye. No power could save them! Carr hurled himself at the guard and tore at the hairy paw which gripped the lever. The throbbing of strange energies filled the air of the room, and Carr's brain pulsed with the maddening rhythm. The red discharge appeared at the projections of the control panels. He forgot the fleet of the Llotta, forgot the menace to his own world. Only Ora mattered now, and he had not the power to save her!

As in a daze he knew he was wrenching mightily at the body of the powerful minion of Rapaju. His fingers encountered heated metal—one of the ray-pistols. He felt the intense vibration of the weapon as its charge was released. But he still lived. The beast who held it had missed! Dimly he was conscious of the screams of Ora; of the yielding of the creature who fought him. An animal cry registered on his consciousness and he shook the suddenly limp Llotta from him. He knew somehow that his last enemy was gone.

A quick glance showed him that Ora was still on her feet, braced against the wall. The red veil was before his eyes. He grasped the controls, and fought desperately to keep his strength and senses. A streamer of horrid whiteness swung across his vision; slithered clammily over the glass of one of the forward ports. They were into the thing! It was the end! He groaned aloud as he fumbled with the mechanisms and strove to formulate a plan of escape.

*   *   *   *   *

The fleet, he knew, was just behind. An enormous mass. The repulsive energy astern would be terrific. He turned it full on. The whiteness obscured his vision. Then it was gone once more. A single streamer waved before him and encompassed them. The movement of these members must be inconceivably rapid, else they'd be invisible at the speed the *Nomad* was traveling. Full speed ahead. The repulsion full on in the direction of the center of the mass as well as astern. The framework of the *Nomad* creaked protestingly from the terrific forces that tore at her vitals.

Then suddenly they were released. The *Nomad* was shooting off into space. The resultant of those combined forces had done the trick. Only the edge of that devil-fish of space, had they touched. Free—they were free of the monster! The red veil lifted. He rushed to Ora's side. She was kneeling at one of the floor ports, breathing heavily but unharmed.

Below them they saw the swiftly receding mass: the fleet of the Llotta diving headlong, drawn inexorably into the rapacious embrace of the vile creature of the heavens. An instant the awful whiteness of the thing closed in greedily about the many spheres of the fleet; swallowed them from sight and contorted madly and with seeming glee over the triumph. Then, in a burst of blinding incandescence, it was gone. The monster, the fleet—everything—blasted into nothingness. The fuel storage compartments of the vessels of Ganymede had exploded! The heavens were rid of the inexplicable growing menace; the inner planets were saved from a terrible invasion. And the *Nomad* was safe. Ora, Detis, Mado—all were safe!

At his side Ora was trembling. Gently he raised her to her feet, and took her into his arms.

CHAPTER X
Vagabonds All

Together they cared for Detis and Mado; made them comfortable in their bunks until the time when the effects of the gas would wear off. Lucky it was that Rapaju had used the gas pistol rather than the ray. Perhaps it had been a mistake. Or perhaps he had needed the scientific knowledge of Detis, the familiarity with the inner planets that was Mado's. At any rate, they had no delusions regarding his designs on Ora or his hatred of Carr. By his own passions had the commander of the fleet been led to the error that cost him his life and made possible the destruction of his fleet.

Carr was torn by conflicting emotions. The delectable little Europan was most disturbing. He'd never had much use for the other sex—on Earth. Too dominating, most of them. And always thrown at his head by designing parents for his money. But Ora was different! Her very nearness set his pulses racing. And he knew that she cared for him as he did for her. Those moments in the control cabin after the explosion! But something had come over him since he cut loose from the old life. Wanderlust—that was it. He'd never go back. Neither would he be content to settle down to a domestic life in Pala-dar. Wanted to be up and going somewhere.

"Oh, Carr, Carr!" Ora's voice called to him. "Mado is awake. He wants you."

Good old Mado! Why couldn't they just continue on their way as they had started out? Roaming the universe in search of other adventures! But the silvery tinkle of Ora's laughter reached his ears. She was irresistible! He forgot his doubts as he hurried to his friend's cabin.

*   *   *   *   *

Mado was staring at the Europan maiden with a ludicrous expression of astonishment—gawping, Carr called it. And Ora was laughing at him.

"Your friend," she gurgled, "doesn't believe he's alive, or that I am, or you. Tell him we are."

Carr grinned. Mado did look funny at that. "Hello, old sock," he said, "had a bad dream?"

"Did I? Oh boy!" Mado rocked to and fro, his head in his hands. Then he displayed sudden intense interest. "Rapaju?" he asked. "His guards—the fleet—what's happened?"

"Ah ha! Now you know you're alive!" Carr laughed. "But the others are dead and gone. The fleet's gone to smash—and how!"

"But Carr. How did you do it? Tell me!"

Mado threw off his covers and clapped his friend on the back, a resounding thump that brought a gasp from Ora.

"Your Sargasso Sea did it. And it's a thing of the past, too. Wait till I tell you about it!"

*   *   *   *   *

Ora tripped from the room as Carr sat on the edge of the bunk to spin his yarn.

"But man alive!" Mado exclaimed when the story was finished. "Don't you know you've done a miraculous thing? I'd never have had the nerve. That damn creature out there had more than four times its former attracting energy. That's what made it impossible for the fleet to get away. And you—you lucky devil—you just doped it out right. The fleet of the Llotta gave you a tremendous push from astern when you used the repulsive energy. If they hadn't been there with their enormous mass to react against we'd all have been mincemeat now along with the Llotta. You Terrestrials sure can think fast! Me, now—Lord, if it had been me, I'd have thought of it after my spirit had departed to its reward—or punishment. Glory be! It's the greatest thing I ever heard of."

"Rats! You'd have done the same as I did. Probably would have missed it a mile instead of nearly getting caught as I did. A good thing the fleet's gone, though. Mars and Terra—Venus, too—they'll never know how close it was for them. Wouldn't have sense enough to appreciate it, anyway."

"They would if they ever got a taste of what the Llotta planned. But what's wrong with you Carr? You act sore. Want to go home?"

"Me? Don't be like that. No—I'd like to carry on as we planned. There's Saturn, Uranus and Neptune yet; Planet 9; a flock of satellites and asteroids. Oh, dammit!"

Mado looked his amazement. "Well, what's to prevent it?" he demanded. "The *Nomad's* still here, and so are we. I'm just as anxious to keep going as you are. Why not?"

But Carr did not reply. Why not, indeed? He strode from the cabin and into the control room. The *Nomad* was drifting in space, subject only to natural forces that swung it in a vast orbit around the sun. He started the generators and drove the vessel from her temporary orbit with rapid acceleration. Out—out into the jeweled blackness of the heavens. There was Jupiter out there, a bright orb that came suddenly very near when he centered it on the cross-hairs of the telescope.

The excited voices of Ora and Detis came to his ears. The booming speech of Mado. Why couldn't he be sensible and companionable as they were? But a perverse demon kept him at the controls. They'd think him a grouch. Well, maybe he was! But the vastness of the universe beckoned. New worlds to explore; mysteries to be solved; a life of countless new experiences! Anyone'd think he was the owner of the *Nomad*, the way he planned for the future.

*   *   *   *   *

They were in the control cabin now—Mado and Detis and Ora. A moment he hesitated, eyes glued to the telescope. Then, with a petulant gesture, he reached for the automatic control; locked it. Shouldn't be this way. They'd think him an awful cad. And they'd be right! He whirled to face them.

Detis was smiling. Mado gazed owlishly solemn. Ora clung to the arm of her father, and her long lashes hid the blue eyes that had played such havoc with the emotions of the Terrestrial.

"Carr," said Detis, gently, "we must thank you. You saved our lives, you know."

"Aw, forget it. Saved my own, too, didn't I? By a lucky break."

"It wasn't luck, Carr." Detis was gripping his hand now. "It was sheer grit and brains. You had them both. If you hadn't used them we'd all be corpses—or disintegrated—excepting Ora, perhaps. And you know the fate that awaited her. Instead, we are alive and well. The fleet is gone. Rapaju's body and that of his guard drift nameless in space where you disposed of them through the air-lock of the *Nomad*. The inner planets need fear no future invasion, for the resources of Ganymede have been expended in the one huge enterprise that has failed. All through your quick wit and bravery. No, it wasn't luck."

"Nonsense, Detis." Carr returned the pressure of the scientist's hand, smiling sheepishly. He pushed him away after a moment. He didn't want their gratitude or praise. Didn't know what he wanted. Ora still avoided meeting his gaze. "Nonsense," he repeated. "And now, please leave me. You, Detis. Mado, too. I'd like to be alone for a while—with Ora. Mind?"

Mado's owlish look broadened to a knowing grin as he backed into the passageway. Detis collided with the huge Martian in his eagerness to be out of the room. They were alone and Carr was on his feet. Nothing mattered now—excepting Ora. Suddenly she was in his arms, the fragrance of her hair in his nostrils.

*　*　*　*　*

Star gazing, the two of them. It was ridiculous! But the wonders of the universe held a new beauty now for Carr. The distant suns had taken on added brilliance. Still they beckoned.

"Carr," the girl whispered, after a time, "where are we going?"

"To Europa. Your home."

"To—to stay?"

"No." Carr was suddenly confident; determined. "We'll stop there to break the news. Then we'll be wedded, you and I, according to the custom of your people. Our honeymoon—years of it—will be spent in the *Nomad*, roving the universe. Mado'll agree, I know. Wanderers of the heavens we'll be, Ora. But we'll have each other; and when we've—you've—had enough of it, I'll be ready to settle down. Anywhere you say. Are you game?"

"Oh, Carr! How did you guess? It's just as we'd planned. Father and Mado and I. Didn't think I'd go, did you, you stupid old dear?"

"Why—why Ora." Carr was stammering now. He'd thought he was being masterful—making the plans himself. But she'd beat him to it, the adorable little minx! "I was a bit afraid," he admitted; "and I still can't believe that it's actually true. You're sure you want to?"

"Positive. Why Carr, I've always been a vagabond at heart. And now that I've found you we'll just be vagabonds together. Father and Mado will leave us very much to each other. Their scientific leanings, you know. And—oh—it'll just be wonderful!"

"It's you that'll make it wonderful, sweetheart."

Carr drew her close. The stars shone still more brightly and beckoned anew. Vagabonds, all of them! Like the gypsies of old, but with vastly more territory to roam. The humdrum routine of his old life seemed very far behind. He wondered what Courtney Davis would say if he could see him now. Wordless happiness had come to him, and he let his thoughts wander out into the limitless expanse of the heavens. Star gazing still—just he and Ora.

Gray Denim

Originally Published In *Astounding Stories*,
December 1930

GRAY DENIM

Beneath the huge central arch in Cooper Square a meeting was in progress—a gathering of the gray-clad workers of the lower levels of New York. Less than two hundred of their number were in evidence, and these huddled in dejected groups around the pedestal from which a fiery-tongued orator was addressing them. Lounging negligently at the edge of the small crowd were a dozen of the red police.

"I tell you, comrades," the speaker was shouting, "the time has come when we must revolt. We must battle to the death with the wearers of the purple. Why work out our lives down here so they can live in the lap of luxury over our heads? Why labor day after day at the oxygen generators to give them the fresh air they breathe?"

The speaker paused uncertainly as a chorus of raucous laughter came to his ears. He glared belligerently at a group of newcomers who stood aloof from his own gathering. Seven or eight of them there were, and they wore the gray with obvious discomfort. Slummers! Well, they'd hear something they could carry back with them when they returned to their homes!

"Why," he continued in rising tones, "do we sit at the controls of the pneumatic tubes which carry thousands of our fellows to tasks equally irksome, while they of the purple ride their air yachts to the pleasure cities of the sky lanes? Never in the history of mankind have the poor been poorer and the rich richer!"

"Yah!" shouted a disrespectful voice from among the newcomers. "You're full o' bunk! Nothing but bunk!"

An ominous murmur swelled from the crowd and the red police roused from their lethargy. The mounting scream of a siren echoed in the vaulted recesses above and re-echoed from the surrounding columns—the call for reserves.

*   *   *   *   *

All was confusion in the Square. The little group of newcomers immediately became the center of a mêlée of dangerous proportions. Some of the more timid of the wearers of the gray struggled to get out of the crowd and away. Others, not in sympathy with the speaker, rushed to the support of the besieged visitors. The police were, for the moment, overwhelmed.

The orator, mad with resentment and injured pride, hurled himself into the group. A knife flashed in his hand; rose and fell. A scream of agony shrilled piercingly above the din of the fighting.

Then came the reserves, and the wielder of the knife turned to escape. He broke away from the milling combatants and made speedily for the shadows that lay beyond the great pillars of the Square. But he never reached them, for one of the red guards raised his riot pistol and fired. There was a dull *plop*, and a rubbery something struck the fleeing man and wrapped powerful tentacles around his body, binding him hand and foot in their swift embrace. He fell crashing to the pavement.

A lieutenant of the red police was shouting his orders and the din in the Square was deafening. With their numbers greatly augmented, the guards were now in control of the situation and their maces struck left and right. Groans and curses came from the gray-clad workers, who now fought desperately to escape.

Then, with startling suddenness, the artificial sunlight of the cavernous Square was gone, leaving the battle to continue in utter darkness.

*   *   *   *   *

Cooper Square, in the year 2108, was the one gathering place in New York City where the wearers of the gray denim were permitted to assemble and discuss their grievances publicly. Deep in the maze of lower-level ways seldom visited by wearers of the purple, the grottolike enclosure bore the name of a philanthropist of the late nineteenth century and still carried a musty air of certain of the traditions of that period.

In Astor Way, on the lowest level of all, there was a tiny book shop. Nestled between two of the great columns that provided foundation support for the eighty levels above, it was safely hidden from the gaze of curious passersby in the Square. Slumming parties from afar, their purple temporarily discarded for the gray, occasionally passed within a stone's throw of the little shop, never suspecting the existence of such a retreat amidst the dark shadows of the pillars. But to the initiated few amongst the wearers of the gray, and to certain of the red police, it was well known.

Rudolph Krassin, proprietor of the establishment, was a bent and withered ancient. His jacket of gray denim hung loosely from his spare frame and his hollow cough bespoke a deep-seated ailment. Looking out from behind thick lenses set in his square-rimmed spectacles, the watery eyes seemed vacant; uncomprehending. But old Rudolph was a scholar—keen-witted—and a gentleman besides. To his many friends of the gray-clad multitude he was an anomaly; they could not understand his devotion to his well-thumbed volumes. But they listened to his words of wisdom and, more frequently than they could afford, parted with precious labor tickets in exchange for reading matter that was usually of the lighter variety.

*   *   *   *   *

When the fighting started in the Square, Rudolph was watching and listening from a point of vantage in the shadows near his shop. This fellow Leontardo, who was the speaker, was an agitator of the worst sort. His arguments always were calculated to arouse the passions of his hearers; to inflame them against the wearers of the purple. He had nothing constructive to offer. Always he spoke of destruction; war; bloodshed. Rudolph marveled at the patience of the red police. To-day, these newcomers, obviously a slumming party of youngsters bent on whatever mischief they could find, were interfering with the speaker. The old man chuckled at the first interruption. But at signs of real trouble he scurried into the shadows and vanished in the blackness of first-level passages known only to himself. He knew where to find the automatic sub-station of the Power Syndicate.

Returning to the darkness he had created in the Square, he was relieved to find that the sounds of the fighting had subsided. Apparently most of the wearers of the gray had escaped. He skirted the avenue of pillars along Astor Way, feeling his way from one to another as he progressed toward his little shop. Peering into the blackness of the square he saw the feeble beams of several flash-lamps in the hands of the police. They were searching for survivors of the fracas, maces and riot pistols held ready for use. A sobbing gasp from close by set his pulses throbbing. He crept stealthily in the direction from which the sound had come.

"Steady now," came a whispered voice. "My uncle's shop is close by. He'll take you in. Here—let me lift you."

*   *   *   *   *

There was a shuffling on the opposite side of the pillar at which Rudolph had halted; another grunt of pain.

"Karl!" hissed the old man. It was his nephew.

"Uncle Rudolph?" came the guarded response.

"Yes. Can I help you?"

"Quick—yes—he's fainted."

The old man was around the huge base of the column in an instant. He groped in the darkness and his hands encountered human bodies.

"Who is it?" he breathed.

"One of the hecklers, Uncle. A young lad; and of the purple I think. He's been knifed."

Together they dragged the inert form into the shelter of the long line of pillars. There was a trampling of many men in the square. That would be a second detachment of reserves. A ray of light filtered through and dancing shadows of the giant columns made grotesque outlines against the walls of the Way. A portable searchlight had been brought to the scene. They must hurry.

Impeded by the dead weight of their burden, they made sorry progress and several times found it necessary to halt in the shadow of a pillar while the red police passed by in their search of the Square. It was with a sigh of relief that Rudolph opened the door of his shop and with still greater satisfaction closed and bolted it securely. His nephew shouldered the limp form of the unconscious youth and carried it to his own bed in one of the rear rooms.

"Ugh!" exclaimed old Rudolph as he ripped open the young man's shirt, "it's a nasty cut. Warm water, Karl."

The gaping wound was washed and bound tightly. Rudolph's experienced fingers told him the knife had not reached a vital spot. The youth would recover.

"But Karl," he objected, "he wears the purple. Under the gray. See! It'll get us in trouble if we keep him."

He was stripping the young man of his clothing to prepare him for bed. Suddenly there was revealed on the white skin a triangular mark. Bright scarlet it was and just over the right hip. He made a hasty attempt to hide it from the watching eyes of Karl.

"Uncle!" snapped his nephew, "—the mark you call cursed! He has it, too!"

*　　*　　*　　*　　*

The tall young man in gray was on his knees, tearing the hands of the old man away. He saw the mark clearly now. There was no further use of attempting to conceal it. Rudolph rose and faced his angered nephew, his watery eyes inscrutable.

"You told me, Rudolph, that it was a brand that cursed me. I have seen it on him, too. You have lied to me."

The old man's eyes wavered. He trembled violently.

"Why did you lie?" demanded Karl. "Am I not your nephew? Am I not really cursed as you've maintained? Tell me—tell me!"

He had the old man by the shoulders, shaking him cruelly.

"Karl—Karl," begged the helpless ancient, "it was for your good. I swear it. You were born to the purple. That's what that mark means—not that you're degraded to the gray, as I said. But there's a reason. Let me explain."

"Bah! A reason! You've kept me in this misery and squalor for a reason! Who's my father?"

He flung Rudolph to the floor, where the old man crouched in apprehensive misery.

"Please Karl—don't! I can explain. Just give me time. It's a long story."

"Time! Time! For twenty-odd years you've lied to me; cheated me. My birthright—where is it?"

He menaced his supposed uncle; was about to strike him. Then suddenly he was ashamed. He turned on his heel.

"I'm leaving," he said shortly.

"Karl—my boy," begged Rudolph Krassin, struggling to his feet. "You can't! That lad in there—he—"

But Karl was too angry to reason.

"To hell with him!" he raged, "and to hell with you! I'm through!"

He stamped from the room and out into the eery shadows of the Way. Karl was done with his old life. He'd go to the upper levels and claim his rights. Some day, too, he'd punish the man who'd stolen them away. God! Born to the purple! To think he'd missed it all! Probably was kidnaped by the old rascal he'd been calling uncle. But he'd find out. Rudolph didn't have to explain. Fingerprint records would clear his name; establish his rightful station in life. He dived into a passage that would lead him to one of the express lifts. He'd soon be overhead.

*   *   *   *   *

A sergeant of the red police looked up startled from his desk as a tall youth in the gray denim of forty levels below appeared before him.

"Well?" he growled. The stalwart young worker had stared belligerently and insolently, he thought.

"I want to check my fingerprint record, Sergeant."

"Hm. Pretty cocky, aren't you? The records for such as you are down below, where you belong."

"Not mine, I think."

"So? And who the devil are you?"

"That's what I'm here to find out. I've got a triangle branded on my right hip."

"A what?"

"Triangle. Here—look!"

The amazing youngster had raised his jacket and was pulling at his shirt. The sergeant stared at what was revealed, his eyes bulging as he looked.

"Lord!" he gasped, "a Van Dorn—in the gray!"

Quickly he turned to the radiovision and made rapid connection with several persons in turn—important ones, by the appearance of the features of each in the brilliant disc of the instrument.

Karl was confused by the sudden turn of things. The sergeant talked so rapidly he could not catch the sense of his words. And that name, Van Dorn, eluded him. He knew he had heard it before, in the little shop down there in Astor Way. But he could not place it. He wished fervently that he had paid more attention to the desires of old Rudolph; had studied more and read the books the old man had begged him to read. His new surroundings confused him, too, and he knew that he was the center of some great new excitement.

*   *   *   *   *

Then they were in the room; two individuals, one in the red uniform of a captain of police, the other a pompous, whiskered man in purple. Others followed and it seemed to Karl that the room was filled with them, strangers all, and they stared at him and chattered incessantly. He experienced an overwhelming impulse to run, but mastered it and faced them boldly.

A square of plate glass was placed under his outstretched fingers. It was smeared with something sticky and he watched the whiskered man as he held it up to the light and studied the impressions. Then there was more confusion. Everyone talked at once and the pompous one in purple made use of the radiovision, holding the square of glass near its disc for observation by the person he had called. The identification number was repeated aloud, a string of figures and letters that were a meaningless jumble to Karl. The room became quiet while the police captain thumbed the pages of a huge book he had taken from among many similar ones that filled a rack behind the desk.

Karl's blood froze in his veins at the rumbling swish of a car speeding through the pneumatic tube beneath their feet. His nerves were on edge. Then the captain of police looked up from the book and there was a peculiar glint in his eyes as he spoke.

"Peter Van Dorn. Missing since 2085. Wanted by Continental Government. Ha!"

The words came to Karl's ears through a growing sensation of unreality. It seemed that the speaker was miles away and that his voice and features were those of a radiovision likeness. Wanted by the great power across the Atlantic! It was unthinkable. Why, he had been but an infant in 2085! What possible crime could he have committed? But the red police captain was speaking again, this time in a chill voice. And the room of the police, thick with the smoke of a dozen cigars, became suddenly stifling.

"Where have you been these twenty-three years, Peter Van Dorn?" asked the captain. "Who have you lived with, I mean?"

*   *   *   *   *

Something warned him to protect old Rudolph. And somehow he wished he had not treated the old fellow as he did when he left. His self-possession returned. A wave of hot resentment swept over him.

"That's my affair," he said defiantly.

The captain shrugged his shoulders. "Oh, well," he said, "you needn't answer—now. We'll find out when it's necessary. In the meanwhile we'll have to turn you over to the Continental Ambassador."

Two of the red police advanced toward him and the rest drew back.

"You mean I'm under arrest?" asked Karl incredulously.

"Certainly. Of course you're not to be harmed."

One of the guards had him by the arm and he saw the glint of handcuffs. They couldn't do this! If it had been for rioting in the Square it would be different. But this! It meant he was a prisoner of a foreign government, for what reason he could not guess. He lost his head completely.

The captain cried out in amazement as one of his huskiest guards went sprawling under a well-planted punch. This youngster must be as crazy as was his father before him. But he was a whirlwind. Before he could be stopped he had tackled the other guard and with a mighty heave flung him halfway across the room where he fell with a thud that left him dazed and gasping. The pompous little man in the purple crawled under the desk as the sergeant leveled a slender tube at the young giant in gray.

Karl ducked instinctively at sight of the weapon, but the spiteful crackle of its mechanism was too quick for him. A faintly luminous ray struck him full in the breast and stopped him in his tracks. A thrill of intense cold chased up his spine and a thunderbolt crashed in his brain. The captain caught his stiffened body as he fell.

* * * * *

Karl—refusing to think of himself as Peter Van Dorn—came to his senses as from a troubled sleep. His head ached miserably and he turned it slowly to view his surroundings. Then, in a flash, he remembered. The paralyzing ray of the red police! They never used it in the lower levels; but overhead—why, the swine! He sat suddenly erect and glared into a pair of green eyes that regarded him curiously.

A quick glance showed him that he was in a small padded compartment like that of the pneumatic tube cars. At one end there was an amazing array of machinery with glittering levers and handwheels—a control board on which numberless tiny lights blinked and flickered in rapid succession. At these controls squatted the twisted figure of a dwarf. A second of the creatures sat at his side and stared with those horrible green eyes.

"Lord!" he muttered. "Am I still asleep?"

"No," smiled the dwarf, "you're awake, Peter Van Dorn." The misshapen creature did not seem unfriendly.

"Then where am I, and who are you?"

"You're in one of the Zar's rocket cars, speeding toward Dorn. We are but two of the Zar's servants—Moon men."

"Rocket car? Moon men?" Karl was aghast. He wanted to pinch himself. But a hollow roar to the rear told him he was in a rapidly moving vessel of some sort. Certainly, too, these dwarfs were not figments of his imagination.

"You've been kept completely ignorant?" asked the dwarf.

"It—it seems so." Karl was bewildered. "You mean we are out in the open—traveling in space—to the Moon perhaps?"

* * * * *

The dwarf laughed. "No, I wish we were," he replied. "But we are about halfway to the capital of the Continental Empire, greatest of world powers. We'll be there in an hour."

"But I don't understand."

"Stupid. Didn't you ever hear of the rocket ships that cross the ocean like a projectile, mounting a thousand miles from the surface and making the trip in two hours?"

"No!" Karl was aghast. "Are we really in such a contraption?" he faltered.

"Say! Are you kidding me?" The dwarf was incredulous. "Do you mean to tell me you know so little of your world as that? Have you never read anything? The news broadcasts, the thought exchangers—don't you follow them at all?"

Karl shook his head in growing wonder. Truly Rudolph had kept him in ignorance. Or was it his own fault? He had refused to dig into the volumes old Krassin had begged him to read. The broadcasts and the thought machines—well, only those of the purple had access to those.

"Hey, Laro!" called the dwarf to his companion, "this mole is as dumb as can be. Doesn't know he's alive hardly. And a Van Dorn!"

The two laughed uproariously and Karl raged inwardly. Mole! So that's what they called wearers of the gray! He clenched his fists and rose unsteadily to his feet.

"Sorry," apologized his tormentor. "Mustn't get sore now. It seems so funny to us though. And listen, kid, you'll never have another chance to hear it all. So, if you'll sit down and calm yourself a bit I'll give you an earful."

*   *   *   *   *

Mollified, Karl listened. A marvelous tale it was, of a disgruntled scientist of the Eastern Hemisphere who had conquered that portion of the world with the aid of the inhabitants he had found on the outer side of the Moon; of the scientist who still ruled the East—Zar of the Continental Empire. A horrible war—in 2085, the year of his own birth—depopulated the countries of Asia, Europe and Africa and reduced them to subjection. There was no combatting the destructive rays and chemical warfare of the Moon men. The United Americas, still weakened from a civil war of their own, remained aloof and, for some strange reason, the Zar left them in peace, contenting himself with his conquest of practically all of the rest of the world. Now, it seemed, the two major powers were as separate as if on different planets, there being no traffic between them save by governmental sanction; and that was rarely given.

It grew uncomfortably warm in the compartment as the rocket car entered the lower atmosphere but Karl listened spellbound to the astounding revelations of the Moon man. There came a pause in the discourse of the dwarf as a number of relays clicked furiously on the control board and the vessel slackened its speed perceptibly.

"But," said Karl, thinking aloud rather than meaning to interrupt, "what has all this to do with me? Why does the government of this Zar want me?"

The dwarf bent close and eyed him cautiously. "Poor kid!" he whispered, "it doesn't seem right that you should suffer for something that happened when you were born; something you know nothing about. But the Zar knows best. You—"

There came a stabbing pencil of light from over Karl's shoulder and the green eyes of the dwarf went wide with horrified surprise. He clutched at his breast where the flame had contacted, then slowly collapsed in a pitiful, distorted heap. Karl recoiled from the odor of putrefaction that immediately filled the compartment. He whirled to face the new danger but saw nothing but the padded walls.

Then they were in darkness save for the blinking lights of the control board. He was thrown forward violently and the piercing screech of compressed air rushing past the vessel told him they had entered the receiving tube at their destination and were being retarded in speed for the landing. This much he had gathered from the explanations of the now silenced dwarf.

Laro, the other Moon man, remained mute at the controls. His companion evidently had talked too much.

*   *   *   *   *

The vessel had stopped and a section of the padded rear wall of the compartment moved back to reveal a second chamber. There were three other occupants of the ship and Karl knew now at whose hands the talkative Moon man had met his death. One of the three—all wearers of the purple—still held the generator of the dazzling ray in his hands. He decided wisely that resistance was useless and followed meekly when he was led from the ship.

Endlessly they rode upward in a high-speed lift, dismounting finally at a pneumatic tube entrance. A special car whisked them roaring into the blackness. Then they were shot forth into the open and Karl saw the light of the sun for the first time in many years. They were on the upper surface of a great city, Dorn, the capital the Continental Empire.

The air was filled with darting ships of all sorts and sizes, most of them being pleasure craft of the wearers of the purple. To Karl it was the sudden realization of his dreams. He was one of them. He, too, should be wearing the purple. Then his heart sank as one of his guards prodded him into action. His dream already was shattered for they stood at the entrance to a great crystal pyramid that rose from the flat expanse of the roofs of Dorn. It was the palace of the Zar.

It seemed then that fairyland had opened its gates to the young man in gray denim. He immediately fell under its influence when they traversed a long lane between rows of brightly colored growing things which filled the air with sweet odors. Feathered creatures fluttered about and twittered and caroled in the sheer joy of being alive. It was sweeter music than he had ever believed possible or even imagined as existing. Again he forgot the menace of the imperial edict which had brought him from the other side of the world.

*   *   *   *   *

Then rudely, he was brought back to earth. He was in the presence of the mighty Zar and his three escorts were bowing themselves from the huge room in which the wizened monarch sat enthroned. They had finished their duties.

A shriveled face; beady eyes; trembling hands with abnormally large knuckles; a cruel and determined mouth— these were the features that most impressed Karl as he stared wordlessly at this Zar of the Eastern Hemisphere. The magnificence of the royal robe was lost on the young wearer of the gray.

"Well, well, so this is Peter Van Dorn, my beloved nephew." The Zar was speaking and the chilly sarcasm in which the words were uttered belied the friendliness they otherwise might have implied.

"That's what I'm told," replied Karl, "though I didn't know I'm supposed to be the nephew of so great a figure as yourself."

Not bad that, for an humble wearer of the gray.

"Oh, yes, yes, indeed. Why else should I have sent for you?"

"I have wondered why—and still wonder."

"Oh, you wonder, eh?" The Zar inspected him carefully and then broke into a cackle of horrible laughter. "A Van Dorn in gray denim!" he chortled. "A mole of the Americas! And to think that even the Zar has been unable to find him in all these years!"

"Stop!" bellowed Karl. "I'll not have your ridicule. Come to the point now and have it over with. Kill me if you will, but tell me the story!" He had seen the slender tube in the Zar's hand.

*   *   *   *   *

An expression of surprise, almost of admiration, flickered in the beady eyes of the Zar and was gone. He spoke coldly.

"Very well, I shall explain. You, Peter, are actually my nephew. Your father, Derek Van Dorn, was my brother; he a king of Belravia and I a poor but experienced scientist. He scorned me and he paid, for I learned of the ancient race of the other side of the Moon, the side we can not see from the earth. I went to them and enlisted their aid in warring upon my brother. When we returned to carry on this war I learned that I had a son. So, too, did Derek. But my son was born in obscurity and Derek's son—you, Peter—in the lap of luxury. The war was short and, to me, sweet. Belravia was first to fall, and I had your father removed from this life by the vibrating death."

"You monster!" cried Karl. But the slender rod menaced him.

"A moment, my hot-headed nephew. I vowed I'd have your life, Peter, but your father had a few friends and one of these spirited you away. So temporarily you escaped. But now I have you where I can keep that vow. You, too, shall die. By the vibration. But first—ha! ha!—I'll give you a taste of the purple. Just so the going will be harder."

Karl kept his temper as best he could. He thought, conscience-stricken, of old Rudolph, that good friend of his father. Then he thought of that youth he had taken from the Square.

"Your son?" he asked gently. "Has he the triangular brand?"

The Zar was taken aback. "He has, yes. Why?" he asked.

"I have seen him in the Americas. He now lies wounded and in peril of his life. What do you think of that?"

Karl was triumphant as the Zar paled.

"You lie, Peter Van Dorn!"

*   *   *   *   *

But the beady eyes saw that the young man was truthful. Sudden fury assailed the monarch of the East. A bell pealed its mellow summons and three Moon men entered the Presence.

"Quick, Taru—the radiovision! Our ambassador in the Americas!" The Zar was on his feet, his hard features terrible in fear and anger. "By God!" he vowed, "I'll lay waste the Americas if harm has come to my son. And you"—turning to Karl—"I'll reserve for you an even more terrible fate than the vibrating death!"

The radiovision was wheeled in and in operation. A frightened face appeared in its disc: the Zar's ambassador across the sea.

"Moreau—my son!" snapped the Zar. "Where is he?"

"Majesty! Have mercy!" gasped Moreau. "Paul has eluded us. He was skylarking—in the lower levels of New York. But our secret agents are combing the passages. We'll have him in twenty-four hours. I promise!"

The rage of the Zar was terrible to see. Karl expected momentarily that the white flame would lay him low, for the anger of the mad ruler was directed first at Moreau, then at himself. But a quick, evil calm succeeded the storm.

"You, Peter," he stated, in tones suddenly silky, "shall have that twenty-four hours—no more. If Moreau has not produced my son in that time you shall be dismembered slowly. A finger; an ear; your tongue; a hand—until you reveal the whereabouts of the heir to my throne!"

"Never! You scum!" Karl was on the dais in a single bound. He had the Zar by the throat, his fingers twisting in the flabby flesh. Might as well have it over at once. "Fratricide—murderer of my father, I'll take you with me!"

* * * * *

But it was not to be. The throne room was filled with retainers of the mad emperor. Strong hands tore him away and he was borne, struggling and fighting, to the floor. A sharp pain in his forearm. A deadening of the muscles. He was powerless, save for the painful ability to crawl to his knees, swaying drunkenly. A delicious languor overcame him. Nothing mattered now. He saw that a tall man in the purple had withdrawn the needle of the hypodermic and was replacing the instrument in its case. Ever so slowly, it seemed.

The Zar was laughing. That horrible cackle. But Karl didn't care. They'd have their sport with him. Let 'em! Then it'd be over. Lord! If only he had been a little quicker. He'd have torn the old Zar's windpipe from its place!

"My word," laughed the Zar. "The sacred word of a Van Dorn. I gave it. He'll wear the purple for a day. Take him from my sight!"

Karl was walking, quite willingly now. The effects of the drug were altering. His muscular strength returned but his mental state underwent a complete change. Always he'd wanted a taste of the purple. For years he'd listened to the orators of the Square, to the conflicting statements of old Krassin. But now he'd see. He'd know the joys of the upper levels; the pleasure cities, perhaps. For one day. But what did it matter? He found himself laughing and joking with his companion, a heavy-set wearer of the purple. They were in a luxurious apartment. Servants! Moon men all of them, but so efficient. They stripped him of his gray denim; discarded it contemptuously. Karl kicked the heap into a corner and laughed delightedly. His bath was waiting.

* * * * *

Much can happen in a day. Clothed in the purple, Karl— Peter Van Dorn, he was, now—expanded. Turgid emotions surged through his new being. He was a new man. In his rightful place. He was delighted with the companionship of his new friend of the purple, Leon Lemaire. An euphonious name! A fine fellow! Fool that the Zar must be, to leave him in the care of so amiable a man. Why, Leon couldn't hold him! None of them could. He'd escape them all—if he wished. Twenty-four hours, indeed!

They were in the midst of a gay company. Wine flowed freely, and Leon had attached to their party a pair of beautiful damsels, young, and easy to know. There was music and dancing. Lights of marvelous color played over the assemblage in the huge hall, swaying their senses at the will of some expert manipulator. Peter was a different person now. He was exhilarated to the point of intoxication, but not by the wine. Somehow he couldn't bear the taste of the amber fluid the others were imbibing with such gusto. The effects of the drug had left a coppery taste in his mouth. But no matter! Rhoda, his lovely companion at the table leaned close. Her breath was hot at his throat. He swept her into his arms. Leon and the other girl laughed approvingly.

There were many such places in the upper levels of Dorn and they traveled from one to another. Now their party was larger, it having been augmented by the appearance of other of Leon's friends. Fine companions, these men of the purple, and the women were incomparable. Especially Rhoda. They understood one another perfectly now. It was all as he had pictured it.

Someone proposed that they visit the intermediate levels. It would be such a lark to watch the mechanicals. They made the drop in a lift. A laughing, riotous party. And Peter was one of them! He felt that he had known them for years. Rhoda clung to his arm, and the languorous glances from under her long lashes set the blood racing madly in his veins.

*   *   *   *   *

In the levels of the mechanicals they romped boisterously. To them the strange robots—creatures of steel and glass and copper—were objects of ridicule. Poor, senseless mechanisms that performed the tasks that made the wearers of the purple independent of labor. Here they saw the preparation of their synthetic food, untouched by human hands. In one chamber a group of mechanicals, soulless and brainless, engaged in the delicate chemical compounding of raw materials that went into the making of their clothing. Here was a nursery, where tiny tots born to the purple were reared to adolescence by unfeeling but efficient mechanical nurses. The mothers of the purple could not be bothered with their offspring until they had reached the age of reason. The whirring machinery of a huge power plant provided much amusement for the feminine members of the party. It was all so massive; throbbing with energy. But dirty! Ugh! Lucky the attendants could be mechanicals.

"We have visited the lower levels," whispered Rhoda in his ear, "but not often. It isn't pleasant. Ignorant fools in the gray denim—too many of them. I don't know why we permit their existence. Fools who will not learn. Education made us as we are, and they won't take it. Sullen looks and evil leers are all that they have for us. Hope nobody suggests going down there now."

"Me, too," said Peter. He had forgotten that once he was Karl Krassin, a wearer of the despised gray.

Someone in the party was becoming restless. They must move on.

"Where to?" asked Peter.

"Sans Dolor, sweet boy. A pleasure city within a hundred kilometers of Dorn. You'll love it, Peter."

A pleasure city! Fondest dream of the wearers of the gray! In the dim past, when he was Karl, he had dreamed it often. Now he was to visit one!

*　　*　　*　　*　　*

They were atop the city now and the crystal palace of the Zar shimmered in the sunlight off there across the flat upper surface of Dorn. But it seemed so far away that Peter did not give it a second thought. He was living in the present.

A swift aero took them into the skies and they roared out above the wilderness that was everywhere between the great cities of earth. Funny nobody thought of leaving the cities and exploring the jungles of the outside. But, of course, it wasn't necessary. They had everything they needed within the cities. All of their wants were supplied by the mechanicals and by the few toilers in the gray who still persisted in ignorance and in some perverse ideas that they must work in order to live. Besides, the jungle was dangerous.

Sans Dolor loomed into view, a great island floating in the air a thousand meters above the tossing waters of the ocean. Peter gave not a thought to the forces that kept it suspended. Dimly he recalled certain words of old Rudolph, words regarding the artificial emanations that had been discovered as capable of counteracting the force of gravity. But his mind was intent on the pleasures to come.

They were over the city. Carefully tended foliage lined its streets and a smooth lagoon glistened in its center. Its towers and spires were decorated with gay colors. The streets were filled with wearers of the purple and the nude bodies of bathers in the lagoon gleamed white in the strong sunlight.

He sensed anew the nearness of Rhoda. Her soft warm hand nestled in his and she responded instantly to his sudden embrace.

There came a shock and the party was stilled in dismay. The aero careened violently and the pilot struggled with controls that were dead. Sans Dolor dropped rapidly away beneath them. They were shooting skyward, drawn by some inexplicable and invisible energy from above.

*   *   *   *   *

Rhoda screamed and held him close, trembling violently. All of the women screamed and the men cursed. Leon arose to his feet and stared at Peter. The friendliness was gone from his features and he spat forth an accusation. A glistening mechanism appeared in his hand as if by magic. A ray generator! He had been appointed by the Zar to guard this upstart and, whatever happened, he'd not let him escape with his life. The girl shuddered at sight of the weapon and extricated herself from his arms. Her affection too had been a pose.

Peter's mind was clearing from the effects of the drug. He had not the slightest idea of what might have caused the quick change in the situation but he resolved he would die fighting, if die he must. Leon fumbled with the catch of the generator. It refused to operate. The force that was drawing them upward had paralyzed all mechanisms aboard the little aero. Flinging it from him in disgust he sprang for Peter.

Their minds befuddled, the rest of the men watched dully. The women huddled together in a corner, whimpering. They were a sorry lot after all, thought Karl. He was no longer Peter Van Dorn, and he thrilled to the joy of battle.

*   *   *   *   *

Leon Lemaire was no mean antagonist. His flailing arms were everywhere and a huge fist caught Karl on the side of his head and sent him reeling. But this only served to clear his mind further and to fill him with a cold rage. He bored in unmercifully and Lemaire soon was on the defensive. A blow to his midsection had him puffing and Karl hammered in rights and lefts to the now sinister face that rocked his opponent to his heels. But the minion of the Zar was crafty. He slid to the floor as if groggy, then with catlike agility, dove for Karl's knees, bringing him down with a crash.

The air whistled by them as the ship was drawn upward with ever-increasing speed. The other passengers cowered in fright as the two men rolled over and over on the floor, banging at each other indiscriminately. Both were hurt. Karl's lip was split, and bleeding profusely. One eye was closing. But now he was on top and he pummeled his opponent to a pulp. Long after he ceased resisting them, the blows continued until the features of Leon Lemaire were unrecognizable. The infuriated Karl did not see that one of the members of the party was creeping up on him from behind. Neither was he aware that the upward motion of the aero had ceased and that they now hung motionless in space. A terrific blow at the base of his skull sent him sprawling. Must have been struck by a rocket, one of those funny ships that crossed the ocean so quickly. A million lights danced before his aching eyeballs.

Lying prone across the inert body of his foe, dimly conscious and fingers clutching weakly, he knew that the cabin was filled with people. Alien voices bellowed commands. There was the screaming of women; the sound of blows; curses ... then all was silence and darkness.

*   *   *   *   *

It was a far cry to the little book shop off Cooper Square, but Karl was calling for Rudolph when he next awoke to the realization that he was still in the land of the living. His head was bandaged and his tongue furry. A terrible hangover. Then he heard voices and they were discussing Peter Van Dorn. He opened one eye as an experiment. The other refused to open. But it might have been worse. At least he was alive; he could see well enough with the one good optic.

"Sh-h!" whispered one of the voices. "He's recovering!"

He looked solemnly into the eyes of an old man; a pair of wise and gentle eyes that reminded him somehow of Rudolph's.

"Quiet now, Peter," said the old man. "You'll be all right in a few minutes. Banged up a bit, you are, but nothing serious."

"Don't call me Peter," objected Karl. He loathed the sound of the name; loathed himself for his recent thoughts and actions. "I am Karl Krassin," he continued, "and as such will remain until I die."

There were others in the room and he saw glances of satisfaction pass between them. This was a strange situation. These men were not of the purple. Neither were they of the gray. Their garments shone with the whiteness of pure silver. And that's what they were; of finely woven metallic cloth. Was he in another world?

"Very well, Karl." The kind old man was speaking once more. "I merely want you to know that you are among friends—your father's friends."

*   *   *   *   *

Surprised into complete wakefulness, Karl struggled to a seated position and surveyed the group that faced him. They were a fine looking lot, mostly older men, but there was a refreshing wholesomeness about them.

"My father?" he faltered. "He's not alive."

"No, my poor boy. Derek Van Dorn left this life at the hands of your uncle, Zar Boris. But we, his friends, are here to avenge him and to restore to you his throne."

"But—but—I still do not understand."

"Of course not, because we've kept ourselves hidden from the world for more than twenty-two years, waiting for this very moment. There are forty-one of us, including Rudolph, my brother. We have lived in the jungle since Boris conquered the Eastern Hemisphere. But amongst our numbers were several scientists, two greater than was Boris, even in his heyday. They have done wonderful things and we are now prepared to take back what was taken from Derek—and more. His life we can not restore—Heaven rest him—but his kingdom we can. And to his son it shall be returned.

"You were given into Rudolph's care when little more than a babe in arms and he has cared for you well. We've watched, you know, in the detectoscopes—long range radiovision mechanisms that can penetrate solid walls, the earth itself, to bring to us the images and voices of persons who may be on the other side of the world. We've followed your every move, my boy, and the first time we feared for you was yesterday when the drug of the Zar's physician stole away your sense of right and wrong. But we were in time to save you, and now we are ready to kneel at your feet and proclaim you our king. First there is the Zar to be dealt with and then we shall set up the new regime. Are you with us?"

*   *   *   *   *

Karl gazed at the speaker in wonder. He a king? Always to live amongst the wearers of the purple? To be responsible for the welfare of half the world? It was unthinkable! But Zar Boris, the murderer of his own father—he must be punished, and at the hands of the son!

"I'll do it," he said simply. "That is, I'll do whatever you have planned in the way of exterminating the Zar. Then we'll talk of the new empire. But how is the Zar to be overcome? I thought he was invincible, with his Moon men and terrible weapons."

"Ah! That, my boy, is where our scientists have triumphed. True, his rays were terrible. They could not be combatted when he first returned. The strange chemicals and gases of the Moon men defied analysis or duplication. His citadel atop the city of Dorn is proof against them all; proof against explosives and rays of all kinds known to him. The disintegration and decomposition rays have no effect on the crystal of its walls. It is hermetically sealed from the outer air so can not be gassed. The vibration impulses have no effect upon its reinforced structure. But there is a ray, a powerful destructive agent, against which it is not proof. And our scientists have developed this agency. You shall have the privilege of pressing the release of the energy that destroys the arch-fiend in his lair. His dominance over, the empire will fall. We shall take it—for you."

A strange exaltation shone from the faces of those in the room, and Karl found that it was contagious. His bosom swelled and he itched to handle the controls of this wonderful ray.

"This ray," continued the brother of old Rudolph, "carries the longest vibrations ever measured, the vibrations of infra-red, the heat-ray. We have succeeded in concentrating a terrific amount of power in its production, and with it are able to produce temperatures in excess of that of the interior of the earth, where all substances are molten or gaseous. The Zar's crystal palace cannot withstand it for a second. He cannot escape!"

"How'll you know he's there at the time?" Karl was greatly excited, but he was curious too.

"Come with me, my boy. I'll show you." The old man led him from the room and the others followed respectfully.

*   *   *   *   *

They stopped at a circular port and Karl saw that they were high above the earth in a vessel that hovered motionless, quivering with what seemed like human eagerness to be off.

"This vessel?" he asked.

"It's a huge sphere; the base of our operations. To it we drew the aero on which you were fighting. A magnetic force discovered by our scientists and differing only slightly from that used in counteracting gravity. We let the rest of them go; foolishly I think. But it's done now and we have no fear. From this larger vessel we shall send forth smaller ones, armed with the heat-ray. The flagship of the fleet is to be yours and you'll lead the attack on Dorn. Here—I'll show you the Zar."

They had reached the room of the detectoscopes—a mass of mechanisms that reminded Karl of nothing so much as the vitals of the intermediate levels which he had visited with Leon—and

Rhoda. He knew that he flushed when he thought of her. What a fool he had been!

A disc glowed as one of the silver-robed strangers manipulated the controls. The upper surface of Dorn swung into view. Rapidly the image drew nearer and they were looking at the crystal pyramid that was the Zar's palace. Down, down to its very tip they passed. Karl recoiled from the image as it seemed they were falling to its glistening sides. The sensation passed. They were through, penetrating solid crystal, masonry, steel and duralumin girders. Room after room was opened to their view. It was magic—the magic of the upper levels.

*   *   *   *   *

Now they were in the throne room. A group of purple-clad men and women stood before the dais. Leon, Rhoda—all of his wild companions were there, facing the dais. The Zar was raging and the words of his speech came raucously to their ears through the sound-producing mechanism.

"You've failed miserably, all of you," he screamed. "He's gotten away and you know the penalty. Taru—the vibrating ray!"

The Moon man already was fussing with a gleaming machine, a machine with bristling appendages having metallic spheres on their ends, a machine in which dozens of vacuum tubes glowed suddenly.

Rhoda screamed. It was a familiar sound to Karl. He noted with satisfaction that Leon could hardly stand on his feet and that his face was covered with plasters. Then, startled, he saw that Leon was shivering as with the ague. His outline on the screen grew dim and indistinct as the rate of vibration increased. Then the body bloated and became misty. He could see through it. The vibrating death! His father had gone the same way!

Karl groaned at the thought. The whine of the distant machine rose in pitch until it passed the limit of audibility. Tiny pin-points of incandescence glowed here and there from the Zar's victims as periods of vibration were reached that coincided with the natural periods of certain of the molecules of their structure. They were no longer recognizable as human beings. Shimmering auras surrounded them. Suddenly they were torches of cold fire, weaving, oscillating with inconceivable rapidity. Then they were gone; vanished utterly.

The Zar laughed—that horrible cackle again.

"Great God!" exclaimed Karl, "let's go! The fiend must not live a moment longer than necessary. Are you ready?"

Rudolph's brother smiled. "We're ready Karl," he said.

*   *   *   *   *

The great vessel hummed with activity. The five torpedo-shaped aeros of the battle fleet were ready to take off from the cavities in the hull. In the flagship Karl was stationed at the control of the heat-ray. His instructions in its operation had been simple. A telescopic sight with crosshairs for the centering of the object to be attacked; a small lever. That was all. He burned with impatience.

Then they were dropping; falling clear of the mother ship. The pilot pressed a button and the electronic motors started. A burst of roaring energy streamed from the tapered stern of their vessel and the earth lurched violently to meet them. Down, down they dived until the rocking surface of Dorn was just beneath them. Then they flattened out and circled the vast upper surface. From the corner of his eye Karl saw that the other four vessels of his fleet were just behind. There was a flurry among the wasplike clouds of pleasure craft over the city. They scurried for cover. Something was amiss!

"Hurry!" shouted Karl. "The warning is out! There is no time to lose!"

He pressed his face to the eye-piece of his sight, his finger on the release lever of the ray. The crystal pyramid crossed his view and was gone. Again it crossed, more slowly this time. And now his sight was dead on it, the gleaming wall rushing toward him. Pressure on the tiny button. They'd crash into the palace in another second! But no, a brilliant flash obscured his vision, a blinding light that made the sun seem dark by comparison. They roared on and upward. He took his eye from the telescope and stared ahead, down. The city was dropping away, and, where the crystal palace had stood, there was a spreading blob of molten material from which searing vapors were drifting. The roofs of the city were sagging all around and great streams of the sparkling, sputtering liquid dripped into the openings that suddenly appeared. Derek Van Dorn was avenged.

"Destroy! Destroy!" yelled Karl madly. A microphone hung before him and his words rang through every vessel of his convoy.

* * * * *

The lust of battle was upon him. A fleet of the Zar's aeros had risen from below; twenty of them at least. These would be manned by Moon creatures, he knew, and would carry all of the dreadful weapons which had originated on that strange body. But he did not know that his own ships were insulated against most of the rays used by the Zar's forces. He knew only that he must fight; fight and kill; exterminate every last one of the Zar's adherents or be exterminated in the attempt.

Kill! Kill! The madness was contagious. His pilot was a marvel and drove his ship straight for the massed ships of the foe. The air was vivid with light-streamers. A ray from an enemy vessel struck the thick glass of the port through which he looked and the outer surface was shattered and pock-marked. But a cloud of vapor and a dripping stream of fiery liquid told him his own ray had taken effect on a vessel of the enemy. One! They wheeled about and spiraled, coming up under another of the Zar's aeros. It vanished in a puff of steam and they narrowly missed being covered by the falling remnants of incandescent liquid. Two! Karl's aim was good and he gloated in the fact. Three! They climbed and turned over, dropping again into the fray. Four!

The air grew stifling, for the expended energy of the enemies' rays must needs be absorbed. It could not disintegrate them nor decompose their bodies, but the contacts were many and the liberation of heat enormous. They were suffocating! But Karl would not desist. They drove on, now beneath, now above an enemy ship. He lost count.

One of his own vessels was in trouble. The report came to him from the little speaker at his ear. He looked around in alarm. A glowing object reeled uncertainly over there between two of the aeros of the Zar. The concentration of beams of vibrations was too much for the sturdy craft. It was red hot and its occupants burned alive where they sat. Suddenly it slipped into a spin and went slithering down into the city, leaving a gaping opening where it fell. This sobered him somewhat, but he went into the battle with renewed fury.

*   *   *   *   *

How many had they brought down? Fifteen? Sixteen? He tore his purple jacket from his body. The perspiration rolled from his pores. His own ship would be next. But what did it matter? Kill! Kill! He shouted once more into the microphone, then dived into battle. Another and another! In Heaven's name, how many were there? It was maddening. If only he could breathe. His lungs were seared; his eyes smarting from the heat. And then it was over.

Three of the Zar's aeros remained, and these turned tail to run for it. No! They were falling, nose down, under full power; diving into the city from which they had come. Suicide? Yes. They couldn't face the recriminations that must come to them. And anything was better than facing that burning death from the strange little fighters which had come from out the skies. Dorn was a mass of wreckage.

Karl tore at the fastenings of the ports, searing his fingers on the heated metal. His pilot had collapsed, the little aero heading madly skyward with no guiding hand. Air! They must have air! He loosened the pilot's jacket; slapped frantically at his wrists in the effort to bring him to consciousness. Then he was at the controls of the vessel, tugging on first one, then the other. The aero circled and spun, executing the most dangerous of sideslips and dives. A little voice was speaking to him—the voice of the radio—instructing him. In a daze he followed instructions as best he could. The whirlings of the earth stabilized after a time and he found he was flying the vessel; climbing rapidly.

*   *   *   *   *

A sense of power came to him as the little voice of the radio continued to instruct. Here were the controls of the electronic motor; there the gravity-energy. He was proceeding in the wrong direction. But what did it matter? He learned the meaning of the tiny figures of the altimeter; the difference between the points of the compass. Still he drove on.

"East! Turn East!" begged the little voice from the radio. "You're heading west. Your speed—a thousand kilometers an hour—it's too fast. Turn back, Zar Peter!"

He tore the loud speaker of the radio from its fastenings. West! He wanted to go west! On and on he sped, becoming more and more familiar with the workings of the little vessel as he progressed. A cooling breeze whistled from the opened ports, a breeze that smelled of the sea. His heart sang with the wonder of it all. He could fly. And fly he did. Zar Peter? Never! He knew now where he belonged; knew what he wanted. He'd find the coast of North America. Follow it until he located New York. A landing would be easy, for had not the voice instructed him in the use of the gravity-energy? He'd make his way to the lower levels, to the little book shop of Rudolph Krassin. A suit of gray denim awaited him there and he'd never discard it.

*   *   *   *   *

Onward he sped into the night, which was falling fast. He held to his westward course like a veteran of the air lanes. The pilot had ceased to breathe and Karl was sorry. Game little devil, that pilot. Have to shove his body overboard. Too bad.

Rudolph's brother would understand. He'd be watching in the detectoscope. And the others—those who had wished to seat him on a throne—they'd understand, too. They'd have to!

Rudolph would forgive him, he knew. Paul Van Dorn—his own cousin—the secret agents of the Zar would never locate him! Too many friends of Rudolph's were of the red police.

He gave himself over to happy thoughts as the little aero sped on in the darkness. Home! He was going home! Back to the gray denim, where he belonged and where now he would remain content.

TERRORS UNSEEN

ORIGINALLY PUBLISHED IN *ASTOUNDING STORIES*, MARCH 1931

Terrors Unseen

Something about the lonely figure of the girl caused Edward Vail to bring his car to a sudden stop at the side of the road. When first he had glimpsed her off there on that narrow strip of rock-bound coast he was mildly surprised, for it was a desolate spot and seldom frequented by bathers so late in the season. Now he was aroused to startled attention by the unnatural posture of the slender body that had just been erect and outlined sharply against the graying September sky. He switched off the ignition and sprang to the ground.

Bent backward and twisted into the attitude of a contortionist, the little figure in the crimson bathing suit was a thing at which to marvel. No human being could maintain that position without falling, yet the girl did not fall to the jagged stones that lay beneath her. She was rigid, straining. Then suddenly her arm waved wildly and she screamed, a wild gasping cry that died in her throat on a note of despairing terror. It seemed that she struggled furiously with an unseen power for one horrible instant. Then the tortured body lurched violently and collapsed in a pitiful quivering heap among the stones.

Eddie Vail was running now, miraculously picking his way over the treacherous footing. The girl had fainted, no doubt of that, and something was seriously wrong with her.

A mysterious mechanical something whizzed past; something that buzzed like a thousand hornets and slithered over the rocks in a series of metallic clanks. Then it was gone—or so it seemed in the confusion of Eddie's mind; but he had seen nothing. Probably a fantasy of his overworked brain, or only the surf breaking against the sea wall. He turned his attention to the girl.

*   *   *   *   *

She was moaning and tossing her head, returning painfully to consciousness. He straightened her limbs and placed his folded coat under the restless head, noting with alarm that vicious red welts marred the whiteness of her arms and shoulders. It was as if she had been beaten cruelly; those marks could never have resulted from her fall. Poor kid. Subject to fits of some sort, he presumed. She was a good looker, too, and no mistake. He smoothed back the rumpled mass of golden hair and studied her features. They were vaguely familiar.

Then she opened her eyes. Stark terror looked out from their ultra-marine depths, and her lips quivered as if she were about to cry. He raised her to a more comfortable position and supported her with an encircling arm. She did cry a little, like a frightened child. Then, with startling abruptness, she sprang to her feet.

"Where is it?" she demanded.

"Where's what?" Eddie was on his feet, peering in all directions. He remembered the queer sounds he had heard or imagined.

"I—I don't know." The girl passed a trembling hand before her eyes as if to wipe away some horrifying vision. "Perhaps it's my imagination, but I felt—it was just as real—one of father's iron monsters. Beating me; bending me. I'd have snapped in a moment. But nothing was there. I—I'm afraid...."

Eddie caught her as she swayed on her feet. "There now," he said soothingly, "you're all right, Miss Shelton. It's gone now, whatever it was." Iron monsters! In a flash it had come to him that this girl he held in his arms was Lina Shelton, daughter of the robot wizard. No wonder she was afflicted with hallucinations! But those bruises were real, as was the forcible twisting of her lithe young body. And he *had* heard something.

*   *   *   *   *

"You know me?" The girl was calmer now and faced him with a surprised look.

"Yes, Miss Shelton. At least I recognize you from the pictures. Society page, you know. And I'm Edward Vail—Eddie for short—on vacation and at your service."

The girl smiled wanly. "You know of father's break with Universal Electric? Of his private experiments?"

"I heard of the scrap and of how he walked out on the outfit, but nothing further." Eddie thought grimly of how nearly he had come to losing his own job when David Shelton broke relations with his employers. He had been too enthusiastic in support of some of the older man's claims.

"It's been terrible," the girl whispered. She clung nervously to his arm as he picked the way back to the road. "The loneliness, and all. No servants will stay out here now, and father spends all of his time in the laboratory. Then—this fear of the mechanical men—they haunt me. I—I guess they've got me a little goofy."

Eddie laughed reassuringly. "Perhaps," he suggested, "you will let me help you. Your father, I believe, will remember me, and I'll be very glad to—"

"No, no!" The girl seemed frightened at the thought. "I'm sure he wouldn't welcome you. He's changed greatly of late and is suspicious of everyone, even keeping things from me. But it's awfully nice of you to offer your assistance, and you've been a perfect peach to take care of me this way. I—I'd better go now."

They had reached the road and Eddie looked uncertainly at his roadster. He hated to think of leaving the girl in this lonely spot. She was obviously in a state of extreme nervous tension and, to him, seemed pathetically helpless, and afraid.

"That the house?" he asked, pointing in the direction of the gloomy old mansion whose dilapidated gables were barely visible over the tree tops.

"Yes." The girl shivered and drew closer to him.

The ensuing silence was broken by the slam of a door. His car! Eddie looked toward it in amazement; he was hearing things again. The springs sagged on the driver's side as under the weight of a very heavy occupant, but the seat was empty. Then came the whine of the starter and the motor purred into life. The gears clashed sickeningly and the car was jerked into the road with a violence that should have stripped the differential. He pulled the girl aside just as it roared past and disappeared around the bend in a cloud of dust. The sound of the exhaust died away rapidly and left them staring into each other's eyes in awed silence.

*   *   *   *   *

David Shelton was prowling around in the shrubbery when they approached the house—a furtive, unkempt creature whom Eddie would hardly have recognized. He straightened up and peered at his daughter's companion with obvious disapproval.

"Lina," he said severely, "I've told you we want no visitors."

"Yes, Dad, I know, but Mr. Vail's car was stolen out in front and there is no way for him to go on. We must look after him."

"His car—stolen? Who stole it?" David Shelton drew close and glared suspiciously at his unwelcome visitor.

"One of your monsters, I think," she replied shakily, "though we could see nothing. And the same thing attacked me and beat me. Look at my bruises!"

Shelton was examining the marks, and his fingers trembled as he touched his daughter's shoulder. He looked piteously into her eyes. "Are you sure, Lina? Sure? Did you see it?"

"No, no. But I felt and heard—the iron arms and the clamps and the buzzing. Oh, it was horrible!" The girl's voice rose hysterically.

"Oh, Lord! What have I done?" groaned Shelton. "It's true, then. Lina, listen: I've succeeded in making them invisible, and one got away this morning. But I thought—I thought—" He looked at Eddie, remembering his presence suddenly. "But I'm talking too much. It seems to me I remember having seen you before, young man."

"You have, sir," Eddie stated. "In the research laboratory of Universal Electric. I work with Borden."

"They've sent you to find me?" Shelton stiffened perceptibly.

"Indeed, not, sir. I'm on vacation and was merely passing by when I saw your daughter in danger, a danger I still do not understand."

"Yes, and he helped me to the road," Lina interposed, "and then lost his car at the hands of—"

"Silence!" the father thundered. But his eyes fell before the fire that instantly flashed in those of the girl.

"Now, you listen to me!" she returned angrily, "I've stayed on here with you until I'm nearly crazy with your everlasting puttering and experimenting—hearing your uncanny machines walking around in the middle of the night—seeing impossible sights—then, this thing I couldn't see but could feel. And you've gotten into such a state that you'll go crazy yourself, if you continue. Something's got to be done, I tell you. I can't stand it!"

*   *   *   *   *

Her voice broke on a choked sob.

"But Lina—"

"Don't but me, Father. I mean it. Mr. Vail discovered your hideout quite by accident and he's been very nice to me. I tell you he means no harm and I want him to stay. If you're not decent to him, if you send him away, I swear I'll go too. I will—I will!"

Shelton's eyes misted and something of the hardness left his expression. A look of haunting fear took its place and he stared pleadingly at Eddie.

"Br-r! I'm cold!" Lina exclaimed irrelevantly. "And—and I believe I'm going to cry." She turned away and raced for the shelter of the gloomy old house without another word.

Eddie turned inquiring eyes on his unwilling host.

"Just like her mother before her," Shelton muttered softly. Then he faced the younger man squarely and his shoulders straightened. "Mr. Vail," he said sheepishly, "I've been a fool and I ask your pardon. But Lina doesn't know. There's something tremendous behind all this, something that's gotten beyond me. I'll send her away for her own safety, but I must stay on. If—if only there was someone I could trust—"

"You can trust me, sir," Eddie stated simply.

The older man paced the ground nervously, and Eddie could see that he was under a most severe mental strain. Several times he halted in his tracks and peered anxiously at his guest. Then he seemed to make a sudden decision.

"Vail," he said sharply, "I need help badly. I want you to stay, if you will. You swear you'll not reveal what I am about to show you?"

"I swear it, sir."

"You'll not report to Universal?"

"Never."

*   *   *   *   *

They surveyed each other appraisingly. Eddie was mystified by the happenings of the day and was curious to learn more concerning these mythical invisible creations. It was inconceivable that the scientist had spoken truly of his accomplishment. Yet, he had done some marvelous things with Universal and, maybe—well, anyway, there was the girl.

"Come with me," Shelton was saying: "I believe you're a square shooter, Vail." He was leading the way along the gravel path at the side of the house. Before them loomed the squat brick building that was the laboratory.

The door crashed open before Shelton's hand had reached the knob, and one of those buzzing, unseen, monstrosities rushed clanking by, knocking the scientist from his feet in its passage. Ponderous, speeding footsteps crunched the gravel of the path, and then, with a wild thrashing of the underbrush alongside, the thing was gone.

Eddie bent over the prostrate man and saw that he was unconscious. A thin trickle of blood ran from a cut in the side of his head.

"Lina! Lina!" called Eddie frantically. For the first time in his life he was genuinely frightened.

*   *   *   *   *

He half carried, half dragged the limp body through the door of the laboratory and propped it in a chair. It required but a moment for him to see that Shelton's injury was inconsequential. He had only been stunned and already showed signs of recovering.

"What is it, Mr. Vail? What's happened?" came the voice of Lina Shelton breathlessly. She was framed in the doorway, dressed now and panting from her exertions in responding to his call. "Oh, it's father," she wailed, dropping to her knees at his side. "He's been hurt. Badly, too."

"No, not badly, Miss Shelton. He'll be around in a minute. I'm sorry to have excited you, but when I called I feared it was worse than it is." He was washing the blood from her father's small wound as he spoke.

She took the basin from his hand, spilling some of the water in her eagerness. "Here, let me have that cloth," she demanded.

Eddie admired her as her deft fingers took up the task. She was as exquisite in a simple sport outfit as she had been in her bathing suit.

The scientist opened his eyes after a moment. Remembrance came at once and he sat erect in the chair, staring.

"Lina!" he exclaimed, grasping her hand conclusively. "You're here, thank God! I dreamed—oh, it was horrible—I dreamed they had you." He clung to her closely.

"They?" she murmured inquiringly.

"Yes. Two of them are loose now. It's danger for you, my dear. You must leave at once. No, no—I can't let you out of my sight until they are captured or destroyed." He rose to his feet in his agitation and shook his head to clear it. He looked pleadingly at Eddie as if expecting him to offer a solution of the difficulty.

"Vail!" he exploded, then, pointing a shaking forefinger at an elaborate short-wave radio transmitter which occupied a corner of the large room. "I ask you to bear witness. That is the source of energy for these creations of mine and it's shut down. How on earth can they keep going? I ask you."

"Perhaps someone else, sir," Eddie suggested doubtfully. "Have you any enemies who might be able to duplicate the impulses of that apparatus?"

"Bah! Enemies, yes—with Universal—but none who could duplicate the complicated frequencies I use. My secrets are my own. I've never even put them on paper."

* * * * *

Eddie was examining the intricate apparatus. "You knew of the first one's escape, didn't you?" he asked. "How did it happen?"

Shelton again became the enthusiastic scientist. "Here," he said, "I'll show you and you can judge for yourself." He strode to the gleaming figure of a seven-foot robot of startlingly human-like appearance.

Lina let forth an exclamation of repugnance and fear.

"No, Mr. Shelton," Eddie objected. "The same thing will occur again. Then there will be three."

"We'll fix that, my boy." The scientist was removing cover plates from the hip joints of the mechanical man. "I'll disconnect the cables that feed the locomotors. He *can't* walk then."

Eddie was still doubtful but dared offer no further objection, especially since Lina Shelton was watching in wide-eyed silence. He examined the monster and saw that it was quite similar in outside appearance to those supplied by Universal for heavy manual labor, excepting that this one was armed as were those used for prison guards. There were the same articulated limbs and the various clamps and hooks for lifting and heavy hauling; the tentacles for grasping; machine guns front and back. Under the helical headpiece that was the antenna this robot seemed to have two eyes—a new feature—but closer examination showed these to be the twin lenses of a stereoscopic motion picture camera. This robot, then, could see. Or at least it could record what the lenses saw for its masters.

"There," Shelton grunted when he had finished his tinkering, "he's paralyzed from the waist down. Let this one try and get away from us."

"Guns aren't loaded, are they?" Eddie asked.

"Lord, no! Never have any of them loaded. That *would* be a fool stunt." Shelton had pulled the starting handle of a motor-generator and its rising whine accompanied his words.

*   *   *   *   *

The vacuum tubes of the transmitter glowed into life and the scientist manipulated the controls rapidly. Lina was watching the robot with fascinated awe. Its arms moved in obedience to the controls, tentacles waved and coiled; the humming of its internal mechanisms filled the room. The locomotion controls had no effect, as the scientist had predicted. Eddie drew a sigh of relief.

"Now, Vail, watch," Shelton exulted. "I'll show you what I was doing with the first one." He closed a switch that lighted another bank of vacuum tubes behind the control panel.

"You can make this one invisible?" Eddie asked incredulously.

"Certainly—from the waist up. This ought to be good."

"Mind telling me the principle?"

"Not at all—now. I've your promise of secrecy. It's a simple matter, Vail, really. Just a problem of wave motions—light. Invisible light; the ultra-violet, you know. My robots are built of specially alloyed metals which permit great freedom of molecular vibration. The insulating materials and even the glass of the camera lenses are possessed of the same property. Get it? I merely set up a wave motion in the atoms of the material that is in synchronism with the frequency of ultra-violet light, which is invisible to the human eye. All visible colors are absorbed, or more accurately, none are reflected excepting the ultra-violet. Perfect transparency is obtained since there is neither refraction nor diffraction of the visible colors. And there you are!"

Eddie stared at the upper half of the robot and saw that it was changing color as Shelton tuned the transmitted wave. Then suddenly it was gone. The entire upper portion of the mechanism had vanished; had just snuffed out like the flame of a candle. He could see down into the tops of the thing's hollow legs. Shelton laughed at him as he stretched forth his hand and hesitatingly felt for the invisible mid-section and upper body. It was there all right, unyielding and cold, that metal body. But no trace of it was visible to the eye. He drew back his fingers as if they had touched a hot stove. The thing was positively uncanny.

"Dad! Turn it off—please," Lina begged. "It's getting on my nerves. Please!"

Obligingly, Shelton pulled the switch. "Now you'll see," he said to Eddie, "whether the same thing happens. Watch."

*   *   *   *   *

Mistily at first, the outlines of the monster's torso and arms came into view, semi-transparent but clouding rapidly to opacity. Then it glinted with the barely visible violet, a solid once more, rigid and motionless. It was a lifeless mechanism, for the source of its energy had been cut off. Eddie had an almost irresistible impulse to pinch himself.

Then he gasped audibly, as did Shelton, for the thing snuffed out of sight again without warning, and the hum of its many motors resumed. There came a terrific clanking as it waved arms and tentacles and violently threshed with its upper body. But the visible portion, its legs, remained rooted to the floor of the laboratory. Lucky it was that the scientist had disconnected those wires; lucky too that the machine guns were empty of ammunition.

"There now—see?" Shelton's voice rose excitedly. "It's been no fault of mine. The power is off but it moves—it moves. What on earth do you suppose—"

Eddie's shout interrupted him. He had seen something at the window: a face pressed against the pane and contorted with unutterable malice. Then it was gone. With the shout of warning still in his throat, Eddie bounded through the door in pursuit of the intruder. Lina's cry of recognition followed him into the twilight. "Carlos!" she had called.

He saw a stocky figure slink around the corner of the laboratory and make for the underbrush beyond. In a flash he was after him. No, he thought grimly, Shelton hadn't any enemy clever enough to duplicate his transmitter! The hell he didn't! Who the devil was this fellow Carlos anyway? He tore savagely at the impeding branches as he plunged deeper and deeper into the thicket.

*   *   *   *   *

It was a fruitless chase and Eddie soon retraced his steps to the laboratory. Swell mess he'd gotten himself into! His car was gone: probably wrapped around a tree by this time. And here was a situation that spelled real danger, a thing with which Shelton was utterly unable to cope. As a matter of fact, he was so impractical—such a visionary cuss, after the fashion of all geniuses—that he'd never be convinced of the seriousness of the matter until it was too late. What to do? The girl was a corker, though, and game as they made 'em. Just the sort a fellow could tie to....

Lina's firm clear voice came to him through the open door of the laboratory. "Dad," she was saying, "why don't you give it up? Let's go back to New York where it is safe for you and for me. Let the things go and forget about them. What do they amount to, after all? We've plenty of money and you already have earned enough fame to last the rest of your life. Come on now—please— for me."

"What do they amount to?" Shelton reiterated, his voice rising querulously. "Lina, it's the most tremendous thing I've ever done. Think for a moment of what my robots could accomplish in the next war. And there'll be a next war as sure as you're alive. Think of it! No sending of our young manhood into the bloody fields of battle; no manning of our air fleets with the cream of our youth; no bloodshed on our side whatsoever. Instead, these robots will fight the war. They'll fight other robots too, no doubt, but the property of invisibility will be an invincible weapon. It will be a war that will end war once and for all. You can't—"

"Nonsense, Father," the girl returned sharply. "You've let your enthusiasm run away with your judgment. See what's happened already?—someone's figured it out before you've even perfected the thing. An enemy of our country could do the same in wartime. Maybe it's a foreign spy who has done what's been done to-day."

*   *   *   *   *

Eddie walked into the laboratory. "Couldn't find him," he announced briefly.

"No difference," said Shelton. "He doesn't count in this. We called to you when you rushed out, but couldn't make you hear."

"Who is he?" Eddie asked shortly. What he had overheard made him more than ever impatient with the older man. So clever and yet so dense, Shelton was.

Lina avoided his gaze.

"Only Carlos—Carlos Savarino," said Shelton, carelessly, "a Chilean, I think. He worked for me for two months during the summer and I fired him for getting fresh with Lina. Good mechanic, but dumb as an ox. Had to tell him every little detail when he was doing something in the shop. I'd have saved time if I'd done it myself."

The girl looked at Eddie squarely now. She was flushing hotly. "And I horsewhipped him," she added.

"Yes," Shelton laughed; "it was rich. He sneaked away like a whipped puppy, and this is the first time we've seen him since."

Eddie whistled. "And you think he doesn't count in this?" he asked.

"Of course not. Too dumb, I tell you. Doesn't know the first principles of science. He thinks the only wave motion is that of the ocean." Shelton chuckled over his own jest.

"I wouldn't be too sure," Eddie snapped. "And I want to tell you something, Mr. Shelton. Through no fault of my own, I heard some of your conversation with Li—with your daughter, before I returned here. I was puzzled over your reasons for working so absorbedly on this thing, but now I know them and I think you're wasting your time and keeping your daughter in needless danger."

"You dare talk to me like this!" Shelton roared.

"I do, sir, and you'll thank me later." Eddie returned the older man's glare with one equally savage.

Lina's gurgle of laughter broke the tension. "He's right, Dad, and you know it," she interposed. "Let him finish."

Eddie needed no such encouragement, though it warmed his heart. And Shelton listened respectfully when he continued, "I'm into this now, sir, and I intend to see it through to the end. I'll keep your secret, too, though I doubt if it'll ever be of much value to you. Know what I think? I think this Carlos is a damn clever fellow instead of the ass you took him to be. He probably just pretended he was ignorant of science. Why shouldn't he? That way he got a liberal education from you in the very things he wanted to find out. Since you tied the can to him he's had plenty of chances to build a duplicate of your control apparatus—with the aid of some foreign government, no doubt—and now they've stolen two of your machines to complete the job. Your secret already is out and in the very hands you've tried to keep it from."

*   *   *   *   *

Shelton paled visibly as Eddie talked. "But—but how—" he stammered.

"How should I know how they did it?" the younger man countered. "Here—let's take a look around. I'll bet they've left their trail right here in this room."

He walked from one end of the laboratory to the other, peering into corners and under work benches as he passed. Shelton trailed him like a shadow, squinting through the square lenses of his spectacles.

They carefully avoided the partially invisible robot, for the humming of its upper motors continued and clanking sounds occasionally issued from the unseen upper portion. The enemies of David Shelton were still at work on their hidden controls.

"Here—what's this?" Eddie exclaimed suddenly, pointing out a glinting object in a dark corner of the laboratory.

Shelton examined it closely, looking over his shoulder. The object he had located seemed to be a mounted and hooded lens, a highly polished glass of about two inches diameter with its mounting attached rigidly to the wall.

"Never saw that before," Shelton stated with conviction. "And—why—it looks like an objective such as those used in the latest automatic television transmitters."

"Just what it is," Eddie grunted. He picked up a pinch bar from a nearby tool rack and drove its end through the glass as he spoke the words.

A violent wrench tore the thing loose and broke away a section of the thin plastered wall. There, in the cleverly concealed cavity behind, was revealed the mechanism of the radio "eye." Somewhere, someone bad been watching their every move. And abruptly the thrashings of the robot ceased and its upper portion again became visible.

*   *   *   *   *

"Well," said David Shelton. "Well! Looks as if you're right, young man. I'm astonished." His watery eyes looked sheepishly over the rims of his glasses.

Lina watched their every move. She seemed to sense the seriousness of the situation far more than did her father.

Then the lights went out. It had darkened to night outside and the blackness and silence in the laboratory was like that of a tomb.

"They've cut the wires," Eddie whispered hoarsely. "Got any weapons here, Shelton?"

"Yes. A couple of automatics. I'll get them." The scientist was no coward, anyway. His whispered words came calmly through the silence.

Eddie heard him shuffle a few steps and fumble with a drawer of the desk. In a moment the cold hard butt of a pistol was thrust into his hand. It had a comforting feel.

"Stay here with Lina," he commanded. "I'll go out and see if I can find them. This looks nasty to me."

"No," came the girl's voice, "I'm going too."

"You are not," Eddie hissed. "You'll stay here or I'll know the reason. It's dark as a pocket outside and my eyes are as good as theirs. I'll get 'em if they're around here. You hear me?"

"Yes," she whispered meekly.

Edward Vail, only that morning headed for rest and quiet, was now out in the night, stalking an unknown and vicious enemy. And—for what? As he asked himself the question, the smile of Lina seemed to answer him from the blackness. Cherchez la femme! He was getting dotty as he neared his thirties. Maybe it was the hard work that had affected his mind.

*　　*　　*　　*　　*

The black hulk of the old house loomed against the scarcely less dark sky. There was no moon, and in only one tiny portion of the heavens were the stars visible. Mighty few of them at that. The swish-swish of the surf came to his ears faintly. Or was it someone creeping along the wall of the house? He held his breath and waited.

They wouldn't use the robots at night. Couldn't follow their movements in the teleview, if such an attachment had been built into their control transmitter. No, the devils would be here in person.

A muttered Teutonic curse sounded close at hand. That wouldn't be Carlos. God! Were the heinies mixed up in this thing? Just like 'em to be swiping a new war machine; but hadn't they gotten enough in 1944? Without warning he was catapulted from his feet by the impact of a heavy body. He struck the ground so violently that the pistol was jarred from his hand. Disarmed before the fight had started!

Then he was rolling over and over, battling desperately with an assailant who was much larger and heavier than himself. He was dazed and weakened from his initial dive to the hard ground. All rules of boxing and wrestling were forgotten. Biting, kicking, gouging, all were the same to this silent and powerful antagonist. It was catch-as-catch-can in the darkness, and mostly the other fellow could and did. He had a grip like the clamp of a robot. Trying to dig out one of his eyes? Eddie saw stars—and lashed out with all his might, his flying fists playing a tattoo on the others ribs. Short arm jabs that brought grunts of agony from his big assailant. Try to blind him, would he?

Eddie somehow managed to get on top; his clutching fingers found the other's collar. Then he let loose with terrific rights and lefts that smacked home to head and face. Those outlanders don't like the good old American fist, and Eddie had room to bring them in from way back, now. The fellow had ceased struggling and Eddie's hands were getting slippery. Blood! Must be, for the stuff was warm and sticky. He rested for a moment, breathing heavily. The other was quiet beneath him—knocked cold. He staggered to his feet triumphantly; wondered how many more of them there were.

*   *   *   *   *

He looked around in the darkness, straining his eyes in vain to pierce its thick veil. There was a glimmer of light over there, through a window. The laboratory! The light flickered a second and vanished. A cold fear gripped him and he stumbled through the grounds blindly, finally colliding painfully with the brick wall. He felt his way toward the door, or where he thought it should be.

He dared not call out for fear the others would hear. Where was that damned door? He rested again and listened. Not a sound was to be heard from within or without. He clawed his way frantically along the unsympathetic wall. It was a mile wide, that laboratory of Shelton's. Ah—at last! Weakly, he staggered within.

"Lina!" he whispered, "Lina! Shelton!"

There was no reply. He fumbled for a match. Funny how slowly his mind worked ... thoughts coming jerkily like a sound film running at quarter speed ... fingers shaking so he could scarcely strike a light. The flare showed the laboratory empty of human beings ... Lina gone ... that crazy robot ... quiet now, and visible ... but grinning at him ... then darkness....

*   *   *   *   *

What a headache! Eddie rolled over and groaned. Astounded by the hardness of his bed and the stiffness of his joints, he roused to instant wakefulness; sat up and stared. Where the devil was he? The laboratory—Shelton's—Lina. He jumped to his feet. Dawn was breaking and its first faint radiance lighted the robot with eery shifting colors. He berated himself: he'd passed out.

He dashed through the door and made a wild circuit of the grounds. Empty! No—there was his automatic, where it had fallen. Blood stains on the grass showed where the encounter had taken place last night. Must have smashed the Dutchman's nose. But he was gone. Everybody was gone. He rushed into the house and from room to room, upstairs and down. The place was deserted.

This was something to think about. Not an automobile around, no neighbors, not even a telephone. When Shelton went into seclusion, he did it thoroughly. Eddie returned to the laboratory and hunched himself in the scientist's chair. Maybe he could think better here.

They had Shelton and his daughter, all right. Kidnapped them. There was probably some detail of his discovery they couldn't dope out, and had decided to force him into telling them. The devils would use Lina's safety as a threat to force him into anything. Horrible, that thought. And Carlos already had made advances to her.

Startled by a sharp click, he turned around. The robot was whirring into life. Fast workers, whoever Shelton's enemies were, and up early! He found the pinch bar with which he had wrecked the television apparatus and, with a few mighty blows, destroyed the antenna and headpiece of the mechanical man. They'd not pull off any devilment with this one, anyway.

A wave meter on one of the benches attracted his attention and he twirled its knob. It gave strong indication at one and a half meters. The wave length of their control transmitter! If only he could find—but there it was: a direction finder. Hastily, he lighted its tubes and tuned to the frequency shown by the meter. He rotated the loop over the compass dial and carefully noted maximum and minimum signals. He had a line on the transmitter! And it must be close by, for the intensity of the carrier wave was tremendous.

*   *   *   *   *

Slipping the automatic into his pocket, he left the laboratory and struck out through the underbrush in the direction Carlos had taken the day before. Fighting his way through the tangled shrubbery, he kept his eyes constantly on the needle of the magnetic compass he had wrenched from the direction finder. It was tough going through the thicket, and just as bad across a swampy clearing where he was mired to the knees before he got across. Up the hill and into the woods he forged, keeping doggedly to the direction he had determined. This was rough country, less than a hundred miles from New York but uncultivated and unsettled excepting for the few summer places along the shore. He'd heard that these backwoods were infested with rum-runners and hijackers, a cutthroat gang.

There was a cabin off there through the trees, almost on the line he was following. Must be what he was looking for. He advanced cautiously, creeping stealthily from tree to tree.

Voices came to his ears, and the throb of a motor-generator. It was the place, all right. He crept closer, and, circling the house, saw that an almost impassable road led to it from the rear. A heavy limousine was parked there in the trees, and another car, a yellow roadster—his own. A feeling of grim satisfaction was quickly dispelled by the sound of a familiar humming. Within a foot of his ear, it seemed to be, and instinctively he ducked.

Click! A powerful clamp had fastened itself to his wrist. One of Shelton's invisible robots! He struck blindly at the unseen monster and was rewarded by a shooting pain up his wrist as one of his knuckles was driven backward by the impact with the hard metal. Bands of writhing metal encompassed his body, pinning his arms to his side and lifting him bodily from the ground. There he hung, kicking and struggling in mid-air, supported by nothing he could see. He closed his eyes and felt of the thing that held him. Cold, hard metal it was—implacable and unyielding.

Clank, clank. The monster was walking with long, jerky strides. The pressure against his ribs brought a gasp of agony from his lips. Each jarring step was an individual and excruciating torture. His breath was cut off by the relentless constriction of one of the tentacles which now encircled his neck. It wouldn't be long now.

*   *   *   *   *

Then, when everything had turned black and he had given up hope, he was dumped unceremoniously on the hard floor of the cabin. A harsh laugh greeted him as he struggled weakly to his knees.

"Thought you could put one over on Al Cadorna, did you?" a voice rasped.

The room spun round as he tried to regain his feet. A mist swam before his eyes. Al Cadorna! The most picturesque figure in gangland. Credited with a dozen killings and with ill-gotten wealth untold, this leader of the underworld openly boasted that the police had never gotten anything on him. And they hadn't. So it was a criminal who had laid hands on Shelton's robots, not a foreign spy. Worse and worse. He thought of what they might be able to do with these invisible mechanical things: make gunmen out of them; safe blowers; house breakers. Why, society would be at their mercy; banks defenceless; the mints, even—

"Stand up on your pins, you worm! Let's have a look at you!" The muzzle of an automatic was thrust in his abdomen, prodding insistently. Things stabilized in the room and he looked up into the cruelest face he had ever seen, and recognizable from the many pictures which had appeared in the yellow press.

Eddie took in the surroundings at a glance. He was in a low-ceilinged room that was almost unfurnished. In one corner there was a replica of Shelton's robot control, teleview disc and all. Carlos had just pulled the switch and the robot was taking visible form. The man who prodded him with the automatic was Cadorna, no doubt of that. His evil leer and yellow eyes marked him at once. The other occupant of the room was a big square-built man with a patch over one eye and strips of adhesive tape across his nose—his antagonist of the night before. Must have sneaked off after he came to; it was safer to send one of the robots after the *verdammt Amerikaner*. Eddie restrained a chuckle at the thought.

"Nothing to laugh at, kid!" Cadorna snarled. "You're goin' for a nice long ride pretty quick. Know that?"

Eddie's head was clearing rapidly, but he pretended to sway on his feet. Lina and her father were not in sight. If only he could spar for a little time.

"What's the idea?" he asked. "Haven't you guys got enough?"

"That's our business. We know what we're doin', and when you butted in you just signed your own papers. Dead men don't talk, you know, kid!"

*   *   *   *   *

There was a door at the other side of the room. If only he could see whether Lina was in there; whether she was alive.

"Tie him up, Gus!" Cadorna kept the pistol pressed into the pit of Eddie's stomach as he gave the order. "Hands and feet—and make it a good job, you wiener."

Eddie shouted then. "Lina!" Resistance was useless, but it would give him some satisfaction to know she still lived even though Cadorna pulled that trigger in the next instant. No reply came from beyond that door.

"So!" Cadorna grinned maliciously. "Another victim! Carlos first, then you, and now—Al Cadorna. If you're worrying about her, kid, you needn't. She'll be perfectly safe with me."

Eddie's roar of rage shook the rafters. Heedless of consequences, he brought his knee up suddenly and violently. Cadorna sank to the floor with a groan, his pistol clattering harmlessly on the rough planks. In a flash Eddie retrieved it, dropping behind the prostrate form of the stricken gangster. Gus had fired and missed. Now he dared not shoot for fear of hitting his chief. Eddie's gun spat fire and the big German clapped his hands over his heart, his good eye widening in surprise. Then he reeled and pitched forward on his face. A feminine cry sounded from the adjoining room and Eddie's heart skipped a beat when he heard it.

Carlos was padding across the floor, trying to get into a position where he could fire without endangering Cadorna. Eddie swung his pistol around and pulled the trigger. A miss! He fired again, but too late. Fingers of steel had gripped his wrist and the king of gangland rolled over on him, twisting the gun from his hand. Clubbed now, the pistol was raised high over that distorted, malicious face. Eddie tried to twist away from under the blow as it started its downward swing, then a thousand steam hammers hit him all at once and ... blackness....

*   *   *   *   *

Something was pounding insistently at the doors of his consciousness. He must pull himself together! They'd left him for dead and he was—almost. But voices as loud and raucous as those would waken the dead. He groaned with pain when he attempted to move his head.

"That for you, you rat." It was Cadorna's voice. "Try to take my woman, will you?"

The pounding resolved itself into the angry barking of an automatic. Someone squealed with mortal agony. Eddie opened his eyes cautiously and saw that the room was full of people. The pungent odor of burned powder assailed his nostrils. There was Cadorna and Carlos, David Shelton and Lina. An undersized, dapper youth stood over the body of the big German, his hands outstretched before his horror-stricken face. A moment he stood thus, like a statue. Then his knees gave way beneath him and he crumpled into a grotesque heap beside the man who had been called Gus. Such was the manner of Cadorna's dealing with those who displeased him.

The door to the adjoining room was open. Lina and her father had been kept in there, with the little thug as their guard. Evidently Cadorna had caught him trying to force his attentions on the girl. Good thing he'd killed him.

Lina was sobbing and the sound brought increased agony to the helpless Eddie. He lay still where they had placed him, beside the table which supported the robot control apparatus. His cheek was against the floor and he saw that a little pool of blood was forming there, blood drawn by the butt of Cadorna's pistol when it contacted with his skull. He was bound hand and foot. They hadn't thought him dead, after all. Keeping him for that ride and a watery grave. Couldn't afford to leave his body around where it might be found.

"What are you going to do with us?" Shelton was asking, his voice bravely defiant. Game old sport at that, he was.

"Don't fret over your daughter. Al Cadorna's her protector now, and she'll be taken care of better'n she's ever been. But you—that's somethin' else again. First off, you're goin' to give Carlos the dope on these trick metals in your machines. He couldn't analyze 'em, or whatever you call it. Then you're goin' to have a nice long ride with your friend over there."

"You'll go to the chair for this, Cadorna. And I'll never tell you the secret of the alloys."

"Tell him, Dad," Lina was crying. "He'll let us go if you do."

"The hell I will, girlie. What I said, goes. We'll make him talk first, too," Cadorna snarled.

"Never!" Shelton shouted.

*   *   *   *   *

Lina had seen Eddie and, with a little cry, she bounded across the room. Carlos was after her like a panther.

"Hands off that dame!" Cadorna yelled. "Let her cry over the boy friend if she wants to. Won't do her any good. You get busy and set one of the tin soldiers goin'. Make the old buzzard talk."

Carlos muttered sullenly as he started the motor-generator. Give him a chance and he'd knife Cadorna in the back—for Lina.

The girl was kneeling at Eddie's side now, examining his bleeding scalp. He opened one eye and gazed at her solemnly, pursing his lips in a warning to silence. She caught her breath and nodded in understanding.

Cadorna was shouting like a madman. "Keep the damn thing so I can see it, you spig! They make me bug-house when you blink 'em off. Besides, I don't trust you."

The bold Cadorna was afraid of something he couldn't see! An idea flashed across Eddie's quickening mind. But he was helpless—bound so tightly that the cords cut his wrists.

One of the robots was clanking across the room. Lina looked up in momentary terror and Eddie saw her eyes stray over the table top where Carlos was working.

"Want to grab the old one?" the Chilean called.

"Yes. Pick him up and squeeze him till his ribs crack. He'll talk."

Lina let a little moan escape her lips. Eddie was watching as the iron monster approached the scientist and flung its tentacles around his madly struggling form. Lina was fussing with him, trying to turn him over. Cadorna's back was to them, his face thrust into that of Shelton, who was fighting desperately to avoid the crushing grip of the robot.

"Give him a squeeze, Carlos."

*   *   *   *   *

Shelton's yell brought another low moan from the girl's set lips. She was working furiously at Eddie's bonds. Lord, she had a knife! Good girl! Must have found it on the table. His hands were free and he wriggled his fingers to bring them to life. Then his feet. He was able to move. Lina whispered in his ear.

"All right?" she asked anxiously.

"Yes," he whispered. Somehow their lips touched and Eddie felt his heart pound at his temples. New life came to him with a rush of exaltation.

Shelton was crying out in pain and Lina sprang to her feet. "You beast!" she shouted at Cadorna. "Let him go."

Then she was across the room, tearing at the unyielding metal bands that pinioned her father and slowly crushed him. Cadorna laughed mirthlessly.

"Tell him to give me the dope," he retorted. "Then I'll let him go—for a while."

Shelton's head hung on his chest, rolling weakly from side to side. Eddie doubted whether he could speak if he wished to. The Chilean was working at the controls, increasing the tension of those terrible tentacles. Eddie raised himself to his knees, watching Cadorna narrowly. He fingered the knife Lina had used in freeing him. No, he couldn't use that. The Chilean would cry out and queer everything. He laid it on the floor, within easy reach.

Cadorna was cursing now, first Shelton and then the girl. His rage was maniacal. "Another notch!" he bellowed.

Eddie rose silently and clamped his fingers on the Chilean's windpipe. Lina's eyes widened as she saw. She did everything in her power to keep Cadorna's attention occupied as Eddie sunk those fingers into Carlos' throat. The Chilean's eyes popped from his head as he struggled furiously to tear away the steel-sinewed hand that had stopped off his breath. Death was staring him in the face, and he could not cry out. His strength left suddenly as the fingers dug in deeper, and Eddie shook him as he would a rat. In a surprisingly short time he had slumped to the floor, and not until his squirmings ceased did Eddie loose that awful grip.

"Another notch, you spiggoty!"

                    *   *   *   *   *

Eddie bent over the controls. Lina's pleadings mingled with the curses of Cadorna. She was cajoling now—telling the brute she'd go with him gladly if only he'd free her father; promising anything, everything, in the desperate attempt to keep him from discovering that his last henchman was out of the picture. But her words served only to spur Eddie to swifter action. He twirled the knobs of the dual control. The second robot was fading from view. He'd give Cadorna a dose of the thing he really feared. He eased off a little on the other control, releasing the pressure on poor Shelton's ribs as much as he dared.

The position indicator of the second robot moved slightly as Eddie started the invisible monster toward the yelling gangster. He watched the screen closely. It was quite a trick, at that, controlling these things you couldn't see. All you had to go by were these sketchy representations in the teleview; tiny flecks of light that outlined the various movable members of the robot.

"Eddie!" Lina screamed suddenly. "Look out!"

But he had seen Cadorna wheel around as he watched his image on the screen. At that moment a tentacle was writhing its way around his thick neck. A bullet whistled past Eddie's ear and buried itself harmlessly in the wall.

Then from the blasphemous mouth of the king of gangland there came a shriek of awful fear. The tightening tentacle shut it off in a choking gurgle. Cadorna was captured at last—by a monster he could not see, a monster that struck terror to his craven soul.

It was the work of but a moment to free David Shelton from the grip of the other robot. The tortured man tottered into Lina's arms for support.

Eddie played with Cadorna now, releasing the grip from his throat and pinioning his arms instead. With rapid fingers he manipulated the controls until the screaming gangster was raised high in the air by the unseen arms of the robot.

"Another notch, Al," he chortled.

Cadorna yelled anew as the clamps tightened, "For God's sake, kid, quit it! Let me down. I'll do anything you say."

"Yeah?" Eddie moved one of the rheostat knobs a trifle.

The prince of racketeers was whimpering now, like a baby. The sharp snap of a rib punctured his outcries.

"Another notch," said Eddie grimly.

But the king of the underworld had fainted.

*   *   *   *   *

An hour later Eddie Vail surveyed the scene complacently. Lina had washed the blood from his head and face and bandaged his wound. Luckily, Cardorna's blow had been a glancing one. The girl was fussing over her father, now, and the scientist was on the point of resenting her attentions; swore he could take care of himself; he wasn't a baby. Carlos and his chief were trussed up like mummies, and had been snarling at each other ever since the Chilean recovered his senses, each blaming the other for their predicament. The robots stood motionless by the wall.

This would be a big haul for the police. Plenty of evidence to send Cadorna to the chair now. The murder of Butch Collins, the undersized thug, had been witnessed by three of them. No, four: Carlos would squeal. He was that kind. There would be rejoicing in the underworld too, for Cadorna had many enemies. They'd be killing each other off in droves though, for the leaders of rival gangs would be battling for his place.

"Guess we'll have to dump them in the limousine," he remarked to Shelton. "Drive them to the nearest town and turn them over to the authorities."

"Yes. Then they can come back for the bodies of the other two." Shelton grimaced as he contemplated the sprawled figures.

"What about your robots?" Eddie asked.

"Why, I'll go ahead with my original plans, of course." The scientist looked surprised.

"Dad!" Lina turned beseeching eyes on Eddie and his heart performed amazingly as he looked into their depths.

"And why not?" asked her father dolefully. "They'll insure the peace of the world. They'll—"

"Listen, Mr. Shelton," Eddie interrupted. "If you'll think a little you'll realize that they'll do no such thing. Has any new and terrible engine of destruction ever accomplished that result? No—the enemy always finds a way of combating the new weapon and of devising another still more terrible. You've discovered a marvelous thing, but its value is quite problematical."

"How can they ever combat a thing they cannot see?"

"Easily. Why, I could devise a teleview attachment in two days that would make them visible. Photo-electric cells are capable of detecting ultra-violet light as you well know. Radium glows under its rays. Why not coat a teleview screen with some radio-active material?"

*   *   *   *   *

Shelton frowned thoughtfully. "You're right. Vail," he said, after a moment of silence; "absolutely right. It was only a dream."

With dragging feet he walked to the transmitter, his expression grim in the realization of failure. He started the motor-generator with a gesture of finality.

"What are you going to do?" Eddie asked fearfully.

"Watch me! At least I can demonstrate another phase of the basic principle I have discovered."

The motors of both robots whirred.

"Don't!" Cadorna wailed. "For God's sake, don't blink 'em out!"

Carlos cursed his chief for a coward.

Shelton was talking rapidly as he manipulated the controls. Instead of building up the wave motion to the frequency of invisible light he was reducing it. Past the other end of the spectrum and into the infra-red. The heat ray! Both monsters were changing color as he marched them through the door and into the open. But now they glowed with a visible red that rapidly intensified to the dazzling whiteness of intense heat. Cadorna babbled in superstitious terror. Then, in an instant, both mechanisms were reduced to shapeless blobs of molten metal. Lina clapped her hands gleefully.

Shelton looked up with enthusiasm once more shining in his face. "Vail, my boy," he said, "we can find some use for that in industry. Let the next war take care of itself."

"You bet!" Eddie was lost in contemplation of the girl—the flush of pleasure that came at her father's words; the shining eyes.

"Then you'll leave the old place down here?" she asked eagerly.

"Yes, as soon as we get rid of these crooks and the other robot. Vail is to spend the rest of his vacation with us, too—if he will."

Would he? Eddie gazed at the girl in rapt admiration and with an inward thrill over his astounding good fortune. Her eyes dropped before the intensity in his and her flush heightened.

David Shelton was wiping his glasses and peering at them with an understanding smile. Good sport, Shelton—and in some ways as wise as they made them. Eddie waited breathlessly for the girl to speak.

"Oh, that's wonderful, Dad," she approved; "and I'm sure that Mr. Vail will agree."

She turned those glorious eyes on Eddie once more and her inquiring smile spoke volumes. He opened his mouth to accept the invitation but the words would not come. He could only nod his head vigorously like an abashed schoolboy.

Some vacation!

The Moon Weed

Originally Published In *Astounding Stories*,
August 1931

THE MOON WEED

Hobart Madison pursed his lips in a whistle of incredulous surprise as he regarded the object that lay in the palm of his hand. An ordinary pebble, it seemed to be, but a pebble in which a strange fire smouldered and showed itself here and there through the dull surface.

"Would you mind repeating what you just said, Van?" he asked.

"You heard me the first time. I say that that's a diamond and that it came from the moon." Carl Vanderventer glared at his friend in resentment of his doubting tone.

"Mean to tell me you've been there? To the moon?"

"Certainly not. I'm not a Jules Verne adventurer. But I'm telling you that stone is a diamond of the first water and that it came from the moon. Weighs over a hundred carats, too. You can have it appraised yourself if you think I'm kidding you."

Bart Madison laughed. "Don't get sore, Van," he said. "I'm not doubting your word. But Lord, man—the thing's so incredible! It takes a little time to soak in. And you say there are more?"

"Sure. This one's the largest of five I've found so far. And there's other stuff, too. Wait till you see. Fossils, beetles and things. I tell you, Bart, the moon was inhabited at one time. I've the evidence and I want you to be the first to see it." The eyes of the young scientist shone with excitement as he saw that his friend was roused to intense interest.

"So that's what all your experimenting has been aimed at. No wonder it cost so much."

"Yes, and you've been a brick for financing me. Never asked a question, either. But Bart, it'll all come back to you now. Know how much that stone's worth?"

"Plenty, I guess. But, forget about the financing and all that. Where's this laboratory of yours?" Madison had pushed his chair back from his desk and was reaching for his hat.

"Over in the Ramapo Mountains, not far from Tuxedo. I'll have you there in two hours. Sure you can spare the time to go out there now?" Vanderventer was enthusiastically eager.

"Spare the time? You just try and keep me from going!"

Neither of them noticed the sinister figure that lurked outside the door which led into the adjoining office. They chattered excitedly as they passed into the outer hall and made for the elevator.

*   *   *   *   *

Vanderventer's laboratory was a small domed structure set in a clearing atop the mountain and well hidden from the winding road which was the only means of approach. Though Bart Madison, who had inherited his father's prosperous brokerage business, had financed his friend's research work ever since the two left college, this was his first visit to the secluded workshop, and its wealth of equipment was revealed to him as a complete surprise. He had always thought of Van's experiments as something beyond his ken; something uncanny and mysterious. Now he was convinced.

The most prominent single piece of apparatus in the laboratory was a twelve-inch reflecting telescope which reared its latticed framework to a slit in the dome overhead. Paralleling its axis and secured to the same equatorial mounting was a shining tube of copper which bristled with handwheels and levers and was connected by heavy insulated cables to an amazing array of electrical machinery that occupied an entire side of the single room.

"Regular young observatory you've got here, Van," Bart commented when he had taken all this in in one sweeping glance of appraisal.

"Yeah, and then some. Not another like it in the world." Van was busying himself with the controls of his electrical equipment, and a powerful motor-generator started up with a click and a whirr as he closed a starting switch.

Madison watched in silence as the swift-fingered scientist fussed with the complicated adjustments of the apparatus and then turned to the massive concrete pedestal on which his telescope was mounted. At his touch of a button the instrument swung over on its polar axis to a new position. The slit in the dome was opened to the afternoon sky, revealing the lunar disc in its daytime faintness.

"You can see it just as well in daylight?" Bart asked as his friend peered through the eyepiece of the telescope and continued his adjustments.

"Sure, the surface is just as bright as at night. Doesn't seem so to your eye, but it's different through the telescope. Here, take a look."

*   *   *   *   *

Bart squinted through the eyepiece and saw a huge crater with a shadowed spire in its center. Like a shell hole in soft earth it appeared—a great splash that had congealed immediately it was made. The cross-hairs of the eyepiece were centered on a small circular shadow near its inner rim.

"That," Van was saying, "is a prominent crater near the Mare Nubium. The spot under the cross-hairs is that from which I have obtained the diamonds—and other things. Watch this now, Bart."

The young broker straightened up and saw that his friend was removing the cover from a crystal bowl that was attached to the lower end of the copper tube that pointed to the heavens at the same ascension and declination as the telescope. The air of the room vibrated to a strange energy when he closed a switch that lighted a dozen vacuum tubes in the apparatus that lined the wall.

"You say you bring the stuff here with a light ray?" he asked.

"No, I said with the speed of light. This tube projects a ray of vibrations—like directional radio, you know—and this ray has a component that disintegrates the object it strikes and brings it back to us as dissociated protons and electrons which are reassembled in the original form and structure in this crystal bowl. Watch."

A misty brilliance filled the bowl's interior. Intangible shadowy forms seemed to be taking shape within a swirling maze of ethereal light that hummed and crackled with astounding vigor. Then, abruptly, the apparatus was silent and the light gone, revealing an odd object that had taken form in the bowl.

"A starfish!" Bart gasped.

"Yeah, and fossilized." Van handed it to him and he took it in his fingers gingerly as if expecting it to burn them.

*　　*　　*　　*　　*

The thing was undoubtedly a starfish, and of light, spongy stone. Its color was a pale blue and the ambulacral suckers were clearly discernible on all five rays.

"Lord! You're sure this is from the moon?" Bart turned the starfish over in his hand and gazed stupidly at his friend.

"Certainly, you nut. Think I had it up my sleeve? But here, watch again, there's something else."

The crackling, misty light again filled the bowl.

"Suppose," Bart ventured, "you bring in something large—big as a house, let's say. What would it do to your machine?"

"Can't. The ray'll only pick up stuff that'll enter the bowl. Look—here's the next arrival."

The mysterious light died down and the scientist picked up the second object with trembling fingers. It was a knife of beautiful workmanship, fashioned from obsidian and obviously the work of human hands.

"There! Didn't I tell you?" Van gloated. "Guess that shows there were living beings on the moon."

He made minute changes in the adjustment of his marvelous instrument and Bart watched in dazed astonishment as object after object materialized before their eyes. There were fragments of strange minerals; more fossils, marine life, mostly; a roughly beaten silver plate; three diamonds, none of which was as large as what Van had taken to New York, but all of considerable value.

"This'll be something for the papers, Van!" Bart Madison was visioning the fame that was to come to his friend.

"Yeah, all but the diamonds."

*　　*　　*　　*　　*

"All but the diamonds is right!"

These words were spoken by a sarcastic voice, chill as an icicle, that came from the open door. They wheeled to look into the muzzles of two automatic pistols that were trained on them by a stocky individual who faced them with a twisted, knowing grin.

"Danny Kelly!" Bart gasped, raising his hands slowly to the level of his shoulders. He knew the ex-army captain was a dead shot with the service pistol, and a desperate man since his disgrace and forced resignation. "What's the big idea?" he demanded.

"You don't need to ask. Refused me a loan this morning, didn't you? Now I'm getting it this way." Kelly turned savagely on Van, prodding his ribs with a pistol. "Get 'em up, you!" he snapped.

Van had been slow in raising his hands, gaping in stupefied amazement at the intruder. Now he reached for the ceiling without delay.

"You'll serve time for this, Danny!" Bart shouted.

"Shut up! I know what I'm doing. And back up, too—where— no, the other door." Kelly was forcing him toward the door of the cellar at the point of one pistol as he kept Van covered with the other.

Bart clenched his fist and brought it down in a sudden sweeping blow that raked Kelly's cheek and ear with stunning force. But the gunman recovered in a flash, dropped the muzzle of his pistol and pulled the trigger. Drilled through the thigh, Bart staggered through the open door and fell the length of the stairs into the darkness of the cellar. Kelly laughed evilly as he slammed the door and turned the key.

"Hold it, you!" he snarled as he swung on Van who had dropped his hands and crouched for a spring. "If I drill you, it won't be through the leg. I'll take those diamonds now."

*   *   *   *   *

He pocketed one of his pistols, and, keeping the other pressed to the pit of Van's stomach, went through his pockets. Then he added those on the tray by the crystal bowl to the collection, and transferred the entire lot to his own pocket.

"Now, you clever engineer," he grinned, "we'll just operate this trick machine of yours for a while and collect some more. Hop to it!" He watched narrowly as Van stretched his fingers to the controls. "No monkey business, either," he grated; "you'll not change a single adjustment. I've been listening to you and I know the clock of the telescope is keeping the ray trained on the same spot. You just operate the ray and nothing else. Get me?"

Van did not think it expedient to tell him of the drift caused by inaccuracies in the clock and perturbations of the moon's motion. He was playing for time, trying to plan a course of action.

"There may not be any more diamonds," he offered as he tripped the release of the ray.

"Oh, there'll be more. Don't try to kid me."

An irregular block of quartz materialized in the bowl and Kelly tossed it to the floor in savage disgust. Then a small diamond, very small; but he pocketed it nevertheless. The next object was a strange one—a dried seed pod about six inches in length and of brilliant red color. The ray had shifted to a new position on the lunar surface. Another and another of the strange legumes followed, one of them bursting open and scattering its contents, bright red like the enclosing pod to rattle over the floor like tiny glass beads. Kelly snorted his disgust.

"Still some sort of vegetation out there," Van muttered. The eternal scientist in the man could not be downed by a mere hold-up.

"Can the chatter!" Kelly snarled as the crystal bowl gave up another of the useless pods and still another. He gathered up the evidence of lunar vegetation, a half dozen of the pods, and threw them through the open doorway with a savage gesture. "You trying to put one over on me?" he bellowed.

"How can I?" Van retorted mildly. "I haven't touched a handwheel." He was wondering vaguely whether this lunar seed would grow in earthly soil; what sort of a plant it would produce under the new environment.

Kelly was becoming nervous now. It seemed that little was to be gained by hanging around this crazy man's laboratory. He had a sizable fortune in rough stones already. That big one alone, when properly cut into smaller stones, would make him independent. Maybe there weren't any more, anyway. And the longer he stayed the greater chance there was of getting caught.

The advent of another of the pods decided him. A quick blow with the butt of his pistol stretched Van on the floor and Kelly fled the scene.

*   *   *   *   *

Bart was pounding furiously on the cellar door when Van first took hazy note of his surroundings. Several uncertain minutes passed before he was able to stagger across the room and release his friend.

"Where is he?" Bart demanded, swaying on his feet and blinking in the sudden light.

"Gone. Socked me and beat it with the diamonds." Van was mopping the blood from his eyes with a handkerchief. "Are you hit bad?" he inquired.

"No, just a flesh wound. Hurts like the devil, though. How about yourself?" Bart limped to his side and sighed with relief when he examined his bleeding scalp. "Not so bad yourself, old man. Where's your first aid kit?"

Van was still somewhat dazed and merely pointed to the cabinet. "Fine pair we turned out to be!" he grumbled after his head had cleared a bit under Bart's vigorous cleansing of the cut on his temple. "Here we stood, meek as a couple of lambs, and let that guy get away with murder."

"Yeah, but those forty-fives made the difference. Ouch!" Bart winced as his friend poured fresh iodine over the wound in his leg. "Have a heart, will you?"

They were startled into silence by a hoarse, strangled scream that came from outside the laboratory. "Help! Help!" someone repeated in a panicky voice—a voice which at once ended on a gurgled note of despair.

"It's Kelly!" Bart whispered. "He's come back. Something's happened to him." He started for the open door.

"Wait a minute. It may be a trick to get us outside where he can pop us off."

"No, it isn't. For God's sake, look!" Bart had reached the door and was pointing at the ground with shaking forefinger.

*   *   *   *   *

The entire clearing seemed to be alive with wriggling things—long rubbery tentacles that crawled along the ground, reaching curling ends high in the air and had even started climbing the trees at the edge of the clearing. Blood red they were, and partially transparent in the light of the setting sun; growing things, attached by their thick ends to swelling mounds of red that seemed anchored to the ground. Translucent stalks rose from the mounds and sprouted huge buds that burst and blossomed into flaming flowers a foot in diameter, then withered and went to seed in a moment of time. But always the weaving tendrils shot forth with lightning speed, reaching and feeling their uncanny way along the ground and over tree stumps into the woods. One of them emerged from a hollow stump with its slender end coiled around the tiny body of a chattering gray squirrel.

"The moon flowers!" Van cried.

"What do you mean—moon flowers?"

"Dried seed pods. They came over into the bowl, and Kelly threw them out. Now look at the damned things. They're alive!"

Kelly's voice came to them once more from behind the barrier of rapidly growing vegetation. "Help!" he screeched. "I'll give back the diamonds—anything! Only get me away from the things!"

"Ought to let 'em get him," Van growled.

Bart shivered. "Too horrible, Van. Got an ax or anything?"

"There's a hatchet around back. Maybe we can—"

*   *   *   *   *

But the young broker had scuttled around the corner of the building and Van looked after him anxiously. The vile red tendrils were reaching for the east wall of the laboratory, and he saw that their inner surfaces were covered with tiny suckers like those on the arms of a devil-fish. Carnivorous plants, undoubtedly, these awful half-animal, half-vegetable things whose seed had been transported across a quarter million miles of space. Man eaters! Deadly, and growing with incredible speed. Even the short-lived flowers were fearsome, as they opened their scarlet pansy-like faces and stared a moment before they folded up and shriveled into the seed cases like those that had materialized in the crystal bowl.

Then he noticed that the pods were opening and spreading more of the terrible seed. Nothing could stop this weird growth, now. It would cover the country like a sea of flaming horror, overcoming and devouring every living thing. Cold fear clutched at Van as he realized the enormity of the calamity that had come to the earth.

Bart was skirting the edge of the clearing with the hatchet in his hand, and Van tried to call out to him, to warn him. But his voice caught in his throat, and instead he ran to his assistance, circling the spreading menace to get around behind where Kelly was still shouting. Damn Kelly anyway! This never would have happened if he hadn't come on the scene!

Kelly was in the woods, wedged into the crotch of a tree and striking wildly at the clutching tendrils with his clubbed pistol. They mashed easily and dripping red, but were not to be deterred from their ghastly purpose. Kelly's time would have indeed been short had not his erstwhile victims come to the rescue. One of the thickest of the twining things encircled his body and had him pinned to the tree. His breath was coming in gasps as its tightening coils increased their pressure. His coarse features were livid and his eyes bulged from their sockets.

Bart hacked and hacked at the rubbery growth until he had him free; jerked him from his perch, blubbering and whining like a schoolboy. His shirt had been torn from his breast and they saw a great red welt where the blood had been drawn through the pores by those terrible suckers.

"Look out, Bart!" Van shouted.

*   *   *   *   *

Another of the creeping things had come through the underbrush and was wrapping its coils around Bart's ankle. Another and another wriggled through, and soon they were battling for their own freedom. Kelly staggered off into the woods and went crashing down the hill, leaving them to take care of themselves as best they might.

The stench of the viscous liquid that oozed from the injured tendrils was nauseous; it had something of a soporific effect; and the two friends found themselves fighting the terror in a growing mist of red that blinded and confused them. Then, miraculously, they were free and Van assisted Bart as they ran through the forest. When they reached the road, weak and out of breath, they were just in time to see Kelly's roadster vanish around the bend.

"Yeah, he'd give back the diamonds—the swine!" Van muttered vindictively. Then, shrugging his shoulders, "Well, they won't be much good to him, anyway. Wouldn't be any good to us either, as far as that goes."

"What do you mean? Aren't they real?" Bart was raising himself painfully into the seat of Van's car, his wounded leg suddenly very much in the way.

"Sure they're real. But don't you realize what this thing means—this ungodly growth that's started?"

"Why—why, no. You mean it'll keep on growing?"

"And how! Those inner stalks drop a new batch of seeds every five minutes or so. Presto!—a flock of new plants spring up ten feet from the first; dozens of them for every pod that drops. You know how geometrical progression works out. They'll cover the whole country—the whole world. Lord!"

"Man alive, this is terrible! I hadn't thought of that before. What'll we do?"

"Yeah, that's the question: what can we do?" Van started his motor and jerked the car to the road. "First off, we're going to get away from here—fast!"

Bart gripped his arm as he shifted into second gear. "Look, Van!" he babbled. "They're out of the woods already. Loose! The red snakes are loose from their stalks. They're alive, I tell you!"

It was true. Several of the slimy red things were wriggling their way over the macadam like great earthworms, but moving with the speed of hurrying pedestrians. Free, and untrammeled by the roots and stems of the mother plants, they had set forth on their own in the search for beings of flesh and blood to destroy. Millions of their kind would follow; billions!

In sudden panic Van stepped on the gas.

*   *   *   *   *

Fifteen minutes later, with shrieking siren, a motorcycle drew alongside and forced them to the curb. "Where's the fire?" the sarcastic voice of a stern-visaged officer demanded, when Van had brought his car to a screeching stop. Seventy-five, the speedometer had read but a moment before.

"It's life and death, officer," Van started to explain. "We must get to the proper officials to warn the—"

"Aw, tell it to the judge! Come on now, follow me."

"But officer, there's death on its way from the hills, I tell you. Red, creeping things that'll be here in a couple of hours—"

"Get away, from that wheel. I'll drive you in meself. You're fulla applejack."

Bart had opened the door on his side and was limping his way around the back of the car. This was serious. They had to get away; had to spread the word in a way that would be believed before it was too late. The officer was tugging at Van's arm, astonishment and black rage showing in his weather-beaten countenance. Speeding, drunk, resisting an officer— they'd never get out of this mess! A swift uppercut interrupted the proceedings. Bart's leg was numb and stiff, but his good right arm was working smoothly and with all its old time precision. His second punch was a haymaker. With his full weight behind it, it drove straight to the chin and stretched the officer on the concrete. Thoughtfully, Bart removed his pistol from its holster before scrambling in at Van's side.

"Boy, now we're in for it!" he gasped.

"And we might as well make a good job while we're at it." Van let in his clutch with a jerk, and again they were breaking all traffic regulations.

*   *   *   *   *

It was dusk when they roared in through the gate at the Rockland County Airport and pulled up at the hangar office. Van rushed in, shouting for Bill Petersen, and Bart followed. A slender, fair-haired youth in rumpled flying togs greeted them.

"Bill, my friend, Bart Madison," Van blurted without pausing for breath. "Listen, we've got to have a plane right away. Got one with a radio?"

"Yes, but what's all the rush? Where you going?"

"Albany. Right away. Make it snappy, will you?"

"Sure, but what's it all about?" Young Petersen was leading them to the field where a sleek mono-plane was in waiting as if they had ordered it. "Warm her up, Joe," he called to the mechanic.

"Listen, Bill—I never lied to you, did I?" Van asked, when they were seated in the plane's cabin.

"Not that I know of. But sometimes I've thought you were lying, until I saw with my own eyes the things you had told me about. What is it this time?"

"Death and destruction. Coming down out of the Ramapos. We've got to warn the country. Plants, Bill—squirmy red plants with long feelers that can twist around a man and devour him. Half animal, they are, and the feelers break loose and crawl by themselves. Multiplying like nothing you ever saw. Millions of them in an hour."

"What?" Petersen stared incredulously as his motor roared into life. Then he gave his attention to the business of taking off. He jerked the thumb of his free hand toward the radio.

*   *   *   *   *

Van's expert fingers manipulated the switches and dials of the portable apparatus, and its vacuum tubes glowed into life. "2BXX calling 2TIM," he droned into the microphone.

"Who's that?" Bart asked. The drone of the motor was barely audible in the closed cabin and did not interfere.

"The *Times*. Trying to get Johnny Forbes. If anyone can get this thing across, he can. Wait a minute, here they are." He closed his eyes as he listened to the murmuring voice in the headphones.

Then he was talking rapidly, forcefully, and the young flyer gazed with owlish solemnity at Bart as they listened to his conversation. It was plain that Bill was but half inclined to believe, though impressed by the earnestness and evident apprehension displayed by his two passengers.

"Yes, 2BXX," Van was saying. "Connect me with Johnny Forbes, please—in a hurry. Yes.... Hello, Johnny, it's Van—Carl Vanderventer, you know. Yes; got a scoop for you, but first I want you to get it in the broadcasts. Get me? It's about a man-eating plant that's starting to overrun the country. No—listen now, I'm not dreaming—listen—"

The frantic scientist rambled on and on about the seed from the moon, the red death that was creeping down from the mountains, the horror of the calamity as he and Bart had visioned it. Then, with a sudden note of despair, his voice trailed off into nothingness and he turned a drawn white face to his two friends.

"Laughed at me. Hung up on me," he groaned. "Good God! We've got to do something—quick!"

"Be in Albany in an hour," the pilot suggested. "What you going to do there?" He believed, now. His expression of horror showed it.

"See the governor. But, man, it's an hour wasted! We must stir up the country—get the word to Washington—everywhere. It might be possible to fight the things some way if we can mobilize State and National resources quickly enough. Bill, Bart, what can we do?"

$$*\quad*\quad*\quad*\quad*$$

The plane sped on through the night under control of her gyro-pilot as the three men racked their brains for a solution of the problem. If a hard-boiled newspaper man would not believe the story, who could?

"I've got it!" Bart shouted suddenly. "Can either of you pound a key—code, I mean?"

"Sure, I can. Then what?" Petersen returned.

"Fake an S. O. S. Don't you see? All broadcasting has to stop, and every ship at sea, every air liner in this part of the country'll be listening—standing by. Give 'em the story in code. Let 'em think we're in a ship from the moon—captured by Lunarians who are here to destroy the world with this weed of theirs— anything. Make it as weird as possible. Most everyone'll think it's a hoax, but there are ten thousand kids—amateurs—who'll be listening in. Somebody'll believe it, and, believe me, there'll be some investigating in the neighborhood of the growth in no time."

"By George, I believe that'll do it!" Van exclaimed. "And the broadcasters listen in for an S. O. S. themselves. Got to, you know, so they know when to start up again. Some smart announcer will tell the story—maybe even believe it. The trick will work, sure as shooting!"

*   *   *   *   *

The pilot glanced at his instruments and saw that the automatic gyro-apparatus was functioning properly. Then he moved over to the radio and threw the switch that put the key in circuit instead of the microphone. Rapidly he ticked off the three dots, three dashes, and again three dots that spelled the dread danger signal of the air. Over and over he repeated the signal, and then he listened for results.

"It worked!" he gloated, after a moment. "They're all signing off—the broadcasters. The Navy Yard in Brooklyn gives me the go-ahead."

He pounded out the absurd message with swift fingers, pausing occasionally to ask a pertinent question of Van or Bart. At Van's request he added a warning to all residents of New York State west of the Hudson River and of northern New Jersey to flee their homes without delay. He even asked that the message be relayed to the governors of the two states, and that Governor Perkins of New York be advised that they were on their way to Albany to discuss the situation. But he balked at the story of the Lunarians, telling instead the equally strange truth regarding the origin of the deadly growth, and adding the names of Van and Bart to lend authenticity to the tale.

Then he signed off and switched the radio receiver to the loud speaker before returning to the pilot's seat.

Bart tuned in on the various broadcasters as they resumed their programs, finally settling on WOR, Newark, whose announcer was reading the strange message to his radio public with appropriate comment. A crime and an outrage he called it, an affront to the industry and to the public. An insult to the government of the United States. But wait! A telephone call had just been received at the station from the village of Sloatesburg. A reputable citizen of that town had reported the red growth at the edge of the State road—huge red earthworms wriggling across the concrete. Another call, and another! The announcer's voice was rising hysterically.

"It *did* work, Bart," Van exulted. "Now the hell starts popping."

*   *   *   *   *

Governor Perkins met them in person when they arrived at the Municipal Airport in Albany. A great crowd had gathered in the shadows outside the brilliance of the flood lights, and a police escort rushed them to the governor's private car.

"Here's where you go to the Bastille for socking that cop," Van observed. His spirits had risen appreciably since that successful S. O. S. call.

But the governor was in a serious mood, as they made their way toward the executive mansion through the milling crowds that lined the hilly streets of the capital city of New York State. Proofs had not been lacking of the truth of Bill Petersen's radio warning. Already the spreading red death had covered a circle some eight miles in diameter, covering farm lands and destroying the crops, blocking the roads and trapping many on the streets and in their homes in nearby towns. More than a hundred had lost their lives, and thousands were fleeing the threatened area. The country was in an uproar.

"Gentlemen," the governor said, when they had reached the privacy of his chambers, "this is a serious matter, and no time must be lost in dealing with it. Nevertheless, I want you, Mr. Vanderventer, to tell your story of the thing to me and to the radio system of the United States Secret Service. The President himself will be listening, as will the chief executives of most of the states. Hold nothing back, as the fate of our people is at stake."

*   *   *   *   *

So Van faced the microphone and related the history of his work in the little laboratory in the Ramapo Mountains. He told of his interest in the earth's satellite, and of his first unsuccessful experiments with ultra-telescopes in the endeavor to explore its surface close at hand; of the failure of a space-ship he had built; of the final discovery of the ray, by means of which it was possible to transport solid objects from the one body to the other. He told of the discovery of man-made relics and of fossils; he told of the diamonds, and of the attack by Dan Kelly which had resulted in the spreading of the seed of the deadly moon weed. He even related the incident of the traffic policeman, at which the governor smiled.

"That has been reported," he said, "and you need have no fear on that score.—The charges will be dropped. I now ask that you give us your opinion as to the best method of combatting this new enemy. Have you any ideas?"

"I have not, sir," Van replied gloomily, "though I believe it can be done only from the air. Possibly bombing, or a gas of some sort—I don't know. It will take time, Mr. Governor."

"Yes, and meanwhile the thing is overwhelming us at what rate?"

"As nearly as I can estimate it, the growth is moving with a speed of four or five miles an hour."

"By morning you expect it will have traveled forty or fifty miles in all directions?"

"I'm afraid so."

A sharp buzz from the instrument on the governor's desk interrupted them. "The President," he whispered.

"That is enough, Governor," came the husky tones of President Alford's voice. "I shall communicate with Secretary Makely at once. All available army bombing-planes will be rushed to the scene. You, sir, will mobilize the militia, as will the governors of the other states. Meanwhile, this young scientist is to report to the Bureau of Scientific Research in Washington— to-night. Have him bring a supply of these seeds with him."

That was all. Governor Perkins offered no comment, but merely rose from his seat to indicate that the discussion was ended. A solemn silence reigned in the room.

"Let's go!" exclaimed Bill Petersen suddenly, unawed by the presence of the governor. "My ship's waiting, and we can stop off for a couple of those pods and still make Washington in two hours. Come on!"

Governor Perkins smiled. "Good luck, boys," he said, as they were ushered from the room. "My car will return you to the airport. And remember, the country will be watching you now, and expecting much from you. Good-by."

They were to recall his words in the dark days ahead.

* * * * *

Before they had reached Newburgh, they saw a dull red glow in the skies that told them the news broadcast to which they had been listening had not exaggerated. The red growth was luminous in darkness. Off there to the south-west, it was as if a vast forest fire were lighting the heavens. No wonder the panics and rioting were getting out of control of the police!

Coming up over Bear Mountain, they caught their first glimpse of the sea of fire that was the red death by night. Like a vast bed of glowing embers it covered the countryside, extending eastward to Haverstraw where it was temporarily halted by the broad Hudson. It was a shimmering, undulating mass of living, luminous things, eating their horrible way through all organic matter that stood in their path. Writhing, squirming, all-absorbing monsters that sent out an advance guard of independent snake-like tendrils to capture and hold for the lagging mother-plants whatever of live stock and humanity they were able to find.

"Think they'll get over the river, Van?" Bart asked.

"Sure they will. Every fugitive who had a narrow escape after being in contact with the things is a potential carrier of the seed. I found several of them sticking to my clothing after we got away. I picked a couple off your coat, but didn't tell you."

"Lord! What did you do with them?"

"Put them in the ash receiver in my car—like a fool. Wouldn't have to go down for more if I'd kept them."

"Well, it can't be helped now. We'll have a job getting some down there now, too."

"I'll say so." Van lapsed into gloomy silence.

* * * * *

They were over the landing field above Tomkins Cove, and Bill turned on the siren whose raucous shriek operated the mechanism of the floodlight switches by sound vibrations. The field sprang into instant illumination, and they circled it once before swooping to a landing. They were but a mile from the advancing terror.

The field was deserted, and the three men started off immediately in the direction of the oncoming weed.

"We'll have to make it snappy," Van grunted. "We've got about twelve minutes to get the pods and get back to the ship. The damn things'll be here by that time."

They scrambled over fences and pushed through thickets. The lighted windows of a deserted farmhouse were directly ahead, and they ran through the open gate and across the fields. Ever, the glow of the weed grew brighter. A terrified horse galloped wildly past them and crashed into the fence, whinnying piteously as it went down with a broken leg. They could see the red rim of the advancing horror just beyond the road.

One of the detached tendrils slithered past, each glowing coil distinctly visible.

"Lucky the things can't see!" Bart shuddered.

"Yeah," said Van. "Have to dodge 'em to get in close enough to one of the plants. Keep your eyes peeled now, you fellows, in case one of us gets caught."

A terrific explosion rocked the ground. They had paid no heed to the roaring of motors overhead. The bombers were on the job! Shooting skyward, a column of flame not a hundred yards from them showed where the high explosive had landed in the red mass. Then, slimy wriggling things rained all about them, fragments of the red weed that still squirmed and crawled and clung. Bill Petersen yelled and clutched at his neck where one of the things had taken hold.

Another warning whistle of a falling bomb. Crash! More of the horror raining down and splattering as it fell. Whistle— crash! A huge blob of quivering, luminous jelly fell before them— a portion of one of the mother-plants. Crash! Crash!

"Run!" Van shouted. "Run for the plane. We'll never make it now. Damn those bombers, anyway!"

All along the advancing front, the bombs were bursting, shattering the air with their detonations and scattering the glowing red stems and tendrils in all directions. The din was appalling, and the increasing brightness of the crimson glow added to the horror of the situation. Stumbling and cursing, they ran for the plane.

"Fools! Fools!" Bill was shouting. "Can't they see the field and the plane? Why in the devil are they dropping them so near?"

*   *   *   *   *

Then Bart was down, clawing at a three-foot length of red tendril that had fallen on him and borne him to the earth.

"Bart! Bart!" Van turned back and was tearing at the thing with fingers that were slippery with the sap that oozed from its torn skin. Monstrous earthworms! Cut them apart and each portion lived on, took on new vigor. And these vile things could sting like a jellyfish! Where each sucker touched the skin a burning sore remained.

Bill helped them break away from the thing, and all three fought on toward the lights of the landing field. Only a short way off now; it seemed they would never reach it. The bombers were dropping their missiles with unceasing regularity, and the red death only spread the faster.

When they scrambled into the cabin of the plane, the red wall of creeping horror was almost upon them. Advancing speedily out from the red-lit darkness, it seemed to halt momentarily, when it emerged into the brilliance of the great arc-lights which illuminated the field. Then, more slowly and with seemingly purposeful deliberation, the wriggling feelers reached out from the mass and bore down upon them. Bill slammed the door and latched it, then fumbled frantically with the starter switch. A most welcome sound was the answering roar of the motor.

The pilot yanked his ship into the air, taking off with the wind rather than running the risk of remaining on the ground long enough to taxi around and head into it. The plane acted like a frightened bird as Bill struggled with the controls, darting this way and that, and once missing a crash by inches as the tail was lifted by the treacherous ground wind. Then they were clear, and slowly gained altitude in a steep climb.

"Whew!" Van exclaimed, mopping his red-splattered forehead with his handkerchief. "That was a narrow squeak, boys. And we haven't got the seeds yet—unless we can find a few on our clothing."

"Who said so?" Bart gloated. "Look at this."

He opened his clenched fist and disclosed one of the pods, unbroken and gleaming horribly scarlet in the dim light of the cabin. Bill heaved a sigh of relief as he banked the ship and swung around toward the south. He had dreaded another landing near the sea of moon weed. Van chortled over their good fortune as he examined the mysterious pod. One good thing the bombers had done, anyway! Blew one of the things into his friend's hands.

*   *   *   *   *

Bart and the young pilot found themselves very much out of the picture when they reported with Van at the Research Building in Washington. The Government had no use for them in this emergency: it was the scientist they wanted, and he was immediately rushed into conference with the heads of the Bureau. His two friends were left to shift for themselves, and they joined the crowds in the street.

The name of Carl Vanderventer was on everyone's tongue. Cursing and reviling him, they were, for the hare-brained experiment which had been the cause of the terrible disaster. Fools! Bart seethed with rage and nearly came to blows with a number of vociferous agitators who were advocating a necktie-party. Why hadn't the officials published the entire story as Van told it over the Secret Service radio? There was no mention of Dan Kelly in the broadcast news, nor of the fact that the police were searching for him in every city and town in the country. Another instance of the results of secrecy in governmental activities!

"We'd better find ourselves a room and turn in," Bart growled. "Let's get out of this mob before I slam somebody."

Bill Petersen was only too willing. He was suddenly very tired.

In the Willard Hotel they were assigned to an excellent room, and Bart insisted on switching on the broadcasts and listening to the news. Far into the night he sat by the loud-speaker, or paced the floor as an exceptionally calamitous happening was reported. But Bill slept through it all.

The army bombers had been recalled. Their efforts had worked more harm than good. The invincible moon weed now had crossed the Hudson River at Nyack and Piermont. Tarrytown was overrun, and many of the inhabitants had lost their lives either in the maws of the insatiable monsters or in the panics and rioting that accompanied the evacuation of the town.

*   *   *   *   *

New Jersey was covered as far south as New Brunswick, and west to Phillipsburg and Belvidere. At Mauch Chunk the contents of twenty oil tanks had been diverted to the Delaware River, and the floating oil film was proving at least a temporary protection to a considerable portion of the state of Pennsylvania. In New York State the growth had buried hill and valley, town and village, as far as Monticello, and, along the Hudson, extended as far north as Kingston. At Poughkeepsie, on the opposite side of the river, frantic householders had armed themselves with rifles and shotguns, and were killing off all refugees who attempted to land from boats at that point. But the militia was on guard at the bridges, assuring safe crossing to the thousands who fled the red death over these routes. There was no keeping the seed of the moon weed from finding its way east.

At some points fire had been used with considerable success as a barrier, hundreds of acres of forest lands being destroyed in the endeavor to stem the crimson tide. But, after the ashes were cool, germination would recur, and the weed would continue on its triumphant way. Acid sprays and poison-gas of various kinds had been tried without appreciable effect. The casualty estimates already ran into the tens of thousands; rumor had it that nearly one hundred thousand had lost their lives in the city of Newark alone. There was no way in which the figures could be checked while everything was in a state of confusion.

Communication lines were broken, roads blocked, gas and electric supply systems paralyzed and the railroads helpless. Trains could not be driven through the glutinous, wriggling mass that piled high on the tracks. Only the radio and the air lines were operative in the stricken area, and even these were of little value to the unfortunates who, in many cases, were surrounded and cut off from all hope of succor.

At four in the morning, with aching heart and reeling brain, Bart threw himself on the bed without undressing and fell into the troubled sleep of exhaustion and despair.

*   *   *   *   *

The next day brought no encouragement, though it was reported that the growth developed with less rapidity after sunrise than it had during the night. Bart endeavored to get Van on the telephone, but was curtly informed by the operator at the Research Building that no incoming calls could be transferred to the laboratory where he was working. Knowing his friend, he pictured him as working feverishly with the Government engineers and giving no thought to sleep or food. He'd kill himself, sure! But such a death, even, was preferable to the red one of the moon weed.

The Canadians and Mexicans had been quick to protect their borders and forbid the landing of any American aircraft or the passage of trains and automobiles. But the seed had reached Europe, one of the twelve-hour night air-liners having carried a thousand refugees who had sufficient foresight and the means to engage passage. It was a world catastrophe they faced!

By mid-afternoon the streets of Washington were almost deserted. It was less than twenty-four hours since the first moon seed took root, and already the crimson growth had progressed nearly a hundred miles southward from the point of origin! Another twenty or thirty hours and it would reach the capital city—unless Van and those engineers over in the Research Building discovered something; a miracle.

Bart tried the telephone once more and was overjoyed when the operator, all apologies now, informed him that Van had been trying to reach him for several hours.

"Listen, old man," his friend's voice came over the wire: "I've been worried as the devil not knowing where you were. I want you and Bill to stick around where I can get you at any time. I may need you. Where are you staying?"

"The Willard. Have you doped out something?" Bart answered in quick excitement.

"Maybe. Can't let anything out yet—not till we've tested it thoroughly. But I can tell you that a hundred factories are already working on machines we've devised. By good luck it only means minor changes to an apparatus that is on the market in large quantity."

"Great stuff. The city's nearly emptied itself, you know, and, boy, how they've been razzing you over the radio and in the papers—howling for your hide, the whole country."

"I know." Van's voice was calm, but Bart sensed in it something of a cold fury that was new to him in his friend. The young scientist was bitterly resentful of the attitude of the public.

"Can we see you, Van?"

"No, nor call me either. Better hang around the hotel and wait for a call from me. So long now, Bart. I've got to get busy."

"So long."

Bart gazed solemnly at Bill Petersen, who had been listening abstractedly to the one-sided conversation. Bill had given up hope and was resigned to the inevitable.

"Says he may need us, Bill," said Bart.

"Yeah? Well, we'll be ready for anything he wants us to do. It's no use though—anything."

"What do you mean—no use? You never saw Van licked yet, did you?"

"Sure I did. By his super-telescopes and the rocket ship."

"But this is different." Bart was a staunch defender of his friend. He glared at Bill for a moment and then switched on the news broadcast which he knew he detested.

*   *   *   *   *

The progress of the moon weed continued unabated. In the city of New York a million souls were reported as having lost their lives, and this in spite of the difficulty experienced by the uncanny moon weed in obtaining a foothold in Manhattan. It had been thought that the asphalt and concrete would prove an effective barrier, and so they did for a time. But, with the seed active in the parks and along the water fronts, it was not long before the powerful roots of the greedy plants worked their way underneath, ripping up pavements and wriggling into cellars as they progressed. The city was a mass of wreckage and a maelstrom of fighting, dying humanity.

Whole regiments of the National Guard were wiped out as they fought off the weed with ax and bayonet, in the effort to provide time for the refugees to clear from their homes in certain localities. All transportation facilities to the south and west were taxed to the utmost. There was fighting and killing for the possession of automobiles and planes and for room in trains and buses. Air-line terminals and railroad stations were the scenes of dreadful massacres as the police and military guards fought off the crazed and desperate creatures who attacked them en masse. And still the news announcers prated of the responsibility of one Carl Vanderventer.

The telephone bell rang, and Bart answered it in relief. At last they were to see some action! But no, it was merely the desk clerk, notifying him that all employees were leaving the hotel and that they would be left to shift for themselves. Yes, there was plenty of food in the kitchens; they were welcome to it. And a permanent telephone connection would be made to their room. The frightened clerk wished them luck.

*   *   *   *   *

In endless monotone, the voice of the news announcer droned on. Binghamton and Elmira, Albany and Schenectady, New Haven, Philadelphia, Allentown—all had succumbed. The casualty estimates now ran into the millions. The mist, the red mist that rose from the steaming weed, was drifting westward and spreading the seed with ever increasing rapidity. For now the monstrous growth from out the sky was adapting itself to its environment; providing the seed with feathery tufts that permitted the winds to carry them far and wide like the seed of a dandelion.

"Turn off that damn thing!" Bill shouted. And he jumped to his feet, his eyes glinting strangely in the twilight gloom of the room. Bill was close to the breaking point.

"Guess you're right," Bart mumbled. "Not good for either of us to listen to that stuff." He switched off the receiver, and they sat in silence as darkness fell over the city.

Bill shivered and felt for the button of the electric light which he pressed with a trembling finger. They blinked in the sudden illumination, but it cheered them somewhat. It was not good to sit in the darkness and think. Besides, they knew that the turbine generators of Potomac Edison were still running. Some brave souls were sticking to their jobs—for a time, at least.

"God!" Bill suddenly groaned, after an endless time of dead silence. "My sister! Lives in Pittsburgh, you know. Wonder if she and the kids got away. It won't be long before the damn stuff gets there."

Bart thanked his lucky stars that he had no family ties. "Oh, they've had plenty of warning," he tried to console Bill. "Hours, you know; and the westbound lines are in good shape from there. I wouldn't worry about them if I were you."

There was utter silence once more. Even the customary street noises was lacking. Both men jumped nervously when the shrill siren of a police motorcycle sounded in the distance. Bart thought grimly of his fracas with the officer who had tried to arrest Van. How long ago that seemed, and how inconsequential an incident!

Their windows faced north, and by midnight they could make out the red glow of the moon weed, that awful band of flickering crimson that painted the horizon the color of blood. The telephone clamored for attention and Bill stifled a hysterical sob as the terrifying sound broke the eery stillness.

Van was on the way to get them! He had a Government car and they were to go to Arlington for Bill's plane. Then what? He refused to commit himself: they must follow him blindly. Anything was better than this inactivity, though. Bart shouted with glee.

*   *   *   *   *

"We're going north," Van replied shortly, in answer to Bart's question when they entered the official car in front of the hotel, "after Dan Kelly."

"After Dan Kelly? Got a line on him?"

"Yes. Secret Service reports him in Toronto. The Canucks are after him now, but, by God, I'm going to get him myself!"

Van was haggard and wan, his eyes gleaming with a fanatical light. The strain had done something to him— something Bart didn't like at all. This was a different Van from the man who had entered his office two days previously. Unshaven and unkempt, he looked and talked like a drunken man on the verge of delirium tremens.

"What's the idea, Van?" he asked gently.

"I'm going to get him. I tell you. The scum! It's his fault the whole world's against me. I'll get him, Bart; I'll kill him with my bare hands!"

So that was it! The combination of gruelling labor in the effort to save mankind from the dread moon weed, and bitter censure from the very people he was trying to save, had been too much for Van. He had developed a fixation, unreasoning and murderous; he'd get even with the man who had caused the trouble. And nothing could deter him from his purpose: Bart could see that. Might as well humor him and help him. It made little difference, anyway, with the red doom spreading at its present rate. They'd all be victims in a few days.

They were speeding through the streets of Washington at a break-neck rate. Van bent over the wheel, and like a demented man glued his wildly staring eyes to the road.

"What about your work?" Bart asked, after a while. "Has anything been accomplished?"

"Yes and no. They'll be ready to shoot in a few hours. Don't know whether it'll be a complete success or not. But I sneaked away anyhow. This other thing's more important to me right now."

"What's the dope? Can you tell us now?"

"Sure. I've got one of the machines in the car and I'll explain when we're on our way to Canada."

This wasn't like Van. Never secretive and always in good humor, he was treating his friends like annoying strangers.

"You can't land in Canada," Bill ventured, as they pulled up at the gate of the airport.

"Like hell I can't! You watch my smoke, and let any bloody Canuck up there try and stop me!"

He was lifting a small black case from the luggage carrier of the car as he replied. Bart silenced the airman with a look.

*   *   *   *   *

When they had taken off and were well under way, Van opened his black case and set a vacuum-tube apparatus in operation. They were nearing the fringe of the glowing sea of red that was the vast blanket of moon weed. It now extended to within a few miles of Baltimore and stretched northward as far as the eye could see.

"It was a cinch," Van was explaining. "When I first saw that the growth slowed up under the arc-lights at Tomkins Cove it gave me the glimmering of an idea. Then, on the following day, when we learned that the weed spread more slowly in sunlight, I was convinced. The stuff is dormant on the moon, you know."

"Why?" Bart asked breathlessly.

"Because there is no atmosphere surrounding the moon, and the sun's rays are not filtered before they reach its surface as they are here. The invisible rays, ultra-violet and such, are present in full proportion. And the moon weed can not flourish when subjected to light of the higher frequencies. It died out when the moon lost its atmosphere, and only revived on being brought to earth—probably a million times more prolific in our dense and damp atmosphere and rich soil. The thing's a cinch to dope out."

"Yeah!" Bart commented drily. Van was now talking and he could have bitten off his tongue for interrupting him.

This machine of Van's was a generator of invisible light in the ultra-indigo range, Van explained. You couldn't see its powerful beam, but they had proved in the laboratory that it was certain doom to the moon weed. They had grown the stuff from seed in steel cages, and played with it until they were all satisfied. Now would come the final test. Ten thousand planes were being equipped with the new generator, which was merely an adaptation of standard directional television transmitters, and to-night these would start out to fight the weed. It was a cinch!

*　　*　　*　　*　　*

Beneath them the red cauldron seethed and tossed as they sped northward; the crimson blanket of death that was steadily covering the country.

"Drop to a thousand feet, Bill," the scientist called, "and then watch below. But, don't slow down. We've got to get to Toronto!"

The ship nosed down and soon leveled off at the prescribed altitude. Van's vacuum tubes lighted to full brilliancy, and a black spot appeared on the glowing surface just beneath them, a black spot that extended into a streak as the plane continued on its way. They were cutting a swath of blackness fifty feet wide through the heart of the growth!

"See that!" Van gloated. "It's killing them by millions! And the best of it is the effect it leaves behind. The soil is permeated to a depth of several inches and the stuff will not germinate in the spots where the ray has contracted. Oh, it works to perfection!"

Bill was exuberant; his hopes revived miraculously. He gave his motor the gun and got out of it every last revolution that it could turn up. He must get Van to Canada! Not such a bad idea, this going after Kelly, at that!

Bart was voluble in his praise, then caught himself short as he remembered that he had doubted Van but a half hour previously: doubted him and despaired. Now Van, lapsing into gloomy silence after his triumph, was again thinking of nothing but revenge. The getting of Dan Kelly meant more to him now than the extinction of the moon weed.

*   *   *   *   *

When they landed at the Toronto Airport they were welcomed with open arms instead of with rifle fire as Bill had anticipated. The news had gone forth. Already a thousand planes flying over the United States were driving back the sea of destruction. The invisible ray was a success, and the name of Carl Vanderventer was now a thing with which to conjure, rather than one on which to heap imprecation and insult. Van grimaced wryly at this last bit of news.

Danny Kelly? No one at the airport had ever heard of him. Van telephoned in to the city; to Police Headquarters. Yes, they had apprehended the fugitive American at the request of Washington, but he was a slippery customer. He had escaped. Van raged and fumed.

Of what use were the congratulations of the night flyers who still loitered in the hangar; of what consolation the radio reports of the success of the ultra-indigo ray in the States and in Europe? He had come after his man and he'd failed. Defeat was a bitter pill.

The news broadcasts from the States were jubilant and became increasingly so during the night. The moon weed was being driven back on a wide front and by morning would be entirely surrounded. There would be no further loss of life and little more destruction of property. Carl Vanderventer had saved the day! Van grunted his disgust whenever an announcer mentioned his name.

When daylight came they prepared to return. Little use there was of searching the highways and byways of Canada for the fugitive. He'd simply have to wait until the Canadians were able to get a line on Dan Kelly again.—It was maddening! But Bart was glad. The light of reason was returning to his friend's eyes in the reaction.

Then there was a telephone call from the city for Van. Police Headquarters wanted him. The fanatical glint returned to his eyes when he ran for the hangar to answer the call. Perhaps they had already captured Kelly! And he had an order in his pocket for the man's return to the States. He'd been made a deputy, and with Kelly released to him anything might happen. Something would happen.

*   *   *   *   *

But the police were reporting the unexplainable reappearance of the moon weed just outside the city limits at a point near Cookesville. Would Mr. Vanderventer be so kind as to fly over there and destroy it before any lives were lost? He would.

The growth had covered an acre of ground by the time they reached the spot designated. But it was the work of only a minute to blast it out of existence with the ultra-indigo ray. Van surveyed the blackened and shriveled mass with satisfaction.

"Let's land and take a look at it," he said.

Bart thought he saw a look of exultation flash over his careworn features.

Soon they were wading deep in the blackened remains of the moon weed. The stems and tendrils snapped and crumbled into powder as they passed through. The stuff was done for, no question of that.

Bill Petersen yelled and pointed a shaking forefinger at an object that lay in the blackened ruin. It was a human skeleton, the bones bare of flesh and gleaming white in the light of the early morning sun. Van was on his knees, quick as a flash, feeling around the grewsome thing: pawing at the shreds of clothing that remained.

Then he was on his feet, his face shining with unholy glee. In his hands were a half dozen small, smooth objects which looked like pebbles. The diamonds!

"I thought so!" he exclaimed. "It's Kelly. Only way the seed could have gotten up here. He had some on his clothes and didn't know it. I couldn't get him myself—but anyway I'm satisfied."

*   *   *   *   *

He staggered and would have fallen, had not Bart caught him in his arms. Poor old Van! Nearly killed him, this thing had, but he'd be himself again, after it was all over. No wonder he'd gone out of his head with the horror of it, and the blame that had been so cruelly laid on him! No wonder he'd become obsessed with this idea of getting square with Dan Kelly! But now he was content: sleeping like a babe in Bart's arms.

Tenderly they carried him to the plane and laid him out on the cushions in back. They'd let him sleep as long as he could; return him to Washington where he'd receive his just dues in recognition for his services. Then would follow the work of reconstruction and rehabilitation. Van would glory in that.

Bart regarded his sleeping friend thoughtfully as they winged their swift way toward the American border. The harsh lines that had showed in his face during the past few hours were smoothed away and in their place was an expression of deep contentment. He was at peace with the world once more. Good old Van.

What a difference there would be when he awakened to full realization of the changed order of things! What satisfaction and relief!

THE COPPER-CLAD WORLD

ORIGINALLY PUBLISHED IN *ASTOUNDING STORIES*,

SEPTEMBER 1931

THE COPPER-CLAD WORLD

CHAPTER I
Into the Unknown

Adrift in space! Blaine Carson worked frantically at the controls, his jaw set in grim lines and his eyes narrowed to anxious slits as he peered into the diamond-studded ebon of the heavens. A million miles astern he knew the red disk of the planet Mars was receding rapidly into the blackness. And the RX8 was streaking into the outer void at a terrific pace—out of control.

Something had warned him when they left Earth; the Martian cargo of k-metal was of enormous value and a direct invitation to piracy. Of course there was the attempt at secrecy and the shippers had sent along those guards. His engineer, Tom Farley, was thoroughly reliable, too. But this failure of the control rocket-tubes, missing their destination as a result—there was something queer about it.

"Tommy," he called into the mike. "Find anything yet?"

"We-e-ll, something," the audio-phone drawled after a moment: "I'm coming up."

"What is it, Tom?" he asked when the engineer's round face appeared at the head of the engine room companionway.

Farley dropped his voice and his customary smile was gone. "I found the stern rocket-tube ignition jammed so it's firing continuously," he said; "and the others are all dead: won't fire at all. That's why she doesn't swing to the controls?"

"Can't you fix it? Lord, man, we're headed out into the belt of planetoids. We'll be wrecked."

"Nothing I can do, Blaine, without shutting down the atomic engines. Then we'd freeze to death and run out of oxygen. These ships ought to have a spare engine just to take care of the heating and air conditioning. I always said so."

"What happened to the ignition system?"

Tom Farley looked over his shoulder apprehensively. "Dirty work, Blaine," he whispered. "I'm sure of it. Tool marks on the breech of the stern tube. And there's one of those guards I don't like the looks of."

"Nonsense. The k-metal people know their men; they picked these three especially for the job."

"Who else could do it? There's only the five of us on board."

There might be something in what Tommy said, at that. A thing like this couldn't just happen by itself. And, come to think of it, one of those guards was a queer looking bird: dwarfed and hunch-backed, sort of, and with long dangling arms. It would be better to investigate.

"Get 'em up here, Tommy," Blaine said.

*   *   *   *   *

The RX8 drove on and on through the uncharted wastes outside the orbit of Mars. None of the space ships of the inner planets ever ventured out this far, and Blaine knew there was grave danger of colliding with some of the small bodies with which the zone was infested. If one of those guards was the traitor he was risking his own neck as well as theirs.

Two of them entered the control room with Tom Farley, big, husky fellows of stolid countenance and armed with regulation flame-ray pistols and gas grenades.

"Where's the other, the dwarf?" Blaine asked, his suspicions mounting immediately.

"In his bunk," Tom replied with a meaning look. "He said he'd be up in a few minutes."

The pilot-commander addressed the guards. "Fellows," he said, "I suppose you know we're in a serious fix. The ship is out of control and we've missed Mars, where your metal was to be delivered. We're speeding out into the unknown, out past the limits of space-travel toward the orbits of Jupiter, Saturn, Uranus—God knows where. And my engineer thinks that one of your number has tampered with the machinery. Know anything about it?" Blaine eyed them keenly.

One of the guards, Mahoney, flushed hotly. "No, sir," he snapped. "At least Kelly and meself had nothin' to do with it.

But we've been suspicionin' that little Antazzo ever since we came out. It's a peculiar way he has about him, the divil."

"You think he—"

* * * * *

An incisive voice from the doorway way interrupted, "Never mind what he thinks, Carson. I'll do the thinking from now on."

At one man they turned to face the speaker. It was the guard, Antazzo, and he was clothed from neck to ankles in a garment of bright metallic stuff that shimmered with shifting colors like those of a soap bubble. A mask of similar stuff covered his face, and in each hand there was a weapon resembling a ray pistol but of strangely unfamiliar design.

Mahoney shot from the hip and his stabbing ray splashed full on the hunchback's chest—but harmlessly. That lustrous garment was an insulating armor; the traitorous guard should have been shriveled to a cinder at the contact. Antazzo laughed evilly as his own weapons loosed strange and terrible energies.

Tom Farley ducked, and Blaine watched in horrified amazement as the crackling streamers of blue radiance from the dwarf's pistols found their marks. Mahoney and Kelly, standing there, bathed for a brief instant in horrid blue fire: tottering, swaying, their mouths opened wide in a last agonized effort, to cry out. Tiny pinpoints of brilliant pyrotechnics flashing and exploding within the columns of blue fire. Then, nothing! Where the two husky guards had stood there was utter emptiness; not even a shred of clothing remained. The air in the control room became heavy and acrid.

"Antazzo!" White-faced and shaking, Blaine cried out in futile protest, "My God, man, what have you done? What does this mean?"

And then, in a blaze of rage, he was on his feet. Murder was in his heart as he set himself for a crashing charge that would sweep the beast from his feet. His own flame-pistol was missing; it was a case of killing this monster with his bare hands. Tom was circling, over there, cursing horribly. One of them would get him. Strangely, Antazzo had lowered the muzzles of his pistols.

*   *   *   *   *

A terrific punch, started from the floor, never reached its mark. Blaine saw a tiny puff of pinkish vapor that spurted from the bosom of that metallic garment. He was coughing and gasping; helpless. Muscles refused to do his bidding. With a moan he dropped into the pilot's seat, knowing that Antazzo's will compelled him. That gas had hypnotic powers. Mechanically, his fingers strayed to the controls.

And Tom—good old Tommy—he was under the influence of the stuff too, creeping there on hands and knees toward the engine room companionway.

Antazzo was talking. "We come now to the matter of instructions," he said. "You, Farley, will assist me in restoring the ignition system to normal. You, Carson, will keep to the controls and will lay a course to Jupiter as soon as the control rocket-tubes will respond. Understand?"

Tom growled reluctant assent from where he was crawling.

Strange, this hypnotic gas! Blaine's mind functioned clearly enough, yet he was utterly at the mercy of this madman's will— a robot of flesh and blood. "Jupiter!" he exclaimed. "Why man, it's nearly a half billion miles from the sun. Not habitable, either."

Antazzo had removed his mask and now smiled a superior smile. "We'll reach it," he said: "the RX8 is very fast. And it's not the planet itself we're bound for, but its second satellite. Io, your astronomers call this body, and it's a world sadly in need of this marvelous k-metal."

"But—but—"

"Enough!" The hunchback snarled his rebuke in Blaine's face and turned to Tom. "Come, Farley," he said, as if talking to a child, "we must get to work."

*   *   *   *   *

In a daze of conflicting emotions, Blaine turned to gaze through the forward port when the two had left the control room. The RX8 was accelerating rapidly under the steady discharge of gases from the stern rocket-tube and had already reached the speed of one thousand miles a second. If one of those tiny asteroids, even one no larger than a marble, should meet up with them it would crash through the hull plates as if they were paper. His heart went cold at the thought.

Oddly enough, he found himself *wanting* to make this trip with the demoniac Antazzo. It was the effects of the pink gas. Even with the misshapen guard down there in the engine room the power of his will was effective. The devil must be an Ionian, he thought. But how in the name of the sky-lane imps had he reached Earth? How had he wormed his way into the confidence of the k-metal people? He must have been there several years, working to this very end.

There was a tinkling crash on the starboard side amidships; a screaming swish as something slithered along the side and caromed off into the void. One of those little planetoids. Probably no bigger than a pea, and luckily they had struck it glancingly. He wiped the sudden perspiration from his forehead.

Pressure on the directive rocket controls brought no response. Would they never finish with that ignition system?

A gleaming light-fleck segregated itself from the mass of stars ahead. At first he thought he imagined it, but a second examination, this time through the telescope, convinced him it was growing larger. Drawing nearer, it was, and resolving itself into a well defined orb that was directly in their path. Fifteen hundred miles a second, the indicator read now! They'd never know what happened when they struck.

"Tommy!" he bellowed into the mike. "Are you fellows ever going to finish down there?"

*   *   *   *   *

There was no reply for a moment, and the blue-white globe drove madly toward them. He consulted the chart. Pallas—an asteroid some three hundred miles in diameter. Not very big as celestial bodies go, but big enough!

"Just one minute now." It was Tommy's voice coming drearily, unnaturally through the audiophone. A minute! Ninety thousand miles! It seemed the asteroid was that close already.

Antazzo was in the control room then, and the effect of his mental dominance became more pronounced. Suddenly the dwarf let out a shriek of terror when he looked through the port and saw the brilliant body that now loomed so close. Blaine experienced a savage joy in the knowledge that the hunchback was mortally afraid.

"Latza! Latza!" In his fear Antazzo lapsed into his own tongue. Then, remembering, he shouted, "We're ready, Carson. Swing wide!"

The directive rockets answered to their controls now. Quick pressure on this, a swift pull on that, swinging the energy value to maximum, brought results. The little vessel groaned and shivered under the strain as a full blast from the forward tubes retarded them. Her hull plates twisted and screeched as the steering tubes belched full energy in swinging them from their course. They were thrown forward violently, though the deceleration compensators were working to the utmost.

Pallas swung around in their field of vision, and there was a fleeting glimpse of sun-lit spires of mountains, shadowed valleys, and mysterious crevasses from which clouds of steam and yellow vapor curled. Still it seemed they must crash against one of those slender pinnacles. Nearer it came like a flash; a dizzying blur, now, that drove directly in their straining faces.

And then, abruptly, it was gone. Already thousands of miles astern, the danger was past. Miraculously, they had escaped.

Antazzo laughed; a hollow mirthless cackle. His fingers shook crazily when he untwisted them from their grip on the port rail.

"Good work, my friend. Very good, indeed," he jabbered, his chin quivering in nervous reaction. "And now we carry on—on to Io."

Blaine Carson, almost wishing they had collided with the spire, set himself grimly to the task. He was powerless to refuse.

CHAPTER II
The Second Satellite

When, eventually, they swung into the orbit of Jupiter and headed in toward the enormous red-belted body, the two Earth men were heartily disgusted with the voyage and with themselves. Repeated doses of the pink gas—the ignominy of their utter subservience to the will of Antazzo—had worn them down no less than had the hard work and loss of sleep. Both were in vile humor. They endured the triumphant chatter of their captor in bitter silence.

"Over there, my friends," he said, pointing; "see? It is our destination. The golden crescent, Io, is something over a quarter million of your miles from the mother planet. See it? It is home, my friends; home to me and for yourselves in the future—if the Zara spares your lives. Lay your course to the body, Carson."

Blaine growled as he sighted through the telescope. Yet, in spite of his fury, he could not overcome the feeling of excitement that came to him when the powerful glass brought the satellite near. This body was like nothing else in the heavens. Antazzo had called it the golden crescent. Rather, it was of gleaming coppery hue, and now, as they swung around, it was fully illuminated—a brilliant sphere of unbroken contour. Smoothly globular, there was not one projection or indentation to indicate the existence of land or sea, mountain or valley, on its surface. It was like a ball of solid copper, scintillant there in the weak sunlight and the reflected light from its great mother planet.

Antazzo laughed over his absorption. "Looks peculiar to you, does it not?" he asked; "rather different from any of the bodies you have visited, you are thinking."

Blaine grunted wordless assent. The globe that was Io rushed in to meet them, growing ever larger in the field of the telescope. Now it appeared that there were tiny seams in the smooth surface, a regular criss-cross pattern of fine lines that looked like—Lord, yes, that was it! The body was constructed from an infinite number of copper plates, riveted or brazed together to form a perfect sphere.

*   *   *   *   *

"Why, the thing's made of copper!" Blaine gasped. "Copper plates. It's a man-made world; artificial. But where are the inhabitants?"

Antazzo laughed uproariously. "Not man-made, my friend," he corrected, "but preserved by man for his own salvation. A dying world, it was, and the cleverest scientists in the universe saved it and themselves from certain death. What you see is merely a shell of copper, the covering they constructed to retain an atmosphere and make continuation of life possible—inside."

"Your people live *inside* that shell?" Blaine was incredulous.

"What else? We must have air to breathe and warmth for our bodies. How else could we have retained it?"

It was staggering, this revelation. The young pilot could not conceive of a completely enclosed world with inhabitants forever shut off from the light of the sun by day and from the beauties of the heavens by night. Yet here it was, drawing ever nearer, a colossal monument to the ingenuity and handiwork of a highly intelligent civilization who had labored probably for centuries to preserve their kind. A titanic task! Who could imagine a sphere of metal more than twenty-four hundred miles in diameter enclosing a world and its peoples? A copper-clad world!

They were coming in close now, and the gravitational pull of the body made itself felt. Blaine was busy with the controls, sending tremendous blasts from the forward rocket-tubes to retard their speed for a safe landing. The incredibly smooth copper surface was just beneath them, stretching miles away to the horizon in all directions.

The inductor compass was functioning. Evidently Io possessed as strong a magnetic field as did the inner planets. Antazzo now consulted a chart which he drew from his pocket, and examined minutely the surface over which they were speeding. Here and there curious designs were etched on the copper plates, and it was from these he determined their course. Obviously there was an entrance to this sealed-in world.

*   *   *   *   *

When they had proceeded some two thousand miles in a northeasterly direction Antazzo gave the order to reduce speed. Off at the horizon there appeared a bulge in the copper surface, a round protuberance that resolved itself into a great dome-shaped structure as they drew nearer. A full two hundred feet it reared itself into the heavens, and Blaine saw a number of large circular hatches in its side that evidently covered air-locked entrances.

"You will land close by the dome, Carson," Antazzo barked, "and both of you will get into your moon-suits."

At his tone Blaine saw red. He realized on the instant that the effect of the pink gas had worn off and that he was his own master once more. All the pent-up emotions of the past few days were unleashed. If only he could get in one good punch. They might get away yet. There was plenty of k-metal to replenish the fuel supply. He whirled suddenly, muscles tensed. He faced the grinning hunchback—and was greeted by a breathtaking spurt of the pink gas. This time it was not merely a subjecting of his own will to that of the master but a complete hypnotism, a somnambulistic state. As in a dream he turned to the controls.

Now it came to him that the dwarf no longer spoke. He worked his will entirely without words; his evil mind possessed fully the mind of his victim. For Blaine Carson there was no further independent thinking. He was an automaton, a sleep-walker.

* * * * *

Like a detached and more or less disinterested observer, he saw that he had landed the ship. Then he noticed three dwarfs in bulky, helmeted moon-suits, shuffling clumsily across the copper plates. Hazily he knew he was with the others in an airlock; the hiss and the throbbing of pumps told him that. Under the great dome there was the latticework of a huge reflecting telescope; strange pigmy figures scuttled here and there, working at curious machines. There was the constant purr of many motors, the gentle pulsation of floor-plates beneath his feet.

With the moon-suit removed, he realized the atmosphere was fetid and stifling. A great pressure bore on his lungs, making breathing labored and difficult. And then they were in a lift that dropped into the depths of its shaft with dizzying speed. Antazzo's grin; Tom's eyes, dull and lifeless, floating there in the haze before his own—it was all a nightmare from which he must soon awaken.

There followed a period of complete unconsciousness of movement and of his surroundings. Light—light everywhere; a blue-white radiance that beat upon his unseeing eyes with unrelenting ferocity. Stabbing pains bored into his very brain, pains that carried with them an unspoken and unintelligible command. Why couldn't they let him alone; leave him to die in peace? He knew he was on his feet, swaying. There were voices, strident and guttural, and then by some magic the veil was lifted. His brain cleared and he saw that he stood before a dais where a much bejeweled and resplendently clad woman sat curled in the luxurious cushions of a golden seat. Chalk-white was her face and her lips crimson; amazing eyes, cat's eyes, pupils red-flecked and glittering, stared out at him.

*   *   *   *   *

"The Zara," Antazzo whispered. "You will make obeisance."

Mechanically, Blaine dropped to his knees and touched his forehead to the floor. Tom Farley, over there, was doing the same, but Antazzo stood erect with arms crossed over his chest and head thrown back. The eyes of the Zara swept him contemptuously from head to foot. All was not well between them.

Blaine arose from his humiliating position at a sharp command from the hunchback. Tommy did likewise and the two exchanged sheepish looks. The effects of the pink gas were wearing off once more. They were in a large hall, obviously the throne room of a palace. Men-at-arms lined the walls on either side of the dais, and these were straight limbed giants with green-bronze skin and regular features—not at all like the deformed Ionian who had captured them and stolen the RX8.

The Zara talked rapidly in throaty gutturals, her fierce gaze directed at Antazzo and her brows drawn together in a scowl that could have but one meaning. She was displeased with the hunchback, displeased and furiously angry. What was it all about? Hadn't he brought home the bacon—the k-metal they were after? Blaine was nonplused.

Then Antazzo replied to the woman who was obviously his queen. His voice rose in shrill disagreement and his scowl was as fierce as the Zara's. Threatening her, he was, the nervy devil. He clenched his fists and raised his arms in an angry gesture, pacing the floor in his fury and thrusting out a pugnacious chin while he raved. This Zara woman rose higher in her cushions, and the look that flashed from those terrible eyes would have warned a less excited human, however justifiable his anger might be. But Antazzo was in too deep to draw back, that was plain to be seen. Blaine held his breath in anticipation of an explosion.

* * * * *

It came then, that explosion, and in a way entirely unexpected and horrible to behold. The tiger woman uttered one fierce sibilant like the hiss of a serpent, a terrifying sound that silenced the hunchback and brought him stiffly to attention, mouth open and eyes bulging with horror. One of those unbelievably white arms stretched forth, threateningly tense, and a jeweled finger leveled itself at the rash Ionian. From it there flashed an intangible something that leaped to bridge the distance with the speed of light, something that screeched as it flew and crashed like breaking glass when it struck Antazzo's horrified face. In an instant he was on the floor, screaming and writhing in mortal agony.

The Zara watched with compressed lips and livid features as a host of black disk-like things covered the squirming body, spinning madly as if driven by atomic energy and emitting a myriad high-pitched tones like the angry buzzing of a swarm of bees. Antazzo's body shriveled as the things hummed on in their devilish work. Soon there was but a tiny heap of clothing with the angry black disks whirling and singing their song of hate. And then, in a puff of thick yellow vapor they were gone, their gruesome work completed. The odor of putrefaction lay heavy on the air.

Blaine shuddered and a fit of nausea twisted his vitals. It served the devil right, of course, but it was a horrible way to go. These damned Ionians, even to their queen, were bloodthirsty creatures. And what devilish ingenuity they had displayed in their development of weapons! His eyes were drawn irresistibly to the flaming orbs of the Zara.

She was actually smiling at him, this beautiful, heartless animal, not a smile of derision but one of deliberate allure. He felt the hot blood mount to his temples. A languid arm beckoned him to her side and the amazing creature settled back in her cushions with the drowsy, contented motions of a lazy feline.

"Watch your step!" Tommy hissed.

That warning was unnecessary. Blaine shook his head and backed away from the dais, an instinctive recoiling from a loathsome thing. The Zara saw and understood; and she went again into a black rage. She sat stiffly erect and called rapid orders to her men-at-arms.

The Earth men were surrounded instantly, their arms and legs pinioned by powerful hands, their feeble resistance overcome by the bronze giants as easily as if they had been children. Helpless and hopeless, they were borne from the room.

                    *   *   *   *   *

This was the end of the story, Blaine thought. Why this Zara woman had not made away with them at once was a mystery. Perhaps they were being reserved for an even more terrible fate than that of the hunchback. They were being carried along a dim-lit passage now, and Tom was cursing his captors in a never-ending stream of invective.

A metal door opened and then clanged shut behind them. They were dumped unceremoniously on metal tables that resembled those of a hospital operating-room on Earth. Woven bands, quickly adjusted by the bronze giants held them fast. Blaine turned his head and saw that Tommy was still struggling against the inevitable. A gag had been placed in his mouth; that was why he had ceased reviling the Zara's servitors.

The room was cluttered with elaborate and complicated mechanisms that Blaine could not recognize in the slightest detail, excepting that there were many banks of slender glass cylinders which bore some resemblance to the vacuum tubes used on the inner planets for radio communication and television. One of the bronze giants, he saw, was bringing a metal cap from which a cable extended to one of the strange machines. This cap was forced down over his head with a none too gentle pressure and he could see no more.

There came a sharp buzz from the machine and a million stinging needles drove into his brain. There was a moment of fleeting visions; strange places he viewed, and strange creatures parading in a fantasmagoria of delirium before his aching eyes. Voices, harsh and guttural, spoke in his drumming ears; voices that were dimly understandable, though uttered in the tongue spoken by Antazzo and the Zara. Then came sudden and merciful unconsciousness.

CHAPTER III
Ilen-dar

When Blaine Carson opened his eyes it was to stare at the blue-white radiance of an illuminated ceiling. He lay on a downy cot and it seemed he had just recovered from a long illness. Weak and sick, he turned his head listlessly to gaze at the ornate embossed designs on a wall of gleaming silvery metal. What place was this? His mind was wool-gathering; dim memories of unspeakable things struggled for mastery over a hazy consciousness. Suddenly then he remembered, and he sat up in his unfamiliar bed, senses acutely alert.

Across the room he saw a figure hunched in a chair; a twisted man-creature who was oddly like someone he had seen. Antazzo! But this one had none of the other's ferocity as he returned Blaine's stare. Rather, there was a look of deep concern in his ugly face. He came immediately to the bedside and looked at Blaine solicitously.

"I see you have recovered," he said. "It is good."

Blaine stared and stared. This creature had spoken in the language of the Zara's subjects, yet he understood his every word! It must be a dream, this impossible thing that had happened. And where was Tom? Abruptly he found that he was talking rapidly in this tongue of an alien race.

"Yes, I've recovered," he said, "and I'm amazed at what I find. How have I acquired this knowledge of your language? Where am I, and where is my friend? Can you enlighten me in these things?"

The other smiled. "I can, Earth man," he replied. "You have been taught our language while you slept. A thought transference process we use for educating the young. You are in the palace of the Zara and your friend is safe in the next room. I may add that you are in high favor with Her Majesty."

The wizened creature lowered his voice on the last words, and his knowing eyes spoke volumes. In favor with that she-devil! Blaine went cold at the thought.

"I want to see my friend," he said shortly.

"Later. My orders are to bring you to the Zara immediately you are strong enough. And Pegrani obeys orders."

*   *   *   *   *

No use to attempt a break now. Blaine was tempted to drive a fist into that ugly countenance and fight his way out of the place. But that would be suicide. He'd wait, get the lay of the land first and then try to dope something out with Tommy.

"All right, Pegrani," he said, "I'm ready to go before this Zara of yours."

As he prepared for the audience, alien thoughts crowded one upon the other in his strangely enlightened mind. With the knowledge of the language had come knowledge of many things relative to the copper-clad world. They'd given him a liberal education. Somehow he knew these stunted creatures like Antazzo and Pegrani were known as Llotta and that, while ruling the sealed-in planet, their kind had originally come from Ganymede, the fifth satellite of Jupiter. Centuries had passed since the inhabitants of Europa and Ganymede had been forced to desert their aging worlds and had settled on Io. During other centuries the widely different peoples had co-operated in constructing the great copper enclosure in order to keep the new world alive and capable of supporting life. Then had come a century of bitter warfare in which the Llotta were victorious. Intense hatred existed between the two races, he knew, and a hazy impression of mechanically imparted knowledge told him that few of the Europans remained alive.

"We are here, Carson," his guide announced, when they stood before the square columns of an enormous portal.

The scene in the throne room was vastly different than when he had first visited it. The Zara sat curled as before, a golden bowl of incense burning at either side of the throne. The men-at-arms were absent and, instead, there were dozens of handmaidens, white-skinned and seductive as their queen, reclining on luxurious cushions that were arranged in a semicircle before the dais. It was a scene of Oriental splendor. A stage carefully set.

*   *   *   *   *

Pegrani knelt and touched his forehead to the floor but Blaine held himself stiffly erect, looking straight into the eyes of the Zara. She smiled and extended her arm in that beckoning gesture.

"You may leave now, Pegrani," she said, without deigning him a glance. "Remain in the corridor until I send for you."

There was a tense silence as the Zara's gaze, ineffably softened now, held Blaine's. Unconsciously he was drawn to the steps of the dais. Unwillingly, yet inexorably, his lagging footsteps brought him to her side. Cool white fingers touched his arm and he saw that the red flecks in the black of those wide eyes were golden now. Surely there was no harm in this woman. But he remembered Antazzo.

"Carson," she purred, "you are more than welcome to Llotta-nar, the land of my people and the ruling power of Antrid, the body you call Io. The freedom of the realm is yours for as long a time as you wish to remain."

This was too good to be true. "You—you mean," he stammered, "that Antazzo exceeded his authority in his act of piracy—in bringing us here?"

The golden flecks flashed red and a cold note was manifest in the throaty voice. "Antazzo," she replied, "was destroyed for his audacious actions. We needed this k-metal of yours, Carson, and he was sent to Earth to get a quantity of the material. By magnetic directional waves was he sent—we have no space-ships—his body disintegrated by my scientists for transmittal, and the atoms of his beastly form reassembled in their proper relation when he arrived there. But he threatened me when he returned successful. The possession of the k-metal and his knowledge of its powers and uses had gone to his head. He demanded my hand in return for his work; demanded that he be permitted to mount the throne of Llotta-nar as my consort. Therefore I destroyed him." The hard eyes softened anew. "And—and for his abominable treatment of you I destroyed him," she concluded.

*   *   *   *   *

Blaine fought off the spell of those gold-flecked eyes; he looked away in sudden panic. This creature was not telling the truth. She was hiding something; a sinister motive lay beneath her smooth speech.

"My friend," he said abruptly: "what of him?"

"For your sake, my Carson," she purred, "he too shall have the freedom of the realm for as long a time as is desired."

The cool fingers crept along his arm, firm and compelling. "Look at me," she whispered.

He thought of the pink gas as his eyes were drawn irresistibly to hers. What he saw in those gold-flecked depths sent a shiver of apprehension chasing down his spine. Savage, devastating desire mingled with ill-concealed rage at his coldness. This beautiful animal could turn like a flash and rend him limb from limb—and would on the slightest provocation.

A commotion in the corridor caused her to release him and sit bolt upright. Temporarily relieved, Blaine wheeled to face the portal. Tommy had broken loose! He heard his strident voice, berating an unseen antagonist in the tongue of the Llotta.

Then they were in the room, Tommy struggling and arguing vociferously with one of the green-bronze guards. The handmaidens had deserted their cushions and were milling about in affrighted confusion. The Zara's sibilant exclamation startled him into looking at her once more. The same cold fury that had greeted Antazzo glinted icy-hard in that grimly beautiful face. It was all over for poor Tommy.

*　　*　　*　　*　　*

But the Zara reached upward and stroked a transparent rod that dangled above the throne, something he had not noticed before. A screaming vibrant note smote the heavy air, a pulsation that beat at the ear drums with painful intensity. Silence fell as the awesome sound died away and echoed faintly from the huge columns that supported the arched ceiling. Tommy cooled off when he saw that Blaine was unharmed.

"Drekan!" The Zara's voice was a whiplash as she addressed the guard. "You will leave my presence and report to your overman for punishment. Never again molest the Earth men. Begone!"

Again this amazing woman curled in her cushions and again she purred. Tommy watched in open mouthed astonishment as she smiled guilelessly on his friend.

"You may leave me now, my Carson," she cooed. "Farley is free to accompany you. Pegrani will guide you and inform you regarding our customs and our people. You will learn much. And then you shall return to Zara Clyone."

Blaine had fully expected that Tommy would die a horrible death before his eyes, and in his sudden relief bent low and kissed the cold white hand of the Zara. A foolish thing to do! She purred and snuggled into the cushions like the feline she was—a dangerous animal; claws drawn in now but ready to strike out, razor sharp, on a moment's notice.

*   *   *   *   *

Pegrani led them along the corridor to a lift. The car shot upward with breath-taking speed.

"Say!" Tommy was growling, in English. "What's the big idea? You've got the old girl ga-ga. Trying to vamp her into letting us off easy?"

"Shut up!" Blaine returned, irritated. "I don't know where we stand any more than you do. But we're going to sit tight now and see what happens. No more rough stuff from you, either."

"What! You're going to just stand around and take it—whatever they hand us?"

"Of course not. But the time isn't ripe yet. We'll have to wait till we know what it's all about."

They were outside then, on the palace roof, and Pegrani motioned them to a railed-in runway that circled its edge. High overhead was the shadowy blackness of the copper shell that enclosed the satellite. Huge latticed columns, line upon line of them, stretched off into the distance as far as the eye could follow; enormous white metal supports that carried the immense weight of the covering which retained the dense and humid atmosphere. Myriads of tiny blue-white suns there seemed to be, stretching off between the columns, carried on thick cables and radiating the artificial daylight of the interior. Hot, damp odors wafted across the roof, the odors of decayed vegetation.

Most amazing of all, were the dwellings. In orderly rows like the columns, they were flat topped cylindrical things that reminded Blaine of nothing so much as the tanks of an oil refinery back home. And the space between was overgrown with dense tropical vegetation, tangled and matted and shooting transparent tubular stems up to a height of a hundred feet or more where they sprouted great spherical growths that looked like enormous sponges. Of a sickly, pale green hue, these growths overran everything; climbed the columns and were lost in the shadows above the multitude of lights. The big sponge-like blossoms expanded and contracted rhythmically. Breathing, they were, like living things. Specially cultivated plant life to assist in maintaining the oxygen supply balance by decomposition of carbon dioxide. A marvelous artificial world!

*   *   *   *   *

"The streets and moving ways are in tunnels beneath the soil," Pegrani was explaining. "What lies before you is the city of Ilen-dar, capital city of the empire, and like all other cities of Antrid, it is self-sustaining. The vegetation is inedible, all of our food is synthetic and highly concentrated. You were fed by intravenous injection while under the influence of the language machines. Our heat and power is obtained from the internal fires of Antrid, and, alas, these are being exhausted with great rapidity. Our shortage of power is becoming acute, and again our peoples are facing extinction."

That explained their need for the k-metal. It came to Blaine in a flash that Antrid was in sore straits and that this expedition to Earth had more back of it than had been revealed. Even with the supply of k-metal Antazzo had stolen, they could not carry on forever.

A screaming object went hurtling through the blackness over their heads. Something, a vehicle of enormous size with rows of lighted ports on the under side, that roared its way under the roof of copper and was gone in an instant.

"One of our monorail cars," Pegrani told them: "a complete system interconnects all cities and divisions. They are capable of circling the globe in a day of your time."

Their familiarity with conditions on Earth was astonishing. Probably Antazzo was but one of many spies who had been sent to the inner planets. Pegrani discussed the speed in their own terms.

*　*　*　*　*

Someone had crept up behind them; a slight, olive-skinned youth who touched Blaine softly on the shoulder. Pegrani did not see. He was pointing into the distance and expounding on the merits of the monorail system. The youth touched a finger to his lips to enjoin silence, and thrust a crumpled ball of metal foil into Blaine's hand before the pilot realized his intention. A message, undoubtedly!

Some instinct, or some slight sound, warned Pegrani and he turned on his heel just as the slender lad was slinking away. Black rage contorted his features and Blaine saw him make a quick motion toward the inner folds of his jacket.

"Pegrani!" he shouted as he saw a glint of steel. "Don't!"

But it was too late and the Llott paid him no attention, anyway. One of those wicked ray pistols sent forth its crackling blue flame and the youth stood there, bathed in the eery blue light; dazzling blasts of exploding atoms were seen within the flare. Then there was the nothingness into which Wahoney and Kelly had gone.

Blaine shouted horrified and angry protest and Tommy rushed in to mix it with their guide. But the glowing ray pistol waved them back. Other guards—the big green-bronze ones—were running in their direction.

"The message!" Pegrani snapped. "Give it to me."

Quick as a flash Blaine crumpled the foil more tightly. A hard little pellet now, he tossed it over the rail far into the matted vegetation below. One might as well hunt for a needle in a haystack as for that tiny ball. But Pegrani would not forget; he'd report to the Zara. They were in for it now.

CHAPTER IV
Before the Council

Pegrani lost no time in reporting the incident to the Zara. The Earth men were hustled to the throne room of the palace where the leopard woman sat in conference with her advisers. An ominous silence greeted their entrance. Ugly faces leered at them from the long table.

"What is it, Pegrani?" The Zara's chalky face went whiter still.

"The Rulans, Your Majesty. They have endeavored to communicate with the prisoners."

"Did they succeed?" Clyone's voice was terrible in its fury.

"They did not. I destroyed the messenger, and the message itself was lost in the jungle where Carson flung it."

The Zara shot a fleeting glance in Blaine's direction and permitted herself the ghost of a smile. "It is well," she breathed. "But it must not happen again. Have Tiedor brought to me."

Pegrani hurried off to do her bidding and Blaine turned uncertainly to follow.

"You will remain, Carson—you and Farley." The incisive voice of the leopard woman halted him in his tracks.

Tiedor was chief of the Rulans, it developed. There was but a handful of them in the realm and they were the last survivors of the civilization of Europa; descendants of those original brave souls who had settled on Io as a last resort in the effort to perpetuate their kind.

He was a magnificent creature, this Tiedor, tall and straight in his muscular leanness and with wide-set gray eyes in the face of a Greek god. Olive-skinned like the messenger, he was, and with the high forehead of an intellectual. He swept the assemblage with a haughty gaze when he faced the Zara.

*   *   *   *   *

"Tiedor," she snarled, "it has come to my ears that a Rulan lad carried a message to one of my guests from Earth. What means this?"

"I know nothing about it, Your Majesty." Tiedor gazed into the wicked eyes, unafraid.

"You lie! There is some treasonable scheme in which you had hoped to enlist their help. You will tell me the entire story, here before the council."

"There is nothing to tell."

"You will confess or I shall destroy every Rulan in the Tritu Nogaru." The Zara's words were clipped short with deadly emphasis.

Tiedor paled and his lips tightened in a grim line, but he stood his ground. "I have nothing to confess," he said.

With a whistling indrawn breath, the leopard woman threw back her head and motioned to one of the green-bronze giants who guarded the entrance. There was a nervous stir around the council table.

At her command the guard drew back a heavy drape that hid an embrasure in the far wall. There, on a stubby pedestal, was revealed a gleaming sphere of crystal, a huge polished ball that shimmered a ghastly green against a background of jet.

Slowly in its depths a milky cloud took shape, swirling and pulsating like a living thing. Then it flashed into dazzling brilliance and the globe cleared to startling transparency. It was as if it did not exist. Rather they looked through an opening in the cosmos that carried their gaze to another and distant point. It was a large open space that was revealed to their eyes; a sort of public square where many of the olive-skinned Rulans were coming and going to and from the entrances of the circular tank-like structures that surrounded the area. They were greeting one another in solemn fashion as they passed and watching furtively the green-bronze guards who were everywhere. The sound of their low voiced conversations came clear and distinct from the depths of the crystal sphere.

"Your choice, Tiedor," the Zara hissed.

"There is nothing—nothing, I tell you!" The Rulan chief's voice was panicky now.

* * * * *

Clyone's snarling command was carried to those guards out there in the Tritu Nogaru by some magic of the crystal sphere. As one man they snapped to attention. With deadly accuracy they released the energy of their ray pistols. It was a shambles, that square of the Tritu Nogaru; a slaughter house. Agonized screams of the doomed Rulans rent the air of the council chamber. They organized hastily and rushed again and again into the crackling blue flame of the disintegrating blasts of the guards' fire. It was hopeless: unarmed and unprotected, they were at the mercy of Clyone's minions.

Sick and trembling, Blaine cried out against the massacre. He was seized instantly by two of the green-bronze guards who had been watching his every move. Tommy, too, was in their clutches once more, fighting valiantly but without avail. The sphere went blank and silent, and the drape was returned to its place. Still muttering disapproval, the members of the council gazed at their queen in alarm. There was no telling what this vile creature might do.

"The slaughter continues. Tiedor," she gloated. "Soon your handful of followers will be no more. And good riddance."

Swaying drunkenly, eyes glazed with the horror of the thing. Tiedor went raving mad. In one wild leap he was upon her, his fingers sinking into the white flesh of her throat. Woman or no woman, he'd have her life.

But it was not to be. A quick move of jeweled fingers was followed by a crashing report. Tiedor staggered and drew back, spinning on his heel to face them all with distended, pain-crazed eyes. Astonishment was there, and horror, but the fire of undying courage remained. His olive skin turned suddenly purple, then black from the poisoned dart that had exploded in his entrails. He collapsed in a still heap at the feet of the Zara.

She stood there a moment in the awful silence, caressing her bruised throat with fluttering fingers. She had faced death for one horrid instant and was obviously shaken.

Then she recovered and flew into a rage. "Out of my sight, all of you!" she screamed. "Out, I say! The Earth men are to be freed and Pegrani will conduct them to their quarters. Go now!"

The councillors made haste to comply, jostling one another in their anxiety to jam through the doorway. Blaine found himself released. He took one step toward Clyone, murderous hatred in his heart. But he recoiled from the expression in those red-flecked eyes; they softened instantly and looked into his very soul, saw through and beyond him into some far place where relief and happiness might be attained. And then, suddenly, they were swimming in tears. The Zara dropped into a seat and buried her sleek coiffured head in outstretched arms, her shoulders shaking with sobs.

An incomprehensible anomaly, this queen of the Llotta; a strange mixture of cruelty and tenderness, of cold hatred and the longing for love. A dual personality hers, susceptible to the deepest emotion or to utter lack of feeling as the mood might dictate.

Blaine tiptoed softly from the room.

* * * * *

They were in the corridor now, and Tommy was blowing off at a great rate. Even Pegrani was stunned and shaken. But Tommy raved.

"Forget it!" Blaine growled. "Where do we go from here?" He couldn't have explained his emotions then, even to himself.

"To our quarters, she said—damn her!" Tom Farley swore in picturesque English. "And we," he wound up his expressive tirade, "are getting in deeper and deeper. We can't do a thing. Why in the devil doesn't she put us out of the way and get it over with? What's she keeping us around for, anyway?"

Blaine was asking himself that very question. Pegrani regarded them with something of understanding in his beady eyes. But he was nervous and apprehensive and broke in on their conversation to urge them into action. The Zara must be obeyed.

The corridor was deserted now and their footsteps echoed hollowly from the bare metal walls. Pegrani was ahead, leading the way, when Blaine was startled by an insistent tap on his shoulder. Another of the Rulans, it was, repeating the gesture of the youth who had been killed on the roof. But this one had no message; he was after something else—telling them in pantomime to make a break for freedom and to follow him.

Blaine caught Tommy's attention. And Pegrani, warned again by that sixth sense of his, turned his head. With a bellow of rage he whirled into action, ray pistol in hand. But Blaine was prepared for him this time. He wasn't going to witness another murder—not now. Flinging Tom Farley aside, he let loose a terrific jab that landed full on Pegrani's mouth. The ray pistol crackled harmlessly, its deadly energy spending itself in searing the metal of the ceiling.

*   *   *   *   *

Then he wrenched the weapon from the astonished Llott and was boring in with body punches that quickly had the dwarf gasping for breath. These creatures knew nothing of fighting with their hands except in the fashion of clumsy wrestlers. The thud of hard fists against yielding flesh was a new and terrifying experience. Pegrani was game, though, and he flailed about with his powerful arms, endeavoring to get his opponent in his grasp.

Sidestepping to avoid one of his rushes, Blaine brought up a terrible uppercut that ended flush upon the Llott's jaw. His head snapped back and his knees gave way beneath him. Down he went in a flabby heap. Suddenly ashamed, the young pilot turned to the Rulan.

Tom's eyes were shining. It was easy to see that he felt better about things now.

"I am a friend," the Rulan whispered in the Llott tongue, "sent by one who would have conversation with you. It is of the highest importance, but we must make haste. Will you trust me?"

Blaine saw deep concern and sincerity in the fellow's blue eyes. "What do you say, Tommy?" he asked, looking to his friend for approval.

"I say, let's go. He seems okay to me."

Their new guide was familiar with the passages and especially so with dark and little used stairways that connected the floors of the huge building. They soon reached the roof through a hatch that opened on a small penthouse which was in deep shadow and entirely hidden from the runways where the green-bronze guards paced constantly.

A slender cable dangled before them, and at its lower end they saw a basket-like car which their guide bid them enter. When they had done so, he tugged on the cable, giving a rapid twitching signal. Instantly they were soaring up into the blackness above the lights of Antrid.

* * * * *

The swift journey ended in a tiny enclosed vehicle where another Rulan operated the cable drum which had made the trip possible. The car was unlighted save for the faint glow of a hand lamp, and it was not until the lower door was closed that they were permitted a view of the interior of the strange vehicle and had a good look at the two Rulans.

"Now," the one who had brought them said, "I can explain. I am Tiedus, son of Tiedor. My companion is Dantus, son of Dantor, the greatest scientist in all Antrid. We are taking you to Dantor who has knowledge of the mad plans of the Llotta and is in need of your help in thwarting them. You are willing?"

"Why—why, yes," Blaine stammered, looking deep into the earnest eyes of Tiedus. "You—you know of the fate of Tiedor?"

"I do." The young Rulan fell silent; then shook his head as if to clear it of unwelcome thoughts. "There are but few of us left, oh Earth man," he said then, "and all expect a like fate sooner or later. But that is beside the point. We have important work to do: work that brooks no delay. We leave now for the Tritu Anu, with your consent."

Tom Farley was examining the machinery of the car with interest. "This one of the monorail cars?" he inquired, when Dantus had seated himself at the controls.

"Indeed not. The Llotta do not even know of the existence of this vehicle. We could not get right of way on the rails, so this gravity car was developed in secrecy. It is provided with variable repulsion energies that can be adjusted to keep it at a fixed distance from the inner surface of the copper shell. Thus it misses cross beams and braces. It is drawn forward by similar energies, or more exactly, by the component of a number of attracting forces. We do not display lights, so are thus comparatively safe from discovery. They'll catch us sooner or later, though, of course." Dantus indulged in a fatalistic shrug of his shoulders as he concluded.

*   *   *   *   *

At his manipulation of a number of tiny levers that were set into the control panels like the stops of an organ, the car lurched forward. Silently, swiftly, they sped on through the gloom under the great copper shell.

Through the viewing glass of a periscope arrangement that let no betraying light escape to the outside, they watched the endless lines of illuminating globes slip by beneath them. Weirdly vast and shadowy in the upper reaches, the latticed supporting columns on either side merged into continuous semi-transparent walls as the car gathered speed.

The city of Ilen-dar was left far behind. Patches of jungle flashed by; other cities. And always the endless rows of blue-white lights. There was neither night nor day in the sealed-in world; only the artificial suns that never set. Continuous subjection to the ultra-violet and visible rays of the vast lighting system was necessary to the growth and reproduction of the plant life that was so essential in keeping the atmosphere breathable.

Tommy had forgotten everything save his interest in the mechanism of the car. He and Dantus were fast friends already.

Chin in hand and eyes avoiding the pain of mourning in Tiedus' fixed gaze, Carson lost himself in gloomy meditation. As he thought back over the events of the past few days he could scarcely believe they had actually occurred or that he was sitting here in a mystery car, speeding through the rank atmosphere of an enclosed world a half billion miles from his own. Home seemed incredibly remote and desirable just then, and the future dark and forbidding.

CHAPTER V
The Tritu Anu

Before the car came to a stop Tiedus rummaged in a locker and stretched forth his hands as if carrying something delicate and fragile.

"It will be necessary for you to put this on," he said: "it will be unsafe otherwise."

Blaine stared, mystified. Was this Rulan kidding him? "Put what on?" he asked.

"A thousand pardons. I had forgotten that you do not know. I hold in my hands a cloak, an invisible thing that will hide you from the guards and from the Zara's crystal. Another secret of my father's. Dantor developed it for him only recently."

Blaine felt the texture of the stuff then; crumpled it in his fingers as its gossamer-like weight dropped in loose folds around his body. But there was nothing there: to the eyes. It simply did not exist except to the touch, and he felt no different with it on than he had before.

"Where's Tommy?" he asked suddenly, seeing that Dantus now sat alone at the controls.

Tiedus laughed. "He has been covered in the same manner," he said, "and is safely hidden from sight as are you."

Incredulous, disbelieving, Blaine called out to his friend in a tremulous voice. And Tom Farley's awed response reassured him.

"Keep close to me," Tiedus told him. The car had stopped and he directed them into the basket of the lift. The two Earth men collided violently and, clinging to each other in their ghastly invisibility, laughed crazily for a moment. As far as any observers might know there were only the two Rulans in the basket.

*   *   *   *   *

Blaine fingered Pegrani's ray pistol when the cable lowered them swiftly to the roof of a huge steel cylinder that rose, a solitary and unlovely structure, in the midst of the jungle a thousand miles from Ilen-dar. The indicator informed him that seven energy charges still remained in the storage chamber of the little weapon. Its possession brought him a measure of confidence.

Careful scrutiny of the roof had shown it to be deserted, so the basket was brought to rest in a deeply shadowed portion. Immediately they stepped out, and it was sent swiftly aloft by remote control of a portable ether-wave that Dantor produced.

They encountered two of the green-bronze guards in one of the passages below and these challenged the Rulan lads with drawn pistols. The alarm was out! Fortunately Pegrani had not recognized Tiedus or all would have been lost. But the Zara was watching every Rulan community and had instructed her guards to take the Earth men into custody at all costs. Those remarkable cloaks were all that saved them. They breathed easier when the guards passed on.

Now they were in a lift, dropping speedily into the depths of the Tritu Anu. When the cage came to rest they were hustled into a maze of winding passageways that led ever downward. A wall of damp stone finally blocked their progress, but at Dantus' touch of a hidden spring a section of the solid rock swung aside to admit them to a concealed room where the lights were bright and where a delegation of Rulans awaited their coming.

With the cloaks of invisibility removed, they were welcomed by Dantor, a tall white-haired Rulan who was startlingly like his son.

They were a solemn lot, these Rulans of the older generation, but they gazed on the Earth men with sympathy and understanding. An entirely different breed from the Llotta.

This room was a secret laboratory, fully equipped for chemical and physical research. Dantor sat before a smaller replica of the Zara's crystal ball as he addressed the visitors.

* * * * *

"No doubt you are puzzled," he began, using the language of the Llotta with an accent that softened its harsh gutturals, "over the calamity that has befallen you. And it is not to be wondered at. But your own danger is as nothing compared with the danger that now threatens our whole solar system. It is to explain that and to ask your cooperation in warding off the holocaust that I have sent for you.

"Since the destruction of the Tritu Nogaru we Rulans number less than one thousand, of whom three hundred are here. The Tritu Anu is foremost of the royal laboratories of Llotta-nar and its work is carried out entirely by our people. It is only on account of our superior accomplishments in science that the Llotta have allowed us to exist for so long a time, and, in this connection, I might say that the Zara has been taken severely to task for her wanton massacre of the Rulans of the Tritu Nogaru. But that is neither here nor there; it is merely a sidelight I am giving you.

"The important thing is this k-metal of yours and its relation to the plans of the Llotta. Antrid, as you know, is a dying world; coming rapidly to the end of its resources. And, as our ancestors did before us, the Llotta have been casting their eyes about for a new home. The inner planets beckoned, especially your Earth, but it was manifestly impossible to reach them as there is insufficient fuel in all Antrid to provide for the voyage of even one space ship. Then, with the long range searching rays of the crystal ball television and sound reproducers, they discovered the use of this k-metal. The sending of Antazzo to your Earth followed.

"The rest you know insofar as his activities are concerned, but what you do not know is this: The Llotta have constructed a huge steel tube that is set deep into the crust of Antrid; an enormous rocket-tube if you please, like one of those on your space ship. They plan to use the energy of this supply of k-metal in setting up tremendous streams of electronic discharges from the great tube and thus to swing the satellite from its natural orbit. They would send this entire world hurtling through space toward the inner planets, and, by proper control of the rocket discharges, bring it close to your Earth where it would become a secondary satellite at close range. Then they could war on you at their leisure and finally take Earth as their new home. Thus have the Llotta planned."

"What!" Blaine exclaimed. "Why, we'd blast them from the skies before they were started. They haven't a chance."

*   *   *   *   *

Dantor nodded gravely. "I am sure of it," he agreed: "I have seen your great guns in the crystal. But they are blind to that possibility. And there are other serious flaws in the plan. The incentive, of course, lies in the certain knowledge that we are using up the internal heat of Antrid so rapidly that less than a century of life now remains to its peoples. Our power is produced by admitting water to the interior through myriads of tubes that serve the double purpose of introducing the water and conveying the generated steam back to the surface, where it produces electricity by driving great turbine generators. This electricity is distributed by charging the copper shell and the ground beneath at high frequency; it is collected from the air between by the heaters and various machines that use it. But the shortage is ever more serious and Antrid is cooling off. Thus the need for the k-metal and thus the sending of Antazzo. And now for the flaws:

"The Zara, in killing Antazzo, frustrated her own plans, as he alone, of all her people, knew how to use this marvelous energy producer. Realizing this, she set about to make friends with you two in the hope that the information might be obtained from you. That was a great mistake and raised an unexpected obstacle."

"Well, I'll be damned!" Blaine exploded. "No wonder she tried her wiles on me. Tried to make a sucker out of me, didn't she?"

Dantor smiled knowingly. "More about Clyone later," he said. "Actually she is enamoured of you, Carson, and besides she is not really responsible for the mad plan herself. But that tale can wait.

"The basic and most serious flaw in the plan is this: It can not possibly succeed, no matter how successful their attempts. What they do not understand and will not believe when I tell them is that the only result of the mad experiment will be the complete destruction of the solar system, Antrid and themselves included. Complete and horrible annihilation, I say!" Dantor paused and eyed his visitors solemnly.

*   *   *   *   *

In his mind's eye, Blaine could not visualize such a thing nor picture the possible explanation. But he saw that Tommy had paled and was clenching his fists. Tommy was more of a scientist; it must be he realized what this enterprise involved.

Dantor was speaking again, in low, intense tones: "What they are refusing to see is that the delicate balance of the solar system will be disturbed if a body as large as Antrid is moved a half billion miles sunward. All bodies are kept in their orbits by a nice balance of mass attraction and centrifugal force; if a single one is altered all others are affected. What would happen is easy to calculate. First off, when Antrid approached the inner planets all bodies in the system would change their paths and the altered forces would cause severe earthquakes, tidal waves and other natural disturbances of disastrous extent.

"These would increase in violence as Antrid drew nearer to the sun, and, if she finally took up her position as a new satellite of the Earth, the entire solar system would be in chaos. By this time, even if life still remained on Earth, it would quickly become extinct, for the vastly increased tidal forces on that body would flood the land to the peaks of the highest mountains. Earth would draw in closer to the sun due to loss of velocity and increased mass of the Earth-moon system. Tremendous new forces would rend asunder the Earth, its moon, and Antrid. Venus and Mars, following suit as the forces equalized, we would have a dead universe."

*   *   *   *   *

Tommy believed him. That was apparent from his furrowed brow and grim set jaw. "I'll never give 'em the secret of the k-metal," he grated. "Nor will Carson; I'll gamble on that. We'll die here before they'll get it out of us."

Blaine seconded his remarks fervently. Then, turning to the Rulan scientist, "Perhaps," he suggested, "we might remain in hiding here for an indefinite period. Perhaps even we might contrive a way of getting to the store of k-metal and regaining possession of it. They'd be licked for sure then."

Dantor beamed. "That is exactly why I sent for you," he said. Then sobering anew, he added, "But I fear that would not be the end. They will not give up. Another emissary would be transmitted to duplicate Antazzo's exploit on Earth and in five of your years the danger would again be faced. They would take infinite precaution to prevent a second failure. We must make it forever impossible—now."

"How can we? My God, it's hopeless!" Blaine groaned.

"Nothing is hopeless, my boy. Consider the plight of the Rulans. No, there is still hope and we will leave you to think it over—if you are willing. It is necessary that we Rulans show our faces above before we arouse the suspicions of the guards."

"Of course we're willing. We'll stay as long as you say—and help." Blaine was intensely earnest and Tommy chimed in with his old time fervor and enthusiasm. But hope of success seemed remote.

A murmur of approval came from the assembled Rulans, and Dantor wiped a trace of moisture from his tired old eyes. "Thank you," he said simply. "This chamber is insulated from the searching rays of the crystal spheres. You are safe for the present and will be supplied with everything you need. And I shall return shortly to discuss the matter in further detail."

*   *   *   *   *

The two Earth men were alone then, in the uncanny silence of the underground retreat, regarding each other with awed comprehension. What patient, hopeless creatures these Rulans were! Knowing they were doomed, and without thought of their own safety, they were bending their every effort to the impossible task of saving the universe from the madness of the Llotta.

"What do you know about that?" Tommy said, after a while.

"It's true, what he said?" Blaine asked. "What would happen to our world, I mean—and to the rest?"

"Not a question of doubt. He's doped it out to a T. Smart guy, this Dantor."

"What do you think? Is there a chance? Think—"

"Hush!" Tommy interrupted him. "Didn't you hear something?"

The silence was ghastly; depressing. Blaine heard distinctly the beating of his own heart.

Then it was there again, that sound—a muffled scream from the other side of the stone door. A woman's scream of desperate entreaty. A shuddering, long-drawn moan, trailing off into deathly silence.

CHAPTER VI
Ulana

Blaine was tugging at the lever he had seen the Rulans use in opening the stone door from the inside. Tommy, less excited, tried to press one of the invisible cloaks into his free hand.

"Here," he begged. "Don't be a damn fool! They'll get you, the devils."

But the great block of stone was swinging already and the young pilot squeezed through and into the passage. He stumbled over the crumpled figure of a young girl and into the arms of one of the green-bronze guards.

Recovering instantly, he prodded the big fellow's ribs with the ray pistol. "Stick 'em up!" he snarled. Then, realizing the words were meaningless to the other, he said, "Raise your hands—above your head! That's right. Stand still now, or I'll use the ray."

The guard, his face ghastly in the dim light, obeyed. But his wary eyes never left Blaine's for an instant.

A short way down the hall was the body of a young Rulan. Blaine shuddered as he saw it was headless. The ray had nearly missed that time, its energy spent before complete disintegration was effected. The girl lay still at his feet. With quick fingers he frisked the guard, finding his ray pistol and one gas grenade. What was he to do with the big fellow? He ought to let him have it, but somehow he couldn't.

Tommy was in the passageway then, invisible. The big guard stifled an amazed cry as his husky voice came out of the nothingness. These devils of Earth men! They had worked their evil magic on the Zara: had she not ordered that their lives be spared? And now there was this! His thoughts were written large on the ordinarily expressionless countenance, and Blaine was tempted to laugh at his affrighted dismay.

"Come on, you bonehead," Tommy was saying in English. "Bring the big bum inside. I'll carry the girl. Hurry; there'll be a million of them in a minute."

The girl's huddled figure was raised by unseen hands. Poised in mid-air for a moment, it floated joggily, unsteadily through the crack of the partly opened stone door. The guard, wide-mouthed and staring, muttered supplication to the war gods of Antrid.

*   *   *   *   *

Safely inside the secret chamber, the Earth men made haste to truss up the guard and gag him. He was as tractable as a child under the invisible fingers of Tom Farley, with eyes imploring the evil spirits for mercy. And when Tommy's head appeared, drifting, unsupported by a body; to be followed by arms and shoulders that seemed to materialize from nothingness, the big fellow struggled panic-stricken in his bonds, shaking with superstitious terror.

Blaine straightened the girl's limbs where she lay on a low couch. She was breathing in low shuddering gasps, but a swift examination assured him she had not been harmed. Her beautifully chiseled ivory features were fixed in an expression of nameless dread. A mass of red-gold hair tumbled in confusion about her face and shoulders and when the pilot smoothed this back his heart did a most peculiar flip-flop. Sort of jumped into his throat and stuck there. This Rulan maiden was a vision of feminine loveliness if there ever was one; a dream.

Tommy watched him with a cynical smile, and said with mock contempt, "So you're the guy who swore you'd never tangle up with a femme! Just a month ago, too. Now look: first you get this Zara woman all het up over you, and now this one's got you all het up over her. You make me sick!"

There was no fitting retort. Besides, this thing that had come to him was too serious; too big. He couldn't kid about it—even with Tom. Why, he'd always pictured this very girl in his thoughts; had always dreamed of meeting her some day. And here she was: a living, breathing reality. She was stirring, too, now; breathing easier. Her eyes opened wide; frightened, innocent ones like a child's, blue-gray and fringed with long lashes that raised dewy from the smooth ivory of her cheeks.

*   *   *   *   *

"Antius, my brother," she exclaimed, remembering, "where is he? I saw—I thought—and the guard; he wanted to take me— oh!"

Hands fluttering to cover her face, she was sobbing now, and Blaine raised her in his arms, clumsily attempting to comfort her.

"Your brother," he said gently; "I'm afraid the guard did away with him. He is no more."

"Y-yes. I remember now; I saw." She shuddered and became still, her tousled golden head somehow finding a comfortable hollow beneath Blaine's shoulder.

And then, bravely, she sat erect and faced him. "I—I suppose I shouldn't feel so badly," she said. "We always expect it. But I was so fond of him, and he was the last. I am alone now."

"Not alone," said Blaine; "you have me—us, that is. We are the Earth men, you know. And you are safe here."

"You are Carson?" she inquired.

"Yes, and my friend is Farley. That is how your people address us, but we had rather you call us Blaine and Tommy."

Tom Farley was grinning like an idiot. Didn't he have any more sense? Blaine thought. The girl would think he was making fun of her.

"I am Ulana," she said simply.

The stone door opened silently and Tiedus slipped in, closing it swiftly behind him. He stared at the girl and at the trussed-up figure of the guard.

"So!" he exclaimed; "this is the explanation." He breathed heavily as if he had run a long way, and his face was flushed with excitement.

"Why? What's wrong?" Blaine sensed a calamity.

"The Zara—she must have seen you in the crystal. She is in a murderous rage and has visited her wrath on the Tritu Anu. Even now Dantor is on his way to Ilen-dar in answer to her summons."

"Tiedus! I'm sorry. It is my fault entirely, but—but we heard Ulana cry out."

"You did quite right, Carson. I should have done the same myself. And actually it makes little difference as far as we Rulans are concerned. We had not long to remain in this life, anyway. It is only that your hiding place might be revealed; that our plans to outwit the Llotta will fail."

"You—you think she will make away with Dantor?"

"No; he is too valuable as a scientist. But the guards are awaiting her orders to repeat what happened in the Tritu Nogaru. She depends on the work of this laboratory a great deal, though it may be she will stay her hand."

*   *   *   *   *

He was fussing with the controls of the small crystal as he spoke, and it sprang into life with the peculiar shifting milkiness. Then, clearly, they were looking into the council chamber at Ilen-dar. Clyone was there, pacing the floor. Dantor had just arrived with two of the green-bronze guards. The Zara, though nervous, was curiously calm and polite in her greeting of the aged scientist.

"Dantor," she said, "I want these Earth men."

"I can not produce them, Your Majesty."

"You will not, you mean." Clyone dropped her voice. "For two reasons, Dantor, I must have these Earth men. And they must not be harmed. We need them on account of this k-metal that was brought by Antazzo, whose ugly body I so foolishly destroyed."

"Two reasons, you said, oh Clyone?" Dantor smiled knowingly.

"Yes, two!" said the Zara defiantly. "I love this Carson, if you must know. And it is the only influence for good that ever has come into my life, Dantor. Oh, can't you see? I *must* have them."

Blaine felt the hot blood mount to his temples. Tommy giggled like a moron. And Ulana drew away, ever so slightly, it was true, but still it was a definite withdrawal. Damn this leopard woman, anyway!

"He is not for you, oh Clyone," Dantor was saying, "To people of his world the very thought of such a woman as yourself is repulsive. A murderess he would call you! Their reactions to the taking of human life are entirely different from those of the Llotta. They are—you will pardon my saying it—more like those of the Rulans. The Llotta hold life cheap; they hold it dear. To your people you are not a bad woman; only a foolish one who sometimes, in the heat of passion, upsets their plans by the sudden snuffing out of a life that is valuable to those plans. Do you not see my point? He is different; to him you are the wickedest woman whom he has ever encountered—a monster."

*   *   *   *   *

This was strong talk. Blaine drew a quick breath, anticipating another of her black rages and sudden death for poor old Dantor.

But Clyone suddenly was on her knees before the old scientist, pleading with him! Creature of strange caprices! Though humanlike in her emotions when in her softer moods, she was more like the feline to which Blaine had likened her, when those soft moods had passed.

Somewhere overhead, in the chambers of the Tritu Anu, there was the sound of a muffled explosion. Its shock was felt even here in the rock-hewn secret apartment. Tiedus went white. Quickly he manipulated the controls of the crystal sphere.

"It can't be," he exclaimed. "The guards would not disobey her, and she has ordered no action."

Swiftly, then, the searching ray of the apparatus swung back to the Tritu Anu itself, boring into the vast structure above them. One of the chemical laboratories was completely wrecked; maimed and dying Rulans were everywhere in the ruins. And those who staggered to their feet were shot down by the green-bronze guards who stood at the doorway.

Then, floor after floor was revealed in the all-seeing crystal. Everywhere it was the same. Merciless, cold-blooded destruction of the Rulan scientists, the most valuable of all in the Llott scheme of things. The Earth men were speechless with horror. Ulana once more buried her head in Carson's shoulder, moaning helplessly.

The scene shifted again to the council chamber of the palace in Ilen-dar. The Zara had not risen from her knees; she was still pleading with Dantor. She knew nothing of the massacre.

"Ianito!" Tiedus gasped. "It must be he."

*　　*　　*　　*　　*

And once more the view was changed. They were in the huge dome through which they had entered this mad world. Near the base of the great telescope a bullet-headed Llott was gazing into the depths of one of the crystal spheres, watching the carnage in the Tritu Anu and shouting his orders to the guards. "Slay, slay, slay!" he yelled. "Not a Rulan shall remain in all Antrid. It is Ianito commanding you, Ianito the Great, master of our destinies, Dictator Supreme. Let not one escape; I command it. Then will come the great day of release; of conquest. A new home, a new world awaits you for the taking."

"It is as I thought," Tiedus groaned: "it is the end. He has taken things in his own hands at last."

The sphere went blank at his touch of a lever. His shoulders drooped and he spread his hands in a gesture of resignation.

"What in the devil!" Tommy exploded. "Can this guy overrule the Zara? Is he that powerful?"

"He is actual ruler of the world that is Antrid; the power behind the throne. Clyone must do his bidding. He has seen that she is softening and resolved to speed things up himself."

A sudden bedlam could be heard in the corridor outside the stone door. This Ianito had gone the Zara one better. He had located them; probably saw the capture of the guard and the rescue of Ulana on the very spot where his minions now hammered for entrance.

"They will take you!" Tiedus whispered. "There is no doubt as to the orders issued by Ianito. They will take you alive and bring you to him. You will be compelled to yield the secret of the metal that energizes."

"Not on your life! We'll refuse." Blaine was very positive.

Tiedus smiled sadly. "There is the pink gas, you know," he reminded him. "No, Carson, there is but one way. You must go out into the jungle and hide for a time. Dantor will return later; it is certain he will be spared. And he will contrive some way of outwitting them. Come; there is a passage."

Blaine saw the wisdom of the argument. It was their only chance. There was a blast that shook the ground beneath their feet, and a huge section of the stone door was blown into the room. He drew Ulana close with a possessive encircling arm.

*　　*　　*　　*　　*

They were in a dark narrow passage now, following the whispered voice of Tiedus. It was damp and rankly odorous there in the darkness, and slimy things wriggled over the floor, brushing their ankles clammily. Behind them there was the roar of another explosion and the shouting of angry voices. The guards were in the secret chamber and hot on their trail.

Tiedus was fumbling with something ahead of them where they had halted; something that rattled and clanked and finally came free. A door opened into the deep-shadowed green of the jungle.

"Go now, quickly," he warned them. "Hide yourselves as far in as you dare go. You will be lost, but will later be directed by a mental message from Dantor. I shall advise him from the spirit world. We do that, you know, we Rulans. But I must leave you now; I must hold back the guards to give you time. Go, friends; farewell."

In his hand Tiedus held the ray pistol they had taken from the captured guard. He would account for a few of the Llotta at least. Blaine reached for him to restrain him; it was unthinkable that this fine lad should sacrifice himself for them. But Tiedus was gone; he had slipped away into the black depths of the passageway.

"Come on, snap into it!" Tommy grated, his voice brittle with suppressed emotion. "The kid's right; let's go." He pushed his way into the matted growth of the jungle.

Holding Ulana close and not daring to look into her eyes lest he should see what he knew was there, Blaine followed his friend. The mysterious depths of the pale green forest closed in about them.

CHAPTER VII
In the Jungle

They had progressed not more than twenty paces into the dense undergrowth when the gleaming wall of the Tritu Anu was entirely hidden from view. The artificial sunlight seeped through the mass of vegetation overhead, a ghostly green twilight that made death masks of their faces. But of the lights themselves, of the great latticed columns, of the enormous sponge-like blossoms of the upper surface of the jungle sea, nothing could be seen. They were deep in a tangled maze of translucent flora that was like nothing so much as a forest of giant seaweed transplanted from its natural element. The moss-like carpet beneath their feet was slushy wet and condensed moisture rained steadily from the matted fronds and tendrils above. The air they breathed was hot and stifling; laden with rank odors and curling mists that assailed throat and head passages with choking effect.

Weird whisperings there were from above and all about them. It seemed almost that the uncanny, weaving green things were alive and voicing indignant protest over the intrusion of the three humans.

Ankle deep in the rain-soaked moss, their clothing drenched and steaming, they pressed ever deeper into the tangle. All sense of direction was lost.

"Guess we'd better rest now," said Blaine, seeing that Ulana was gasping from her exertions, "They'll never trail us here."

"How about this crystal thing—the searching ray?" Tommy ventured.

"It can not follow us," the girl explained, "Certain juices of the plants provide an insulator against the ray. In fact, it was an extract of these that was used in protecting the underground laboratory we just left. We are safe now and I am very tired."

So that was the reason Tiedus had been so certain they would be safe in the jungle! Blaine had wondered about that searching ray, and now Ulana's statement had stilled his doubts. Poor kid—she was all in! Her shoulders drooped and she leaned on his arm for support. His conscience troubled him for having forced the pace in the difficult footing. They need not have come so far in.

*   *   *   *   *

A glint of light through the close packed stems caught his eye; something phosphorescent it was, shining there in the green twilight. A giant mushroom! Towering seven feet from the ground, the great umbrella-like top was aglow with sulphurous light on its under side. And, beneath its ten foot spread, the mossy carpet was dry. An ideal shelter. Here Ulana might find the rest she so sorely needed, and in comparative comfort.

She curled up beside the huge stem and, half buried in warm, dry moss, immediately fell asleep. The Earth men sat gazing solemnly at each other; speechless. In the dim distance the roar of a monorail car rose faintly at first, then grew louder and louder, only to fade away once more into the whispering silence. A steady patter of jungle rain drummed on the mushroom top.

"God!" Tommy muttered, after a while. "I'd give my right eye for a cigarette."

"Me too." Blaine was hugging his knees, nodding drowsily. "A nice rare steak with mushroom sauce wouldn't go so bad, either," he drawled.

"Aw, have a heart. I'm so sick of these vitamin pills of theirs I never want to see one again."

"Yeah, but they're better than nothing. We haven't any of those even."

"Say!" Tommy jumped to his feet in sudden remembrance. "I saw a bush, back there about fifty feet, with bunches of big red berries on it. Like grapes, they looked. May be good to eat."

"Sure, they *may* be. And then again they may be poison. We can't take any chances like that. Leave 'em alone."

*   *   *   *   *

Tommy growled unintelligibly and fell to walking around their shelter with nervous strides, keeping just within the dry area and glaring savagely into the steaming jungle. Blaine smiled grimly. Nerves! Tommy always was like that; always had to be on the go and doing something. His own nerves were jumpy to-day. They were in hot water this time, for sure. Had to keep on though; they were still alive, or at least half alive; and the solar system was intact as yet. If only Tom Farley would quit his infernal tramping!

"Cut it out!" Blaine snapped peevishly. "You'll have us both bughouse. Can't you sit down and take it easy?"

Tommy stopped in his tracks. "Sorry, Blaine," he said. But he remained standing, staring off into the jungle. Then, suddenly he exclaimed, "Say, I'm going for some of those grapes, or whatever they are. I'll bring a mess of them back and we can wait till Ulana wakes up. She'll know whether they're poison or not."

"Oh, go ahead. But don't get yourself lost. Yell out if you can't find us and I'll answer."

"Okay. Don't worry about me." And in three steps Tommy was swallowed up in the undergrowth.

Blaine stole a glance at the girl and something caught at his throat. God, she was beautiful! There must be some way of getting her out of this mess. Dantor, perhaps, might show the way. He ought to be sending that message soon—a mental one, Tiedus said. Poor kid, Tiedus; gone to the happy hunting grounds now, no question of that. And he intended to advise Dantor from the spirit world. As simple as that, it was. They were game, these Rulans. Fatalists, though, and resigned to the inevitable; hopeless. But a wonderful people in a rotten world.

Soon he felt his head droop and in a moment he began to doze.

When he awoke it was to the touch of Ulana's soft fingers on his arm. "We are alone?" she asked.

"Lord!" he exclaimed, rising stiffly and rubbing the sleep from his eyes. "How long have I napped? I shouldn't have."

A swift look around the small clearing disclosed the fact that Tommy was missing. He shouldn't have let him go. A sudden panic gripped him.

"Tommy! Tommy!" he called out.

* * * * *

There was not even an echo in reply. Only the whispering of the jungle overhead and all around them. His friend was gone.

"Ulana," he said, his voice trembling, "we *are* alone. Farley is lost; swallowed up in this terrible forest."

And then, suddenly, she was in his arms. Those wondrous blue eyes, swimming in tears, looked into his own. Soft red lips, upturned, met his lips; clung there.

"I am sorry, my Carson," she said softly, when he had released her: "sorry that your good friend is lost. But perhaps," more brightly—"he has but strayed away. When the mental message comes you will be reunited. He will hear it as well as you."

Blaine shook his head. In his own heart he knew he would never see Tommy again. He had wandered too close to the Tritu Anu and had been overpowered by the green-bronze guards. Their ray pistols—he shuddered at the thought.

"I have *you* now, my Carson," the girl was saying. "Only you."

In a daze of pain and happiness intermingled, he knew he was holding her close, drawing her fiercely to him. And then, raising dull eyes to stare over the precious head and into the jungle that hid his friend, he froze with horror.

A flat serpent head with wide slavering mouth and beady eyes swayed there directly behind her. Pendant, it was, on a scaly and slimy length of undulating body that coiled high above in the matted growths of the jungle. As he watched, rooted to the spot, the great head drew back and poised, vibrating, ready to strike.

* * * * *

In one quick movement he flung the girl aside and whipped out the ray pistol he had taken from Pegrani. He pressed the release and a whirring sound came from the little weapon. But no crackling blue flame sprang forth to blast this creature into nothingness. Jumping aside, he was thrown to the ground by its lashing body as the great snake struck and missed.

But the pistol was useless. Short circuited by moisture, no doubt. He crouched there, calling huskily to Ulana. She must run for it; force her way into the thick undergrowth where the thing could not reach her. She lay there, helpless with terror. Then, in a flash, she was on her feet dashing to his side. God, the huge head was poised there again! Pulsating! The glittering avid eyes upon them!

Instinctively Blaine raised the pistol just as the head darted downward. The release clicked home. And, wonder of wonders, the blue flame crackled spitefully. Exploding atoms, dazzling in the green twilight. Mighty thrashings of the huge coils high up in the tangled foliage. Crashing and tearing of great stems and rope-like tendrils. But the enormous body was headless; a dead thing in the throes of its final reflexes. Only the one charge had been spoiled; the little pistol had served them well.

He drew Ulana into the thickest of the undergrowth for protection against the tremendous lashing thing that crashed into the small clearing where the giant mushroom grew. Their shelter was destroyed. He must find another; he must be forever on guard over this girl whose hand clung so confidently to his own as they wedged their way into the thicket.

"Carson! Ulana!" A familiar voice rose above the whisperings of the jungle. A voice familiar, yet unreal; supernatural; a calm, commanding one that did not sound but echoed only in the consciousness.

"Hark!" Ulana gripped his hand more tightly. "Did you hear? It is Dantor. The message Tiedus promised."

In awed silence they waited. A tiny ball of orange fire flamed suddenly in the depths of the rushes directly before them. A sign!

"Ah, you are there!" the voice broke in. "I have your mental reactions. You will follow the orange beacon to the Tritu Anu where I await your coming. Be of good cheer, my children."

*   *   *   *   *

What magic was this? The science of the Rulans was beyond the comprehension of the Earth man. Here was telepathy in its most perfect form. Communications from the spirit plane; the orange flame—it was all so utterly fantastic that Blaine had to look earnestly at the girl to assure himself it was not a dream. She smiled confidently.

And the orange flame was moving off into the undergrowth. They must follow its beckoning, flickering light.

It was a nightmare, that journey back through the jungle to the Tritu Anu. Dantor must be in a fearful hurry, for the orange flame moved swiftly. If they stopped a moment to rest it danced there impatiently, then receded into the green shadows until they were forced to follow for fear of losing it. Ulana's light robe was torn and sodden with moisture. The perfectly rounded ivory shoulders, bare now, were scratched and bleeding from contact with thorny protuberances that covered some of the lighter reed-like stems.

But the brave girl was uncomplaining. She clung doggedly to the Earth man's hand when they were able to walk erect: followed swiftly and unquestioningly when they were compelled to crawl or wriggle through an almost impenetrable thicket.

Once she cried out in alarm and Blaine turned back to see that the wiry tendrils of a spiny, globular plant had wound themselves around her slim body and held her fast. As he grasped her hand to draw her away, others of the tendrils curled about his wrist and he too was imprisoned. They burned the flesh, those writhing things, and tugged mightily. Ulana screamed with the pain of the many that held her in their tightening grasp.

*   *   *   *   *

It was alive, this thing that grew there, a huge ball with a thousand stinging tentacles. A carnivorous plant. Even as the realization flashed across his mind he saw that the spiny sphere was opening. Split vertically, the two halves fell apart to disclose the steaming interior whose walls were lined with sharp dagger-like projections a foot in length. And the wiry tendrils were drawing them in!

Almost insane with horror, Blaine released the disintegrating energy of the weapon he still carried in his free hand. Twice he pressed its release and twice the searing blue flame spurted from the glass tube that was its muzzle. Only a few charges remained now in the marvelous weapon but once more it had served then well. The open-mouthed plant monster vanished with the clearing of the blue vapor and the ensnaring tendrils relaxed, falling from their bodies like so many loosened cords. Blaine caught the swooning girl in his arms.

Half carrying her, he struggled on after the orange flare. The base of one of the latticed supporting columns loomed vast in the eery twilight gloom, and he leaned a moment against one of its vine-wrapped members. The girl was exhausted and hung limp in his circling right arm. Still the orange beacon danced on. If only Dantor would ease up a bit. Couldn't he give them a little time?

*   *   *   *   *

On and on he staggered, ploughing through the sloppy footing and the dripping clinging greens that were everywhere in his path. Slimy fronds wrapped themselves around them, impeding his progress; clinging as if they too were alive. The whispering silence closed in on them, vast and mysterious. Menacing; awful....

And then he stumbled against a metallic wall. The curved side of the Tritu Anu! His brain cleared and courage returned with a rush. The tiny orange flame danced merrily, leading him along the wall toward the door he knew was there.

Breathing easier now, his pace quickened as Dantor's guiding light slithered along the gleaming wall. Sometimes it was almost hidden from sight by the curvature of the welded plates and he was forced into a jog trot to keep it in view.

Grimly, tenderly, he clung to the delectable creature whose soft body drooped against him.

The door! The selfsame passage through which they had escaped opened before him. Grateful even for this doubtful protection, he crossed the threshold and trudged wearily along with his precious burden. Blindly trusting in the miraculous powers of Dantor, he followed the orange beacon which now seemed to smile cheerfully as it lighted his way through the winding rock-walled tunnel.

Dazed and spent, he collapsed in the arms of the aged Rulan when he reached the end of the passage.

CHAPTER VIII
Last of the Rulans

Bathed and fed and attired in dry clothing provided by Dantor, the Earth man and Rulan maiden were much refreshed and heartened when, together, they finally faced the aged scientist in the laboratory of the secret apartment. He hadn't allowed them to talk as yet.

Blaine glanced at the ragged opening where the stone door had been blown away. "We are safe from intrusion here?" he asked.

Dantor shrugged expressive shoulders. "The Tritu Anu is empty of life," he said; "a sepulchre. Those of our people who were not completely disintegrated lie blackened corpses in the chambers and corridors overhead. The gas grenades, you know. The guards went to Ianito with Farley and reported you dead: lost in the jungle from which none return."

"Farley!" Blaine shouted. "He is alive?" A wild hope sprang into being, intensified to a certainty as Dantor nodded.

"Why, yes. I thought you knew. They captured him very soon after the escape, but were unable to find you and Ulana. Ianito has mechanized him; he is in a hypnotic state of complete subjection to the Dictator. A quantity of k-metal has been taken to the laboratory at the breech of the great rocket-tube, and Farley now works there with Ianito's crew, initiating them into the mysteries of the metal's uses. Things look very bad."

"Wh-a-at!" Blaine lost his elation over the knowledge that his friend was alive. Tommy was doomed, anyway. They all were doomed. "Why did you bring us back?" he asked, turning away. Blaine felt it was better to have died in the jungle than to face this certainty of lingering torture. Ianito had triumphed; the universe was fated for utter annihilation and Ulana would suffer for weeks, perhaps months, before the final swift dissolution.

*   *   *   *   *

Understanding, Dantor smiled gravely. "My boy," he said, "we still live, and while we live there is hope. That is the reason I brought you back. Tiedus' message came to me as his spirit left the body and I made haste to come here as soon as the Zara released me and I knew the coast was clear."

"What hope can there be?" Appalled by the enormity of the disaster that threatened the solar system, certain of the ultimate fate that would be meted out to Tom Farley, and convinced of their own helplessness, Blaine was gloomily unenthusiastic.

"That remains to be seen, Carson. I confess it seems impossible of remedy, but the situation must be faced and studied carefully. Insignificant as we are in the vastness of the cosmos, we may yet prove to be the ones to circumvent the mad plans of the Llotta and prevent the catastrophe which is inevitable if they succeed. We must not give up while we still breathe."

The indomitable spirit of the old scientist glistened in his keen eyes, and he stepped to the controls of the crystal sphere.

"He will not give up, oh Dantor," Ulana exclaimed loyally. "He is with us to the end. Do I speak truth, my Carson?"

Her arm slipped through his and he thrilled anew at her fragrant nearness. Give up? Never! Not with Ulana to fight for. Blaine nodded wordless agreement, silenced by the expression of Dantor's face as the crystal vibrated to a musically throbbing note.

*   *   *   *   *

There in the crystal ball was pictured a vast underground workshop somewhat like the one in the great dome through which they had entered the copper-clad world. In place of the telescope there was the butt of a gigantic cannon-like tube that towered and was lost in the shadows of the vaulted chamber. Tom Farley, moving jerkily and staring with glazed unseeing eyes, was working there with a cube of the glittering k-metal. In the open breech block of the tube was a heaped-up cone of dry soil, the material they would disintegrate in producing the blast of electronic forces. Blaine groaned as his friend called for the equivalent of a milligram of radium. Though his voice was listless and his movements uncertain, Tommy knew what he was doing and was giving away the secret, powerless to resist the command Ianito had implanted in his completely subjective mind.

"Ah," Dantor breathed: "progressive annihilation of energy: a thing we never have accomplished. You excite ordinary material such as this dry soil by means of atoms exploded from this k-metal which is in turn excited by ordinary radium that can be used over and over as the primary excitant. Am I correct?"

"You are. There are precise ratios of atomic weights to be considered, of course, but it looks as if my friend is being extremely accurate in spite of his dazed condition. Man alive! There is enough material there to provide power for the entire planet Venus for a month!"

"And enough to start Antrid from her orbit," Dantor returned. "Enough to send her on her fatal journey sunward?"

"Only for the first acceleration. A vast amount of energy is needed, Carson, since the gravitational attraction of the planet you call Jupiter is enormous. Antrid will be speeded up in its orbit and the increased centrifugal force will cause it to take up a new and larger orbit where the forces will equalize. Several charges will be required in order to free her entirely from the mother body."

*   *   *   *   *

"There's time then!" Blaine exclaimed excitedly. "What can we do to put a stop to the thing? Something to counteract this control by Ianito; to cause Tommy to err in his proportions."

"Yes, that would do it—temporarily at least," Dantor agreed, his brow wrinkled in thought; "and there are the invisible cloaks. It is a bare chance if you want to take it. I can show you the way to this underground laboratory, and, in invisibility, you might even be able to change the ratios yourself. Yes, yes, it is a very good idea." The scientist brightened in renewed hope.

"Of course I'll chance it. When do I start?"

Dantor grinned in appreciation and Ulana looked up at him starry-eyed. "I'm going with you," she stated simply.

"Not on your life! There'll be danger. I won't have it!"

"Nevertheless, I'm going. There's another cloak and besides the danger would be greater if I were alone. Where you go I go, and if you die I die with you—gladly." She twined her fingers with his and gazed at him appealingly.

"Dantor! This can't be!" He turned to the scientist for support.

The aged scientist studied the two a little while, and then said quietly, "I'm afraid it is better as she wishes, Carson. I am unable to protect her, my boy, and there is no one else who might give her shelter. We are the last of the Rulans, she and I. The very last."

"Oh-h!" Ulana moaned, pale and distraught. "All—all are gone?"

"All, my dear. In his rage the Dictator destroyed the Tritu Deanu and the Tritu Raortu when he had finished here. Those were the last settlements remaining, you know. We alone are left behind, Ulana." Dantor bowed his head and the girl sobbed silently.

"Good Heavens!" Blaine Carson was aghast at the revelation. A monstrous deed, this last one of Ianito's. He was a fit master of a world gone mad. A monster in the twisted semblance of human form.

*   *   *   *   *

"He will be searching for you, oh Dantor," the girl said with sudden conviction. She had mastered her emotions and was instantly alert to every angle of the situation.

"That is true," said the old man gravely. "For myself I have nothing to fear, of course. Though insanely jealous of my accomplishments, he maintains an armed truce with me. He dares not do otherwise as the Supreme Council is aware of his shortcomings and cognizant of my superior knowledge of science. But there is danger to you two. You must make haste."

A trembling of the ground beneath them lent added emphasis to his final words. A quick glance into the crystal told them that the initial charge was at work in the huge rocket-tube. The laboratory there at its base was in confusion indescribable, the workmen running hither and yon in the effort to escape the terrific heat that radiated from the red hot breech of the tube.

They jammed the exits in their anxiety to be anywhere but near this monster source of energy whose pulsating roar drowned out all other sounds in the vast chamber.

Already Antrid was accelerating in velocity. Her vitals were wrenched and twisted, groaning in protest.

"Quick now!" Blaine was adjusting one of the invisible cloaks for Ulana. He'd *have* to take her with him. And a silent prayer for her safety was on his lips.

Invisible now, and hand in hand, they followed Dantor through the deserted passageways to the lift which carried them quickly to the roof. A drumming sound came to their ears as they stood there looking up into the blackness above the blue-white lights of Antrid. Vibrating to the tremendous roar of the rocket-tube, the copper shell emitted a constantly increasing reverberation that was like a long drawn peal of thunder on Earth or Venus. It was awe-inspiring, that sonorous bombilation; deafening.

*   *   *   *   *

Dantor was fumbling with the mechanisms of the remote control which Tiedus had used in returning the basket lift to the car that had brought the two Earth men from Ilen-dar. Again and again he returned to his manipulations after peering anxiously upward. But the basket did not respond to the call. They were marooned atop the empty shell of the Tritu Anu!

"Carson! Ulana! Where are you?" the aged scientist shouted above the din, his face a tragic mask, his lips compressed with anxiety and disappointment.

They grasped him to reassure him, each taking a hand. Carson, placing his lips close to the old man's ear, inquired anxiously, "What's the trouble?"

"The car does not respond. Something has happened to the motors, probably on account of the vibration. I can do nothing."

And then, piercingly through the thunderings of the copper shell, a voice broke in—Ianito's voice. "Dantor!" it shrieked. "At last I have found you. I need your help immediately. Wait there for the monorail."

Dantor gripped them tightly to enjoin silence. Ianito had located the scientist with the searching ray and was still watching and listening at his crystal. He seemed not to know that Blaine and Ulana were there.

"Very well, oh Ianito. I shall wait," Dantor shouted.

"It is good. There is important work to be done." Ianito's words trailed off into the maelstrom of sound that swirled about them.

"He's cut off," the scientist yelled. "There is but one chance now. You must come with me, depending on absolute silence and your cloaks to deceive them. It is the only way."

*   *   *   *   *

Ulana clung to him there in the terrifying bedlam and Blaine's fingers strayed to the comforting butt of the ray pistol. Whatever happened there were a few charges left; blasts of energy that would serve at least to postpone the end for Ulana. Or, if worse came to worst—

The sudden rush of a monorail car high overhead interrupted his thoughts. "Close to me now!" Dantor shouted; "but have a care lest one of them touch you and discover—"

A cable-hung cage dropped swiftly to the roof and they crowded in beside the scientist. Quickly it whisked them aloft to the higher plane.

In the monorail car Blaine held the girl close, and they trod softly as they dodged the guard at the porthole and stepped into the passenger compartment. Two of Ianito's technical experts were there and a crew of at least a dozen of the green-bronze giants. Unseen by any, the couple tiptoed to the farthest corner of the compartment and took seats in a recessed section.

With a quick jerk and the rising whine of motors, the suspended vehicle started back in the direction of Ilen-dar. In earnest conversation with Ianito's engineers, Dantor affected an air of nonchalance that was artfully disarming. The Llotta suspected nothing as the car continued on its way.

And then there came an ominous grinding sound from underneath the very seat occupied by the invisible fugitives. A puff of dense black smoke followed and Ulana coughed spasmodically, uncontrollably. They were coming now, two of the green-bronze ones, to investigate. There was no escape from this narrow space. And—Ulana was gone! She had slipped from his grasp in the coughing fit and he could not find her with his wildly searching hands. Another betraying cough over there. The green-bronze ones were between them. He saw one of them draw back in amazement, then clench his fingers and twist.

The ripping sound of torn material followed and the girl's head and startled face appeared: floating there, unsupported, her body and limbs as yet invisible. But they'd found her; she was lost!

CHAPTER IX
Ianito

Quickly stripping the protecting cloak from her body, the green-bronze one held the struggling girl gingerly but with a grip of iron. His eyes bulged from their sockets, and the other guard staggered backward with hands outstretched as if to ward off an evil spell that might be cast by this supernatural visitant.

Blaine thrust his arm through the folds of his coat, ray pistol in hand. A crazy laugh forced itself to his lips at sight of the detached member, stretched there, tensed, drifting in mid-air. The pistol prodded Ulana's captor viciously.

"Hands off of her!" the voice behind the lone arm was snarling. "Hands off, or I fire!"

The girl slipped to the floor in a heap as the amazed guard loosed his grip. And, in the same instant, the blue flame spurted. He had not intended to press the release; it was useless anyway to battle the entire outfit. But the blood lust was upon him and a savage joy in the destruction of this beast who had dared lay hands on Ulana impelled him to turn on the other. Blindly he swung, clubbing the pistol and beating in the ghastly face that wobbled there upon the spineless, superstition-bound body.

Others were coming then, hundreds of them it seemed. The pale face of Dantor appeared for an instant in the background, through the red haze that was blinding him. He only knew he was fighting desperately, viciously, and against impossible odds. The satisfying crunch of his left fist against a leering green-bronze face was followed by an excruciating pain as one of his knuckles was driven back. Hardly knowing he had pressed the release of the ray, he was mildly astonished to see that two of the guards were enveloped in the blue vapor. Scintillant tiny sunbursts within the blue. Two less of those devils! His pistol was empty and he flung it into a grinning face; he saw the blood spurt and the face change shape, crushed beyond human resemblance.

He was down then, gasping for breath against the floor plates. The weight upon him was enormous; crushing. If only they'd quit squirming so ... and pounding ... reminded him of his old football days ... some scrimmage!

Abruptly came the blankness of insensibility.

*   *   *   *   *

Dimly at first, in the painful throbbings of returning consciousness, Blaine knew he was in one of the Llott workshops where machines hummed and pounded and where many operatives were busily engaged. A cool hand stroked his aching brow and he opened his eyes. Ulana! They had spared her. Alert on the instant, he was acutely aware of the babbling of voices close at hand. Ianito was there, at the base of the huge telescope, talking with Dantor, his voice raised excitedly. The monorail crew stood by, and he noted with grim satisfaction that several of them were as badly damaged as he could wish.

His gaze returned to the sweet face that bent so near. Weakly he drew the golden head to his breast; held it there a moment, thinking, hoping, planning. Then he sat up on the edge of the low couch on which he had been placed, regarding her anxiously. Evidently they had not harmed her—as yet.

Ianito had dismissed the green-bronze ones and was approaching the couch. Dantor was with him, lagging a little and pressing a finger to his lips; shaking his head gravely to warn them. They must not speak of the plans made in the Tritu Anu; must not talk.

The Dictator was regarding them now with hard eyes. But it seemed almost that something of admiration or respect, something of human-like emotion was in his cold stare.

"Hah!" he grunted, at last. "These two are in love, Dantor. It is as you explained. It is good, and fits in with my plans to a nicety. I shall spare the life of the Earth man on account of his knowledge of the inner planets; I can use him later. The girl I shall spare for a different reason, and that fits in with my plans as well."

*　*　*　*　*

What did he mean by that last crack, the grinning devil? A sinister intent was there, behind his smooth talk. Blaine half rose from his seat in quick anger, but the girl's gentle touch on his arm restrained him. She depended on him now and he'd have to go easy until the proper time came.

"Impetuous, aren't they?" Ianito was saying, "these Earth men. A characteristic that must get them into much trouble, even in their own world."

Laughing at him, this hell-hound! Blaine gritted his teeth.

The Dictator addressed him directly. "You are a fortunate young man," he drawled sarcastically. "You have slain several of my trusted retainers and by so doing have forfeited your right to life. But Ianito is forgiving. Mechanized, you will be of value to me when the great day comes. And it pleases me that you are so deeply attached to the Rulan maiden; it pleases me greatly."

"Why?" Blaine snapped, a great rage consuming him. Only the pressure of Ulana's fingers held him back. He would have to control his temper or he'd make a mess of things.

"Because, my dear Carson, it will so displease the Zara."

With this cryptic remark he turned on his heel and left them. A number of his technical experts awaited him at the eyepiece of the great telescope.

Dantor whispered swiftly before following him, "Keep up your courage, Carson. A way may yet be found."

The group by the telescope was an excited one. Something had occurred which must be of great moment. It came to Blaine in a flash that the reverberations of the copper shell of Antrid had ceased. The rocket-tube was silent.

"I don't know why we shouldn't be in on this," he said to the girl. "Let's go over there and see what it's all about."

*　*　*　*　*

One of the astronomers was reporting to Ianito, referring to a sheet of calculations he held in nervous fingers. "Our orbital velocity has increased greatly," he was saying, "and the new path lies at an average distance of eighty-three erds from the mother planet. According to my figures it will require six more charges to free us from her pull and another to redirect us toward our destination."

Eighty-three erds! Practically a million Earth miles. Already they had swung out to a new orbit between those of Ganymede and Callisto. And what of the effect on the other satellites? Blaine listened carefully as the astronomer continued.

"Perturbations in the movements of the other bodies in our own system are marked, and, in the case of the first satellite, have proved disastrous. It has commenced its inward journey and soon will have fallen into the gaseous envelope of the mother body. But this need occasion us no concern; it is small and there will be stabilization of the others after the second charge is fired."

Colossal conceit! What amazing ignorance or oversight of natural laws! These Llott scientists could see no farther than their snub noses, or at least no farther than the satellite system of Jupiter. And Ianito was complimenting the astronomer on his good work!

The group broke up now and the Dictator turned to the controls of his crystal sphere. Blaine and Ulana caught the view of the underground laboratory at the base of the great rocket-tube.

All was as it had been when they first saw this chamber. The breech of the huge cannon had cooled and its massive block was open. Tommy was there, fishing the radium capsule from the powdery residue in order that it might be used in exciting the next charge. A mechanical precision marked his every motion.

"It is good," Ianito grunted, flicking a lever that cut off the view. "We are progressing nicely, thanks to the generosity of the Earth beings in providing this k-metal."

His sarcastic grin was infuriating. Dantor cast a warning look in the Earth man's direction. It wouldn't do to lock horns with this self-satisfied despot; at any rate, not now. Blaine's mien was expressionless as he faced him.

*   *   *   *   *

The view in the crystal was another familiar one when Ianito made a quick readjustment: the throne room in the palace of the Zara! The Dictator snorted when he saw that Clyone was reclining lazily on her golden couch, submitting graciously to the ministrations of her handmaidens.

"Faithless creature!" he snarled. "Harlot! Parricide! But at last Ianito will have his revenge."

The hate in his voice and in those terrible glass-hard eyes was devastating in its intensity: implacable, relentless. Yet Blaine could not down the exultant feeling that came to him when he saw that this monster could suffer, too.

"What's the matter?" he sneered. "Did she throw you down?" He could have bitten off his tongue as he spoke. Ulana gasped.

And if Ianito had been in a rage before he was a madman now. Despite his contempt of the misshapen creature, Blaine quailed before the murderous glare that answered his rash words. But the Dictator was master of himself, at that; his lips tightened in a thin line and he held his peace. He actually smiled after a moment, the devil, a smile, though, of evil triumph. He turned once more to the crystal and switched on the sound mechanism.

"Clyone," he called, in velvety voice; "it is Ianito."

She looked up, startled, her chalky face gone whiter still. Her jeweled fingers fluttered to the smooth throat.

"I hear you," she replied shakily. "What do you wish of me."

"Nothing much—this time. I have visitors who request an audience with you, oh Clyone. Can you see them at once?"

"Who—who are they?" Her eyes widened at his insinuating tone.

"An Earth man—Carson—and the Rulan maiden who is to become his mate." Ianito chuckled evilly as he watched her expression.

"Carson?" she whispered, her wild eyes softening, "He—he lives?" Black hatred replaced the wondering joy that had glowed in her face. She was thinking of the statement regarding the Rulan maiden. "Why, yes," she snapped, suddenly very much alert; "I can see them. Send them immediately."

The Dictator chortled as he switched off the power. Dantor paled and looked away. So this was his scheme! He was sending Ulana to certain death at the hands of the leopard woman.

Blaine bit his lips until they bled. If only he had one of their ray
pistols again. If he had—

*   *   *   *   *

Ianito was at his side, whispering. But he couldn't see him;
the devil had donned one of Dantor's invisible cloaks. Something
hard pressed deep into his ribs.

"I shall be with you," the Dictator told him, "but she will not
know. It is necessary, of course, that I watch over you in order
that your deportment be suitable to the occasion. The death ray
of Antrid is ready in my hands. Proceed, you and the Rulan
maid, and see to it that you give her every attention while in the
Zara's presence."

Dantor interposed an objection, "But, Ianito, you promised to
spare them. I learned to love these two and want no harm to
come their way."

"I keep my promise, oh Dantor. Ianito will not harm them."

"But the Zara."

"What Clyone does is none of my concern. Silence, Dantor; I
command it! You will remain here." The voice of the Dictator cut
like a knife.

The old Rulan scientist bowed his head and turned away.
Good old Dantor! He'd done all in his power to help them. This
was the end; not a question of doubt. Blaine Carson drew the
Rulan maiden fiercely to him. This Clyone might meet some
opposition if she attempted to wreak her spite on Ulana; she
would meet it. There was no need for Ianito to ask that he pay
every attention to the lovely, frightened girl who clung to him so
trustingly.

They were in the lift then, dropping swiftly into the palace
beneath the great dome that topped Antrid.

"This Clyone," Ulana whispered, "she has great power of
enticement, my Carson. I fear for your loss—to me. She will take
you from me, and I shall be alone—or dead. Death would be the
better."

"Never!" said Blaine huskily. "Never, my dear. She has no
power over me; nor will I permit her to bring suffering to you."

Ianito laughed then, an ugly cackle that came out of the
unseen.

CHAPTER X
Clyone and Ulana

The Zara received them in the throne room, alone. Blaine hesitated as he crossed the threshold, Ulana's trembling fingers tightly clasped in his own. The quick prod of the invisible ray pistol warned him that Ianito was at his heels.

Clyone uncurled her sinuous, black-sheathed body and rose to her feet as they neared the dais.

"Welcome, oh Carson," she purred. "Clyone has mourned you as dead, but she mourns no longer. A kind fate has returned you."

The gold-flecked eyes were all for him; it was as if she did not see his companion. Blaine fought the spell of her with all that was in him. He did not reply.

"Come to me, Carson," she pleaded, her lashes lowered. "Leave this Rulan girl and come to me."

"Where I go she goes," he replied firmly.

"Very well then," said the Zara meekly, "bring her with you. I would converse with her as with you."

Something new, this was: a gentleness Blaine had never thought the leopard woman could exhibit, even in sham. And her eyes, when she raised them, still were gentle. She extended a white arm and smiled provocatively. If this was a ruse, if she meant harm to the Rulan maid, her acting was superb. And, from what he had seen of the woman previously, he was almost convinced of her sincerity. A nature like hers was incapable of successful dissimulation. Still, he was suspicious and he shielded Ulana with his body as they came up to the throne. The Zara studied them in silence for a while. Then she spoke.

"Let me look at you, my dear," she said to the Rulan maiden.

*   *   *   *   *

And Ulana, unafraid, faced her boldly. His muscles tensed, Blaine watched every movement of the Zara's straying fingers. But her gaze was direct and kindly; there was no dissembling here. It was not the same Clyone he had previously known.

"You are very beautiful, Ulana," she said softly. "Do you love this Earth man very much?"

"I do, Your Majesty."

"And you, Carson, you love her—very much?"

His answer was wordless. A sudden lump in his throat choked back the vigorous affirmative and he merely nodded, mute, as he enfolded the slight form of Ulana in his arms.

"Carson—are you sure?" Clyone was pleading, her eyes compelling; tender. Ulana drew away from his arms, waiting.

What had come over the leopard woman? She was a creature of mad vagaries, he knew, and yet this was the most convincing mood he had seen. Despite his knowledge of her past; despite his better judgment, he was drawn toward her. A step, and then quick revulsion of feeling. He recoiled and turned swiftly to Ulana.

Clyone saw and understood. Her tender mood was over in a flash and she crouched there, terrible jealous eyes fixed on the Rulan maiden. She extended a white arm with jeweled fingers, pointing. Blaine swung quickly, brushing the arm aside just as that intangible something flashed from her hand. The energy of the black disks! It had missed Ulana by inches, but crashed home—on something!

*　　*　　*　　*　　*

A scream of terror rang out in the chamber, and there on the floor a dozen paces from the dais the thing that had been Ianito wriggled under the heap of whirring black things that suddenly covered the invisible form. He wriggled and then lay still as the angry buzzing of the black destroyers rose in triumphant, discordant song.

"Ianito!" the Zara exclaimed, thunderstruck. "He was here?"

"He was," Blaine assured her in an awed voice, "invisible, oh Zara, in a cloak contrived by Dantor, the Rulan scientist." Then blind rage overcame him. She had tried to kill Ulana; before his eyes! "You she-devil!" he roared. "I've half a mind to choke the vile life from your tainted body. Damn you! May the heat devils of Mercury burn and sear and shrivel you in everlasting torment."

She cowered as if he had struck her, and, unaccountably, he was ashamed. Cursing her like a schoolboy and using the language of the lower class Venerians!

"Please, Carson, please," she moaned; "do it. Choke me if you will and release me from my torment. I am yours to do with as you please." Throwing back her proud head, she bared her throat.

Blaine took a step forward, his knees weak beneath him.

"Carson!" It was Ulana, her hand soft on his arm.

He drew the back of his hand across his eyes. This was madness! But was ever a woman so deserving of death? Incomprehensible half-animal creature, she sat there rocking to and fro, waiting.

"No!" he said. "No! Only let us go in peace, Clyone. Your sins be on your own head. Your realization of them is punishment enough."

"Wait!" Controlling herself now, she rose once more, and her face was transfigured. Almost it seemed that she was happy. "Wait!" she repeated. "You are free to go when I have finished, but first Clyone wishes to bid you farewell."

*   *   *   *   *

They faced her in silent wonderment.

"Ianito is gone," she continued, "and the Llotta are helpless without him, unless I take over their leadership in fact. He was my master, I admit. But Clyone is able to carry on with the plans he conceived; able, but no longer willing. Clyone is abdicating. It but remains for you, Carson, to put a stop to this thing they are doing down there at the great rocket-tube. You can do it, I am certain. Go now; and think not too badly of Clyone when you have gone. Farewell."

With a quick motion she raised her fingers to her lips, then tossed a small vial crashing to the floor.

"Carson—she has taken something," Ulana stifled a hysterical sob as she spoke. "Go to her. It is the least you can do."

Blaine caught the leopard woman in his arms and lowered her gently to the luxurious cushions of the throne she had occupied for so long a time, a queen in name only. Already the gold-flecked eyes were glazing and they begged him piteously.

"Kiss me." Her lips formed the words, but no sound came.

Ulana was there, on her knees and crying. "Carson, you must," she urged him.

The spirit of Clyone, with its great burden of evil and some little of good, left the beautiful body as the Earth man pressed his lips to hers. An unwonted smile, placid and content, wreathed the still features.

The Zara was no more.

*   *   *   *   *

Stunned and shaken by what they had seen, they hurried from the chamber of death. Blaine located the lift and they were quickly carried to the laboratory.

Dantor was there, working with the astronomers, and Blaine drew him aside, whispering the story in his ear in swift disjointed sentences. The aged scientist could scarcely credit his senses.

The thrumming of the copper shell to the energy of the second rocket-tube charge came but faintly to their ears in this place, since the vacuum of outer space surrounded the great domed structure. But the vibration and quakings of the satellite were transmitted to the floorplates on which they stood. They knew that Antrid was swinging ever outward from the mother planet.

"You must do it alone," Dantor was saying; "you and Ulana. I have no control over these Llotta. I am here only on sufferance of Ianito, and Ianito is no more. But they know it not. These in the dome think he is with you now, cloaked in invisibility. The tale of the cloaks has been broadcast. You are safe for the present and can descend to the base of the rocket with impunity. Ianito's name is the password. And here is a ray pistol, fully charged; two of them. He left them in his desk. Go now, quickly."

"The way—how do we get there?" Blaine's fingers closed lovingly over the butts of the pistols and he thrust them in his pockets.

"Oh yes. The lift—the one that carried you to the palace—its shaft ends deep down beneath the natural surface of Antrid in a tunnel where a moving platform will carry you to your friend. May your God and the gods of ancient Antrid be with you."

Once more they were in the cage of the lift, dropping with breath-taking speed. Down into the bowels of the satellite they sped and it seemed the shaft would never end.

*   *   *   *   *

Then they were in the tunnel Dantor had told them about, smooth walls speeding past as the swiftly moving platform carried them on. The great arched chamber opened before them at last and they saw that the workmen were returning to their tasks. The huge breech of the rocket-tube had cooled to a dimly visible red, the second charge having done its work.

Hands in his pockets and walking stiffly as if mechanized, the Earth man presented himself before the guard at the entrance, Ulana pressed close to his side. He feigned the hypnotic state.

"I-an-i-to," he repeated in jerky syllables, acting the part, "he—sent us—with message—for Farley."

The guard grinned. Even here the story of the Earth man and the Rulan maiden was known. The strange leniency of Ianito in permitting them to remain together was the topic of the day. He waved them through with an indulgent gesture. Ianito knew what he was about, and would have his little joke—later.

Tom Farley was there, waiting with the Llott scientists until the breech block should have cooled sufficiently to permit them to open it and prepare the third charge. A flicker of recognition in his glazed eyes told Blaine he was not altogether gone, but Tommy gave no other outward sign. Perhaps with Ianito no longer alive, the mental control would become ineffective.

They had not long to wait, for the breech was water-jacketed and cooled rapidly. Blaine puttered around with unfamiliar test tubes and retorts, watching for a chance to get a word with Tommy in private. He was almost certain that his friend was recovering. Ulana sat there on a greasy bench, regarding the scene with anxious eyes. She was a brick: game as they made them.

Tommy was beside him then, weighing a heap of the dry soil for the next charge. "Are you all right?" Blaine whispered.

But Tom Farley stared back with not a glimmer of comprehension: He was still a victim of the mechanizing process of the Llotta. With a carefully planned but seemingly careless gesture, Blaine slid back the weight on the scale arm. This charge would be short of the proper ratio of dry soil. He wondered what the effect would be.

*   *   *   *   *

One of the Llott scientists came over then with the radium capsule, and Tommy attached it to the clamp that would hold it in contact with the cube of k-metal. The dry soil was shoveled into the breech block by the unsuspecting Llotta and the thing was ready for the placing of the excitant.

The great breech block swung home and a siren shrieked. All work in the laboratory was suspended and the workmen stood around in expectant silence. Blaine found himself worrying as to the possible result of his tampering.

"I saw you!" Tommy hissed then in his ear. "There'll be hell to pay now. We gotta beat it."

Good old Tommy! He'd recovered after all. He, too, had been shamming at the last. Blaine saw they were unobserved and thrust one of the pistols in his hand.

"Now!" his friend rasped. "Before they get wise. Grab the girl and we'll make a break for the tunnel entrance: over there."

Ulana took in the situation at a glance and was at his side. They moved swiftly in the direction of the entrance through which they had come.

A terrific roar came from the base of the rocket tube and the Llotta broke into excited screechings. Something different about it this time. There was a terrible menacing note in the jarring thump which preceded the roar. A muffled boom high in the five mile depth of rock strata above them spelled disaster of an unknown and terrifying nature. The breech of the tube was white with heat in an instant of time.

Pandemonium broke loose now and the Earth men were running for the exit to the lift, covering their retreat with brandished ray pistols. Ulana, brave girl, ran alongside, swinging a pinch bar she had picked up, ready to help.

CHAPTER XI
Disaster

The great crystal sphere on the central pedestal was ablaze with the scarlet warning signal of the Supreme Council. A sonorous voice from its depths boomed out above the clamor.

"Kill them! Kill the Earth men," it roared. "The Zara is dead and Ianito has vanished. Denari has mounted the throne, and it is he who commands you. Kill the traitors!"

But the Llotta and the green-bronze guards needed no command from the new ruler of Antrid. These devils from Earth had tampered with the last rocket-tube charge; probably had caused serious damage to the tube itself. They must die.

Only the guards were armed, and the Llotta swarmed so closely in pursuit of the fugitives that it was impossible for them to use their ray pistols. At the great iron gate that now closed the exit stood the guard who had admitted them. Tommy's pistol spurted blue flame and he was enveloped by the destroying energy.

Ulana screamed as a Llott grasped her, wrenching the iron bar from her hands. Blaine covered the intervening distance in a bound and his fist crashed to the fellow's jaw, snapping back his head and lifting him off his feet. He crashed to the floor plates an inert heap and the Earth man recovered the pinch bar.

Pocketing his pistol, he swung the bar with both hands in mighty circles that took terrible toll of the Llotta. They fell back before the onslaught of the infuriated Terrestrial, leaving eight of their number dead or dying with crashed skulls and broken ribs and arms.

*   *   *   *   *

"Open the gate, Tommy," he shouted. "Use your pistol on the lock if you have to." A guard was coming at him and he ducked to the floor as the blue flame crackled, singeing the hair from his head and blistering the scalp as it spent its charge in fusing a cross member from one of the steel columns nearby.

He fired from under his prostrate body and the guard thrashed his arms wildly in the blue mist, then stiffened to a sparkling vanishing figure within the dissipating vapor.

A gas grenade burst at his side and Blaine sprang to his feet, running from the spreading sulphurous cloud. The gate was open and its lock dropped molten metal. Good old Tommy!

The poison gas hid them from their pursuers for the moment and they were through the gate, all three.

"Get back!" Blaine shouted: "the gas!" He held his breath and closed his eyes as he slammed the gate and wedged it with the pinch bar he still carried. That would hold them for a while.

The gas was upon him and his skin flamed scorching hot from the contact. He mustn't breathe: mustn't open his eyes. He groped there in the scalding vapor, blindly. Tommy had him by the wrist then, dragging him away. Ulana was calling somewhere there in the darkness. His lungs were bursting. And then he knew the air was pure, and he exhaled the long pent breath noisily, and inhaled deeply.

Eyes smarting and head reeling, he saw Ulana through a haze of dancing smoke wisps he knew were illusory. She was safe, thank God! They were on the moving platform then, on the return side, and his strength was returning. Narrow escape, he'd had, from that lung-rotting gas. Ulana smiled happily when his vision cleared.

* * * * *

The speeding platform carried them swiftly toward the lift that had brought them down. What if the lift would not operate? This Denari might well have shut off the power or even returned the cage to the upper end of the shaft.

"Boy, oh boy," Tommy was saying, "you sure did gum up the works. Know what happened?"

"Plenty, from the look of things," Blaine smiled grimly.

"I'll say. You cut down the dry soil ratio a third. Not sure of the exact reaction, but the expansion was too rapid. Explosion followed before the air could be driven from the tube. I'll bet the big cannon was wrecked somewhere overhead. Boy, what a blast!"

As if the last sentence were a prophecy, there came a terrific jar that twisted the platform violently from under them. They were thrown headlong and an awe-inspiring rumbling came up from the vitals of Antrid. An earthquake! The tortured satellite could not withstand the strains set up by the tremendous reactive force of the rocket-tube. The lights snuffed out and the platform came to a grinding stop. One of the underground power plants was out of commission and they were trapped here in the stifling darkness.

"Nice fix we're in now!" Tommy grunted where he had fallen.

Blaine, having located Ulana, was relieved to find that she was unharmed. "Yes," he said slowly; "but there's one thing sure: they can't follow us here unless they walk."

"Why can't we walk?" Ulana asked with forced cheerfulness. "It isn't far now."

"Oh, we can walk all right; we'll have to. And here's hoping we get somewhere." Tommy, at least, was undaunted so far.

* * * * *

It was their only chance now. Blaine held fast to the girl as they felt their way along the smooth tunnel wall, and Tom Farley, behind them there in the darkness, kept up a running fire of small talk that was utterly irrelevant. Nothing could keep that Irishman down.

After what seemed like miles of steady plodding they glimpsed a light ahead. They quickened their pace. It was the open door at the base of the shaft, and the cage of the lift was there, fully lighted and waiting. Denari had not shut off the power after all. But of course! It came to Blaine in a flash; this was a private shaft, used by Ianito in his clandestine visits to the palace of the Zara and for his own use in descending to the sub-surface chamber at the base of the rocket-tube. Denari did not even know it existed.

Strange they had not been followed. Surely the Llotta could have forced that gate back there in a comparatively short time. A mass of falling rock, shaken loose by the temblor that cut off their light and stopped the moving platform, must have closed the tunnel.

They were in the cage now, shooting aloft with smooth acceleration. Tommy fidgeted and paced the floor in the narrow confines like a caged animal.

"Lord, man," he said, after a while, "what I wouldn't give for a cigarette!"

"Is that all you can think of?" Blaine was sarcastic. His own nerves were on edge. They were nearing the upper end of the shaft. "Try to do a little thinking about what's going to happen up there above Ilen-dar. We've got to do some tall figuring and some swift scrapping before we're through."

"Sure." Tommy shrugged his shoulders. "There'll be a lot of fireworks, I guess. But I wish I had a smoke just the same."

Ulana pouted. They spoke in English and she did not understand. But the expression of their faces forced a laugh to her lips, one of those silvery tinkles that caught at Blaine's heart strings. All that mattered now was to see her to safety—and happiness.

*   *   *   *   *

The cage slowed up and came to rest as the automatic control of its gravity energy functioned. The door rolled back and Blaine thrust his head through the opening, pistol in hand.

There on the floor of the corridor that led to the great dome room was a crumpled figure. Dantor! It couldn't be that they had slain him! Blaine was on his knees by the body, raising the blood-smeared head with gentle hands. A deep gash extended from over the right temple up into the scalp and the skull was crushed; a mortal wound. But the doughty heart of the aged scientist still beat on, weakly, but with determination. He opened his eyes and smiled.

"Ah, you have come at last," he sighed. "I have waited here to warn you and advise you."

"Easy now." Blaine straightened the helpless limbs and cradled the drooping head on his knees. Ulana was beside him, bravely holding back the sobs that were in her throat.

"I saw—in the crystal," Dantor whispered. "And Denari struck me down when I expressed relief at your escape. Carson—Ulana—Farley—you can escape if you do as I say. Antrid is doomed; the incorrectly proportioned charge burst the rocket-tube in several places and tore the muzzle asunder where it projected from the copper shell of our world. With the explosion at the muzzle a huge section of the copper casing was blown away and the atmosphere of Antrid is now escaping rapidly into the vacuum of space...."

Dantor closed his eyes, and a spasm of pain twisted his features.

Tommy expelled a shuddering breath, solemnly expressive.

*   *   *   *   *

The aged scientist fought off the grim spectre valiantly. He patted Ulana's hand as his weak voice resumed. "You will take care of her I know, Carson. Take her with you to your own world; make her happy." He fell silent once more.

"But how?" Blaine whispered.

"Oh yes, I am forgetting. The side passage—next one on the right—it leads to a storeroom of the oxygen helmets and vacuum-tight suits in which you can step forth from the adjoining airlock. Your space ship is there ... unharmed.... In it you will be able to return ... and...."

But Dantor's spirit had fled the pain-racked body. Blaine closed his lids and stretched him on the hard metal floor, crossing the thin hands on his breast. Ulana sobbed openly for a moment and then bowed her head in silence.

"The last of the Rulans," Blaine said softly, looking down at all that was mortal of the Rulan scientist.

"No," Ulana whispered, "I am the last, my Carson."

"You'll become a good American, sweetheart," he said gently. "That is, if we get away from here." There was no time to be lost, at that. At any moment this Denari might find them. "Come," he begged, drawing her from the body, "we must hurry."

Following the passage indicated by Dantor they came at last to an open door. A noticeable draft blew outward and Blaine thought grimly of the scenes that were being enacted throughout all Antrid. The air that made life possible was escaping. And the news broadcasts from Ilen-dar would have notified the entire population by this time. There would be rioting, panics, murder and suicide in the cities of the accursed Llotta and in their subject countries. A frantic effort of the scientists to stop the gap would avail them nothing: it was an impossible task now. The construction of the great shell had been a different matter; there was some natural atmosphere remaining in those days. And, finally, they would suffocate, every last one of them. They'd die miserably, purple of face and with swollen tongues protruding.

*   *   *   *   *

The open door led to a railed-in balcony that looked out over the dome room. Machines still hummed there but the place was deserted save for a few scattered corpses: probably those of the Llotta who had objected when Denari usurped the throne.

A second door opened from the balcony into the store room of the moon-suits. At least these helmeted contraptions resembled the so-called moon-suits used by inhabitants of the inner planets when they visited a body having no atmosphere.

Ulana needed some assistance with the bulky equipment, and then Blaine climbed into another of the suits and locked his helmet. A moment later they were in the air-lock with Tommy, who had attired himself more quickly and was operating the controls.

At the outer hatch they waited until the air pressure reduced to a practically complete vacuum. Their suits distended ludicrously now by the pressure within, they unclamped the hatch and stepped out to the surface of the great copper shell. It vibrated under their feet to the blast from the huge gap that was not five miles distant.

The RX8 was there as Dantor had said, a slim tapered, cylinder that gleamed, a thing of beauty, in the reflected light of Jupiter which now was millions of miles distant. The sun was not visible and the light of the mother planet cast long shadows on the copper plates. Pelting ice particles clattered resoundingly against the metal helmets: frozen moisture from the escaping air of Antrid.

Blaine cried out in surprise; then remembered his companions could not hear him. There were moving shadows over there, four of them, nearing the hull of the RX8. The Llotta had beat them to it. Denari, no doubt, intending to escape with a chosen few of his subjects. He broke into a run through the now blinding hail storm. He would have to head them off; else, Ulana was lost, they all were lost.

CHAPTER XII
The Last of Antrid

Tommy was running beside him now and Ulana was not far
behind. They too had seen the danger. If they could not reach the
vessel ahead of the Llotta; would not fight them off and gain
possession, it was all off. They'd die here, horribly, on the roof of
Antrid.

And the ray pistols were useless: they could not be fired
inside the ballooning fabric of their suits without destroying it
and themselves. There were only the hooks that were attached
to the bulging sleeves—iron hooks for lifting—but these were
heavy and sharp pointed. They might be of some use, at that.

Once they were completely blinded by a deluge of ice
particles, Blaine could see neither the RX8 nor the waddling
figures of the Llotta. He clung to his companions by means of the
hooks, interlocking his with theirs, and waited for the storm to
ease off. If ever it would! Pressing the thick glass window of his
helmet against that of Ulana's, he saw that her eyes were wide
with terror. But she smiled bravely and nodded encouragement.
What a girl!

There was a momentary clearing a little way from the white
wall and he saw the hull of the ship, a dim shape that loomed
suddenly distinct and near. They dashed for the open port, still
holding together.

One of the bulging, helmeted Llotta had reached the port and
was scrambling inside. Blaine loosed himself and pounced on
him, swinging one of his hooks in a sweeping, clawing arc. It
caught in the fabric of the fellow's suit, ripping a foot-long slit.
Like a punctured ballon it deflated and became a shriveled,
clinging thing. The Llott hung there over the rim of the port,
instantly suffocated and frozen stiff in the vacuum and intense
cold of space as the air and heat of the suit was dissipated.

* * * * *

Blaine dragged the rigid body from the opening and flung it
to the white powdered copper surface. Wheeling, he saw that
another of the Llotta had engaged Tommy. Two of them: in fact,
there were three swollen figures in that mix-up. And the fourth

was advancing on a smaller figure that turned and ran. Ulana! In a flash he was after them. Tom Farley would have to look out for himself, poor devil. With two of them against him, the outcome was dubious.

And then came a second snow-like deluge of white particles. He stumbled on, groping blindly; slipping, sliding in the precarious footing. It was ankle deep now, that powdery carpet of ice particles. Oh God, if that Llott devil got Ulana! He groaned aloud, a hideous mournful echo in the confines of the helmet. Groping, staggering there in the white silence, he gave up hope. The white-carpeted shell of Antrid heaved mightily from the force of some new concussion within, and threw Blaine scrambling.

Crawling now, feeling his way over the shuddering surface, he saw a dim huddled mass there in the pelting rain of ice. Moving, it was! Two bloated figures, one large and one small, rolling over and over: Ulana and the Llott who had chased her! He was there in one mad scramble and had dragged the fellow from her; was astride the rubbery inflated covering, clawing and tearing. The thing collapsed and went flat between his knees. He saw the mist of moisture-laden escaping air; felt the quick swelling and the jarring collapse as internal organs exploded from the atmospheric pressure inside the brute's body. Nauseated, he crawled away from the dead, grotesque-looking figure.

Ulana was on her knees, endeavoring to get to her feet. She had not been harmed, thanks to his good fortune in finding them. But where was the RX8? In the awful white silence, broken only by the eery patter of the ice particles on helmets and fabric, all sense of direction was lost. Through the double thickness of helmet lenses he looked into Ulana's eyes: for the last time, he thought.

*   *   *   *   *

And then the white shroud lifted once more. The ship was there, not a hundred yards distant! Tommy still battled one of the Llotta, desperately circling the wary, grotesquely bobbing figure and swinging those terrible slashing hooks. The other was down, almost covered with white. Out of the picture, that one, but the remaining Llott was giving his friend a tough time of it. With the girl clinging to him, their arms hooked fast, he scuttled over the treacherous, ice-powdered copper. He had to get there quickly, and help.

Tom Farley slipped and fell heavily. The Llott was on him in a flash and they struggled madly there in splashings of white that hid them from view for a moment. Then one of them was up and the other lay still, a surprisingly shrunken and motionless figure.

The victor was coming at him then, bloated arms lashing out in swift, vicious circles. He had got Tommy, the damned swine! Blaine met his rush with a flying tackle that brought him down crashing. He lay still, the devil, knocked out probably by the metal helmet contacting with his skull. With arm poised for that slashing swing that would send him into eternity, Blaine peered through the lens of his helmet. His heart stopped beating and the upraised arm fell limp. This was no Llott: it was Tom Farley! Good Lord, he would have killed him in another second!

He tried to shake him; to bring him to. But he couldn't get hold of the bulging suit anywhere without danger of slashing it with one of those hooks. What if that fall had been fatal! Ulana was at his side now and he stared at her, white-faced, trembling in his uncertainty and horror.

And then Tommy opened his eyes. They saw him shake his head to clear it and then he, too, stared in horror. How close a call! Friend killing friend, out here in the air-less cold on the shivering shell of the dying alien world!

They helped him to his feet and through the entrance manhole. His mind awhirl with emotion, Blaine saw that Ulana was inside and then followed as in a dream. He bolted the outer cover and turned the valve that would admit air to the lock. Soon they would be inside. With their protecting coverings discarded there would be the fresh air of the interior; light; warmth. Safety for Ulana. Away from the copper-clad world, they'd be on their way—home.

*   *   *   *   *

A little later, Blaine Carson sat at the controls of the RX8, Ulana at his side. Tommy was below, polishing and oiling and fondling his beloved machines. The surface of Antrid was visible through the viewing port, twenty miles beneath them and receding rapidly. Swinging in its new orbit, Antrid was gasping its last.

Over there, a few miles to the east, there spouted a column of white vapor that rose from a heaped up crater of ice which extended in a circle now many miles in diameter. Heavily laden with moisture as it was, the artificial atmosphere of Antrid provided a vast storm of frozen particles as it escaped into the absolute zero of space. For many days this would continue and the pressure within would drop gradually, down, down, until the air was so rare it would no longer sustain life. And there was no hope of repairing the break: the mountain of ice prevented getting at it from outside, and the rush of air from within made the handling of patch plates and brazing torches impossible. Besides, an area of supporting columns of more than a mile diameter had been wrecked by the blast of the rocket-tube. It would require an Earth year to make such a repair, even if they could retain that atmosphere. Antrid was done for, this time.

Abruptly, Blaine turned his head from the port and gave his attention to the controls. The RX8 pointed her nose upward, away from this terrible world of disaster and death—homeward bound. With a tremendous blast from the stern rocket-tubes she headed swiftly into the heavens. A thousand miles, five, ten, they shot into space with ever increasing acceleration.

*   *   *   *   *

And then a blazing orb was visible off to one side of the swiftly receding globe that was Antrid. Through the floor ports it shone, casting cheerful rays upward to the ceiling where they made a patchwork pattern of the gleaming metal.

"The sun," Ulana breathed, in awe. "I—I've never seen it, my Carson. It is most beautiful."

He drew her to him tenderly. "You'll see it every day, dear," he whispered, "when we're home."

Home—a wonderful thought! He'd not hoped to see it again; hadn't dared to since Antarro showed his hand back there in the asteroid belt. And now it was a reality. He was going home, and with him he was taking—Ulana.

"You—you think they will approve of me?" she was saying as he sent blasts from the steering rockets to swing them around on a new course sunward. "Your people, I mean. They will approve of your choice, my Carson?"

Anxiety showed in her wide-eyed gaze and she drew closer as if fearful of losing him.

If only she knew! If only he had words to tell her!

"Approve of you!" he said huskily. "Lord, girl, they'll love you! But not as I love you. It is the biggest thing—"

Tommy's discreet cough came from the head of the companionway. Blaine turned to glare savagely. His friend was standing there, grinning like an idiot and extending a paper-wrapped package.

"Look," he exclaimed guilelessly: "cigarettes. I found them, a whole carton."

"Well, I'll be damned!" Blaine exploded, careful that he spoke in English. "All you think of, all you've talked about since we left the vessel, is your hankering for a cigarette. For God's sake, get out of here and go smoke yourself to death."

But Tommy was advancing, still grinning, still extending the package. "Come on, old kid, have one," he insisted. "It'll do you good; quiet your nerves."

And his friend dropped a tantalizing eyelid. In spite of his annoyance Blaine was forced to laugh. "Oh, all right," he said, reaching for the package of smokes; "I'll take one. Just to please you. But, beat it then, will you?"

*　　*　　*　　*　　*

Swaggering as he went and casting knowing glances over his shoulder, he was gone. Great little Irishman, Tommy: always smiling, always there in a pinch, never worried, he was the best friend a man could have. They'd catch hell when they got back, for losing a part of their precious cargo. Those miserly k-metal people wouldn't give them credit for salvaging nine-tenths of the stuff (luckily only about a tenth had been removed by the Llotta): they'd only cry about the amount that was lost. And Tom Farley would laugh it off: kid them out of it.

Ulana was smiling as if she understood. She *did* understand, God bless her. She saw into this wonderful friendship and was glad. It was great to have a friend like that—and a girl like this.

Hand in hand, they gazed into the heavens before them. To the girl it was a most marvelous sight, an omen of good fortune and of happiness to come. She nestled her head into the shoulder of the Earth man as she watched; spellbound.

For a long time the silence was broken only by the steady muffled purr of the stern rocket-tubes. The aroma of cigarette smoke drifted up the companionway.

Out there in the heavens was the sun, Mars, Earth, Venus; the dear old solar system was still intact, undisturbed excepting for the slight perturbation in the region of Jupiter. Blaine doubted if the influence was measurable insofar as changes in the motions of the inner planets were concerned.

He turned to the eyepiece of the telescope and swung the instrument around to bear on the Earth. A cool green crescent was there in the field of vision: the eastern coast line of the Americas outlined clear and distinct.

"Look, dear," he whispered. "Home! Your new home is there; our home together."

She sighed happily as she gazed at the inviting sunlit outlines. "Home," she repeated, softly, reverently, "with you, oh my Carson—for all eternity."

CREATURES OF VIBRATION
A SEQUEL TO "VAGABONDS OF SPACE"

ORIGINALLY PUBLISHED IN *ASTOUNDING STORIES*,
JANUARY 1932

CREATURES OF VIBRATION
A SEQUEL TO "VAGABONDS OF SPACE"

Carr Parker sat day-dreaming at the *Nomad's* controls. More than a week of Earth time had passed since the self-styled "vagabonds of space" had left Europa, and now they were fast approaching the great ringed orb of Saturn with the intention of exploring her satellites.

Behind him, his Martian friend, Mado, was manipulating the mechanism of the *rulden*, that remarkable Europan optical instrument which Detis had installed in the vessel before they left. Mado was utterly fascinated by the machine, having spent most of his time during the voyage searching the surfaces of Saturn's moons for signs of human habitation. Now, as they headed directly for Titan, the sixth satellite, he was completely absorbed in an examination of the heavy cloud layer that covered it.

But Carr's thoughts were of his bride, who still slumbered in their stateroom amidships. In his bachelor days he never had imagined he could find such contentment as had come with his marriage to Ora. He had fought shy of the fair sex on Earth. Somehow, the women he knew back home had bored him; angling for a man's money and position, most of them, and incapable of giving real love and companionship in return for the luxuries they demanded. He was resigned to his single state.

But all that was changed by the little blue-eyed girl he had met in Paladar. She was a different sort; worth a hundred of those others and fulfilling to perfection the ideal he had always set up. On her world, Jupiter's satellite, Europa, he had neither wealth nor influence; he'd left these behind when he deserted Earth for a life of vagabondage among the stars. But, to the daughter of Detis, this lack meant less than nothing; his love, and hers, meant everything.

*   *   *   *   *

And, what a good sport she had been! When they were threatened by Rapaju and his minions; when they barely escaped being swallowed up by that monster of space which Mado had likened to the Sargasso Sea of Earth; when she herself proposed joining them in their rovings throughout the universe.

She was a companion of whom even the phlegmatic Martian was proud, she brought with her presence on the *Nomad* a subtle something that made of the coldly mechanical space-ship a thing of new beauty and a place of cheerfulness—a home. And, to think he had won her for his own. To think....

"Carr!" Mado's sharp exclamation startled him from his pleasant thoughts. "Come here and take a look at this," the Martian demanded, his voice betraying an excitement unusual for him. "Something is wrong on this satellite we're heading for."

Locking the controls in the automatic position, Carr turned to join his friend at the viewing-disk of the rulden. Mado had found an opening in the heavy cloud layer, and before them was an unobstructed view of a rugged countryside where huge boulders had been scattered by the mighty hand of creation and where the sun shone weakly on the rim of a yawning crater in which sulphurous vapors curled. They saw this strange land as from an altitude of a few hundred feet, though the *Nomad* was still more than a million miles from the satellite.

"What's wrong about that?" Carr grunted. "Excepting that it's just another of these barren and useless bodies that doesn't even provide us with an attracting interest."

"Wait," Mado replied, "You'll see in a moment. Something—"

*   *   *   *   *

At that instant there came a puff of blue flame from out the pit, carrying on its heated breath a drifting sheet of incandescence that fluttered and pulsated like a thing alive. Mado switched on the sound mechanism of the rulden and the roaring of the pillar of flame came to their ears. There were other sounds as well; the babble of alien voices and the rumble of drums.

Immediately the rough ground in the vicinity was filled with creatures of human mold, half naked red-skinned beings that rose up from behind the boulders and rushed toward the pit of fire and the uncanny heat mantle that wandered ghost-like along its rim. Two of them carried something between them, a struggling writhing something which they stood erect at the crater's edge. It was a girl!—a slim, bronzed figure that swayed there an instant uncertainly as the throb of the drums rose high and the voices of the assembled savages swelled in a monotony of exultant chanting.

"Good Lord!" Carr gasped. "A human sacrifice!"

A quick push, a piercing scream immediately drowned out by the cries of the multitude, and the girl was flung headlong into the welcoming folds of the white-hot ghost-mantle which hovered there like some greedy monster of the lava pools of Mercury. The thing closed in around the wildly struggling body, enwrapping it with exultant constrictions of its hell-born substance and diving, flapping, smoking heat devil, into the flame from whence it had sprung. Mado touched a lever with quick trembling fingers and the rulden's disk went blank.

* * * * *

Sickened by what they had seen, the two friends stared at one another, white-faced.

"No place for us," Mado said, after a moment. "Not with Ora."

"Right!" Carr agreed grimly. "But I'd like to get in close enough to see more of Titan. How high is this cloud layer?"

"About a mile above the surface. We can dive through and look them over; perhaps give them a taste of the disintegrator."

"Attaboy! You took the words out of my mouth. The devils! Who'd ever dream of such a horror in the twenty-fourth century—even out here?"

"What's the reason for this serious discussion?" The voice of Detis broke in on them from the door of the control room.

"Plenty!" Carr exclaimed. And the Europan listened gravely as he described the awful thing they had witnessed.

"I am not surprised," he said calmly, when the Terrestrial ended his recital. "There are certain emanations from the mother planet that most certainly will affect the mentality and baser instincts of a race living within their influence. I have been studying these vibrations for several hours."

They turned to the forward port as the scientist indicated the great orb of Saturn with its gleaming rings. Now, as they drew near to the enormous planet, it did indeed seem that there was a sinister quality in its shifting luminosity. Carr shivered, thinking of Ora.

"You mean," Mado asked, "that there are vibrations in the ether hereabouts that are set up electrically by the planet?"

"Precisely. Or rather I should say they are set up by the vast number of whirling particles of which its encircling rings are composed. The wave form propagated is of a characteristic that is in tune with those portions of the brain which control the savage impulses. We may certainly expect to find superstition-ridden ignorance and all manner of vice prevalent in the races of Titan."

"You think these vibrations will affect us?" Carr inquired anxiously.

"Not if we make our visit short. The intensity is quite low."

"It'll be a short visit, all right. We'll be in Titan's atmosphere in about forty minutes now, and, if I have my say, we'll be out of it and away again inside of an hour."

"Best thing you've said today," Mado approved. "But let's have another look in the rulden. We may find other gaps in the clouds."

*   *   *   *   *

The mechanism of the radio telescope whirred into life as he spoke and its disk shone bright with the reflected light of Titan as it pictured the body. The *Nomad* was speeding toward the ill-omened satellite at the rate of more than a thousand miles a second.

But the surface was nowhere visible and Mado adjusted the focus so that the view of the billowy cloud-covering fell rapidly away. Though actually they were approaching the satellite with tremendous velocity, it receded swiftly in the rulden's disk until the entire body showed as a perfect sphere of uniform brilliancy. All surface markings were concealed by the blanket of clouds.

"Just a moment, Mado," said Detis. "I believe I saw something."

The Martian pressed a button and the image was stationary. A tiny black spot had appeared near one edge of the satellite's disk and this now spread rapidly like a blot of spilled ink. Then it stretched out into a wriggling line that quickly streaked its way across the equator, completely banding the body as they watched. A moment it lay there like a great serpent encircling the globe, and then it vanished in a flash of intense light that left them blinking in amazement. It was as if a trail of gunpowder had been laid across the surface and then set off by a torch in the hand of some unseen giant of the cosmos. A strange electrical storm that agitated the cloud blanket mightily, then left it more densely closed in than before.

Through the forward port the satellite could be seen with the naked eye, growing larger now and resolving itself into a tiny globe. To Carr it seemed that the diminutive moon winked provocatively as he turned to regard it without the rulden's aid. Off to the west, Saturn and her rings almost filled the sky, and their baleful light shone cold and menacing against the black velvet of the heavens.

*   *   *   *   *

Mado took the controls when the *Nomad* entered the atmosphere of Titan and drifted over the sea of clouds. He corrected the altimeter for the mass of this body of three thousand miles diameter, and noted that they were up about six thousand feet. Test samples indicated that the outside air, although thin, was pure. But they did not open the ports as they had no intention of landing.

Ora had not yet awakened and Carr hoped fervently that she would not do so until they had left the immediate vicinity of Titan. It was vastly better if she missed seeing anything of the barbarians of the cloudy satellite. Besides, with her adventuresome and fearless nature, she'd not be satisfied merely to look on from afar—she'd want them to land. And that must not be done.

Something tinkled metallically against the hull plates of the vessel. Again and again the sound was repeated, and soon they saw that the air was filled with driving particles which clattered on the thick glass of the ports and contacted resoundingly with the hull. A vast cloud of black loomed directly ahead, springing up from the tossing cloud banks; and Mado yanked at the controls, swerving the *Nomad* sharply from her course.

But there was no escaping the fury of that sudden squall; they were in the thick of it in an instant, and the ship was buffeted and tossed about as if it were a toy. Millions of the driving particles battered the *Nomad* and the din of their pounding was terrific as the ship was whirled deeper into the midst of the tempest.

*   *   *   *   *

Carr saw that the black particles were piling up around the rim of the port, sticking fast to the metal of the hull. They were bristling in fantastic array, like iron filings adhering to the poles of a magnet. In a flash it came to him that these particles were magnetic; the *Nomad* was covered with them and they piled on ever more thickly, soon weighting her down so heavily that she lost altitude. They were at the mercy of a furious electrical storm of mysterious nature.

"Imps of the canals!" Mado shouted above the din. "We're finished! The machinery is paralyzed. This iron hail is charged."

The viewing port was completely covered over now with particles that arched across from rim to rim, slender rod-like things about two inches long and of the thickness of heavy wire. Black, they were, as black as graphite. Detis worked frantically with Mado at the useless controls, vainly endeavoring to stabilize the pitching vessel.

Dazed by the suddenness of the calamity, Carr turned to look at the altimeter. Five thousand feet, forty-five hundred, four thousand! Nose down, and reeling drunkenly, the *Nomad* was diving to certain disaster on the rocky ground of Titan. He dashed from the control room, calling distractedly to Ora as he raced along the passageway.

She staggered from the stateroom and into his arms, a slim, boyish figure in her snug leather jacket and breeches. Together they were flung violently against the partition by a heavy lurch of the vessel.

"What is it?" she gasped, clinging to him for support.

"A freak storm, in Titan's atmosphere. Guess the *Nomad's* done for." Carr drew her fiercely close as an awful picture flashed across his mind—of Ora's body mangled in twisted wreckage; of the savages finding it, down there....

The metal floor-plates seemed to buckle and hurl themselves aft with a grinding crash of disrupted joints. Holding desperately to the precious little body within his arms, Carr was thrown off his feet. There was a detonation as if the universe had been blasted into oblivion—then darkness, and numbed silence.

* * * * *

"Carr, you're hurt!" Ora moaned.

He was—a little. His head was splitting and the taste of blood was in his mouth, but it was nothing serious. He'd been half knocked out, but his head was clearing already. Of far greater importance was the fact that Ora was unharmed; he satisfied himself of that immediately.

"I'm all right," he grunted, struggling to his feet and feeling around in the blackness.

The lights in the passage were out and he groped blindly along the partition, the metal of which had suddenly become very hot to the touch. There was a curious feeling of lightness as if his body had no weight at all; the ship rolled gently and he knew they were falling swiftly to the inevitable crash. Yet he clung fast to Ora, and, together, they made their way to the control room.

Faint daylight streamed in through the ports there and he saw Mado and Detis, both bleeding from injuries they had received when the mysterious shock hurled them amongst the control mechanisms. They were working furiously with the exciter-generator, which had stopped. The *Nomad* was without power and helpless to exert her anti-gravity energy.

"The iron hail!" gasped the Europan scientist. "It gave up its charge, Carr—exploded. Here, give us a hand and see if we can get the generators started."

The ports were clear of the black particles and Carr saw that the outer surface of the glass was cracked and darkened from the heat of the blast. He understood, remembering the black band and the flash they had seen across the cloud layer from afar. And in the instant of remembering he saw that the ground was very near, rushing upward to meet them. A coil of the exciter-armature broke away in his fingers; the thing had been burned out by the electric storm, and the *Nomad* was doomed.

The altimeter needle moved with sickening speed and already registered but little more than five hundred feet. Four hundred! Carr braced himself for the impending crash and gathered Ora in his arms.

And then a strange thing happened. Four light rays, dazzling in intensity, stabbed up at them from the forest beneath them and converged on the vessel's hull. The *Nomad* staggered, then came to an even keel and slackened in her mad dash to the surface. She vibrated from stem to stern under the mighty conflict of energies and they felt themselves pressed hard against the floor-plate. But the mysterious energy beams had come too late to save them. A densely wooded slope loomed directly ahead. There was a crashing of branches and the rending of mighty trunks, and the *Nomad* came to a jarring stop.

*   *   *   *   *

"Devils of Terra!" Mado ejaculated. "We're in a fine fix now. We'll have to set foot on Titan whether we want to or not."

Carr had laughed, somewhat shakily, in relief. They were safe, all of them, and no one much hurt. And the generator coils could be rewound. But he sobered instantly at Mado's words; they'd have to produce copper and insulating materials for the job.

"Right," he agreed. "And that's not so good."

"What's so terrible about landing here?" Ora inquired. "I thought we were expecting to explore this satellite." She looked up from her ministrations to Detis, who had a nasty scalp wound.

"The people here are dangerous savages," Carr answered gravely. "At least some of them are; we saw them in the rulden. You'll have to remain aboard while we look up the ones who projected those rays and do some bargaining with them."

"What! You expect me to hide in the vessel while you're at work outside? Not much! I want to see something of Titan while we are here." Her pretty chin was set in that determined manner she had.

"I tell you it's too risky!" Carr was firm, but he looked at Mado beseechingly, signaling for his support.

But the Martian only grinned owlishly. He knew as well as did Carr that Ora would have her way.

"Risky—pooh!" she returned. "I'm not afraid. We have our ray pistols and the funny torpedoes you brought from Mars. Besides, I don't believe it's as bad as you think."

Carr shrugged his shoulders. After all, they probably would not encounter any of the savages here in the forest. Beings of far greater intelligence were responsible for those rays, that much was certain. Besides, they'd be three able-bodied men out there to watch over her, and he'd make sure she didn't get too far away from the ship.

*   *   *   *   *

Carr was first to step from the opened manhole to the soft carpet of the Titanese forest. He found the air cool and crisp, with a tang of ozone assailing his nostrils. There was a pulsating motion in it that he could hardly define; it seemed that it massaged his cheeks and raised the short hairs at the nape of his neck and on his forearms as if they were electrified. Those vibrations Detis had told them about were actively at work.

The gravity was even less than on Mars, though slightly greater than that of Europa. Mado was entirely at ease, and the Europans would not be bothered by the slight change in their weight. But Carr would have to take it easy, as he'd done ever since leaving Earth. His muscles were too powerful for his body on these smaller worlds, though this was a mighty advantage if he took care not to over-exert.

A melodious whistling note rose high somewhere in the depths of the forest and trailed off into eery silence. The sky was overcast with gray clouds and the light was poor, of little more than twilight intensity on Terra, this being partly due to the masking of the sun by the clouds and partly to their tremendous distance from that radiant body. Odd that it was not colder, he thought. Probably those vibratory radiations of Saturn's rings had something to do with the temperature in addition to their other effects.

Detis was on his knees, examining a queer specimen of purplish moss which had drawn his eye. The eternal scientist in the man could not be downed. Mado had come out armed with one of the bulky kalbite torpedo-projectors and was looking around belligerently.

Ora drew herself erect and took a deep breath as soon as her feet touched the ground, her eyes bright and her cheeks flushed with excitement. "Oh, Carr," she breathed, "it's marvelous; an honest-to-goodness virgin forest. We've neither of us ever seen one, you know. Aren't you thrilled?"

"We-e-ll," he admitted, "I've always looked forward to wandering in just such places. But, with you along, and thinking of those barbarians we saw—"

"Silly. I'm as capable as any of you. And, even if I couldn't look out for myself, I know that you will be at my side." She pursed her lips and tossed back her head provocatively.

What was a man to do?

*   *   *   *   *

A deep-toned booming note came then from the hills, commencing like the warning siren of a space liner approaching its berth and swelling to a bombilation of ear-shattering sound that set the steel of the *Nomad's* hull vibrating and their very flesh and bones a-tingle. Then it died away as had the bird note which was the first sound of this world to greet them.

"Jupiter! What's that?" Mado unslung his torpedo-projector.

As if in answer to his startled question, a weird object drifted over the treetops and poised directly above them, about fifty feet up. An egg-shaped thing, six or seven feet in length, and seemingly made of white metal. It swayed there gently, without visible means of support, and they could make out a transparent disk on its side, back of which there was a human head with eyes that regarded them curiously.

Mado raised his torpedo tube and took aim.

"Hold it!" Carr warned him. "This fellow's no savage. Probably he's one of those who tried to break our fall. Friendly, perhaps."

Two more of the ovoids drifted in from the woods and joined the first one, all three settling a few feet lower and their occupants staring intently at the intruders.

"I'll get the psycho-ray apparatus," Detis said excitedly. "We may be able to get thought contact with them." He dived through the *Nomad's* entrance-manhole as he spoke.

"Nothing so frightening about these creatures," Ora murmured, her eyes reproaching Carr. "Why, they seem anxious to know that *we* are not enemies."

And, indeed, this seemed to be the case, for the strange ovoids wafted still lower, dropping until a faint humming of the internal gravity mechanism came to their ears. These were a highly developed people of scientific attainment; civilized beings. But Mado kept firm hold of his torpedo tube, and Carr fingered the ray pistol at his belt.

The booming note from the hills came then, frightfully near this time, and the three ovoids moved with sudden roaring of their motors, literally hurling themselves skyward. But the menace they sought to escape was real, and not to be outdone in speed. A vast black something whirred out from beyond the treetops and flung itself upon them.

"A pterodactyl!" Mado gasped. "One of the prehistoric monsters of Terra!"

"Carr, there are men riding it!" Ora exclaimed. "Red men!"

*   *   *   *   *

It was true; the pteranodon, a horrid bat-like thing with a wing-spread of fully twenty feet, carried three of the bronzed savages clinging to a sort of harness that encircled its body just back of the crested head. The huge flying reptile whistled raucously as it flew and one of the savages was whirling a sling which held a stone as large as his own head. They watched in amazement as the swift aerial steed flapped its way after the rising ovoids. And then the savage let loose an end of his thong and released its missile, which crashed full against the transparent disk of an ovoid and tore its way through.

The damaged ovoid careened violently and then fell end over end, crashing in the forest. With a bellow of fury, Mado fired with the kalbite tube at his hip. There was the twang of the propelling ray, and the slender arrow-like torpedo sped forth on its message of death, singing spitefully as it cleaved the air of Titan.

It was a fair hit, catching the pteranodon just ahead of its trailing legs and exploding with the characteristic screaming roar of the deadly kalbite. The monstrous reptile and its crew of barbarians vanished in a blaze that lighted the clouds above them and brought a babble of excited shoutings from the depths of the forest on all sides. They were surrounded by the uncivilized ones of Titan! And those of the ovoids had run off at the first sign of danger.

The din from the forest was augmented by the whistlings of a second pteranodon which darted after the remaining ovoids, following swiftly as these retreated with ludicrous, wabbling haste.

* * * * *

Ora screamed and struck out at something with her fist. A naked arm had reached out from the underbrush and grasped her wrist. Carr wheeled and his ray pistol spat crackling flame. The savage, an undersized red man with an enormous head, rose unsteadily from his hiding place, a look of terrible hate in his contorted features. Then, like a punctured balloon, his body collapsed into the nothingness of complete disintegration.

"Back, back to the *Nomad!*" Carr roared, dragging Ora with him and leveling his pistol at a group of the bronze brutes who rushed into the space where the vessel lay amongst the trees.

Mado was busy with his torpedo tube and a vast explosion shook the ground beneath them as a trio of the savages were blasted out of existence. A great tree toppled and crashed across the nose of the *Nomad,* its roots ripped from the soil by the concussion.

Ora had whipped out her own pistol and was firing as they fell back. Game kid, she was! Carr gloated as he saw she was making each shot tell. But this couldn't last; there were hundreds of them now, long-armed and big-headed red devils swarming in from every direction. Carr dodged none too quickly to save his skull from a swift-flung stone, which clanged against the *Nomad's* hull. There was a perfect hail of the missiles now:

one struck his left arm a numbing blow, and he heard a sickening thud and Ora's moan as she was hit. And there were winged darts, from blow-guns.

A dusky moon-face leered into his own, horribly close, and he yelled his rage as he drove it back with a swift uppercut. But the horde of savages came on in ever increasing numbers and with renewed vigor.

"Quick—inside!" Carr hissed in Ora's ear as his fingers found the rim of the manhole. He'd have her safely within in a moment.

Detis clambered out with the thought machine in his arms, and a singing dart from one of the blow-guns pierced him through and through. A look of astonishment spread over his kindly features, and he fell forward, dying.

And then Carr looked up into a grinning face behind a huge club that was swinging downward. He threw up his arm to break the force of the blow, but the club fell too swiftly; the enormous weight of it crashed down on his skull, and he knew no more.

* * * * *

When he awakened it was to stare for a dazed moment into a pair of blue eyes that looked down upon him in a place of dim light and stuffy atmosphere. The eyes were only vaguely familiar in his befuddled memory. Beautiful eyes, though, and incredibly dear....

"Ora!" he exclaimed, in wondering remembrance, trying to sit up as he grasped her hand.

"Hush!" she warned him, placing a finger-tip to his lips. "Be quiet now and perhaps they'll leave us alone for a while."

"They! Did they capture us?" he whispered. "Are you hurt?"

"We're prisoners, all right, excepting poor father. But they didn't harm *me* much, outside of the rough handling."

"The devils. What of Detis?" He was growing stronger by the minute and now saw that they were in an open-mouthed cave and that Mado was sitting hunched dejectedly in a corner, his massive shoulders drooping and his proud head bowed on his chest.

"Father—they killed him," Ora sighed almost inaudibly. "Have you forgotten? We saw the dart strike him and I—I saw it sticking from his chest. Oh, Carr!" A dry sob caught in her throat.

"Yes—yes. Lord!" Carr groaned, sick at heart with the sudden recollection and full of compassion for the stricken girl.

He patted her hand with clumsy tenderness as she turned her head and gazed out through the cave mouth in silence that was fraught with intense pain. She would take it like that: with little to say but with much inward suffering.

And then he noticed a fourth occupant of the cavern, a young lad of Titan. Like one of the savages in his small stature and in the large size of his head, he was much lighter in color and his body was encased in a snug one-piece garment of shimmering material of silky texture. And there was a different light in his eyes, the light of intelligence and culture.

"Who is that?" Carr whispered.

Ora stared when she saw that the stranger was on his feet. "Oh," she exclaimed, "I'm glad he has recovered. He's one of the civilized ones; they captured him with his ovoid when the second pteranodon went out after them."

*   *   *   *   *

Mado was standing now, endeavoring to communicate with the lad by means of signs and the drawing of crude pictures in the red sand of the cavern floor. The graceful little fellow watched him with understanding and with a smile of amused tolerance. Then he halted the big Martian with an imperious motion, addressing him in velvety voice.

"Nazu," he said simply, placing a forefinger on his breast and bowing before the astonished Mado.

"Imps of the canals!" the Martian exclaimed, grinning delightedly as he cast a swift look at Carr and Ora. "He's telling me his name." "Mine's Mado," he said, turning his eyes to the keen gray ones that smiled up at him. "Mado," he repeated, placing a huge fist against his own chest and bending his body in awkward imitation of the lad's courtly gesture.

They made no attempt to converse in tongues that would convey no meaning, but there was no mistaking the quick friendship that sprang up between the incongruous pair. Mado was the boy's slave from that moment, and Nazu looked up to the Martian with all of youth's admiration for his vast bulk and rippling muscles.

Suddenly they were without light and Carr saw that a curtain of woven rushes had been dropped over the mouth of the cave. There were soft padding footsteps on every side and he drew back against the rock wall with Ora clasped in his arms. A sinewy hand grasped his wrist and twisted his right arm free. He lashed out in the darkness and was rewarded by a grunt of pain as his fist contacted with an unseen face. Nazu's voice rose in anguish, and Mado's wrathful bellow was followed by a frightful commotion as he tore into his assailants.

They were everywhere in the blackness, these slippery little savages of Titan, their half naked bodies crowding him and stifling him with their sweaty nearness. Again and again Carr struck out, but it was like fighting a horde of squirming and clawing feline creatures that swarmed over him and bore him down by sheer weight of numbers. They dragged Ora from his arms and quickly overpowered him. Thongs of rawhide twisted deeply into the flesh of his wrists and he was hauled forth into the daylight.

*   *   *   *   *

Securely tied, hand and foot, Carr was propped sitting with his back to a huge boulder. He saw they had been carried to the place they had viewed in the disk of the rulden. A dozen paces away, Ora and Mado sat similarly bound. The Martian had been gagged as well and Carr was forced to smile despite the seriousness of the situation. His mad bellowings must have proved as painful to the ears of the red dwarfs as had his fists to their bodies.

Nazu, unbound and walking proudly erect, was being marched to the edge of a smoking fissure by two of the savages. No others of the red men were in sight.

Carr shuddered. It was the place of sacrifice they had seen in the rulden, and the natives were in hiding as before. Nazu would be first to go; then Ora, most likely. He strained desperately at his bonds when he realized the awful significance of their position. It was incredible that Ora was here and in the hands of these unspeakable monsters. Why, she'd be thrown into the incandescent folds of the flapping fire-god, along with the rest of them! He groaned in an agony of self-recrimination; he should not have allowed her to come on this mad voyage.

Then came that roaring column of flame from out the crater, and the weird fluttering thing whose intense heat radiated across the intervening space like the breath of a blast furnace. The rumble of drums commenced, and thousands of the red men dashed over the rocky area to worship at the shrine of their pitiless god.

As their monotonous chant rose high, Nazu was rushed to the edge of the pit. The ghastly, shimmering heat-ghost drifted hungrily to await the flinging of the slight form into its consuming embrace. Carr was glad to see that Ora had turned her head.

*   *   *   *   *

And then there came a sucking noise from the depths of the crater, and the pillar of blue flame vanished abruptly, the incandescent ghost-shape flapping disconsolately in its wake. The chant of the savages trailed off into a chorus of disgruntled murmurings and the booming of the drums died down in disappointment. The worshippers had been cheated of their sadistic pleasure. There was something wrong with the timing of the rite; their mysterious fire-god had granted the captives a reprieve.

But the prisoners were not deceived by the solicitous treatment accorded them by their captors when they were returned to the cave and their bonds were severed. For well they knew that at the next appearance of the phenomenon of the pit they would be dragged off to the sacrifice. Sooner or later all of them were to meet the fate of those given into the embrace of the heat-demon.

A guard of fifty or more of the savages, armed with blow-guns and stone hatchets, paraded continuously before the mouth of the cave as one of their number returned with a huge woven container of fruits and nuts of strange form and color. This was set before them and the bearer withdrew.

"Humph!" Mado grunted. "Seems like they want to fatten us up for this heated sheet of theirs. Like hogs fattened for the market."

But he reached for the striped yellow melon atop the heap, and, at a bright nod of approval from Nazu, bit into its smooth skin.

Carr's stomach rebelled when he looked at the food. He could not bear the sight of the stuff, sitting there in the damp cavern with Ora's blue eyes regarding him in the dim light. Those wide eyes held a gleam of hope and trust that would not be discouraged.

*   *   *   *   *

He gazed out through the cave mouth and calculated their chances. There were none. Not against that horde of barbarians; there were too many of the devils to fight with their bare hands. If only they had their ray pistols, or a torpedo projector. At least they could sell their lives dearly. His eyes narrowed speculatively when they came to rest on a peculiar egg-shaped object that stood out there in the open. It was Nazu's ovoid. Here was an idea!

But he saw that its entrance door was open and that the space inside was too small for any of them excepting one of the small stature of the Titanese. It was crammed with machinery. Nazu was the only one of their number who could squeeze into the thing; in fact he alone knew how to operate the queer flying machine. There must be others of his kind, plenty of them; another country, or a city full of them at least. Perhaps he might obtain aid if only he could be made to understand, and if they could get him out there safely somehow.

"Mado," he called, pointing, "do you suppose we could dope out a way of getting Nazu aboard his sky vehicle to go for help?"

The Martian stared, his mouth stuffed with food and his jaws in full action. He strained suddenly to swallow the huge mouthful so he could make reply.

"Not a chance," he grunted. "Why, there's a million of them out there. You won't catch them napping."

But he turned his attention from the basket of fruit and made a desperate effort to convey the idea to Nazu, whose bright eyes took in his every significant motion and whose sensitive fingers traced images in the sand that conveyed his own thoughts to the mind of the Martian in rapid succession.

"He's got it!" Mado gloated. "The game little cuss would go in a minute if we could get him to the ovoid. He's got a picture of a big island here, so help me! An island covered with circular dwellings, made of metal like the ovoids, he indicates. Look here."

*   *   *   *   *

Carr and Ora moved over to watch the swift sketching of the Titanese lad. By means of pantomime and his carefully drawn pictures, he told them of his people, making it clear that they were forced to live in insulated dwellings and travel only in the ovoids, which likewise were insulated against the devastating vibrations that emanated from Saturn's rings. He sketched those rings, illustrating the vibrations and tapping his own forehead in explanation of the effect on the brain; pointing to the savages to indicate the ultimate fate of his kind. The protective insulation, it appeared, was not permanent; sooner or later, all of them would become barbarians like the others.

The savages out there were their fathers, mothers, sisters and brothers, gone mad; their skins darkened by continued action of the vibrations after they fled their insulated homes. His pictures of the family life were meticulously drawn. His people never warred upon these savage kin of theirs—naturally— though the reverse was not always true. However, Nazu pointed to the ovoid and showed his willingness to help the strangers. But he shook his head sadly as he counted the barbarians on his fingers, multiplying the number endlessly by clapping his hands. There were too many of them; the thing was impossible.

"Good Lord!" Carr exclaimed. "He's a marvel at communicating his thoughts without words. But I'd think his people would beat it for the hills without waiting. Might as well have it over with."

"But, they're still working on the problem," Ora objected. "With their wisdom, they'll finally get the thing under control. And they probably hope to discover a way of restoring their maddened relatives."

She was doing something with the red sand; wetting her fingers in a trickle of water that oozed from the wall and making a red paste which she smeared on her white forearm and then rubbed off.

"I guess you're right," Carr admitted. Then, watching her strange performance, he asked, "What are you doing?"

She looked up with sparkling eyes and stretched forth her arm. "It stains, Carr, see!" she exclaimed excitedly. "We can fix up Nazu to resemble one of the savages. It is the exact color of their skin."

"Mado!" he called, sensing at once the possibilities of her discovery. They could make up Nazu to perfection. Mingling with the barbarians unsuspected, he might get possession of the ovoid.

*   *   *   *   *

The Titanese lad fell in with the idea at once and the two men started work on him with water and the powdery stuff they had taken for red sand. They stripped him of his silken garment and smeared him from head to foot, Carr taking especial care to see that his upper body and face were thoroughly covered. Then, after using his own clothing to swab off the coating, they stepped back to view the result. He was exactly like one of the red men in color now, and he stood there twisting his face in a wicked grin to heighten the similarity.

"The little devil!" Mado chuckled. "He gets the idea perfectly. We'll have to muss his hair now and fix him up with a kirtle like theirs."

Removing his suede jacket and turning it inside out, he draped it about the slim hips of Nazu, then slapped his chest approvingly. "There you are, lad," he told the grinning youngster. "A tough-looking kid we've made of you, too."

The words were lost on the young Titanese, but his bright eyes showed that he fully comprehended the humor as well as the gravity of the situation. The improvised covering would pass without question as one of the untanned hides the barbarians wore dangling from their waists. The disguise was faultless.

Ora had been watching at the mouth of the cave. Now she called out in low-voiced warning, "Hurry! One of them is coming."

Carr moved forward swiftly to face the opening, while Mado stood with his great bulk hiding the now unrecognizable Nazu. The savage entered, proceeding directly to where Carr was standing. He bent over the fruit basket and then the Earth-man was upon him.

The wiry red man struggled furiously, but Carr had a grip on his windpipe that stopped his attempts to cry out and quickly reduced him to a state of flabby subjection. Then he bound and gagged his captive, tearing strips of linen from his own shirt to provide the necessary material. In a moment they had bundled the trussed-up dwarf into a dark corner of the cavern, and Nazu stepped forth blithely to lift the basket to his shoulder.

*   *   *   *   *

Everything seemed to happen at once after that. Nazu stalked boldly out among the savages, who paid him no attention whatsoever. He passed out of their field of vision for a moment, and then they saw him at the circular door of the ovoid. In a flash he was inside and the thing soared speedily into the air and out of sight. The red men broke forth in a babel of excited jabbering and then they were crowding into the cave, hundreds of them it seemed, shrieking their rage as they attacked the hapless prisoners.

Carr went down fighting madly but to no avail. He hadn't counted on this; he should have known better. A crushing weight of them was upon him, clawing and beating at him as he struggled to rise. They were suffocating him with their rank animal odors.

And then he was dragged into the open air. Battered and dazed, he saw they had found their fellow, the one he had bound and gagged. Ora was considerably mussed up, but unharmed, he observed with relief; but Mado lay there inert. This was the first time Carr had ever seen him take the count at the hands of man.

When they had untied the one whose place had been taken by Nazu, he came straight for the Earth-man and would have brained him with a huge stone had not his fellows interfered. He objected strenuously, his eyes red with hate and a torrent of harsh gutturals pouring from his lips. But the others held him off; this strange white giant from the machine of the skies was to be saved for the embrace of the fire-god.

*   *   *   *   *

With the entire blame for Nazu's escape thus placed upon the Terrestrial, Ora and Mado were returned to the cavern and left unmolested. But Carr was prodded into moving over against a boulder and was surrounded by a semi-circle of the dwarfs who squatted calmly to watch him, blow-guns in their hands and stone hatchets on the ground within easy reach. They were taking no more chances with this one.

The long day of Titan dragged interminably but the watchful eyes of his guards never strayed from their prisoner. At any moment the fire-god might make an appearance and the rite of sacrifice take place. Carr supposed that the thing made more or less regular appearances, like a geyser of Earth. And, next time, there would be no escape.

Night fell, and still those eyes watched intently in the light reflected against the low-flung clouds from the seething crater nearby. Nothing had been seen of Nazu or any of the ovoids. Probably it was useless to expect them; they could not bring themselves to do battle against these savage kin of theirs. Anyway, he was glad the little fellow had gotten away; he hoped he was safely in bed—if they had beds in those insulated dwellings.

He could not sleep. All through the night he sat with bowed head, alternately planning rescue attempts and cursing himself for bringing Ora to this horrible end. Detis was dead; the *Nomad* was hopelessly beyond repair for many days, even if they could make their escape and locate it; Nazu had saved his own skin, and they were left to the mercy of these vibration-crazed brutes who waited there in the flickering red twilight all around him. It was a revolting ending for an adventure that had started so auspiciously.

*   *   *   *   *

With the first faint light of dawn came the roaring of the pillar of flame from out the crater. Instantly there rose the hollow booming of the drums and the chanting of thousands of the barbarous worshippers. The place was swarming with them almost instantly, and Carr's guards closed in on him with evil glee.

Ora was brought out into the open, her arms held fast by two of the red devils who yanked her roughly along between them. Carr roared out in blind rage and in awful fear for the girl. He struck out viciously into the first grinning face that pressed near. Something in his brain seemed to snap then, and he became a snarling, fighting animal, battling against overwhelming odds in defence of his mate. A dart buried itself in his arm and a stone hatchet bit into his shoulder, but he scarcely felt the hurts. All that mattered now was Ora; they were taking her away—taking her to the folds of that incredible hot thing that flapped there at the crater's rim. An arm snapped like a pipestem in his fingers and he heard the squeal of pain from somewhere in the tangled mass of savages around him.

And then they were falling back; easing up on him. The din was increasing, but it seemed that a note of fear had crept in to replace the exultant frenzy of those chanting voices. The drums were stilled.

Wiping the blood from his eyes with the back of his hand, he saw the barbarians running everywhere; they were screaming in superstitious terror and fighting one another in their desperate anxiety to escape the vicinity of their precious fire-god. A tremendous voice boomed out over the hubbub, a voice that came from the crater in vast commanding gutturals that struck terror into the souls of the panicky barbarians. Yet somehow that mightily sonorous voice carried a familiar ring.

Carr raised astonished eyes to the pillar of blue flame and was seized with a well-nigh uncontrollable impulse to flee with the red men. For a monstrous image of Detis swayed there in the hot vapors, a massive arm raised menacingly and an equally Brobdingnagian voice issuing from his lips in fierce syllables of the red man's tongue!

"Detis!" Carr shouted. "Detis! Ora—Mado!"

*   *   *   *   *

And then he was running toward the crater's edge in bounding strides that carried him twenty feet at a leap. He understood now. Detis had recovered from his wound and was reversing the rulden's energy. He was projecting his own image and voice, many times amplified, into the column of fire to terrify the savages!

Ora was lying there, on the rim of the pit. She had fainted at sight of the ghost-shape, whose white-hot folds flapped there, reaching to engulf her in their all-consuming embrace. Carr babbled like a madman as he pulled her away from the horrible thing that pulsated with eager flutterings not three feet away, its hot breath singeing her silken lashes and brows.

Mado was there, encouraging him and yelling something else he couldn't understand; pointing skyward. And then he saw it; the *Nomad*, with its sleek, tapered cylinder of a body nosing down toward them with the silvery aura of its propulsive energy gleaming like a beacon of hope against the dull clouds of the satellite of terror. And there was something else: one of the ovoids of Titan, clinging there to the vessel's hull plates, alongside the open manhole. Nazu had not failed them after all. His mind refused to question the miracle further.

Somehow, when the vessel landed, he managed to reach the manhole with his precious burden. He staggered through the passageway and into their stateroom, tenderly stretching Ora on her own bed. In the next instant he was rummaging in the medicine closet. He found ointment for her burns; smelling salts; damp cloths. With trembling fingers he ministered to her, a great joy welling up within him as he saw she was recovering. Another minute, back there at the crater, and he'd have lost her forever. He swallowed hard at the thought, his eyes misty as he looked down at her and remembered.

Impatiently he jerked the barbed dart from his arm and poured a powerful antiseptic into the open wound, unmindful of the pain. As best he could, he disinfected his other cuts and bandaged them. Ora had raised herself and now sat there, swaying weakly and regarding him with anxious gaze.

*   *   *   *   *

A little later they made their way forward to the control room. The *Nomad* had taken off and was drifting slowly higher. At the controls sat a strange, bedaubed figure. Nazu!

Mado was peering through the coils of a helix of silver ribbon that had been erected beside the rulden.

"Father!" Ora darted past him and dropped to her knees on the floor-plates at the Martian's side. The body of Detis was slumped there a ghastly corpse within those gleaming coils. But his kind features were fixed in a serene smile. He had gone to his reward with content in his heart.

Only then did Carr remember. One could not subject his body to the reversed energies of the rulden without certain expectation of death. A few short seconds with those terrible oscillations surging through his being, carrying the amplified visual and oral reproduction through the ether, and the Europan scientist had perished. Knowingly, willingly, Detis had given his life that the rest of them might live! Recovered miraculously from his first serious injury, he had done this magnificent thing deliberately and gladly....

A great lump rose in Carr's throat as Ora's sobbing came to his ears. With his vision blurred by tears, he turned to the pilot's seat, where Nazu faced him with solemn eyes.

"Nazu go now," the amazing young Titanese stated. He spoke in halting syllables of Cos, the language of the inner planets!

*   *   *   *   *

Carr stared agape, scarcely believing his ears.

"Detis great man," Nazu continued, relinquishing his seat to the dazed Earthman. "Nazu find him in ship. My people already there with him. They want to help when you come. Return after capture and heal dart wound of Detis. Bring wire and help him fix motors. Work very quick, my people. Detis have brain machine. Talk with Nazu; teach him words, also very quick. Nazu tell where you are and we come to help. Then he scare away red men—and die. That is all. Now I go—and you go also. Quickly."

"So that's how it happened," Carr muttered, slowly mulling over the amazing things he had heard. He watched the Titanese lad keenly as his eyes wandered in Mado's direction. He saw the admiring light that came into them as the big Martian removed the body of Detis from the helix and carried it gently away.

"Wait a minute," he interposed, as Nazu made as if to leave. "Mado would like to talk to you."

"Must go soon." The youngster drew himself up proudly. "Nazu is prince of his people. They need him. And you—you must go at once. Vibrations of mother planet's rings work on you too long already. Must be quick. Else you be wild men—like those down there."

He waved his arm in a gesture that embraced all Titan. Anxiety was written large on his countenance and his gaze traveled nervously to the door through which Mado must return.

The big Martian was not long in coming. He had carried the body of Detis aft, leaving Ora there with her dead. Carr's heart ached for her; he knew how silently and terribly she suffered. Knowing that her father had been healed of his deadly wound by the friendly Titanese, only to be taken from her afterwards by his own heroic act, made the blow doubly hard.

Later they would give Detis a decent burial, sending him through the airlock to drift aimlessly in space, preserved through the ages by the intense cold and the absence of air. A fitting tomb for the noblest of the vagabonds!

*   *   *   *   *

Mado chattered endlessly with Nazu, who was impatient to be off. Seeing that it was impossible to detain him, and realizing at last the stern necessity of hastening their own departure, he finally let him go. The youngster bid Carr a sober, friendly farewell and followed Mado to the airlock.

Carr heard the clang of the manhole cover as it swung home, and was bolted to its seat. The ovoid drifted away from the vessel and dropped toward the forest beneath them. Nazu had gone to rejoin his people.

His fingers strayed to the controls. They must get away from the evil influence of those vibrations; he had felt something of their degrading power in the fighting down there. He had almost become a savage himself, he remembered with a revulsion of feeling.

The feel of the levers brought to him a renewed sense of confidence and responsibility. A while back he thought he'd never perform such simple duties again. The *Nomad* responded instantly and rose swiftly to hover over the pit of the fire-god. The flame had partly subsided and the ghost-shape wabbled there, changing form rapidly with darkening colors. Some weird phenomenon of nature that those brutes had set up as a deity.

Carr increased the repulsion energy once more and the *Nomad* shot skyward like a rocket. Through the floor port he saw Nazu's tiny ovoid scudding over the treetops. Then it had vanished.

"We're getting away none too soon," said Mado, rejoining him.

"Right." Carr watched the temperature indicator as he increased speed to the maximum they could withstand in the atmosphere.

They were out above the cloud layer then and he cast apprehensive eyes on the enormous flat disks encircling the great globe that was Saturn. Something like a hundred and seventy thousand miles across them, he remembered. But the astronomers of the inner planets had little actual knowledge of their composition; they knew nothing at all of their terrible power or their strange inhabitants.

*   *   *   *   *

The *Nomad* left Titan with tremendous acceleration now, as he increased the speed of the rejuvenated generators. They'd go on, on toward Uranus, Neptune—anywhere, away from this ringed planet that was responsible for the death of one of their number; away from the region that was soon to become the tomb of Detis.

There was silence then as the *Nomad* raced on through the blackness. Mado gripped the rail of the port and peered long and earnestly at the tiny pinpoint of light that now was Titan.

"Great kid, that Nazu," the Martian said, after a while. "Too bad he couldn't come along with us."

"Yes." Carr was thinking of the different life there would be on board the *Nomad*; and well he knew that Mado was thinking of the same thing. The Martian had missed the close companionship of his Terrestrial friend since his marriage to Ora; missed it more than he would admit, even to himself. And the lad, Nazu, had appealed to him; he would have fathered him as only a lonely bachelor can. Suddenly Carr's own friendship for the big fellow seemed a wonderful thing.

"Never mind, old man," he whispered, reaching over and gripping Mado's hand mightily, "We'll be a three-cornered family, Ora and you and I. And, who knows but that you'll find the one and only girl yourself, some fine day?"

"Oh, shut up!" Mado grunted.

But a big hand closed down hard on Carr's fingers, and the Earthman knew that their friendship was more firmly cemented than ever before.

Vulcan's Workshop

Originally Published In *Astounding Stories*,
June 1932

VULCAN'S WORKSHOP

Savagely cursing, Luke Fenton reeled backward from the porthole, his great hairy paws clapped over his eyes. No one had warned him, and he did not know that total blindness might result from gazing too earnestly into the sun's unscreened flaming orb, especially with that body not more than twenty million miles distant in space.

He did not know, in fact, that the ethership was that close: Luke had not the faintest notion of the vast distances of the universe or of the absence of air in space which permitted the full intensity of the dazzling rays to strike into his optics unfiltered save by the thick but clear glass which covered the port. He knew only that the sun, evidently very near, was many times its usual size and of infinitely greater brilliance. And he was painfully aware of the fact that the fantastically enlarged and blazing body had seared his eyeballs and caused the floating black spots which now completely obscured his vision.

Stumbling in his blindness, he fell across the hard cot that was the sole article of furniture in the cell he had occupied for more than two weeks. Lying there half dazed and with splitting head, he cursed the guard who had opened the inner cover of the port; cursed anew the fish-eyed Martian judge who had sentenced him to a term in Vulcan's Workshop.

Several of Luke's thirty-eight years had been spent in jails and sundry other penal institutions devised by Earthman and Martian for the punishment of offenders against the laws of organized society. And yet they had failed to break his defiant spirit or to convince him of the infallibility of his creed that might makes right. Nor had they taken from him the gorillalike strength that was in his broad squat body, the magnificent brute lustihood that made him a terror to police and citizen alike. Instead, the many periods of incarceration had only served to increase his hatred of mankind and his contempt of the forces of law and order. Especially was he contemptuous of the book-learning that gave the authorities their power.

As the pain back of his eyes abated, Luke could see dimly the shaft of light that slanted down from the porthole to the bare steel floor. His sight was returning, yet he lay there still, growling in his throat, his mind occupied with thoughts of his checkered past.

*   *   *   *   *

Steel-worker, mechanic, roustabout, he had worked in most of the populous cities of Earth and had managed to get into serious trouble wherever he went. It was his boast that he had never killed a man except in fair fight. And yet, at thirty, finding himself wanted by the police of a half dozen cities of Earth, he had signed up in the black gang of a tramp ethership bound for Mars, knowing he would never return and caring not at all.

At first, he had been riotously happy in the changed life on the new world. There had been plenty of soul-satisfying brawls and plenty of chulco, the fiery Martian distillate. On his many and frequent jobs there were excellent opportunities to rebel against authority, and he had fomented numerous mutinies in which he was always victorious but which usually landed him in one of the malodorous Martian jails for a more or less extended stay.

Then had come that final fracas in the Copau foundry on the bank of Canal Pyramus. Overly optimistic, Luke's new boss had struck out at the chunky, red-headed Earthman during an inconsequential argument and had promptly measured his length in a sand pile as a hamlike fist crashed home in return. They had picked up the foreman and taken him to the infirmary where it was found that his skull was fractured and that he had little chance for life. There were the red police after that, and Luke, single-handed, trounced four of them so soundly and thoroughly that someone sent in a riot call. It had taken a dozen of the reserves to club him into submission at the last.

That was too much for Martian justice. In pronouncing sentence the judge had termed Luke an incurably vicious character and a menace to society such as the planet had never harbored. And Luke, his head swathed in bandages from which his wiry red hair bristled like the comb of a gamecock, had grinned evilly and snarled his defiance.

And so they were taking him to the dread prison camp known as Vulcan's Workshop, a mysterious place of horror and hardship from which no convict had ever returned. Vaguely Luke knew that it was located on still another world, away off somewhere in the heavens. He had seen the lips of men go white when they were condemned to its reputed torture, had heard them plead for death in preference. Yet its terrors had not awed him; they did not awe him now. He had beaten the law before; he'd beat it again—even in Vulcan's Workshop.

*   *   *   *   *

A key rattled in the lock and Luke Fenton leaped to his feet, facing the barred door with feet spread wide and with his massive shoulders hunched expectantly. He could see now, with much blinking and watering of his still aching eyes, and he looked out with sneering disapproval at the three guards in the corridor. They were afraid of him, singly, these Martian cops, even though armed with the deadly dart guns and with shot-loaded billies. So afraid, Luke chuckled inwardly, that they had kept him from the other prisoners throughout the trip, kept him in solitary confinement.

The door was opening and it came to Luke that the ethership was strangely and hollowly silent. The rocket tubes were stilled, that was it, and even the motors that drove the great ventilating fans had been stopped. They had arrived.

No time now to start anything. He would have to submit tamely to whatever they might mete out to him in the way of punishment—until he got the lay of the land. It would require some time to study things out and to plan. But plan he would, and act; they'd never hold him here until he died of whatever it was that killed men quickly in Vulcan's Workshop. Not Luke Fenton.

Sullenly docile, he was prodded forward to the air-lock. A draft of hot fetid air swept through the corridor, carrying with it the forewarning of unspeakable things to come. And a shriek of mortal terror wafted in from outside by the stinking breeze, told of some poor devil already demoralized. The thick muscles of

Luke's biceps tightened to hard knots under his black prison jacket.

*   *   *   *   *

They were outside then and Luke essayed a deep breath, a breath that was chokingly acrid in his throat.

"Waugh!" he coughed, and spat. One of the guards laughed.

Any foul epithet that might have formed on Fenton's lips was forgotten in the sight that met his eyes. A barren and rugged terrain stretched out from the landing stage, a land utterly desolate of vegetation and incapable of supporting life. Pockmarked with craters and seamed with yawning fissures from which dense vapors curled, it was seemingly devoid of habitation. And the scene was visible only in the lurid half light of flame-shot mists that hung low over all. In the all too near distance, awesomely vast and ruddy columns of fire rose and fell with monotonous regularity. For the first time, Luke experienced something of the superstitious fear exhibited by even the most hardened criminals when faced with a term at Vulcan's Workshop. That term, to them, meant horror and misery, torture and swift death. And he, too, was ready to believe it now.

He was prodded down an incline that led from the landing stage to the rocks below. The guards from the ethership, he saw, remained behind on the platform and there were new guards awaiting him below. Husky fellows, these were, in strange bulky clothing and armed with the highest powered dart guns. The other prisoners from the vessel were already down there, a huddled and frightened mass—a squashed pile, almost—silent now and watchful of their jailers.

*   *   *   *   *

"Come on, show some speed, tough guy!" a guard yelled from the foot of the runway. "Think this is a reception?"

Another of the guards guffawed hoarsely, and Luke choked back the blasting retort that rose in his throat. Plenty of time yet before he'd be ready to make things hot for those birds.

The runway, he observed, was a strip of yielding metal that glowed faintly with an unnatural greenish light. He was nearing its lower end when the siren of the ethership shrieked and he heard the clang of the outer door of its air-lock as it swung to its seat.

Then he stepped out to the smooth stone slab on which the nearest of the guards was standing. Immediately it was as if a tremendous weight was flung upon him, bearing him down until his knees buckled beneath him. He was rooted to the spot by an enormous force which dragged at his vitals and weighted his limbs to leaden uselessness. With a mighty effort he raised his head to look up into the grinning yellow face of the guard, and his thick neck muscles were taut gnarled ridges under the strain.

"Damn your hide!" he howled. "It's a trick. I'll break you in two for this, you slob!"

His huge biceps tensed and his fists came up. But they came up slowly and ineffectually, ponderous things he could scarcely lift. A great roaring of rocket tubes was in his ears then, and the ethership screamed off through the red mists while he dabbed futilely at the leering yellow face. And vile curses rasped from between his set teeth at the laughter of the guards.

*   *   *   *   *

Luke Fenton never had taken the trouble to learn or he would have known something about this planet Vulcan on which he was a prisoner. As far back as 1859, by Earth chronology, its existence within the orbit of Mercury had been reported by one Lescarbault, a French physician. But other astronomers had failed to confirm, in fact had ridiculed his discovery, and it was not until some years after the establishing of interplanetary travel in the first decade of the twenty-first century that the body was definitely located.

Vulcan, the smallest and innermost of the planets, circles the sun with great rapidity at a mean distance of twenty million miles. Its periods of rotation and revolution are equal, so that it always presents the same face toward the solar system's great center of heat and light—for which reason one side is terrifically hot and the other, that facing into outer space, unbearably cold.

There is no life native to the body, and mankind has found it possible to exist only in the narrow belt immediately on the dark side of the terminator, the line of demarcation between night and day. Here there are the dense vapors, illuminated perpetually by refracted light from the daylight side and by the internal fires of the planet itself, fires which erupt at regular intervals through many fissures and craters. And it is only under greatest hardship that man can exist even here, what with the noxious gases and the extremes of heat and cold to which his body it subjected. There is no natural source of water or of food, so these essentials must of necessity be conveyed from Mars or Earth by ethership.

In spite of all this, man has persisted in establishing himself in the vapor belt of Vulcan for the sake of wresting from the rocky soil its vast deposits of rare ores, and a great number of mining operations are continually in progress. All of these are commercial projects and are worked by adventurous seekers of fortune, save only the penal colony known as Vulcan's Workshop: But no Terrestrial or Martian, however greedy for riches, would dare to remain longer than two lunar months, which is the average time limit of human endurance. Only the condemned remain, and these remain to die.

*   *   *   *   *

Though hardly more than two hundred miles in diameter, Vulcan is possessed of a surface gravity almost six times greater than that on Earth. This is due to the planet's core of neutronium, the densest known substance of the universe, a little understood concentration of matter whose atoms comprise only nuclei from which all negative electrons have been stripped by some stupendous cataclysm of nature.

And so it was that Luke Fenton, uninsulated from the tremendous gravity pull when he stepped from the charged metal of the runway, was struggling against his own bodily weight, suddenly increased to more than twelve hundred pounds.

Doggedly, the Earthman pitted his mighty sinews against the force he could not understand. Here was an intangible thing, yet it was a power that challenged his own brute strength, and he exerted himself to the limit in accepting the challenge. With legs spread wide and with sweat oozing from every pore, he heaved himself erect, straightening knees and spine and standing there firmly on his two feet.

"He's carrying it!" came the husky whisper of a guard. "This bird *is* tough."

Craftily, Luke bared his white, even teeth in a good-humored grin. He had seen what they were doing with the other prisoners, fitting them one by one with the strange bulky breeches—garments that gave forth a faint greenish glow like that of the runway. And each of the men, so attired, was enabled somehow to get to his feet easily and walk about as if unhampered by the force which had flattened him to the rocks and which still held Luke's straining body in its grip.

* * * * *

The yellow-skinned guard, a Terrestrial of Asiatic origin, was solemnly engaged now in lacing the slitted legs of a similar garment to Luke's rigid nether limbs. Yet there was no cessation of that awful weight when the thing was done. The guard stepped back and leered wickedly. He had slung his dart gun over his shoulder and now produced a slender black tube which he leveled at Luke's midsection.

"You walk now, Fenton," he snarled.

The Earthman rose upward as if he would leave the ground. Two or three inches seemed added to his stature, and his muscles trembled from the sudden release. He stepped a pace forward.

Then a light beam flashed forth from the black tube and Luke sagged down with an astonished oath squeezed grunting from his throat. The swift renewal of the inexplicable force had caught him off balance and he dropped ignominiously to his knees.

"Ha!" gloated the Oriental. "It is thus we control the tough ones, Fenton. I've given you a warning; now get up—and march!"

On the last word came blessed release and the return of Luke's strength. He marched, meekly falling in with the file of new prisoners. He even smiled through the red stubble of his beard. But black hatred was in his heart, and renewed determination that he'd get away from this place somehow—alive.

Time would show him the way.

*   *   *   *   *

Fenton's slow but retentive mind absorbed many things during the succeeding few days. There was neither day nor night in this hellish place—only the flame-lit mists; but they had clocks like those of Earth, and you worked fourteen hours on the slope or in the smelter and had the rest of each so-called day of twenty-four hours in which to eat and sleep.

The food was coarse, but there was plenty of it. There was only water to drink, lukewarm stinking stuff, doled out sparingly in rusty tin cups. And, during the sleeping periods, you were required to take off the gravity-insulated garments and sleep in huts with insulated floor coverings. The charged floor, of course, allowed you to sleep without being smashed flat on the uncomfortable cots. But they had you safe in these sleeping huts; they took away your clothes and you couldn't step out of the door without taking on the weight of a half a dozen men.

The Workshop itself was in a vast excavation from whose slopes a silvery-veined ore was being removed. There were the blast furnace and reduction plant on the one side and the convicts' huts and more pretentious houses of the guards on the other. And the choking mists, and the lurid flame behind. The stifling heat, Luke learned, too, that every ninth day, with what they called the libration of Vulcan, there came an equal period of raw and biting cold to replace the heat. As bad or worse, that would be.

There were perhaps three hundred prisoners here, Luke guessed, and a guard allotted to each squad of fifteen men. Not many guards for so large a number of convicts—but enough. The weird gravity of Vulcan had taken care of that, and the flashlight things they always carried—queer lights that would instantly neutralize the insulating property of his clothing and render a man helpless.

*   *   *   *   *

Luke was working high up on the slope, with rock drill and pick. The group to which he had been assigned was composed entirely of new prisoners, mostly white men, but with a few blacks and one coppery-skinned drylander of Mars. Whimpering, hopeless creatures, all of them; not worth his notice. All day he labored without speaking to any of them and the quantities of ore he removed gave mute evidence of his tireless vigor. If Kulan, the giant Martian guard, took any notice of it he gave no sign.

During the sleeping period, which they persisted in calling night, things were different. No guards were needed in the escape-proof huts and there was some surreptitious fraternizing among the prisoners. As long as they made no undue noise, they were left to their own devices. But for the most part they went to sleep heavily and wordlessly as soon as they flung into their bunks. A broken-spirited lot.

Luke saw men suffering from some horrible malady that made them cough and scream and bleed from nose and mouth. Old-timers, these were, men who had survived for as many as three of four months. He saw them, in their agony, beg the guards for merciful death; heard the brutal laughter of their tormentors. Only when they were no longer able to rise from their bunks were they put out of their misery by one of the singing darts from the senior guard's gun.

Novak had it, this malady known as X.C.—Novak, the scar-faced, yellow-fanged rat who occupied the bunk beneath Luke's and who talked to him in hoarse whispers long after the others had gone to sleep. It was from Novak that Luke was learning, and the knowledge he gained by listening to the doomed man served only to intensify the flame of hate that smoldered deep in his barrel-like chest.

After three red-lit days of grueling labor and three similarly red-lit nights of listening to Novak, he reached the grudging conclusion that escape from this place was impossible. With this conviction there came to him a deeper bitterness and the resolve that he, Luke Fenton, would have his revenge before he went the way of the rest.

Perhaps the law had him for keeps this time—it certainly seemed so; but he'd leave his mark on its representatives yet.

*   *   *   *   *

At inspection preceding the next labor period, Luke began doing things.

The prisoners were lined up and the guards were parading the line, reassigning them to new working squads, which were shifted and rearranged every third day. Kulan, the big Martian, selected Luke.

"You, Fenton," he snapped, "ten paces forward."

Luke grinned but made no move.

Amazed, the guard stepped closer. "You heard me!" he roared. "I'm keepin' you in my squad, tough guy."

A ripple of astonished comment ran along the line and the other guards bellowed for silence. Kulan fingered the black tube of his neutro-beam and his broad face was chalky white.

Luke advanced two paces, still grinning. And he looked up sneeringly into the grim face that was a foot above his own.

"That's right, you big ape," he grated, "you ain't man enough to fight the way men fight. Gotta use dart guns, or gravity."

It was sheer baiting of the big Martian. Fenton was shrewd and he knew the fellow's kind, quick to resent insult and prouder of their physical size and prowess than of any other possession. He saw the flush that rose to replace the guard's pallor, saw the huge lithe body go tense. Laughing derisively, he completed his ten paces with leisurely aplomb.

Speechless with rage, Kulan stood rigid. Furtive boos and a few hoarse cheers came from somewhere in the long line of convicts, and Luke saw several men flattened to the ground by swift darting neutro-beams.

And then the head guard came running from the small bastion. "What the hell?" he demanded of Kulan. "Any trouble?"

Kulan saluted, and his eyes were narrow slits. "No sir," he returned stiffly, "no trouble."

Eyeing Luke suspiciously, the senior guard grunted, then moved on along the line. And the work of reallotting squads went on.

*   *   *   *   *

It was exactly as Fenton had expected. This Kulan, a head over him in stature and broad in proportion, was sure in his mind that he could handle the red-headed Earthman without resort to weapons. And the taunt as to his physical ability had struck home. In some way that guard would maneuver matters so the encounter could come about. Besides, he would endeavor to keep Luke in his squad where he would be able to drive him to the utmost. The guards, Novak had said, were on the job only a month when they were replaced by fresh recruits—and their pay was based on the productivity of the squads they commanded. Kulan had seen that the Earthman was a real sapper; worth three of the others. And he'd try to keep it so.

That working period was a highly gratifying one to Luke. With the rankling hatred concentrated and directed at Kulan, he was positively gleeful. And yet he was content to bide his time. He swung his pick and wielded his rock drill with joyful abandon, so that three men were kept busy loading the ore he removed.

Kulan, he saw with satisfaction, was sullen and watchful. But no word passed between the two. And the Earthman knew he had planted a seed that was bound to sprout and grow until it bore fruit.

* * * * *

At the midday mess it happened. The shifting of men had brought Novak in the same squad with Luke and they came in to sit at the long table together. Kulan eyed them narrowly from the head of the board.

"Say," Novak whispered, "yuh got under Kuley's skin, know it? He'll run yuh ragged."

"Yes?" Luke looked up at the guard, saw he was scowling darkly in their direction, and grinned evilly. "I'll run him, you mean. I'll bust him in two if I get my hands on him."

"Yuh ain't got a chance, I tell yuh. I seen a guy once, take a poke at a guard, and what they done to him was plenty. They——"

With that, the wasted body of Novak bent double and he dropped to the ground screaming. Blood gushed from his nostrils. Luke had seen the same thing happen to several others and he knew what to expect. It was all over for Novak, or nearly over.

Kulan came running and turned the stricken man face up.

"You'll last another period," he snarled. "Get up and eat."

He yanked Novak to his feet and shook him as he would a sack of meal. The sick man moaned and begged, his head rolling from side to side and his eyes filmed with pain.

"Let me have it," he whimpered. "I'm done, I tell yuh Kuley. Get Gannett, if yuh don't believe me."

Kulan slapped him heavily with the flat of his massive hand. "You'll work another period, sewer rat, if I have to prop you up!"

Then Luke Fenton took a chance. He didn't care particularly for Novak, nor was he overly concerned by what might happen to him. But this gave him an excuse, an opening.

He hooked his thick fingers in the collar of Kulan's jacket and twisted until the big Martian loosed Novak and whirled around. Then Luke drove a hard fist to his jaw—a pulled punch so as not to betray his real strength. Nevertheless it set the guard back on his heels and split the taut skin where it landed.

*   *   *   *   *

Pandemonium broke loose in the mess hall. Gannett, the senior guard, came bellowing down the aisle, and the squad guards were on their feet in an instant, neutro-tubes and dart guns ready. The uproar of the prisoners died down.

Kulan shook his shaggy head and crouched low as he circled the Earthman. Murder was in his heart, and the urge to break this tough guy Fenton with his bare hands. But Gannett was between them.

"Hell's bells!" he yelped. "What goes on here?"

Then he saw Novak—and heard him. Novak was writhing on the ground, begging for death. And the chief guard's dart gun twanged as its needlelike missile sped forth and drove into the sick man's breast where it sang its shrill song of vibratory dissolution.

In the twinkling of an eye where Novak had lain was only the dust of complete disintegration and a few scintillating, dancing light flecks that swiftly snuffed out. A speedy and merciful end.

In the silence that followed, Gannett turned on Kulan. "Why didn't you send for me?" he demanded.

The guard, white with rage, indicated Luke.

"So—the tough guy Fenton again. Can't you handle him?"

Kulan's yellow eyes flashed fire. "Sure I can; I will. But I want your permission, sir. With my hands."

"No,"—flatly. And then Gannett whirled to look over the mess tables, whence a few scattered hisses had arisen.

His gaze was solemn when he returned it to Kulan. Swiftly his black eyes measured the Martian's giant body, and then they swung to Luke. The comparison evidently pleased him, for he changed his mind.

"On second thought, yes," he said to Kulan. "It'll be good for discipline. Only don't disable him; he's too valuable a worker."

Luke concealed his unholy glee; stood glowering savagely. "In fair fight?" he put in.

"In fair fight," sneered Gannett. He took personal charge of Kulan's weapons. "All right, you," he yelled then to the mess, "you can watch this. But if there's a sound or a move from any one of you there'll be the neutro-broadcast and full gravity for an hour for the whole flea-bitten gang of you."

He drew back, motioning Luke and Kulan to an open space nearby. There was not the slightest doubt in his mind as to the outcome, for the Martian towered over his stocky opponent and was fully fifty pounds heavier. This irregular procedure would put a stop to some of the open homage paid to this reputed tough guy by the prisoners, and to the restlessness among them which his coming had occasioned.

*   *   *   *   *

They fought instantly and with silent deadliness of purpose, these two. Luke drove in two terrible blows to the big Martian's body in the split-second before they closed, breathtaking punches that rocked Kulan yet did not slow him up in the least. And then the tangle of arms and legs and bodies of the two was so swift moving and violent that the watchers could not follow them.

Now they were up, slugging, clinching; now down, rolling over and over, straining and tearing at each other like beasts of the jungle. Once, breaking free, Luke was seen to batter Kulan's face to a bloody mass with swift, hammering fists that thudded too rapidly to count. And then the Martian had flung him to the rocky ground so heavily that it seemed certain the Earthman's end had come. But such was not the case, for there was a flailing scramble and Luke Fenton rose up with the great body of Kulan across his shoulders. He spread his legs wide and heaved mightily.

The Martian guard kicked and squirmed, lashing out with his huge fists at the squarely-built and squarely-planted body of the Earthman below him. But to no avail. Grasping a shoulder and a thigh, Fenton straightened his thick arms and Kulan was hoisted aloft. Amazingly then, the madly struggling guard was flung out and away to land with a sickening thud, smashed and crumpled on the rocks.

Luke stood swaying on those spreadeagled legs and his lungs were near bursting from the exertion in the noxious atmosphere. "There you are, Gannett," he howled through swollen lips. "That fair enough for you?"

In the ominous silence a cracked voice yelped: "Attaboy Fenton!"

Wild disorder followed. Immediately there was the raucous call of the general alarm siren and a flashing light from the bastion that paled the red mists to a sickly, luminous pink. Full gravity coming down with crushing force on the hapless prisoners.

Luke, as he was flattened, gasping painfully under the enormous pressure, saw that Gannett and the rest of the guards were not affected by the neutro-broadcast. They stood erect and moved freely among the prisoners who sprawled everywhere in grotesque squashed heaps. Queer. There was no way of beating the authorities at this game.

*   *   *   *   *

Gannett transferred Luke to the dreaded sealed cell in the reduction plant, a room spoken of in hushed whispers by the convicts, and in which it was reported an inmate suffered indescribable tortures for the better part of three weeks. Then he died in horrible misery, for one could not survive longer than that.

Kulan had not been killed. He would recover, but was pretty well smashed up, with a fractured hip and several broken ribs, one of which had punctured a lung. It would be necessary to return him to Mars on the next ethership, due in two days. Strangely, the news brought Luke no great amount of satisfaction.

When they locked him up in the sealed cell for his first period of labor he saw there was only one other occupant. A tall lanky Earthman with narrow aristocratic features and keen gray eyes. He was perhaps forty-five, slightly stooped, and with thin graying hair. Luke had seen him several times at mess and had contemptuously classed him as a highbrow. Fuller, his name was.

This was a small room where several slender chutes brought down tumbling crystals of a silvery salt from somewhere above, emptying it into glass containers that stood in endless rows in wooden racks. You filled these containers with the salt, then sealed them in lead tubes and packed them for shipment. There was a faint pungent odor in the air of the room, a new smell that widened Luke's nostrils and caught at his throat and lungs.

In this place you were watched by a guard who came regularly each half hour and spied on you through a peephole.

Child's play, the work in the sealed cell. Luke went at it half-heartedly and he spoke no word to Fuller after the heavy door had closed them in. After ten minutes of silence he caught himself watching his companion furtively.

What was there about Fuller that marked him as superior to Luke and the rest of the convicts? A good gust of wind would blow the man away; a woman might easily beat him in a rough and tumble. Yet this man had something which unmistakably proclaimed greatness, the same something that gave authority and power to the smart guys of Earth and Mars. Brains—book-learning! Luke snorted.

Fuller was looking at him with calmly appraising gaze. Luke scowled darkly, but the keen eyes that measured him did not waver.

"You're a fool, Fenton," came from the thin lips.

"What!" Luke advanced threateningly.

"I repeat: you are a fool." Still the gray eyes were unwavering.

"Why, you—you——" Spasmodically Luke's fingers closed down on the spare shoulder with crushing force.

*   *   *   *   *

By not so much as the flicker of an eyelash did Fuller betray the pain that must have come with that grip. He did not even wince, but swiftly lashed out with a bony fist, raking Luke's cheek with sharp knuckles. The blow stung, but was utterly futile. With a single cuff Luke could send the man sprawling; with a single wrench of his powerful hands, snap his spine. Yet he did neither, and the impulse to laugh coarsely died in his throat. Here was courage of a kind he never had encountered; here a man in whose bright eyes fearlessness and defiance mingled with a cool disdain that brought the first real feeling of inferiority Luke ever had experienced.

He relaxed his grip of Fuller's shoulder and his big hands fell loosely at his sides. It was that action which saved Fenton. He did not know it at the time, nor would he have believed it. But he was to remember many times and finally to realize it, though he never fully understood.

"That's better," breathed Fuller. And the ghost of a smile crinkled the corner of his mouth.

At the old man's warning Luke returned to his own work bench and was industriously engaged when the guard's eye showed at the peephole. Then the eye was gone and he grinned over at Fuller.

"How long you been in here?" he ventured.

"Five days in the sealed cell; ten altogether in the Workshop."

Luke pondered this. "How'd you get in the cell?"

"Same way you did—I struck a guard."

"No!" marveled Luke. "Mean to tell me you——"

"I had a reason to get in here," Fuller broke in mildly.

"You—you *wanted* to get in?" Luke was incredulous.

"I did."

"My God, you ain't crazy, are you—wantin' to get yourself killed off quicker?"

*   *   *   *   *

"No, that isn't it," Fuller explained patiently. "I've a plan to escape and only by taking the chance of spending some time here could I obtain access to the necessary materials. Fenton, I'm a scientist and I know——"

"Escape!" Luke snorted. "You *are* crazy. Where you goin' to go?"

"Listen, Fenton." The other dropped his voice. "I'm not doing this blindly; I have friends outside. And you can help me. You can get away yourself, alive. I called you a fool and by that I meant that you have relied too much on brute force in your lifetime and had not sense enough to realize that this brought only trouble. Combine your brawn with my brains, now, and do as I say—if you will I promise you freedom. Will you do it, or do you want to keep on being a fool?"

Luke bristled, but the earnestness of that steady gaze served to check his rising temper. "I still think you're nuts," he growled, "but hell, I ain't fool enough to pass up any kind of chance of gettin' outa here. Gimme the dope."

Fuller coughed slightly and a fleck of red-tinged foam appeared at his lips. "It'll have to be to-day," he whispered. "One more day in this place and it'll be too late for me."

X.C.! Luke stared, horrified. Fuller had it already and didn't know it. Poor devil; he was a goner before he started this crazy break of his. Strangely, Luke was deeply concerned. It was a new experience, this feeling of compassion for a fellow man.

"To-day!" he grunted. "You ain't figurin' on gettin' out to-day?"

"Positively—it must be to-day. I'll explain."

*   *   *   *   *

Much of what followed was unintelligible to Luke Fenton, but he absorbed enough of the scientist's explanation to understand that his plan was not impossible of realization. He waxed enthusiastic.

Tom Fuller was vague concerning his own past, but Luke gathered that a political crime had been responsible for his sentence to the Workshop. There was much bitterness in the scientist's refusal to dwell on this point. This, too, Luke was able to understand. The bond between them strengthened.

"It's like this," Fuller told him: "these suits which enable us to move about comfortably in Vulcan's gravity are really quite simple in their functioning. A maze of fine wires is woven into the fabric, and these wires are charged with anti-gravity energies from tiny capsules which are inserted under the belt of the garment. The capsules are really miniature atomic generators and are replaced with fresh ones each night during the sleeping period, since the initial charge lasts only eighteen hours. The generated energies neutralize more than eighty percent of the effect of gravity and our weight thus becomes approximately the same as it is on Earth. Such garments are worn by all prospectors and other visitors to Vulcan."

"How come the neutro-beams?" asked Luke.

They are used only here in the Workshop and they operate the same as the neutro-broadcast from the bastion, the only difference being that the broadcast blankets an area of about two miles in all directions. In both cases vibratory ether waves are sent out and these are of such frequency and wave form as to neutralize the anti-gravity energies originating in our capsules. They render our suits useless, but those of the guards are provided with insulating coverings which block off the waves and thus permit their own garments to function even when the neutro-broadcast is in operation."

"Smart guys," commented Luke. "Too smart. How the devil we gonna get away, then? They'll send out the alarm and——"

"Ah, that is where we fool them, Fenton. With the radium."

"Radium!"

*   *   *   *   *

"Yes, didn't you know? This ore we mine here contains a higher percentage of that valuable element than any on Earth or Mars. Its emanations, together with certain atmospheric gases of Vulcan, are what cause X.C.—a swift destruction of tissue in the lungs and other vital organs. And this concentrate"—Fuller waved his hand toward the rows of tubes before him—"is most highly radioactive of all the products of the Workshop. That is why the sealed cell is so very dangerous to work in. But it is this radioactive salt that gives us the means for escape——"

Both men turned quickly to their labors on hearing the footsteps of the guard.

"My suit is already prepared," continued Fuller, when the eye had gone from the peephole. "Now to prepare yours. I discovered that this radioactivity can be used to defeat the purpose of the neutro-rays as well or better than the regular insulation, which, of course, we can not obtain. That is why I wanted to be in the sealed cell for a time. We merely pack a quantity of the radioactive salt around the capsules in the lining of our garments, and the radium emanations continue the excitation of the tiny atomic generators even under the influence of the neutralizing vibrations. Do you follow me?"

"Yes."

Luke did comprehend, even though the technical explanation was beyond his understanding. They would be able to defy this terrible gravity of Vulcan. They could fight unhampered; walk, or run—to meet these mysterious friends of Fuller's. The flashlights and the broadcast would be useless against them.

The lanky scientist outlined the further details of his plan in swift whispers while he worked with the energizing capsule of Luke's garment.

* * * * *

Actual escape was surprisingly easy. They waited until the labor period was finished, when Chan Dai, the yellow-skinned guard, came to unlock the door. As agreed, Tom Fuller came out first and Luke held back, dragging his feet and cursing softly to himself.

"What'd you say?" the guard snarled.

Luke grinned disarmingly. "Nothin'," he drawled. Still he hung back, scarcely moving from where he stood just within the door.

"Come on, tough guy, a little speed." Chan Dai reached for him.

And then Luke was upon him. The neutro-beam flashed harmlessly. Luke's big hands moved with lightning swiftness, his left one scooping the guard's dart gun from its shoulder strap and his right closing on the astonished Oriental's wind-pipe. It was the work of only an instant to choke him in unconsciousness and lock him in the sealed cell.

"Quick, the chute!" hissed Fuller. He dived head foremost into a rectangular wooden trough that was used for the disposal of the gangue from a crushing mill above. This chute, Fuller had said, led to the outside at the back of the reduction plant.

Across the passage Luke saw a squad of convicts and two guards emerging from the lift. Then he plunged down the steeply inclined trough after Fuller. As he slid and tumbled into the darkness, he heard the hoarse shouting of the guards.

He landed heavily in the pile of gangue at the base of the chute; then was scrambling and slipping down with an avalanche of the sharp edged stone. At the bottom, he saw that Fuller had already started up the slope of the great pit which enclosed the Workshop. Luke darted after him.

*   *   *   *   *

They were hidden from the bastion by the buildings of the smelter and reduction plant. But the loud yelling of guards back there in the pit gave evidence that word of the escape was being passed along to Gannett. Before they were halfway up the slope there was the shriek of the alarm siren, and Luke felt his body sag with a sudden increase of weight. Fool that he had been to trust the scrawny scientist!

"It's the broadcast," panted Fuller, beside him. There is some effect, of course. You're probably carrying fifty extra pounds."

"Huh!" Luke hoped it would be no worse.

Fuller slipped into a narrow crevasse that ran slantwise of the slope and extended upward to the rim of the pit. The going was much easier here and they made rapid progress toward the top. Suddenly Luke realized that it was growing very cold; there was a bite to the foul air, and moisture from the red mist was frosting his beard. The liberation of the tiny planet and consequent shifting of the terminator was bringing frigidity to Vulcan's Workshop.

They came up out of the crevasse at the top of the pit and Luke could not resist looking back. Every convict in sight was flattened to the ground. They sprawled singly and in heaps, each one a squashed inert thing that would not move again until the neutro-broadcast was discontinued. The guards, confident they would find the escaped prisoners in like condition, were searching the slope below them.

Luke raised Chan Dai's, dart gun to his shoulder.

Fuller struck aside the muzzle of the weapon. "No!" he protested, "No unnecessary killing, Fenton. They're completely fooled, and we'll be well on our way before they know the truth."

Grumbling, Luke drew back from the rim of the excavation.

*   *   *   *   *

Up here the ground was fairly level, but there were many fissures and small craters which made the footing precarious. The mists were so dense they could see scarcely two hundred feet ahead.

"We'll be lost in the vapors when they finally wake up and come out after us," Fuller said. "And look Fenton, off there to the left are the three columns of fire that mark the rendezvous."

They plunged on through the red mist toward the flaming pillars. Those beacons, even though they subsided at regular intervals, quickly reappeared after each cessation. And their brilliance penetrated the mists with ease at this distance of about two miles. There was no fear of missing their destination.

"Sure your friends'll be there?" Luke asked doubtingly. He was beginning to have some misgivings about the matter—the scientist had been anything but explicit as to who these friends were. And the longer his thoughts dwelt upon the things Fuller had told him the more suspicious he became. Pretty cagey about everything but the actual getting away from the Workshop, Fuller had been.

"Certainly they will; they've been waiting two days." Fuller's tone was impatient and his words came painfully. "You leave that part of it to me, Fenton," he gasped. There was a fleck of blood at his lips.

As the scientist stumbled on through the mists, Luke's doubts increased and he began to lose his respect for the man's intellect and for the cunning which had enabled him to outwit the neutralizing energies used by the guards. After all, he was a weak and puny specimen. They all were, the smart guys who held the people of two worlds in their power by exercising the knowledge they had learned from books. And this one had failed even in that; whatever he might have been, he had run afoul of the law himself and was already a doomed man. Tricks! This trick of Fuller's had gotten them away, but of what use was it without the brute force necessary to carry on to a successful end?

The brawn Tom had spoken of so slightingly was what they needed from this time on, and nothing else would save them. Luke had that brawn; Fuller did not. The scientist slipped and nearly lost his balance at the edge of a fissure, but Luke made no move to help him. It was every man for himself at this stage of the game.

*   *   *   *   *

Increasing difficulty came with every step. Now they were sliding and rolling into a deep crater, now scrambling up its steep sides with hands torn and bodies bruised by the jagged boulders. A yawning crevasse opened before them and they were forced to skirt its edge for fully a half mile in the wrong direction before they found a crossing. And the cold was unbelievably intense. Numbed and silent, with their eyes half blinded and lungs seared by the frosty air, they struggled on toward the three pillars of flame.

And still Tom Fuller carried on, though Luke was now in the lead.

They had covered probably half the distance to the flaming columns when shouts arose behind them. The guards were on their trail.

"Can't—find us," Fuller panted. "The mists——"

"Hell, the mists are clearing," Luke snarled. "You ain't so damn smart as you think."

What he said was true. Though there was less light on account of the new angle with the sun farther below the horizon, the red mist was definitely lighter in color, noticeably less dense. Visibility was good to several hundred yards. Luke turned his head, but could see nothing of their pursuers.

"They can't," Fuller insisted weakly.

Luke, pushed on with renewed vigor, ignoring him, cursing.

And then there came faintly to his ears the twang of a dart gun; the shrill scream of its deadly vibrating missile; a violent blow that flung him headlong.

*   *   *   *   *

Like a cat, he bounced to his feet, crouching with Chan Dai's dart gun at his shoulder. A strangely grotesque heap was at his feet—Tom Fuller. Off there in the thinning mist he saw a shadowy figure and he fired at it twice. Whether his darts found their mark he was never to know, for a wall of white swept down suddenly to obscure his vision. Snow! Great massed flakes falling endlessly—the moisture of the mist crystallized and closing in on him to hide him even more safely, than had the mists themselves.

He was on his knees then at Fuller's side. A brilliant flash and a screaming roar over amongst the rocks apprised him of the fact that the guard's dart had gone wide. And yet Fuller was down, moaning with pain. Luke tried to turn him over and found that his body had taken on tremendous weight. He was flattened, crushed to the rocky surface of Vulcan by the full force of its gravity!

"What the devil!" he grunted as he heaved and strained. "What'd they do to you, old man?"

With great effort he succeeded in turning the scientist face up. Then he saw what had happened, and knew in a flash that Fuller had saved him from the singing dart whose energy was making a sizzling puddle of the stones where it had landed. The missile, in passing, had carried away the belt and part of the fabric of Tom's garment—carried away the capsule and the radium that energized it. Made the thing worse than useless. And Fuller had done this for him; he had flung himself upon Luke to shove him out of the line of fire ... risking his own life gladly ... lucky the deadly dart had missed his body, but....

*   *   *   *   *

"You go on, Fenton," the scientist was whispering through lips that were blue and stiff. "Leave me here. I'm licked. But you can carry on the work; go to my friends and tell them—everything. Tell them what you saw back there—tell them——"

"Shut up!" Luke's words were softly growled. There was a new and utterly unaccountable huskiness in his voice as he straddled the prone body and locked his strong fingers underneath. "You ain't gonna be left behind," he grunted. "We're goin' on, brother, together."

His back straightened and Fuller was swung clear of the ground. His huge biceps tensed and the scrawny scientist was in the air, up and above the bowed head, then let down gently to rest across the broad shoulders of Luke Fenton. Fuller hung there, bent double by the immense weight of him, crushed to painful contact with the taut muscles that carried the strain.

On Earth, Fuller might have tipped the scales at a scant one hundred and thirty pounds; now his sagging body was a load in excess of seven hundredweight. With that load upon him, and glorying in the effort it cost, Luke staggered on toward the triple red glow, which, even in the blinding whiteness of the snowfall, marked the location of the columns of fire.

That all feeling had left his limbs in the deep-biting cold meant nothing; that his lungs were near bursting under the terrific strain meant even less. Luke Fenton had found a man. One he would fight for, not against. And, miraculously, he had found himself.

*   *   *   *   *

After that there was a blur of interminable torture. Reeling and stumbling, his leg and back muscles shot through with stabbing pain as the frost worked slowly upward, Luke plodded doggedly ahead. An occasional shout came from far behind where the guards still searched the rocky plateau.

Across his great shoulders, Luke's burden was a dead weight, of corpselike rigidity and stillness. Yet Luke clung to it tenaciously, disposing the drooping leaden limbs as comfortably as possible by the judicious spreading of his own brawny arms.

Fuller, he was sure, had not long to live in any event. X.C. had already progressed to such a point that it was hardly possible he could recover. And yet, these smart guys Luke always had detested—the doctors and surgeons and such—they might be able to do something for the poor devil. Anyway, he determined, he'd get the scientist to his friends dead or alive, and he'd see to it that they treated him right. If they didn't....

The red glow was suddenly very bright and a silvery metallic shape loomed up before him in the whiteness. An ethership! Luke tried to call out but his bellowing voice was gone; only faint gurgling sounds came from his throat. He pushed forward with a savage summoning of his last ounce of energy and Fuller's weight was that of a mastodon upon him. The curved hull of the vessel was overhead when he slipped and fell to one knee in the thick carpet of snow.

Luke saw them then, a dozen strangers running from the open air-lock of the ship. In uniform, some of them—government officials of Earth and Mars. Damn them, it was a trap!

Knowing vaguely that they had surrounded him, he let Fuller slip from his shoulders and lowered him gently to the snow. Lurching to his feet, he stood swaying above the scientist's body, ready to defend the helpless man against any who came to take him. Defiant curses died in his paralyzed throat as darkness swooped down to blot out all consciousness. His steel-sinewed body, beaten at last, slumped protectingly over the lanky form of his new-found friend.

*   *   *   *   *

When Luke next saw the light he stared long and hard at immaculate white walls and ceiling that shut him in. A gentle purring was in his ears and he knew he was in an ethership that was under way. He lay weak and helpless beneath snowy covers, on an iron hospital bed.

There were voices in the room, hushed, awed voices, and Luke moved his head painfully to stare across the room. Fuller, he saw, was stretched on another cot, pale and still. And a white-clad nurse was there, bending over him, talking softly to a doctor. The words that passed between them brought enlightenment to Luke—and more. They brought a new elation, and understanding, and hope.

When the doctor and nurse had left, Luke lay for a long time with his thoughts. There was a man—Tom Fuller. Unafraid, as an agent of a special governmental committee investigating prison conditions he had volunteered to get the evidence on Vulcan's Workshop. And he had done it, even though it was almost certain that his own life was to be the price. He had dared the misery and hardship, dared X.C. and the horrible death it brought, that this hellhole of Vulcan might be exposed, that it might be wiped out of existence by government agreement. Vulcan's Workshop, where the gold dust of a certain political clique, brought torture and disease and extinction to hapless prisoners who might otherwise be remade into useful members of society by the use of scientific methods—all this was to be no more.

Fuller had succeeded where many others had failed. And Fuller was not to die. Only one of his lungs had been affected by X.C. and this not too extensively to respond to treatment. Many months of careful attendance would be required, and many more months of convalescence. But Fuller, they were sure, would live, Luke gloated.

From what he had heard, Luke gathered that there was to be no trouble about his own pardon. Oddly enough, this gave him no satisfaction. Something had happened to him—inside. For the first time he realised his debt to society and would have preferred that just sentence be carried out upon him. But not in that place, not in Vulcan's Workshop! Luke shuddered.

* * * * *

And lying there, he swore a mighty oath that the remainder of his life was to be devoted to entirely different pursuits. It was not too late to face about, not too late to learn. If Fuller would help him, he *would* learn. He had acquired a healthy respect for the book-learning he formerly ridiculed, and he wanted some of it for himself—as much as he could get. His old creed was forgotten, and his bitterness vanished.

"Luke!" At the scientist's husky whisper he turned his head. Fuller was gazing at him with wide, solemn eyes.

"Thanks, Luke," the thin lips murmured.

"Thanks yourself. Where'd we be right now if it wasn't for your radium?"

There was silence as they regarded one another.

"I need you, Luke," Fuller whispered then, "in my laboratory back home. I'll be laid up for a long time, you know, and there's much to be done. Your brawn and my brain—we'll both profit. What do you say to that, Fenton, will you do it?"

Luke grinned. "Will I? Just watch me!"

Then, with a queer lump choking him, Luke looked away. He could think of no words to suit the occasion; he couldn't think at all somehow.

Blissfully, he fell asleep.

WANDERER OF INFINITY

ORIGINALLY PUBLISHED IN *ASTOUNDING STORIES*,
MARCH 1932

Wanderer of Infinity

Lenville! Bert Redmond had never heard of the place until he received Joan's letter. But here it was, a tiny straggling village cuddled amongst the Ramapo hills of lower New York State, only a few miles from Tuxedo. There was a prim, white-painted church, a general store with the inevitable gasoline pump at the curb, and a dozen or so of weatherbeaten frame houses. That was all. It was a typical, dusty cross-roads hamlet of the vintage of thirty years before, utterly isolated and apart from the rushing life of the broad concrete highway so short a distance away.

Bert stopped his ancient and battered flivver at the corner where a group of overalled loungers was gathered. Its asthmatic motor died with a despairing cough as he cut the ignition.

"Anyone tell me where to find the Carmody place?" he sang out.

No one answered, and for a moment there was no movement amongst his listeners. Then one of the loungers, an old man with a stubble of gray beard, drew near and regarded him through thick spectacles.

"You ain't aimin' to go up there alone, be you?" the old fellow asked in a thin cracked voice.

"Certainly. Why?" Bert caught a peculiar gleam in the watery old eyes that were enlarged so enormously by the thick lenses. It was fear of the supernatural that lurked there, stark terror, almost.

"Don't you go up to the Carmody place, young feller. They's queer doin's in the big house, is why. Blue lights at night, an' noises inside—an'—an' cracklin' like thunder overhead—"

"Aw shet up, Gramp!" Another of the idlers, a youngster with chubby features, and downy of lip and chin, sauntered over from the group, interrupting the old man's discourse. "Don't listen to him," he said to Bert. "He's cracked a mite—been seein' things. The big house is up yonder on the hill. See, with the red chimbley showin' through the trees. They's a windin' road down here a piece."

Bert followed the pointing finger with suddenly anxious gaze. It was not an inviting spot, that tangle of second-growth timber and underbrush that hid the big house on the lonely hillside; it might conceal almost anything. And Joan Parker was there!

The one called Gramp was screeching invectives at the grinning bystanders. "You passel o' young idjits!" he stormed. "I seen it, I tell you. An'—an' heard things, too, The devil hisself is up there—an' his imps. We'd oughtn't to let this feller go...."

Bert waited to hear no more. Unreasoning fear came to him that something was very much amiss up there at the big house, and he started the flivver with a thunderous barrage of its exhaust.

The words of Joan's note were vivid in his mind: "Come to me, Bert, at the Carmody place in Lenville. Believe me, I need you." Only that, but it had been sufficient to bring young Redmond across three states to this measly town that wasn't even on the road maps.

Bert yanked the bouncing car into the winding road that led up the hill, and thought grimly of the quarrel with Joan two years before. He had told her then, arrogantly, that she'd need him some day. But now that his words had proved true the fact brought him no consolation nor the slightest elation. Joan was there in this lonely spot, and she did need him. That was enough.

He ran nervous fingers through his already tousled mop of sandy hair—a habit he had when disturbed—and nearly wrecked the car on a gray boulder that encroached on one of the two ruts which, together, had been termed a road.

Stupid, that quarrel of theirs. And how stubborn both had been! Joan had insisted on going to the big city to follow the career her brother had chosen for her. Chemistry, biology, laboratory work! Bert sniffed, even now. But he had been equally stubborn in his insistence that she marry him instead and settle down on the middle-Western fruit farm.

With a sudden twist, the road turned in at the entrance of a sadly neglected estate. The grounds of the place were overrun with rank growths and the driveway was covered with weeds. The tumble-down gables of a descrepit frame house peeped out through the trees. It was a rambling old building that once had been a mansion—the "big house" of the natives. A musty air of decay was upon it, and crazily askew window shutters proclaimed deep-shrouded mystery within.

Bert drew up at the rickety porch and stopped the flivver with its usual shuddering jerk.

* * * * *

As if his coming had been watched for through the stained glass of its windows, the door was flung violently open. A white-clad figure darted across the porch, but not before Bert had untangled the lean six feet of him from under the flivver's wheel and bounded up the steps.

"Joan!"

"Bert! I—I'm sorry."

"Me too." Swallowing hard, Bert Redmond held her close.

"But I won't go back to Indiana!" The girl raised her chin and the old defiance was in her tearful gaze.

Bert stared. Joan was white and wan, a mere shadow of her old self. And she was trembling, hysterical.

"That's all right," he whispered. "But tell me now, what is it? What's wrong?"

With sudden vigor she was drawing him into the house. "It's Tom," she quavered. "I can't do a thing with him; can't get him to leave here. And something terrible is about to happen, I know. I thought perhaps you could help, even if—"

"Tom Parker here?" Bert was surprised that the fastidious older brother should leave his comfortable city quarters and lose himself in this God-forsaken place. "Sure, I'll help, dear—if I can."

"You can; oh, I'm sure you can," the girl went on tremulously. A spot of color flared in either cheek. "It's his experiments. He came over from New York about a year ago and rented this old house. The city laboratory wasn't secluded enough. And I've helped him until now in everything. But I'm frightened; he's playing with dangerous forces. He doesn't understand—won't understand. But I saw...."

And then Joan Parker slumped into a high-backed chair that stood in the ancient paneled hall. Soft waves of her chestnut hair framed the pinched, terrified face, and wide eyes looked up at Bert, with the same horror he had seen in those of the old fellow the village. A surge of the old tenderness welled up in him and he wanted to take her in his arms.

"Wait," she said, swiftly rising. "I'll let you judge for yourself. Here—go into the laboratory and talk with Tom."

She pushed him forward and through a door that closed softly behind him. He was in a large room that was cluttered with the most bewildering array of electrical mechanisms he had ever seen. Joan had remained outside.

*   *   *   *   *

Tom Parker, his hair grayer and forehead higher than when Bert had seen him last, rose from where he was stooping over a work bench. He advanced, smiling, and his black eyes were alight with genuine pleasure. Bert had anticipated a less cordial welcome.

"Albert Redmond!" exclaimed the older man. "This is a surprise. Glad to see you, boy, glad to see you."

He meant it, Tom did, and Bert wrung the extended hand heartily. Yet he dared not tell of Joan's note. The two men had always been the very best of friends—except in the matter of Joan's future.

"You haven't changed much," Bert ventured.

Tom Parker laughed. "Not about Joan, if that is what you mean. She likes the work and will go far in it. Why, Bert—"

"Sa-ay, wait a minute." Bert Redmond's mien was solemn. "I saw her outside, Tom, and was shocked. She isn't herself—doesn't look at all well. Haven't you noticed, man?"

The older man sobered and a puzzled frown crossed his brow. "I have noticed, yes. But it's nonsense, Bert, I swear it is. She has been having dreams—worrying a lot, it seems. Guess I'll have to send her to the doctor?"

"Dreams? Worry?" Bert thought of the old man called Gramp.

"Yes. I'll tell you all about it—what we're working on here—and show you. It's no wonder she gets that way, I guess. I've been a bit loony with the marvel of it myself at times. Come here."

Tom led him to an intricate apparatus which bore some resemblance to a television radio. There were countless vacuum tubes and their controls, tiny motors belted to slotted disks that would spin when power was applied, and a double eyepiece.

"Before I let you look," Tom was saying, "I'll give you an idea of it, to prepare you. This is a mechanism I've developed for a study of the less-understood dimensions. The results have more than justified my expectations—they're astounding. Bert, we can actually see into these realms that were hitherto unexplored. We can examine at close range the life of these other planes. Think of it!"

"Life—plane—dimensions?" said Bert blankly. "Remember, I know very little about this science of yours."

* * * * *

"Haven't you read the news-paper accounts of Einstein's researches and of others who have delved into the theory of relativity?"

"Sa-ay! I read them, but they don't tell me a thing. It's over my head a mile."

"Well, listen: this universe of ours—space and all it contains—is a thing of five dimensions, a continuum we have never begun to contemplate in its true complexity and immensity. There are three of its dimensions with which we are familiar. Our normal senses perceive and understand them— length, breadth and thickness. The fourth dimension, time, or, more properly, the time-space interval, we have only recently understood. And this fifth dimension, Bert, is something no man on earth has delved into—excepting myself."

"You don't say." Bert was properly impressed; the old gleam of the enthusiastic scientist was in Tom's keen eyes.

"Surest thing. I have called this fifth dimension the interval of oscillation, though the term is not precisely correct. It has to do with the arrangement, the speed and direction of movement, and the polarity of protonic and electronic energy charges of which matter is comprised. It upsets some of our old and accepted natural laws—one in particular. Bert, two objects can occupy the same space at the same time, though only one is perceptible to our earthbound senses. Their differently constituted atoms exist in the same location without interference—merely vibrating in different planes. There are many such planes in this fifth dimension of space, all around us, some actually inhabited. Each plane has a different atomic structure of matter, its own oscillation interval of the energy that is matter, and a set of natural laws peculiar to itself. I can't begin to tell you; in fact, I've explored only a fraction. But here— look!"

*   *   *   *   *

Tom's instrument set up a soft purring at his touch of a lever, and eery blue light flickered from behind the double eyepiece, casting grotesque shadows on walls and ceiling, and paling to insignificance the light of day that filtered through the long-unwashed windows.

Bert squinted through the hooded twin lenses. At first he was dazzled and confused by the rapidly whirling light-images, but these quickly resolved into geometric figures, an inconceivable number of them, extending off into limitless space in a huge arc, revolving and tumbling like the colored particles in an old-fashioned kaleidoscope. Cubes, pyramids and cones of variegated hues. Swift-rushing spheres and long slim cylinders of brilliant blue-white; gleaming disks of polished jet, spinning....

Abruptly the view stabilized, and clear-cut stationary objects sprang into being. An unbroken vista of seamed chalky cliffs beside an inky sea whose waters rose and fell rhythmically yet did not break against the towering palisade. Wave-less, glass-smooth, these waters. A huge blood-red sun hanging low in a leaden though cloudless sky, reflecting scintillating flecks of gold and purple brilliance from the ocean's black surface.

At first there was no sign of life to be seen. Then a mound was rising up from the sea near the cliff, a huge tortoiselike shape that stretched forth several flat members which adhered to the vertical white wall is if held by suction disks. Ponderously the thing turned over and headed up from the inky depths, spewing out from its concave under side an army of furry brown bipeds. Creatures with bloated torsos in which head and body merged so closely as to be indistinguishable one from the other, balanced precariously on two spindly legs, and with long thin arms like tentacles, waving and coiling. Spiderlike beings ran out over the smooth dark surface of the sea as if it were solid ground.

*   *   *   *   *

"Jupiter!" Bert looked up from the eyepiece, blinking into the triumphant grinning face of Tom Parker. "You mean to tell me these creatures are real?" he demanded. "Living here, all around us, in another plane where we can't see them without this machine of yours?"

"Surest thing. And this is but one of many such planes."

"They can't get through, to our plane?"

"Lord no, man, how could they?"

A sharp crackling peal of thunder rang out overhead and Tom Parker went suddenly white. Outside, the sky was cloudless.

"And that—what's that?" Bert remembered the warning of the old man of the village, and Joan's obvious fear.

"It—it's only a physical manifestation of the forces I use in obtaining visual connection, one of the things that worries Joan. Yet I can't find any cause for alarm...."

The scientist's voice droned on endlessly, technically. But Bert knew there was something Tom did not understand, something he was trying desperately to explain to himself.

Thunder rumbled once more, and Bert returned his eyes to the instrument. Directly before him in the field of vision a group of the spider men advanced over the pitchy sea with a curiously constructed cage of woven transparent material which they set down at a point so close by that it seemed he could touch it if he stretched out his hand. The illusion of physical nearness was perfect. The evil eyes of the creatures were fastened upon him; tentacle arms uncoiled and reached forth as if to break down the barrier that separated them.

And then a scream penetrated his consciousness, wrenching him back to consideration of his immediate surroundings. The laboratory door burst open and Joan, pale and disheveled, dashed into the room.

*   *   *   *   *

Tom shouted, running forward to intercept her, and Bert saw what he had not seen before, a ten-foot circle of blue-white metal set in the floor and illuminated by a shaft of light from a reflector on the ceiling above Tom's machine.

"Joan—the force area!" Tom was yelling. "Keep away!"

Tom had reached the distraught girl and was struggling with her over on the far side of the disk.

There came a throbbing of the very air surrounding them, and Bert saw Tom and Joan on the other side of the force area, their white faces indistinct and wavering as if blurred by heat waves rising between. The rumblings and cracklings overhead increased in intensity until the old house swayed and creaked with the concussions. Hazy forms materialized on the lighted disk—the cage of the transparent, woven basket—dark spidery forms within. The creatures from that other plane!

"Joan! Tom!" Bert's voice was soundless as he tried to shout, and his muscles were paralyzed when he attempted to hurl himself across to them. The blue-white light had spread and formed a huge bubble of white brilliance, a transparent elastic solid that flung him back when he attacked it in vain with his fists.

Within its confines he saw Joan and her brother scuffling with the spider men, tearing at the tentacle arms that encircled them and drew them relentlessly into the basket-weave cage. There was a tremendous thump and the warping of the very universe about them all. Bert Redmond, his body racked by insupportable tortures, was hurled into the black abyss of infinity....

*   *   *   *   *

This was not death nor was it a dream from which he would awaken. After that moment of mental agony and ghastly physical pain, after a dizzying rush through inky nothingness, Bert knew suddenly that he was very much alive. If he had lost consciousness at all, it had been for no great length of time. And yet there was this sense of strangeness in his surroundings, a feeling that he had been transported over some nameless gulf of space. He had dropped to his knees, but with the swift return of normal faculties he jumped to his feet.

A tall stranger confronted him, a half-nude giant with bronzed skin and of solemn visage. The stalwart build of him and the smooth contours of cheek and jaw proclaimed him a man not yet past middle age, but his uncropped hair was white as the driven snow.

They stood in a spherical chamber of silvery metal, Bert and this giant, and the gentle vibration of delicately balanced machinery made itself felt in the structure. Of Joan and Tom there was no sign.

"Where am I?" Bert demanded. "And where are my friends? Why am I with you, without them?"

Compassion was in the tall stranger's gaze—and something more. The pain of a great sorrow filled the brown eyes that looked down at Bert, and resignation to a fate that was shrouded in ineffable mystery.

"Trust me," he said in a mellow slurring voice. "Where you are, you shall soon learn. You are safe. And your friends will be located."

"*Will* be located! Don't you *know* where they are?" Bert laid hands on the big man's wrists and shook him impatiently. The stranger was too calm and unmoved in the face of this tremendous thing which had come to pass.

"I know where they have been taken, yes. But there is no need of haste out here in infra-dimensional space, for time stands still. We will find it a simple matter to reach the plane of their captors, the Bardeks, within a few seconds after your friends arrive there. My plane segregator—this sphere—will accomplish this in due season."

*   *   *   *   *

Strangely, Bert believed him. This talk of dimensions and planes and of the halting of time was incomprehensible, but somehow there was communicated to his own restless nature something of the placid serenity of the white-haired stranger. He regarded the man more closely, saw there was an alien look about him that marked him as different and apart from the men of Earth. His sole garment was a wide breech clout of silvery stuff that glinted with changing colors—hues foreign to nature on Earth. His was a superhuman perfection of muscular development, and there was an indescribable mingling of gentleness and sternness in his demeanor. With a start, Bert noted that his fingers were webbed, as were his toes.

"Sa-ay," Bert exclaimed, "who are you, anyway?"

The stranger permitted himself the merest ghost of a smile. "You may call me Wanderer," he said. "I am the Wanderer of Infinity."

"Infinity! You are not of my world?"

"But no."

"You speak my language."

"It is one of many with which I am familiar."

"I—I don't understand." Bert Redmond was like a man in a trance, completely under the spell of his amazing host's personality.

"It is given to few men, to understand." The Wanderer fell silent, his arms folded across his broad chest. And his great shoulders bowed as under the weight of centuries of mankind's cares. "Yet I would have you understand, O Man-Called-Bert, for the tale is a strange one and is heavy upon me."

It was uncanny that this Wanderer should address him by name. Bert thrilled to a new sense of awe.

"But," he objected, "my friends are in the hands of the spider men. You said we'd go to them. Good Lord, man, I've got to do it!"

"You forget that time means nothing here. We will go to them in precise synchronism with the proper time as existent in that plane."

*   *   *   *   *

The Wanderer's intense gaze held Bert speechless, hypnotized. A swift dimming of the sphere's diffused illumination came immediately, and darkness swept down like a blanket, thick and stifling. This was no ordinary darkness, but utter absence of light—the total obscurity of Erebus. And the hidden motors throbbed with sudden new vigor.

"Behold!" At the Wanderer's exclamation the enclosing sphere became transparent and they were in the midst of a dizzying maelstrom of flashing color. Brilliant geometric shapes, there were, whirling off into the vastness of space; as Bert had seen them in Tom Parker's instrument. A gigantic arc of rushing light-forms spanning the black gulf of an unknown cosmos. And in the foreground directly under the sphere was a blue-white disk, horizontally fixed—a substantial and familiar object, with hazy surroundings likewise familiar.

"Isn't that the metal platform in my friend's laboratory?" asked Bert, marveling.

"It is indeed." The mellow voice of the Wanderer was grave, and he laid a hand on Bert's arm. "And for so long as it exists it constitutes a serious menace to your civilization. It is a gateway to your world, a means of contact with your plane of existence for those many vicious hordes that dwell in other planes of the fifth dimension. Without it, the Bardeks had not been able to enter and effect the kidnaping of your friends. Oh, I tried so hard to warn them—Parker and the girl—but could not do it in time."

A measure of understanding came to Bert Redmond. This was the thing Joan had feared and which Tom Parker had neglected to consider. The forces which enabled the scientist to see into the mysterious planes of this uncharted realm were likewise capable of providing physical contact between the planes, or actual travel from one to the other. Tom had not learned how to use the forces in this manner, but the Bardeks had.

*   *   *   *   *

"We travel now along a different set of coordinates, those of space-time," said the Wanderer. "We go into the past, through eons of time as it is counted in your world."

"Into the past," Bert repeated. He stared foolishly at his host, whose eyes glittered strangely in the flickering light.

"Yes, we go to my home—to what was my home."

"To your home? Why?" Bert shrank before the awful contorted face of the Wanderer. A spasm of ferocity had crossed it on his last words. Some fearful secret must be gnawing at the big man's vitals.

"Again you must trust me. To understand, it is necessary that you see."

The gentle whir of machinery rose to a piercing shriek as the Wanderer manipulated the tiny levers of a control board that was set in the smooth transparent wall. And the rushing light-forms outside became a blur at first, then a solid stream of cold liquid fire into which they plunged at breakneck speed.

There was no perceptible motion of the sphere, however. It was the only object that seemed substantial and fixed in an intangible and madly gyrating universe. Its curved wall, though transparent, was solid, comforting to the touch.

Standing by his instrument board, the Wanderer was engrossed in a tabulation of mathematical data he was apparently using in setting the many control knobs before him. Plotting their course through infinity! His placid serenity of countenance had returned, but there was a new eagerness in his intense gaze and his strong fingers trembled while he manipulated the tiny levers and dials.

*   *   *   *   *

Outside the apparently motionless sphere, a never-ending riot of color surged swiftly and silently by, now swirling violently in great sweeping arcs of blinding magnificence, now changing character and driving down from dizzying heights as a dim-lit column of gray that might have been a blast of steam from some huge inverted geyser of the cosmos. Always there were the intermittent black bands that flashed swiftly across the brightness, momentarily darkening the sphere and then passing on into the limbo of this strange realm between planes.

Abruptly then, like the turning of a page in some gigantic book, the swift-moving phantasmagoria swung back into the blackness of the infinite and was gone. Before them stretched a landscape of rolling hills and fertile valleys. Overhead, the skies were a deep blue, almost violet, and twin suns shone down on the scene. The sphere drifted along a few hundred feet from the surface.

"Urtraria!" the Wanderer breathed reverently. His white head was bowed and his great hands clutched the small rail of the control board.

In a daze of conflicting emotions, Bert watched as this land of peace and plenty slipped past beneath them. This, he knew, had been the home of Wanderer. In what past age or at how great a distance it was from his own world, he could only imagine. But that the big man who called himself Wanderer loved this country there was not the slightest doubt. It was a fetish with him, a past he was in duty bound to revisit time and again, and to mourn over.

Smooth broad lakes, there were, and glistening streams that ran their winding courses through well-kept and productive farmlands. And scattered communities with orderly streets and spacious parks. Roads, stretching endless ribbons of wide metallic surface across the countryside. Long two-wheeled vehicles skimming over the roads with speed so great the eye could scarcely follow them. Flapping-winged ships of the air, flying high and low in all directions. A great city of magnificent dome-topped buildings looming up suddenly at the horizon.

The sphere proceeded swiftly toward the city. Once a great air liner, flapping huge gossamerlike wings, drove directly toward them. Bert cried out in alarm and ducked instinctively, but the ship passed *through* them and on its way. It was as if they did not exist in this spherical vehicle of the dimensions.

*　　*　　*　　*　　*

"We are here only as onlookers," the Wanderer explained sadly, "and can have no material existence here. We can not enter this plane, for there is no gateway. Would that there were."

Now they were over the city and the sphere came to rest above a spacious flat roof where there were luxurious gardens and pools, and a small glass-domed observatory. A woman was seated by one of the pools, a beautiful woman with long golden hair that fell in soft profusion over her ivory shoulders and bosom. Two children, handsome stalwart boys of probably ten and twelve, romped with a domestic animal which resembled a foxhound of Earth but had glossy short-haired fur and flippers like these of a seal. Suddenly these three took to the water and splashed with much vigor and joyful shouting.

The Wanderer gripped Bert's arm with painful force. "My home!" he groaned. "Understand, Earthling? This was my home, these my wife and children—destroyed through my folly. Destroyed, I say, in ancient days. And by my accursed hand— when the metal monsters came."

There was madness in the Wanderer's glassy stare, the madness of a tortured soul within. Bert began to fear him.

"We should leave," he said. "Why torment yourself with such memories? My friends...."

"Have patience, Earthling. Don't you understand that I sinned and am therefore condemned to this torment? Can't you see that I *must* unburden my soul of its ages-old load, that I must revisit the scene of my crime, that others must see and know? It is part of my punishment, and you, perforce, must bear witness. Moreover, it is to help your friends and your world that I bring you here. Behold!"

*   *   *   *   *

A man was coming out of the observatory, a tall man with bronzed skin and raven locks. It was the Wanderer himself, the Wanderer of the past, as he had been in the days of his youth and happiness.

The woman by the pool had risen from her seat and was advancing eagerly toward her mate. Bert saw that the man hardly glanced in her direction, so intent was he upon an object over which he stood. The object was a shimmering bowl some eight or ten feet across, which was mounted on a tripod near the observatory, and over whose metallic surface a queer bluish light was playing.

It was a wordless pantomime, the ensuing scene, and Bert watched in amazement. This woman of another race, another age, another plane, was pleading with her man. Sobbing soundlessly, wretchedly. And the man was unheeding, impatient with her demonstrations. He shoved her aside as she attempted to interfere with his manipulations of some elaborate mechanical contrivance at the side of the bowl.

And then there was a sudden roaring vibration, a flash of light leaping from the bowl, and the materialization of a spherical vessel that swallowed up the man and vanished in the shaft of light like a moth in the flame of a candle.

At Bert's side, the Wanderer was a grim and silent figure, misty and unreal when compared with those material, emotion-torn beings of the rooftop. The woman, swooning, had wilted over the rim of the bowl, and the two boys with their strange amphibious pet splashed out from the pool and came running to her, wide-eyed and dripping.

The Wanderer touched a lever and again there was the sensation as of a great page turned across the vastness of the universe. All was hazy and indistinct outside the sphere that held them, with a rushing blur of dimly gray light-forms. Beneath them remained only the bright outline of the bowl, an object distinct and real and fixed in space.

"It was thus I left my loved ones," the Wanderer said hollowly. "In fanatical devotion to my science, but in blind disregard of those things which really mattered. Observe, O Man-Called-Bert, that the bowl is still existent in infra-dimensional space—the gateway I left open to Urtraria. So it remained while I, fool that I was, explored those planes of the fifth dimension that were all around us though we saw and felt them not. Only I had seen, even as your friend Tom has seen. And, like him, I heeded not the menace of the things I had witnessed. We go now to the plane of the metal monsters. Behold!"

*   *   *   *   *

The sphere shuddered to the increased power of its hidden motors and another huge page seemed to turn slowly over, lurching sickeningly as it came to rest in the new and material plane of existence. Here, Bert understood now, the structure of matter was entirely different. Atoms were comprised of protons and electrons whirling at different velocities and in different orbits—possibly some of the electrons in reverse direction to those of the atomic structure of matter in Urtraria. And these coexisted with those others in the same relative position in time and in space. Ages before, the thing had happened, and he was seeing it now.

They were in the midst of a forest of conical spires whose sides were of dark glittering stuff that reminded Bert of the crystals of carborundum before pulverizing for commercial use. A myriad of deep colors were reflected from the sharply pointed piles in the light of a great cold moon that hung low in the heavens above them.

In the half light down there between the circular bases of the cones, weird creatures were moving. Like great earthworms they moved, sluggishly and with writhing contortions of their many-jointed bodies. Long cylindrical things with glistening gray hide, like armor plate and with fearsome heads that reared upward occasionally to reveal the single flaming eye and massive iron jaws each contained. There were riveted joints and levers, wheels and gears that moved as the creatures moved; darting lights that flashed forth from trunnion-mounted cases like the searchlights of a battleship of Earth; great swiveled arms with grappling hooks attached. They were mechanical contrivances— the metal monsters of which the Wanderer had spoken. Whether their brains were comprised of active living cells or whether they were cold, calculating machines of metallic parts, Bert was never to know.

"See, the gateway," the Wanderer was saying. "They are investigating. It is the beginning of the end of Urtraria—all as it occurred in the dim and distant past."

He gripped Bert's arm, pointing a trembling finger, and his face was a terrible thing to see in the eery light of their sphere.

*   *   *   *   *

A sharply outlined circle of blue-white appeared down there in the midst of the squirming monsters. The sphere drifted lower and Bert was able to see that a complicated machine was being trundled out from an arched doorway in the base of one of the conical dwellings. It was moved to the edge of the light circle which was the bowl on that rooftop of Urtraria. The same bowl! A force area like that used by Tom Parker, an area existent in many planes of the fifth dimension simultaneously, an area where the various components of wave motion merged and became as one. The gateway between planes!

The machine of the metal monsters was provided with a huge lens and a reflector, and these were trained on the bowl. Wheels and levers of the machine moved swiftly. There came an orange light from within that was focused upon lens and reflector to strike down and mingle with the cold light of the bowl. A startling transformation ensued, for the entire area within view was encompassed with a milky diffused brightness in which two worlds seemed to intermingle and fuse. There were the rooftops of the city in Urtraria and its magnificent domes, a transparent yet substantial reality superimposed upon the gloomy city of cones of the metal monsters.

"Jupiter!" Bert breathed. "They're going through!"

"They are, Earthling. More accurately, they did—thousands of them; millions." Even as the Wanderer spoke, the metal monsters were wriggling through between the two planes, their enormous bodies moving with menacing deliberation.

On the rooftops back in Urtraria could be seen the frantic, fleeing forms of humanlike beings—the Wanderer's people.

There was a sharp click from the control panel and the scene was blotted out by the familiar maze of geometric shapes, the whirling, dancing light-forms that rushed madly past over the vast arch which spanned infinity.

*   *   *   *   *

"Where were you at the time?" asked Bert. Awed by what he had seen and with pity in his heart for the man who had unwittingly let loose the horde of metal monsters on his own loved ones and his own land, he stared at the Wanderer.

The big man was standing with face averted, hands clutching the rail of the control panel desperately. "I?" he whispered. "I was roaming the planes, exploring, experimenting, immersed in the pursuits that went with my insatiable thirst for scientific data and the broadening of my knowledge of this complex universe of ours. Forgetting my responsibilities. Unknowing, unsuspecting."

"You returned—to your home?"

"Too late I returned. You shall see; we return now by the same route I then followed."

"No!" Bert shouted, suddenly panicky at thought of what might be happening to Joan and Tom in the land of the Bardeks. "No, Wanderer—tell me, but don't show me. I can imagine. Seeing those loathsome big worms of iron and steel, I can well visualize what they did. Come now, have a heart, man; take me to my friends before...."

"Ah-h!" The Wanderer looked up and a benign look came to take the place of the pain and horror which had contorted his features. "It is well, O Man-Called-Bert. I shall do as you request, for I now see that my mission has been well accomplished. We go to your friends, and fear you not that we shall arrive too late."

"Your—your mission?" Bert calmed immediately under the spell of the Wanderer's new mood.

"My mission throughout eternity, Earthling—can't you sense it? Forever and ever I shall roam infra-dimensional space, watching and waiting for evidence that a similar catastrophe might be visited on another land where warm-blooded thinking humans of similar mold to my own may be living out their short lives of happiness or near-happiness. Never again shall so great a calamity come to mankind anywhere if it be within the Wanderer's power to prevent it. And that is why I snatched you up from your friend's laboratory. That is why I have shown to you the—"

"Me, why me?" Bert exclaimed.

"Attend, O Earthling, and you shall hear."

The mysterious intangibilities of the cosmos whirled by unheeded by either as the Wanderer's tale unfolded.

*   *   *   *   *

"When I returned," he said, "the gateway was closed forever. I could not reenter my own plane of existence. The metal monsters had taken possession; they had found a better and richer land than their own, and when they had completed their migration they destroyed the generator of my force area. They had shut me out; but I could visit Urtraria—as an outsider, as a wraith—and I saw what they had done. I saw the desolation and the blackness of my once fair land. I saw that—that none of my own kind remained. All, all were gone.

"For a time my reason deserted me and I roamed infra-dimensional space a madman, self-condemned to the outer realms where there is no real material existence, no human companionship, no love, no comfort. When reason returned, I set myself to the task of visiting other planes where beings of my own kind might be found and I soon learned that it was impossible to do this in the body. To these people I was a ghostly visitant, if they sensed my presence at all, for my roamings between planes had altered the characteristics of atomic structure of my being. I could no longer adapt myself to material existence in these planes of the fifth dimension. The orbits of electrons in the atoms comprising my substance had become fixed in a new and outcast oscillation interval. I had remained away too long. I was an outcast, a wanderer—the Wanderer of Infinity."

There was silence in the sphere for a space, save only for the gentle whirring of the motors. Then the Wanderer continued:

"Nevertheless, I roamed these planes as a nonexistent visitor in so far as their peoples were concerned. I learned their languages and came to think of them as my own, and I found that many of their scientific workers were experimenting along lines similar to those which had brought disaster to Urtraria. I swore a mighty oath to spend my lifetime in warning them, in warding off a repetition of so terrible a mistake as I had made. On several occasions I have succeeded.

"And then I found that my lifetime was to be for all eternity. In the outer realms time stands still, as I have told you, and in the plane of existence which was now mine—an extra-material plane—I had no prospect of aging or of death. My vow, therefore, is for so long as our universe may endure instead of for merely a lifetime. For this I am duly thankful, for I shall miss nothing until the end of time.

"I visited planes where other monsters, as clever and as vicious as the metal ones who devastated Urtraria, were bending every effort of their sciences toward obtaining actual contact with other planes of the fifth dimension. And I learned that such contact was utterly impossible of attainment without a gateway in the realm to which they wished to pass—a gateway such as I had provided for the metal monsters and such as that which your friend Tom Parker has provided for the Bardeks, or spider men, as you term them.

"In intra-dimensional space I saw the glow of Tom Parker's force area and I made my way to your world quickly. But Tom could not get my warning: he was too stubbornly and deeply engrossed in the work he was engaged in. The girl Joan was slightly more susceptible, and I believe she was beginning to sense my telepathic messages when she sent for you. Still and all, I had begun to give up hope when you came on the scene. I took you away just as the spider men succeeded in capturing your friends, and now my hope has revived. I feel sure that my warning shall not have been in vain."

"But," objected Bert, "you've warned *me*, not the scientist of my world who is able to prevent the thing—"

"Yes, *you*," the Wanderer broke in. "It is better so. This Tom Parker is a zealot even as was I—a man of science thinking only of his own discoveries. I am not sure he would discontinue his experiments even were he to receive my warning in all its horrible details. But you, O Man-Called-Bert, through your love of his sister and by your influence over him, will be able to do what I can not do myself: bring about the destruction of this apparatus of his; impress upon him the grave necessity of discontinuing his investigations. You can do it, and you alone, now that you fully understand."

"Sa-ay! You're putting it up to me entirely?"

"Nearly so, and there is no alternative. I believe I have not misjudged you; you will not fail, of that I am certain. For the sake of your own kind, for the love of Joan Parker—you will not fail. And for me—for this small measure of atonement it is permitted that I make or help to make possible—"

"No, I'll not fail. Take me to them, quick." Bert grinned understandingly as the Wanderer straightened his broad shoulders and extended his hand.

There was no lack of substantiality in the mighty grip of those closing fingers.

*   *   *   *   *

Again the sphere's invisible motors increased speed, and again the dizzying kaleidoscope of color swept past them more furiously.

"We will now overtake them—your friends," said the Wanderer, "in the very act of passing between planes."

"Overtake them...." Bert mumbled. "I don't get it at all, this time traveling. It's over my head a mile."

"It isn't time travel really," explained the Wanderer. "We are merely closing up the time-space interval, moving to the precise spot in the universe where your friend's laboratory existed at the moment of contact between planes with your world and that of the Bardeks. We shall reach there a few seconds after the actual capture."

"No chance of missing?" Bert watched the Wanderer as he consulted his mathematical data and made new adjustments of the controls.

"Not the slightest; it is calculated to a nicety. We could, if we wished, stop just short of the exact time and would see the re-occurrence of their capture. But only as unseen observers—you can not enter the plane as a material being during your own actual past, for your entity would then be duplicated. Of course, I can not enter in any case. But, moving on to the instant after the event, as we shall do, you may enter either plane as a material being or move between the two planes at will by means of the gateway provided by Tom Parker's force area. Do you not now understand the manner in which you will be enabled to carry out the required procedure?"

"H-hmm!" Bert wasn't sure at all. "But this moving through time," he asked helplessly, "and the change from one plane of oscillation to another—they're all mixed up—what have they to do with each other?"

"All five dimensions of our universe are definitely interrelated and dependent one upon the other for the existence of matter in any form whatsoever. You see—but here we are."

*   *   *   *   *

The motors slowed down and a titanic page seemed to turn over in the cosmos with a vanishing blaze of magnificence. Directly beneath them glowed the disk of blue-white light that was Tom's force area. The sphere swooped down within its influence and came to rest.

"Make haste," the Wanderer said. "I shall be here in the gateway though you see me not. Bring them here, speedily."

On the one side Bert saw familiar objects in Tom's laboratory, on the other side the white cliff and the pitchy sea of the Bardek realm. And the cage of basket-weave between, with his friends inside struggling with the spider men. It was the instant after the capture.

"Joan! Tom!" Bert shouted.

A side of the sphere had opened and he plunged through and into the Bardek plane—to the inky surface of the sea, fully expecting to sink in its forbidding depths. But the stuff was an elastic solid, springy under his feet and bearing him up as would an air-inflated cushion. He threw himself upon the cage and tore at it with his fingers.

The whimpering screams of the spider men were in his ears, and he saw from the corner of his eye that other of the tortoiselike mounds were rising up out of the viscid black depths, dozens of them, and that hundreds of the Bardeks were closing in on him from all directions. Weapons were in their hands, and a huge engine of warfare like a caterpillar tractor was skimming over the sea from the cliff wall with a great grinding and clanking of its mechanisms.

But the cage was pulling apart in his clutches as if made of reeds. With Joan in one encircling arm he was battling the spider men, driving swift short-arm jabs into their soft bloated bodies with devastating effect. And Tom, recovering from the first surprise of his capture, was doing a good job himself, his flailing arms scattering the Bardeks like ninepins. The Wanderer and his sphere, both doomed to material existence only in infra-dimensional space, had vanished from sight.

A bedlam rose up from the reinforcing hordes as they came in to enter the force area. But Bert sensed the guiding touch of the Wanderer's unseen hand, heard his placid voice urging him, and, in a single wild leap was inside the sphere with the girl.

With Joan safely in the Wanderer's care, he rushed out again for Tom. Then followed a nightmare of battling those twining tentacles and the puffy crowding bodies of the spider men. Wrestling tactics and swinging fists were all that the two

Earthlings had to rely upon, but, between them, they managed to fight off a half score of the Bardeks and work their way back into the glowing force area.

"It's no use," Tom gasped. "We can't get back."

"Sure we can. We've a friend—here—in the force area."

Tom Parker staggered: his strength was giving out. "No, no, Bert," he moaned, "I can't. You go on. Leave me here."

"Not on your life!" Bert swung him up bodily into the sphere as he contacted with the invisible metal of its hull. Kicking off the nearest of the spider men, he clambered in after the scientist.

*   *   *   *   *

The tableau then presented in the sphere's interior was to remain forever imprinted on Bert's memory, though it was only a momentary flash in his consciousness at the time: the Wanderer, calm and erect at the control panel, his benign countenance alight with satisfaction; Tom Parker, pulling himself to his feet, clutching at the big man's free arm, his mouth opened in astonishment; Joan, seated at the Wanderer's feet with awed and reverent eyes upturned.

There is no passing directly between the planes. One must have the force area as a gateway, and, besides, a medium such as the cage of the Bardeks, the orange light of the metal monsters, or the sphere of the Wanderer. Bert knew this instinctively as the sphere darkened and the flashing light-forms leaped across the blackness.

The motors screamed in rising crescendo as their speed increased. Then, abruptly, the sound broke off into deathly silence as the limit of audibility was passed. Against the brilliant background of swift color changes and geometric light-shapes that so quickly merged into the familiar blur, Bert saw his companions as dim wraithlike forms. He moved toward Joan, groping.

Then came the tremendous thump, the swinging of a colossal page across the void, the warping of the very universe about them, the physical torture and the swift rush through Stygian inkiness....

"Farewell." A single word, whispered like a benediction in the Wanderer's mellow voice, was in Bert's consciousness. He knew that their benefactor had slipped away into the mysterious regions of intra-dimensional space.

*   *   *   *   *

Raising himself slowly and dazedly from where he had been flung, he saw they were in Tom's laboratory. Joan lay over there white and still, a pitiful crumpled heap. Panicky, Bert crossed to her. His trembling fingers found her pulse; a sobbing breath of relief escaped his lips. She had merely swooned.

Tom Parker, exhausted from his efforts in that other plane and with the very foundations of his being wrenched by the passage through the fifth dimension, was unable to rise. Only semiconscious, his eyes were glazed with pain, and incoherent moaning sounds came from his white lips when he attempted to speak.

Bert's mind was clearing rapidly. That diabolical machine of Tom's was still operating, the drone of its motors being the only sound in the laboratory as the inventor closed his mouth grimly and made a desperate effort to raise his head. But Bert had seen shapes materializing on the lighted disk that was the gateway between planes and he rushed to the controls of the instrument. That starting lever must be shifted without delay.

"Don't!" Tom Parker had found his voice; his frantic warning was a hoarse whistling gasp. He had struggled to his knees. "It will kill you, Bert. Those things in the force area—partly through—the reaction will destroy the machine and all of us if you turn it off. Don't, I say!"

"What then?" Bert fell back appalled. Hazily, the steel prow of a war machine was forming itself on the metal disk; caterpillar treads moved like ghostly shadows beneath. It was the vanguard of the Bardek hordes!

"Can't do it that way!" Tom had gotten to his feet and was stumbling toward the force area. "Only one way—during the change of oscillation periods. Must mingle other atoms with those before they stabilize in our plane. Must localize annihilating force. Must—"

What was the fool doing? He'd be in the force area in another moment. Bert thrust forward to intercept him; saw that Joan had regained consciousness and was sitting erect, swaying weakly. Her eyes widened with horror as they took in the scene and she screamed once despairingly and was on her feet, tottering.

"Back!" Tom Parker yelled, wheeling. "Save yourselves."

* * * * *

Bert lunged toward him but was too late. Tom had already burst into the force area and cast himself upon the semitransparent tank of the spider men. A blast of searing heat radiated from the disk and the motors of Tom's machine groaned as they slowed down under a tremendous overload.

Joan cried out in awful despair and moved to follow, but her knees gave way beneath her. Moaning and shuddering, she slumped into Bert's arms and he drew her back from the awful heat of the force area.

Then, horrified, they watched as Tom Parker melted into the misty shape of the Bardek war machine. Swiftly his body merged with the half-substance of the tank and became an integral part of the mass. For a horrible instant Tom, too, was transparent—a ghost shape writhing in a ghostly throbbing mechanism of another world. His own atomic structure mingled with that of the alien thing and yet, for a moment, he retained his Earthly form. His lean face was peaceful in death, satisfied, like the Wanderer's when they had last seen him.

A terrific thunderclap rent the air and a column of flame roared up from the force area. Tom's apparatus glowed to instant white heat, then melted down into sizzling liquid metal and glass. The laboratory was in sudden twilight gloom, save for the tongue of fire that licked up from the force area to the paneled ceiling. On the metal disk, now glowing redly, was no visible thing. The gateway was closed forever.

* * * * *

What more fearful calamity might have befallen had the machine been switched off instead, Bert was never to know. Nor did he know how he reached his parked flivver with Joan a limp sobbing bundle in his arms. He only knew that Tom Parker's sacrifice had saved them, had undoubtedly prevented a horrible invasion of Earth; and that the efforts of the Wanderer had not been in vain.

The old house was burning furiously when he climbed in under the wheel of his car. He held Joan very close and watched that blazing funeral pyre in wordless sorrow as the bereaved girl dropped her head to his shoulder.

A group of men came up the winding road, a straggling group, running—the loungers from the village. In the forefront was the beardless youth who had directed Bert, and, bringing up the rear, limping and scurrying, was the old man they had called Gramp. He was puffing prodigiously when the others gathered around the car, demanding information.

And the old fellow with the thick spectacles talked them all down.

"What'd I tell you?" he screeched. "Didn't I say they was queer doin's up here? Didn't I say the devil was here with his imps—an' the thunder? You're a passel o' idjits like I said—"

The roar of Bert's starting motor drowned out the rest, but the old fellow was still gesticulating and dancing about when they clattered off down the winding road to Lenville.

*   *   *   *   *

An hour later Joan had fallen asleep, exhausted.

Night had fallen and, as mile after mile of smooth concrete unrolled beneath the flivver's wheels, Bert gave himself over to thoughts he had not dared to entertain in nearly two years. They'd be happy, he and Joan, and there'd be no further argument. If she still objected to living on the fruit farm, that could be managed easily. They'd live in Indianapolis and he'd buy a new car, a good one, to run back and forth. If, when her grief for Tom had lessened, she wanted to go on with laboratory work and such—well, that was easy, too. Only there would be no fooling around with this dimensional stuff—she'd had enough of that, he knew.

He drew her close with his free arm and his thoughts shifted—moved far out in infra-dimensional space to dwell upon the man of the past who had called himself Wanderer of Infinity. He who would go on and on until the end of time, until the end of all things, watching over the many worlds and planes. Warning peoples of humanlike mold and emotions wherever they might dwell. Helping them. Atoning throughout infinity. Suffering.

Also From Resurrected Press
Science Fiction Authors Resurrected

Fyfe Resurrected - The Stories of H. B. Fyfe
Stories from the Golden Age of Science Fiction by the author of D-99. dealing with the interaction of humans and aliens on far off worlds in ways that were as creative as they were imaginative.

Schmitz Resurrected - Selected Stories of James H. Schmitz
Includes "An Incident on Route 12", "Watch the Sky", "The Other Likeness", "The Star Hyacinths", "Oneness", "The Winds of Time", "Ham Sandwich" and "Gone Fishing".

Sheckly Resurrected - The Early Stories of Robert Sheckley
Resurrected Press has collected some of the best of these from the 50's including "Warrior Race", "The Leech", "Watchbird", "Warm", "Diplomatic Immunity", "The Hour of Battle", "Besides Still Waters", "Keep Your Shape", "One Man's Poison", 'Ask a Foolish Question", "Cost of Living", "Death Wish Forever".

Dick Resurrected - The Early Stories of Philip K. Dick
Early stories from the author of the novels that inspired "Blade Runner," "Total Recall," and "A Scanner Darkly".

Hamilton Resurrected - Classic Stories of Edmond Hamilton
Edmond Hamilton was one of the most popular writers during the 30's and 40's, the period that saw the first flowering of modern science fiction.

Smith Resurrected - Selected Stories of Evelyn E. Smith ton
During an era when women rarely appeared in science fiction magazines, Evelyn E. Smith appeared regularly in the pages of Galaxy and Fantastic Universe. Resurrected Press is proud to return these stories to print.

OTHER CLASSIC SCIENCE FICTION NOVELS

TALENTS, INCORPORATED - BY MURRAY LEINSTER

When a Mekinese fleet conquers his home planet, Captain Bors turns to Talents, Incorporated for help using their collection of individuals with unusual abilities to defeat the enemy and save the galaxy.

THE PIRATES OF ERSATZ - BY MURRAY LEINSTER

Bran Hodden just wanted to be an electronic engineer and marry a delightful girl. But when he's framed by the powers on Walden he's forced to turn back to his family's trade, piracy. Also published as The Pirates of Zan.

EMPIRE - BY CLIFFORD SIMAK

Spencer Chambers and Interplanetary Power owned the Solar System because they controlled the source of power. It fell to Russell Page and Harry Wilson to challenge that control if they had to cross the universe to do it.

NIGHT OF THE LONG KNIVES - THE CREATURE FROM THE CLEVELAND DEPTHS - BY FRITZ LEIBER

Two classic novellas set in the not too distant future from a classic master of science fiction.

ARMAGEDDON - 2419 A.D. - THE AIR LORDS OF HAN - BY PHILLIP FRANCIS NOWLAN

The two novels that introduced the world to that intrepid hero of the 25th Century, Buck Rogers. Buck Rogers must save the world from the clutches of the insidious Han.

Resurrected Press Fiction by Randall Garrett

Anything You Can Do...

What do you do when an alien with exceptional physical abilities crash lands on Earth and leaves a path of death and destruction in its wake? You use biological modification to create an enhanced human able to match the alien in strength and speed. But is the result still human?

Unwise Child

After two unsuccessful and seemingly random attempts on his life in the space of as many hours, Michael Raphael Gabriel finds himself called on to act as engineering officer on a new type of spacecraft designed for one mission only, to carry a giant computer to a distant destination before it can destroy the Earth. But once under way he discovers there is a murderer on board and the computer has gone crazy.

By Randall Garrett and Laurence Janifer

Pagan Passions

The Gods and Goddesses of the Ancient Greece and Rome have returned to rule Earth. William Forrester, a mortal teacher, dedicated to the pleasures of the mind, finds himself caught up in the power struggles of the immortals and seduced by the pleasures of the flesh.

The Fictional Detective
by Greg Fowlkes

Who killed Ezekial O. Handler?

A beautiful dame, a hard-boiled private eye − and a dead body.

It started like any other case. When a famous writer dies in a mysterious car crash, private detective Frank Slade is called in to find answers, but all he finds is more questions. Who killed Ezekial Handler? Who is Janet Nielsen and why is she so interested in finding out? Who is leaving the neatly typed clues? And as Slade tries to find answers to these questions he starts to wonder if the ultimate answer will threaten his very existence.

Read about it in
The Fictional Detective

Visit www.thefictionaldetective.com

About Resurrected Press

A division of Intrepid Ink, LLC, Resurrected Press is dedicated to bringing high quality, vintage books back into publication. See our entire catalogue and find out more at www.ResurrectedPress.com.

About Intrepid Ink, LLC

Intrepid Ink, LLC provides full publishing services to authors of fiction and non-fiction books, eBooks and websites. From editing to formatting, from publishing to marketing, Intrepid Ink gets your creative works into the hands of the people who want to read them. Find out more at www.IntrepidInk.com.

www.ingramcontent.com/pod-product-compliance
Lightning Source LLC
Chambersburg PA
CBHW070353260626
47161CB00001B/121